Praise for Debra Lee Won't Break

Hooked me from the first page. . . . [Pickett] has created a protagonist with grit, resilience, and a heart so big that it beats through every page of this well-crafted novel.

—Michelle Brafman, author of *Swimming with Ghosts* and
Draw Near to Me

Moving, inspiring, gorgeously written . . . *Debra Lee Won't Break* is the ride of a lifetime!

—*New York Times* bestselling author Michael Levin

An electrifying tale of grit, heart, and unshakable resolve. . . . Katherine Pickett is a masterful storyteller whose words don't just tell a story—they pull you in, wrap around your heart, and linger long after the last page.

—Suzie Housley, *Midwest Book Review*

Debra Lee Won't Break will have you rooting for its eponymous heroine from page one. Written with warmth and sensitivity and notable for its realistic portrayal of a life with multiple sclerosis, this heartening story of family and friendship suggests it just may be possible to go home again after all.

—Hillary Adrienne Stern, author of *The Garment Maker's Daughter*

Heartwarming. . . . An inspiring tale of an unlikely heroine who discovers a wellspring of strength within herself, encouraging us all to push past our limits with persistence and grit.

—Lisa Doggett, MD, author of *Up the Down Escalator: Medicine, Motherhood, and Multiple Sclerosis*

It is amazing how you took the time to even listen to us in our chats. Thank you for making MS an actual disease.

—Jenny Barbieri, blogger at *A Girl with MS and a Dream*

Debra Lee Won't Break is a touching novel about the limits we all face—in our own bodies, hearts, and minds as well as in our relationships—and how we overcome them. . . . [Deb's] story sheds light on the true importance of friends, family, and perseverance. Like the bike race at its center, this book is a journey well worth taking.

—Jennifer Savran Kelly, author of *Endpapers*

DEBRA LEE WON'T BREAK

A Novel

Katherine Pickett

Hop On Publishing

Silver Spring, Maryland

Hop On Publishing
11003 Lombardy Road
Silver Spring, MD 20901
www.HopOnPublishing.com

Publisher's Note: This is a work of fiction. Names, characters, places, and incidents are a product of the author's imagination. Locales and public names are sometimes used for atmospheric purposes. Any resemblance to actual people, living or dead, or to businesses, companies, events, institutions, or locales is completely coincidental.

Interior design © 2017 BookDesignTemplates.com
Cover design by Paul Nylander, Illustrada Design

Debra Lee Won't Break / Katherine Pickett. -- 1st ed.
ISBN 978-0-9914991-8-2 (paperback)
ISBN 978-0-9914991-9-9 (epub)

To the members of the "Stay-at-Home" Virtual MS Support Group,
who helped me to understand

Content Warning

This story contains descriptions of sexual assault and death at home. Readers are encouraged to practice self-care when engaging with the material.

DEBRA
LEE
WON'T
BREAK

A Novel

One

At the age of thirty-seven, Deb knew the face of misfortune better than her own. As a teenager she had danced with it, shared its bed, and carried its child, then ran away to Texas. But not even big old Texas could shield her from its reaches. A lesser person might have grown hard-hearted and rigid under the circumstances, expecting tragedy at every turn. But not Deb. Deb was determined to live life on her own terms.

Behind the wheel of her blue Honda Odyssey, she cranked up the A/C for the drive home from Central Market. An oversized sheet cake emblazoned with "Congratulations, Grad!" balanced precariously on the passenger seat, and she didn't want the Texas heat to melt the writing. She'd attempted to secure the behemoth with the safety belt but still worried as she wound along Lamar Boulevard back to her house on Austin's south side. Seeing the size of the cake now, she thought perhaps she had overordered. Paula had invited her entire graduating class, but surely they wouldn't all show.

She heard the siren before she saw the ambulance whip past her, causing Deb to quickly pull over. The rush of air shook the van. She took a deep breath. It was the summer solstice, a day that always made her think of sirens—deafening noise, streaking lights, carrying tragedy with them. Until two years ago she had loved the paradox of the solstice. The longest day of the year setting off the steady march to deep winter. The stuff of Greek legends. But not anymore. She checked on the cake then reentered the flow of traffic.

Another red light and Deb braked carefully. Her phone buzzed but she chose to ignore it. Paula, most likely. The drive was taking longer than she'd expected, and after her husband's life-changing accident, being even a few minutes late prompted angst in both her children. The light turned green and she was off again. A driver in a white pickup cut her off just as she was about to change lanes, and she swerved to avoid a collision. "Asshole!" She looked over to where Luis should have been, shaking his fist in faux rage, knowing exactly how to make her relax, and a laugh caught in her throat. But he wasn't there. She absorbed the familiar pang of loss and turned her attention back to the road.

Deb's heart twisted at the idea of having a party on the solstice. It was, after all, the anniversary of her husband's death. But she trusted her beloved Luis would understand. He'd always been more practical, less superstitious than Deb. And to be fair, she'd tried to schedule it for another day—really, *any other day*—but she worked full-time, Paula was leaving for a postgraduation summer abroad next week, young Marco had already started summer camp, and no other weekend was available. In the end she decided it was meant to be. New memories and all that.

At last she pulled up in front of the one-story rambler where she lived, and sat a moment to collect her thoughts. Paula was off to Prague in a few days. After that, college in Chicago. Deb's heart twisted again as she thought about it. She would miss her daughter, yes, but she was also looking forward to starting a new chapter in her life. Marco at eight years old was becoming more self-sufficient, and Deb was making mental plans for taking back her life. Maybe an art class or two? Get back in shape? She'd been a single teen mom, pregnant with Paula when she arrived from Silver Spring eighteen years ago, and that had meant putting off living her own life. College deferred. Life deferred. Until Luis came along. Deb reveled in his Mexican heritage, so different yet somehow akin to her German-Irish upbringing. Both featured big families and larger-than-life personalities, an emphasis on tradition and respect for your elders. They did college together, married, brought a son into the world. Luis was gone now, but the really deep sadness of the past two years was lifting. She would always love her husband, yet she also knew she had a life to live—she should live it.

Her cell buzzed again, moving Deb to action. She got out of the van and opened the passenger door, unbuckled the cake, then struggled to lift it out of the seat. Yes, definitely too big. The adrenaline from driving had worn her out and she would've liked to have her cane to lean on, but carrying the cake and the cane at the same time would've been impossible. She took a deep breath, hefted up the cake, and locked the car, then walked to the front door and rang the bell. Balancing the heavy cake in her hands, she wasn't about to try her key. She hoped she wouldn't have to wait long.

Soon enough the door opened to reveal Marco, brown haired and brown eyed—a carbon copy of his father—wearing a light blue soccer jersey, green athletic shorts, and black socks pulled up to his knees. Deb walked inside. "Sweetie, I thought I asked you to get dressed." She carefully set the cake on the dining table. "The guests will be here soon."

Marco was a boy with an abundance of anxious energy. While he talked he bounced in place. "The phone's been ringing."

"Here too? I heard my cell but thought it was Paula checking up on me."

Paula appeared from the back bedroom dressed in a navy mini-dress. She was combing her long blond hair, which accentuated her naturally golden skin tone. "It wasn't me. Did you get the cake?"

"Yes, I got it. It's on the dining table. Go see."

While Paula inspected the cake, Deb pulled her phone out from her purse. Three missed calls. She didn't recognize the number but they had left a message. Maryland area code. Her mother? Thoughts of sirens returned. The landline rang then, startling her, and she hurried to answer it.

"Mom?" The receiver trembled in her hand as she spoke. "What's wrong?"

Two

The dog was hurt. From Deb's position thirty feet away, on the sidewalk in front of Marco's new school, she could see its back leg was injured. Flies were buzzing the wound, and the pup, whimpering, walked in nervous circles. Several young kids began to crowd around it, and the whimpering turned to snarls. Deb dropped her walking stick and Marco's hand and rushed to the scene.

Standing between the kids and the dog, she put on her most authoritative voice. "The last bell is about to ring. Go on to class now, please." These children didn't know her, but a confident attitude went a long way, especially with elementary students. The dog continued to walk in circles behind her but seemed to understand Deb was in command. He began to relax.

As the other students filtered into the school building, Marco caught up. "Mom, should you be doing that?"

Deb had squatted next to the dog and was holding it by the scruff, stroking its chest to calm it. "I am taking care of this dog. I think it was hit by a car. I'm going to call the Humane Society."

Marco shifted his backpack up and down, then turned to peer over his shoulder. Relief washed over his face. "Here comes Mrs. Cook. She'll know what to do."

Deb looked up. A tall, trim, red-haired woman was striding toward them. "Marco, it's fine," his mother said. "I know what to do. Now go on to class."

Before Marco could answer, the redhead called out. "Hello! I heard the disturbance over here. Can I be of service?"

Deb, already feeling defensive, prepared to reject the offer. She peered up at the woman. Mrs. Cook seemed to be about Deb's age, late thirties, but taller, more fit. More self-assured. From her squatted position in the grass, Deb suddenly felt feeble. Maybe she could use some help.

Mrs. Cook stepped closer and recognition dawned on Deb.

"Caroline?" she gasped.

"Yes?" The woman cocked her head to the side as she peered down at Deb. "Oh my gosh! Debra? Someone told me Debra Lee was back in town. Now I know it's true. How good to see you!" Caroline beamed. "My son Jacob goes here. I volunteer with the PTA to help with arrivals. Is this one yours?" She gestured at Marco, still standing by his mother's side.

"Yes. This is Marco."

"Hello, Marco," Caroline said kindly. "I've seen you around."

Marco blushed but didn't respond.

Deb gazed at her old friend. She'd worried about running into old schoolmates ever since she moved back, but she'd begun to think they'd all moved away. Never did she expect to see Caroline again. Last Deb heard she was in New York. "You look amazing, Caroline. I love the short hair."

"Do you?" Her hand flew to the nape of her neck. "Thank you. I— Oh, that poor dog! Is that what all the kids were so excited about?"

Deb looked at the desperate animal next to her. It was shaking again. Its coarse yellow fur was rubbed off on its left hind leg and it was bleeding. The injury looked bad but not life-threatening. "There's no collar. I was going to call the Humane Society."

"That's far away from here," Caroline said. "We should take him to the animal hospital instead. I can drive."

"I told you Mrs. Cook would know what to do." Marco smiled knowingly at his mom.

Deb looked at her son without humor. "Marco, I told you to get to class. I will pick you up this afternoon."

"Aw, fine." His shoulders slumped as he shuffled toward the school building.

"I love you," Deb called after him.

"Love you too."

Caroline stood before Deb with her hands on her hips. "I have a blanket in my car. We can use that to wrap up the dog and load him in the car."

Deb agreed, and Caroline trotted off. She came back a few minutes later with her SUV. Hopping out, she unfurled a fuzzy blue blanket and wrapped the dog in it. Then the two women loaded the injured pup into the back seat.

"I can take it from here," Caroline said triumphantly. Deb felt control slipping from her grasp.

"Are you sure? I don't have work this morning." Deb hoped the fib would go unquestioned. Truth was she was between jobs, but why advertise that when there was an injured dog to take care of?

Caroline was sure. "I have a friend at the animal hospital nearby. It's no trouble."

But still Deb hesitated. Was she really going to slip back into her old role with Caroline? They hadn't seen each other in twenty years, yet here she was, deferring to her again, after five minutes in her presence. Deb should offer to go with her. Be the one in charge.

Caroline was looking at her expectantly.

Say something.

Why not let Caroline take the dog?

Deb's multiple sclerosis was sure to act up after all the excitement from the morning, and she needed to get back to her mother. What difference did it make?

"Okay then," Deb relented. "Thanks."

She watched as Caroline hopped into the driver's seat, but instead of driving off, she leaned over while the passenger window slowly lowered. "I know it's late notice," she called to Deb, "but I'm having some people over for dinner tonight. Want to come? We can talk. Kids welcome."

As Caroline drove off, the injured dog in the back seat, Deb wondered why she'd accepted the invitation. What was she hoping would happen? When she left Silver Spring for Austin, no one knew she was pregnant, and she intended to keep it that way. No visits home. No ten-year reunion. She'd created a new life for herself, and she was happy. Then she got that call from her mother. Another stroke. Signs of dementia. Living alone was no longer an option. Deb knew she had to come back. Now here she was, in the thick of it. Did having dinner with Caroline mean they would rekindle their friendship? Did she even want to?

Still pondering the night ahead, Deb brushed off her hands, reclaimed her walking stick, and headed home.

Three

Marco was jumping up and down on Caroline's enormous stone porch, while Deb wondered what she'd gotten herself into. She'd realized on the drive over, this wasn't just dinner with Caroline. It was a dinner *party*, and she hadn't thought to ask who else was invited.

"Can I ring the bell?" Marco asked when Deb mounted the last step. Fifteen stone steps. She was exhausted.

"Sure. Why don't you."

Marco tapped the doorbell, and a camera flashed. A moment later the door opened.

"Hello, hello! You must be Debra Lee." A handsome thirtysomething man in a yellow pullover and dark jeans held the door open. His blond hair was thick and wavy, and his blue eyes sparkled.

"Yep, and this is Marco." Deb smiled broadly as she put her arm around her son.

"Welcome. I'm Robbie, Caroline's husband. Come in, come in."

She should've known Caroline's husband would be fit and preppy. Just like Caroline.

Robbie opened the door wide, and Deb and Marco passed through. The house, Deb immediately could see, was exceptional. Expansive adobe-tile floors stretched back to the kitchen, with spacious rooms opening on either side. One appeared to be the formal living room, with overstuffed sofas and soft beige carpet, while the other must have been a den or an office. She could also see a formal dining room off the kitchen. What looked to be original artwork decorated every wall, and a delicate vase was stationed on a pedestal in the hallway. She did her best not to gape. Marco openly marveled.

"Go on through to the kitchen. The sliding doors will take you to the patio," Robbie said, following behind them. "I'll be right there. I'm gonna hit the head."

"Will do." Deb smiled again, trying not to appear as overwhelmed as she felt. This place was amazing. She and Caroline had grown up on the same block, and their houses did not look like this.

Marco led the way to the back door. Sometimes Deb really appreciated her son's outgoing personality. She'd been outgoing, too, when she was young, married, and healthy. All of the baggage she now carried could get in the way of making friends.

Deb reached the sliding doors and stopped. This was it. Caroline and who knew who else were waiting on the other side. She closed her eyes and took another deep breath.

"You all right, Mom? Maybe you should've brought your cane."

"Yes, honey. I'm fine. You know it just takes me a minute sometimes."

You got this, she said to herself and stepped out onto the patio.

"Debra Lee, you made it! Come, have a seat."

Caroline was standing at the head of a glass-and-wrought-iron table, looking taller and more self-assured than ever. She wore a vibrant orange-and-yellow sundress with a brown wrap that complimented her fair skin and copper hair. Oversized brown sunglasses rested on top of her head. The early March sun had begun to set, and strings of lights created a warm glow around the table. Beyond the patio was a large yard dominated by a garden of wildflowers. There must have been a fence somewhere, but it was obscured by ornamental grasses and abundant trees. Deb, her son by her side, felt as though they had stepped into a wonderland of vegetation and beauty.

Already seated and deep in conversation were another couple and two young boys. Deb searched the faces but was sure she didn't know any of these people in her past life. She relaxed just a bit.

"Caroline, thank you for inviting us. Your home is amazing." Deb turned, arms spread, to indicate the whole scene.

"Thank you! Here. Sit here." Caroline gestured to an open chair to her right and sat down at the head of the extra-long table. "And Marco," she said, looking him in the eye, "you can have a seat next to Jacob and PJ." She nodded toward the far end.

Marco looked at his mom, knitting his eyebrows. "Will you be all right?"

"Yes, sweetie, I'll be fine. Go on and have a seat."

Bodies and chairs mingled as those already at the table made room for the new arrivals. Deb watched as Marco immediately settled into conversation with the other boys. The older one, who looked conspicuously like Caroline with the same copper hair and blue eyes, had a deck of Uno cards, and all three huddled around to play. Deb wished the adults had a game of their own to play—anything to ease the conversation.

She looked back at her old friend to discover Caroline staring at her, a smile plastered to her face. "Let me introduce you," she said. Starting with the side across from Deb, she announced, "Here we have Philippe, Rosa, and their son, PJ." PJ, in the seat next to Marco, was dwarfed by the older boys, and looked to be around six years old. "You know Marco." Marco looked up at the sound of his name but immediately went back to his cards. "Then we have Jacob, my son—can you believe he's ten?—and next to you is Robbie. Welcome back, Robbie." Caroline smiled at her husband, and he blew her a kiss.

It was a small group of friendly faces, and Deb was glad to see her son wasn't the only one there with brown skin. She raised her eyebrows and opened her mouth, but before she could speak, someone's cell phone buzzed. Robbie announced, "Salmon's ready. Be right back."

"I'll help you," Caroline said, standing. She put a hand on Deb's shoulder. "You'll be all right, won't you?"

"Of course," Deb said. "Go on."

Deb turned back to the table to realize she was essentially alone with Philippe and Rosa, as the three boys were engaged in their own activity at the other end. Two empty plates sat between them—had someone canceled?

"So, Deb, what brought you back to town?" Rosa asked, a slight Spanish lilt accenting her words. "Caroline mentioned you grew up here."

"Yeah, I did. Lived here till I was eighteen. I moved to Austin for college and loved it so much I stayed. But I'm back now. My mom needs care, so we moved home."

"How long have you been back?" Philippe asked.

"A few months now. It took time to wrap things up—"

"Heads up, coming through!" Robbie called, reappearing on the patio with a tray of food. "Hope everyone's hungry."

Conversation paused while Caroline, coming up behind him, set down platters of baked salmon, steamed asparagus, and roasted red potatoes, and the guests began to serve themselves.

"Robbie, this looks and smells delicious," Philippe said as he took a filet of fish. The others murmured their agreement.

Deb helped herself to some of everything and made sure Marco did the same. This was made somewhat awkward by the overly long table, but eventually he did as she asked. She assessed her plate. Nothing too challenging here. Any worries of spilling food or choking were quickly fading. But what to talk about? Not her past. She looked across at Philippe. He was tall and athletic-looking with dark brown skin and kind eyes. "So, Philippe, how do you know Caroline?" she ventured.

Philippe smiled, chewed, and swallowed. "Rosa and I live across the street. Moved in when PJ was two. He thinks the world of Jacob." He spoke with a strong, clear tone that seemed to welcome all listeners. The faint musical quality to his voice was pleasing.

Caroline chimed in. "It's true. They play together whenever they can. Video games, soccer, hide-and-seek, you name it." She took a dainty bite of salmon.

"That's wonderful," Deb said. "Marco loves soccer. He must have twenty team jerseys. His uncle sends him a new one every few months. It's all he'll wear."

"True? Marco," Philippe called from the other end of the table, "can I see your jersey?"

"What?" Marco was perplexed.

"What is the design on your shirt?" Philippe asked, pointing to his chest.

Marco looked down at his own chest and then back at Philippe. "It's the logo for the Mexican fútbol team." He stood up so Philippe could get a better look.

"Oh, are you a soccer fan too? In Haiti it's what all the kids played. It's still my favorite sport."

"You're from Haiti? Do you know Jean-Jacques Pierre?" Marco sounded awed.

Philippe laughed. "You mean the footballer? Well, I know who he is, but we never met, I'm afraid. I did meet Manno Sanon once. He was in the stands after a game. I got his autograph."

"Wow. You did?" Marco said, eyes wide. "I don't know who that is." The adults at the table all chuckled, and Marco, looking slightly baffled, went back to talking to his new friends.

Deb tucked into her meal, and the conversation quieted down. "Are you expecting another couple?" she asked, motioning to the empty places.

Caroline looked up. "I guess I could've removed those. Our friends Meg and Jason were supposed to come, but they canceled last minute." Caroline shook her head, and Deb wondered what wasn't being said.

"How's Meg these days?" Rosa asked. "Is she still working with the support dogs?"

"Yes!" Caroline waved her hand dramatically. "Have you seen the latest video she posted? It's hysterical!" She laughed loudly. Seeing the questioning look on Deb's face, Caroline explained. "Our friend Meg makes videos with support dogs doing tricks. She's a magician with these animals. You should see it—it's aaa-mazing."

Rosa nodded emphatically. "Those support dogs are something else. My cousin has one. She has multiple sclerosis and the dog has really helped."

"Your cousin has MS?" Deb couldn't hide the surprise in her voice.

"Yes, she does, sadly. But she manages well. Why? Do you know someone with it too?"

Deb considered her response. She hadn't told Caroline about her diagnosis and hadn't planned on discussing it tonight. Not that she was hiding it, exactly. Much like being unemployed, being diagnosed with a chronic debilitating illness wasn't the kind of thing you broadcast on social media. Well, some people did, but not Deb.

"I have MS." She smiled. She sensed Rosa's surprise. She was also aware of Caroline's eyes on her, and she avoided looking at her now. "It took a lot to get me here tonight. But mine isn't as bad as a lot of people's. I can still do most things. I've been very fortunate." Deb's cheeks burned as she spoke. She didn't know why she often felt like she had to apologize for not being more sickly. She expected to see horror on the other guests' faces, but they seemed to have taken the news in stride.

"Wow. When were you diagnosed?" Rosa asked. "I mean, if you don't mind my asking."

"I was going to ask the same thing," Caroline said, her head cocked to one side.

Deb was now in territory she'd hoped to avoid. But Rosa's open personality made her respond in kind. "Seven years ago. It started well before that, with numbness in my toes and a lot of fatigue. I also developed some spasticity in my calves, kinda like charley horses that don't go away, although that has mostly subsided with medication. It took some time to figure out what was going on, but now that we have a name for it, I know how to manage it."

Robbie leaned back in his chair. "All I know about MS is that there's a bike ride to raise money for it. It was called the MS-150 when my friend did it in Philly. Here I think they call it the Chesapeake Challenge."

"I've done that ride," Philippe said. "I raised money for Rosa's cousin three or four years ago now. I'm planning to do it again this summer."

"What's that again?" Caroline leaned in.

"One hundred and fifty miles of biking over two days to support multiple sclerosis research," Philippe said.

Robbie whistled. "That's a lot of biking."

Caroline looked at Deb. "You used to bike. Is that—?"

Deb met Caroline's eyes. An arrow of panic shot through her. She gave a quick shake of the head, hoping Caroline would drop it. Deb had been an avid cyclist once, but that was in the past.

Robbie said, "Didn't the girl on *Facts of Life* have MS?" Everyone looked at him curiously.

"No, that was muscular dystrophy," Caroline corrected, her mouth tight. Deb read embarrassment on her face.

"Oh, right. Like Jerry's Kids," Robbie said, nodding with understanding. Caroline rolled her eyes and Deb suppressed a smile.

The conversation stalled, until Robbie broke the silence. "Well, you're very brave," he said to Deb. It was the kind of sentimentality Deb hated, and she quickly changed the subject.

"Thanks. These days I'm more focused on my mom. She had a couple of strokes and now I'm the one taking care of her. It's a difficult role reversal." Deb thought again about the phone call that changed her world. So much for doing something for herself. She took a bite of food and looked down the table at Marco. He had just finished his meal and was waving at her. She nodded to let him know she was listening even though her mouth was full, but apparently he didn't understand, because he kept waving. She nearly choked from laughing. She swallowed and had some water. "What is it, Marco?"

"Can I go inside with Jacob and PJ and play video games?" His bright eyes shone. "Please?"

"That's fine with me if the other parents don't object."

The others gave their permission, and the three boys got up from the table. As they ran inside, Jacob gave PJ a hard shove and sprinted ahead. Deb couldn't tell what PJ thought of that. Brotherly play or bullying? The other parents didn't seem to notice.

The sun was down by then, and Deb watched as a cool breeze blew through the tall grass, revealing a small sign in the garden. She could just make it out: "Certified Wildlife Habitat." Could you really pay someone to create a wildlife habitat in your own backyard? Oh, the things money could buy.

Caroline refilled her wineglass. "So, Rosa, how's PJ? Did you get everything worked out with his teacher?"

"No, not yet. It's such a headache." Rosa looked at Deb. "We are working with PJ's teachers to get more language assistance, but it has been really hard. He's a sweet boy, but he is young. He needs guidance and extra time with his studies. I thought a kindergarten teacher would understand that, but this one . . . I'm not sure she does."

"Oh, I'm sorry to hear that. Marco and I are still new to the school, but so far we have only had good interactions."

Deb's sole complaint was that Marco had been slow to make

friends. Entering school midyear had put him at a disadvantage, and the usually gregarious nine-year-old had yet to connect with many of his classmates.

"You're lucky. Marco, he's bilingual?"

"Yes, well, he was." Deb explained that since Marco's dad died a few years ago, Marco had lost most of his fluency with Spanish. Now he only spoke the language with his uncle. "PJ speaks French?"

Rosa nodded. "Yes, French, Spanish, and English. He amazes me so much. But he is behind in his English reading, and his teacher, she does not like that."

Deb was sympathetic. "It will come. Give him time."

"Thank you! See, Philippe. Deb agrees with me." She tapped her husband lightly on his chest as she spoke. "As long as there is forward progress, I'm okay."

Caroline had been listening intently while Rosa and Deb got to know each other, and she leaned forward now. "I have an idea. You could get Marco and PJ together to practice their language skills. They could be study buddies."

Robbie laughed, but Caroline scowled. "What? It might work."

Deb looked at Rosa to gauge her reaction. Rosa looked back with the same cautious expression. "If nothing else, it will give Marco another friend at school," Deb ventured. She very much wanted to be Rosa's friend too. "He might like reading to PJ for practice. We used to read together every night. Now he mostly reads to himself."

Rosa smiled. "That would be great. I'll try anything to get this teacher off my back."

The conversation turned to other topics then, and Deb marveled at how open Caroline's friends were. She wondered at her earlier fears of discomfort. Maybe this was a lesson for her: She needed to take more risks. Sometimes they paid off.

Robbie stood up then. "Is everyone ready for dessert? It's a special occasion, after all."

"It is?" Deb looked at Caroline. "It's not your birthday."

Caroline put her hand on Deb's arm. "It's not a big deal. I'm going to have an opening at an art gallery downtown, that's all."

"Not a big deal? This is huge! Are these your photos?" Caroline had been a photographer for the school newspaper in high school. Deb could only guess she had continued her pursuit.

"Yes. A retrospective of sorts."

Deb was happy for Caroline. Her own show. At the same time, she felt anxious to leave. Her intuition told her Caroline was about to invite her to the art show, and that felt like more of a commitment than she was ready to make.

"Papi! Papi!"

PJ came rushing out of the house, tears streaming. He ran to Philippe's side, saying something in French, and Philippe and Rosa did their best to soothe him. Deb recalled the hard shove and wondered what more had transpired. While the others were occupied with PJ, she took the opportunity to escape. "Well, I think Marco and I better hurry on home," she said to Caroline.

"Oh, no. So soon?" Caroline said. "What about dessert?"

"I wish we could, but it's a school night, and Mom's expecting me." She also had a call with Paula but was careful not to mention it. "Thank you, Caroline and Robbie, for hosting. Everything was just perfect." Deb stood up to leave.

"Thank you for coming." Caroline stood and gave Deb a hug. "Let me walk you out."

"Not necessary. I'll just round up Marco and be on my way. I insist you stay here and enjoy these delightful people." Deb made a dramatic bow.

Caroline laughed. "Okay, if you insist." She hugged Deb again. "Really, Debra Lee is back! It's so good to see you. Text me, okay?"

"I will," she said, though she wasn't sure she would. "It was wonderful meeting you," she said to Rosa and Philippe.

Philippe, one arm around PJ, saluted. Rosa leaned forward, her brown eyes full of sincerity. "Listen, I know people in the MS community here. If you need anything, please, you can call me anytime. I could put you in touch with my cousin."

Deb thanked her for her kindness. Then Rosa cocked her head to the side, a thoughtful look on her face. "Did you say you used to bike too?"

"Yes. I still do, though it's been a few years. Why?"

"You should think about doing the Chesapeake Challenge. Before you can't, I mean. If you don't mind my saying."

"Rosa. No." Philippe shook his head at her.

"What? Deb knows what I'm talking about." She turned back to Deb, an earnest look on her face. "My cousin says she wishes she'd done it before things got bad. She offered to help Philippe with fundraising, but I think she really wishes she could be on the route."

"I can understand that feeling, but two days on a bike? I don't know."

"Think about it. That's all I'm saying."

With that, Deb walked into the house to find Marco, her emotions a swirl of relief and regret to be leaving so soon.

Four

"Well, that was fun," Caroline said as she began to load plates into the dishwasher, and Robbie agreed. The guests had all gone home, and she and Robbie were cleaning up after the dinner party. Jacob was in his room, getting changed for bed.

"What did you think of Debra? Do you think she had a good time?"

"She seemed fine. A little quiet. Not what I was expecting after how you described her."

Caroline paused, dirty silverware held in midair. "Yeah. I don't remember her being so secretive." Her mind flashed to the scared look on Deb's face when they were talking about the bike ride. What was it about the Chesapeake Challenge that seemed so familiar? After all these years it was a blur. "She left in a hurry too."

Robbie looked at Caroline askance. "Didn't she say she has to take care of her mom?"

Caroline was used to Robbie dismissing her intuition. It bothered her, but she didn't want to ruin the good feeling from the party. "Maybe you're right, but I still plan on finding out."

"Did you know she had MS?" Robbie asked.

"No, I didn't. See what I mean? Secretive."

"Or private," Robbie offered.

Dismissing me again. "Are you working tonight?"

"Not sure. I have to see what came in since I was last on. I'll do that now."

Jacob walked into the kitchen as his dad was walking out. Robbie gave him a friendly tap on the shoulder with his fist, and Jacob giggled. He tried to tap Robbie back but missed, and Robbie disappeared around the corner. Jacob asked Caroline, "What were you talking about?"

"None of your beeswax," she said. She smiled at Jacob, who frowned back. "Do you need something to eat?"

"No, I had enough at dinner."

"All right. Well, get your homework in your book bag and then brush your teeth. Dad'll be up soon to say good night."

"Fine." His tone was grumpy, not uncommon when talking to Caroline these days.

Caroline hugged her son, his arms loosely wrapped around her. She remembered when she used to be the favorite parent, the one Jacob requested to tuck him in every night. It had felt like a burden then, but now she missed it. She worried about their relationship as he grew older and they seemed to have less and less in common. He was ten years old, on the cusp of being a teenager. If they didn't have a strong bond now, how would they weather the turmoil of the teen years? They still had their good days; she noticed they did better when she was able to walk him to school instead of driving. But much of their communication seemed to be her telling him what to do and him not doing it. Whereas they used to create art projects together and go for hikes in the woods, completing homework at the kitchen table and reading together before bed, now he often chose to play video games by himself or spend time at PJ's house instead. Sometimes it felt inevitable that she would lose him.

She kissed the top of his head and released him. As he ran off she called after him, "Get that homework in your bag!"

Deb and Marco walked through the garage and into the kitchen still thinking about the night's events. The yellow light over the stove cast a warm glow. Compared to Caroline's place, Betty Lee's three-bedroom bungalow wasn't much, but it was comfortable and clean, and it was where Deb felt most safe.

"Mom, are you up?" Deb called.

She sent Marco to his bedroom to get his pajamas on, then found her mom sitting in her recliner in the living room. A midsize room with outdated carpet and sixties-style furniture, it was the main area for socializing but not for eating. The square dining table, butted up against the shared kitchen wall, had been taken over by a half-completed jigsaw puzzle, a present for Deb after Paula's trip to Prague. She glanced at it with regret as she walked into the room. One more hobby she never seemed to have time for.

Betty shut off the television and greeted her daughter. Deb noted the crumpled-up chocolate wrappers sitting on the TV tray next to her mom's chair but didn't comment.

"Debbie, how'd it go? You forgot your cane."

Deb stifled her annoyance. She used a walking stick or a cane to help with her fatigue. She liked the walking stick best when she'd be outside, because it didn't automatically mark her as ill. The cane was smaller and better suited for indoor use. But when she could get away with it, she preferred not to carry either.

"Hi, Mom. I know, I left it here on purpose. I didn't want to make a scene." While she talked, she picked up a small trash can, brushed the wrappers from the tray into the can, and set the can back in place.

"Oh, you mustn't think of it that way. What if you'd fallen? What kind of scene would that've been?"

Deb stepped back and considered Betty. Her first reaction was irritation, but she reminded herself to be more patient. "You're right, Mom. But it worked out all right. Thank you for your concern."

"Who did you have dinner with, again?" Betty asked.

"Do you remember Caroline Simmonds? Her family lived down the street when we were in high school. She's Caroline Cook now. Lives in a mansion. Must've been six bedrooms, a huge backyard. Hard to believe we're in the same school district."

"Well, good for her, doing well for herself." Betty patted Deb's hand.

Deb felt admonished by her mother's generous spirit when she herself thought Caroline's house bordered on ostentatious. Who would pay to turn their backyard into a certified wildlife habitat? Deb sat on the couch and kicked off her shoes. Marco came out of his room dressed in his pajamas, and Deb sent him to the kitchen for a snack. "Did Nurse Lydia come by?" she asked Betty.

"Yes, she did. Gave me my insulin and meds. Laurie called while she was here, so I answered." Deb furrowed her brow at her sister's name, and Betty quickly added, "I know you don't like me answering the phone when you're out, but I figured you'd want me to pick up for my daughter."

How to respond to that? *Be diplomatic.* Her mother was clearly confused. It happened sometimes, especially at night. Laurie hadn't called anyone in twenty-five years. "Do you mean Paula? *My* daughter?"

"Yes, of course. Isn't that what I said?"

"No, but that's okay." Confronting Betty with the mistake would only embarrass her. "What did Paula say? We weren't supposed to talk until nine thirty."

"She can't talk tonight. She has plans. A study group or something. Said she'd call another day."

Deb checked her phone. No texts. The time showed 8:45. "Marco, let's go. Time to brush your teeth."

"But we forgot to play the game," Marco said, walking out of the kitchen and into the living room. His shoulders slumped theatrically.

"And which game is that?" Deb asked, smiling at his antics.

"The rose-bud-thorn game." Marco shook his head at his mother's forgetfulness. Never mind that they had played it only a handful of times. Betty, who practiced mindfulness as part of her stroke recovery, had taught Marco and Deb how to play. Marco had taken to it right away, and Deb found it a useful way of keeping up with what Marco found important. Deb was ready to skip it, given the time, but as often happened, she was too slow.

"You're right, Marco. Should we play it now?" Betty asked.

"Yes!"

Deb reached out her arm to her son. "Come sit with me and we'll play real quick. Mom, do you want to go first?"

"Sure, I can go first. Let me think a minute." She touched her finger to her lips, and Deb noticed how dry they were. She made a mental note to add lip balm to her shopping list.

Betty cleared her throat. "Okay, I'm ready. Rose: I held my Warrior II pose for thirty seconds during yoga class this afternoon before falling over. That's a first. Thorn: I missed the answer to Final Jeopardy."

"Aw," Deb and Marco said.

"Thanks. It was about backgammon. I was never going to get it." She shrugged. "Now for the bud. Hmm." She paused. "I know, I look forward to another chance tomorrow." Her tone was triumphant.

"Very good, Mom." Deb smiled good-naturedly as she realized Betty's habit of speaking in platitudes applied even to her self-talk.

"My turn," Marco said. "Thorn: I ate lunch by myself today."

"Tomorrow will be better," Betty said.

Deb's heart ached but she said nothing.

"Rose: I finished my bear this afternoon."

Deb's eyebrows shot up. "You did? Can we see it?"

Marco's uncle had sent him a whittling kit shortly after they landed in Silver Spring. Like most gifts from Julian, it was something Deb never would have bought, but Marco enjoyed it. He'd been working on it off and on ever since it arrived. He ran to his room now to get the finished piece.

Deb held the small carved bear in her palm. The wood was soft and lightweight and felt pleasant in her hand. "This is so good, sweetie. I love it!"

She passed the bear to her mother. Betty complimented Marco on his perseverance. "It turned out beautifully. Well done."

Marco accepted their praise with a thank-you, then returned to the last part of the game, the bud. "Let's see . . . Oh! Pizza night on Saturday." Marco beamed and pumped his fist.

"Who said we're having pizza on Saturday?" Deb furrowed her brow at her son, but her tone was playful.

"I don't know. Can we? I don't have anything else to look forward to." Marco's brown eyes were hopeful.

Deb squeezed his side, evoking a giggle. "I'll think about it."

"Your turn, Mom."

"Your turn, Debbie."

"Okay, let's see. I'll start with the rose. Meeting Caroline's friends, Rosa and Philippe, tonight. They were so nice! I would love to get to know them better. Thorn: Still no reply from the last batch of job applications I sent out." She shook her head in frustration. It had been more than three months. She'd never had so much trouble finding a job. "And bud." Deb paused, then smiled devilishly. "Pizza on Saturday night!"

Betty laughed and Marco whooped. "You're the best, Mom."

"Thanks, sweetie. I think you're the best too." She looked at the time again and spoke to Betty. "It's nine o'clock, Ma. Can I help you to bed?"

"Help Marco first. He needs you. I can wait."

"As you wish." Deb took a deep breath, hefted herself up to standing, and headed toward the bedrooms, with Marco several steps ahead.

Lying in the dark that night, Marco and Betty tucked safely in bed, Deb listened to the sounds around her. Three months since the big move and she still found it hard to believe she was sleeping in the room she grew up in. The room was the same, but was she? Thoughts of Luis drifted through her mind, followed by images of Paula as a laughing newborn, a shy kindergartner, and Marco too. And always the sirens. No, she was not the same. She was like a cat, on her fourth or fifth life.

And Caroline! She had entered Deb's world in high school, just a few months after Deb lost her sister, Laurie—the first cut. Deb had turned inward after that, but Caroline's way of loving herself and taking chances reminded Deb that life was about more than just survival. When they met sophomore year, Deb was in the process of watching all of the VHS tapes Laurie had acquired. Her sister loved offbeat superheroes and had the movie collection to prove it. *The Crow. Tank Girl. Batman and Robin.* Plus old superhero flicks. *Superman I* through *IV. Tron. Howard the Duck.* One day after school, Deb invited Caroline to watch *The Return of Swamp Thing* and Caroline said yes. It turned out Caroline was also a lover of B movies. And although Caroline's life often looked perfect, she'd had her own tough times and knew how to let Deb grieve. In that way, she had saved Deb.

Yet Deb wondered, did she really want to rekindle their friendship? Tonight had gone better than she'd expected, true, but she hadn't even mentioned Paula. Did she dare to be that vulnerable again after what Caroline had done? Deb had lost so much. She didn't want to go through that again.

Now, Philippe and Rosa were another story. They were just the kind of people she needed more of in her life. Rosa saw right to the heart of her. It was as if she knew Deb yearned to complete the Chesapeake Challenge. That would really show her MS who was boss! Surely she could get back in shape. It wouldn't be easy, but she could do it. That had been one of her goals in Austin, before the call from her mother. Maybe this was fate knocking.

Then again, she wasn't so young anymore. A hundred and fifty miles would be her longest ride ever, and that wasn't something you could do off the couch. Who would watch Marco while she was away for the weekend? Plus training time? Who would care for her mom? There were so many obstacles. Sure, she loved cycling, but she also knew there were just some things she couldn't do now that she had MS. She had tried the ride before and it didn't work out. Like Rosa's cousin, she had missed her chance.

Or had she?

Five

Sunday night, Deb signed on to the video chat a few minutes early. Marco and Betty were already in bed, and Deb had set up in the kitchen so she could talk to Paula without disturbing the house. She grabbed her glass of water, put on her computer glasses, stuffed earbuds into her ears, and fixed her hair. *Ding.* Paula arrived.

"Hi, honey!" Deb smiled broadly at seeing her daughter on the screen. Paula grinned back. She was wearing a workout shirt and had her hair pulled up in a ponytail. Deb guessed she would have been playing a pickup game of basketball with her friends not long before the call. Today Deb could see she was calling from the common area outside her dorm room, other students visible in the background. Paula was a tall, healthy girl who took her studies and her friendships seriously. Deb was proud of the young woman she had grown into.

They caught up on Paula's week of social work classes, and Deb reported back about Marco and Betty. Then Deb asked about the new study group Paula had joined.

Paula's face brightened. "It was really good! The other kids are super smart."

"You're smart too, sweetie." Deb didn't like it when Paula downplayed her talents.

"I know, Mom. That's not what I mean." Paula huffed gently. "I'm just saying I can learn a lot from them."

"Oh, okay, honey." Deb regretted her words. She didn't always say the right things, and she worried it hurt her relationship with her kids. With Paula especially. It was times like these when she missed Luis the most. He rarely suffered from foot-in-mouth disease.

"Sorry I had to miss our call, by the way. Does this time work for you?"

"Yes, this works. You won't get to talk to Marco, but you two can arrange a different time for the rest of the semester."

"Uh, yeah, I don't know when, but that's a good idea. I don't want to abandon him."

"Maybe you could write him a letter. He loves to open the mail. You two could be pen pals."

"Yeah. Pen pals. I'll do that."

Deb turned the conversation to dinner at Caroline's. She hadn't stopped thinking about the Chesapeake Challenge. "I really like Rosa. She's a dynamo. Her husband is doing the MS-150, and she said I should think about doing it too." Deb held her breath while she awaited her daughter's response.

"Really? Isn't that a bit strenuous?" Paula's face crumpled with concern.

Deb's chest tightened as she sensed Paula's disapproval. It was not the reaction she had been hoping for. "Yes, but people do it. I used to be a pretty good cyclist myself back in the day. Anyway, I didn't say I was going to do it. I know that with MS I don't always get to do what I want."

"Sorry, Mom. I didn't mean to rain on your parade."

Deb exhaled. "It's okay, Paula. I know you're just looking out for me. I'm thankful every day for you."

Paula leaned back, and Deb noticed a young woman in the background talking to two young men. They were laughing and shoving each other. The attempts of the two men to outperform each other were almost painful to witness. She dragged her eyes back to Paula and smiled.

Paula said, "How's everything in Silver Spring? Is it pretty in the springtime?"

Paula's voice had turned wistful, putting Deb on edge. Now that Deb lived back in her hometown, she wondered how much longer she could put off a visit from Paula. She loved her daughter, but she had good reason for keeping her two worlds separate.

"I'll send you pictures, how's that?" Deb's voice was harsher than she intended. Paula's face turned red, and Deb's heart splintered. Message received. She felt the knot in her stomach release. "I'm sorry. Yes, it's very nice here," she said. "How's Chicago? Has it stopped snowing?"

Paula nodded. "Mostly. I've heard there can be lake-effect snow as late as April, but I'm hoping that's just a rumor. I'm ready for the sun to return."

"Hang in there, sweetie. The sun always returns."

As they wrapped up their call, Deb took in her daughter. Nineteen. The same age she was when Paula was born. "I love you," she said. Despite their troubles, she hoped her daughter knew she meant it.

"Love you too, Mom."

Paula's screen went dark, and Deb sat at the computer a minute or two longer. She felt slightly bereft. Deflated. She realized she'd been hoping to get Paula's encouragement for the bike ride, but that hadn't happened. The more she'd thought about a long ride, the more she wanted to try it. It had been twenty years since she last attempted something this big, and she'd had to drop out. This could be her last chance. But—Paula was a cautious person and always very practical. Doing the ride didn't make sense. Deb could see that. Still, does a person always have to make the practical decision? Maybe when they have people counting on them, they do.

She couldn't blame Paula for being protective. Her daughter had only one parent now. Paula never knew her biological dad. Early on Deb had told her he ran off, and left it at that. But the secret ate at Deb. She didn't dare return to Silver Spring with a baby. She couldn't face the questioning looks she was sure to get. As time went on, Betty stopped asking when she was coming home, resigned to visit Deb in Austin when she wanted to see her granddaughter. Then Deb met Luis at UT and her fears subsided. He started coming around after class for study sessions, and he took to Paula right away. Deb could still picture the joy in Paula's eyes when Luis would toss her in the air. He was such an uplifting soul, like a rising tide. Paula was four when they married, and he had steadied their ship. Adding Marco to the family had been a sign of Deb's mooring. Now, with Luis gone, it was up to Deb to make sure they weren't once again set adrift.

Six

"I wonder what you'll talk about with Mrs. Lupinski today," Caroline said brightly as she and Jacob walked up the path to the elementary school. Forty-foot-tall birch trees lined one side, while the school's front lawn rose up on the other.

Jacob didn't answer. Something had caught his eye and he took off running. Caroline was left peering over the rise to try to see where he'd gone. When she crested the hill, she could just make out Marco and Deb in front of the school building. Jacob was with them. Then he and Marco disappeared. Debra was leaning on a walking stick.

"Good morning," Caroline called and waved. Deb waved back with her free hand and Caroline jogged to catch up.

"How are you this morning?" Deb asked when Caroline came to a stop beside her.

"Oh, a little frazzled. You know, Jacob just took off running when he saw Marco. We were in the middle of a conversation and *bang, zoom*, off he went." She sighed and shook her head. "He used to be so loving. Now it seems like he can't get away from me fast enough. I don't know, maybe it's normal. Is Marco like that?"

"I don't know. I don't think you can compare the two. Since Marco's dad died, he's been much more interested in taking care of me. Maybe too interested."

Caroline shook her head again. She had assumed the boys would be nearby but she didn't see them. "Where are they now?"

Deb jutted out her chin to indicate the side of the building. "Just over at the playground. I told them they had five minutes." As if on cue, the first bell rang.

Caroline and Debra walked to the playground, where Jacob and Marco were hanging from the monkey bars. Their backpacks were resting in the mulch. The playground consisted of several types of slides, three sets of rings, and a dome-shaped apparatus that the younger kids used for hide-and-seek. Caroline thought the school could do better, but the students didn't seem to mind.

"Jacob," Caroline said when she had reached him, "let's go. That was the bell. Now, please be sure to turn in your homework this morning. I got a message from your teacher saying you left it at home the past two days."

"I know, Mom. I have it." Jacob dropped to the ground and so did Marco, kicking up mulch as they did so. Both boys picked up their backpacks.

"Show me," Caroline said sternly. She had learned not to trust everything Jacob said.

"What?" Jacob's face showed disbelief.

"Open your book bag. Show me your homework." She crossed her arms in front of her chest and gave him a no-nonsense look.

Jacob sighed, unzipped his bag, and scrunched up his face. "Oh, no!"

Caroline's eyes flashed with anger. "Jacob, do not tell me you left your schoolwork at home again! I told you last night to get that folder in your book bag."

Jacob's cheeks flushed and his eyes were wide. "I know, Mom. I thought I did."

"Well, that's not good enough. You are in fourth grade. You should be more responsible than this. I should not have to remind you every day to do the littlest things."

Debra switched her weight to her other leg, and Caroline realized she was making a scene. She lowered her voice and said, "I'm sorry, we shouldn't be arguing. Jacob, you'll have to tell your teacher you messed up. See if she'll accept the work tomorrow."

"Mom, can't you tell her? Or could you bring my folder up to school?" Jacob sounded hopeful with this second option.

"No, I cannot tell her, and I cannot bring your folder up to school. I have work, you know. Anyway, this is your responsibility. If you didn't spend so much time on video games—"

"Aw, Mom, don't start on me about that. I play a lot less than most of my friends do."

Debra broke in. "Marco, give me a hug. It's time to go." Marco, who had been entranced by the quarrel surrounding him, walked over and hugged Debra.

"I love you," she said.

"I love you too," he said, then ran inside.

Caroline noticed Marco run off and stopped the argument. She didn't want Debra to get the wrong impression. "All right, Jacob. We'll talk about this at home. Have a good day at school." She opened her arms for a hug, but Jacob turned and ran inside without hugging her.

Caroline watched him go, her heart aching and embarrassment swelling inside. Meanwhile, Debra had already started the trek back to her vehicle alone, walking stick at her side. Caroline fell in line next to her a moment later. "Sorry about that. I don't know what to do with Jacob sometimes. He can be so sweet and responsible and grown-up, but then he turns around and acts like a teenager, huffing at me over the slightest request. If this is ten, what is thirteen going to be like?"

"You can say that again." Deb smiled as a warm breeze blew through the trees. The branches were dotted with springtime buds.

"And he wants me to pick up the slack," Caroline continued, oblivious to the beautiful day. "I just don't understand."

"It doesn't get easier," Debra said.

Caroline paused when she reached her SUV. "Hey, we didn't really get to catch up at dinner the other night, did we? Would you like to get some coffee?"

"I can't." Deb's mouth turned down, and Caroline wondered if she meant she didn't ever want to meet for coffee. Then Deb seemed to reconsider. "What about tomorrow?"

"Maybe. Let me check." Caroline took out her phone and opened her calendar. "I have a call at ten o'clock but am free before then. Want to meet after drop-off?"

Debra nodded. "Sure, I'd like that. Have you tried the little coffee shop at the strip mall? Mishna's? It's actually pretty good."

"Sounds perfect." Caroline beamed. "See you tomorrow!" With the coffee date settled, she swiftly lobbed herself into her vehicle, started the engine, and drove off, leaving Debra Lee alone on the sidewalk.

Deb marveled as she watched Caroline drive away. When she had looked backward down the school path ten minutes earlier and spotted Caroline, she had suddenly wished she'd left her walking stick at home. She was sure Caroline noticed it. What must her old friend think of her now? She was hardly the same Debra Lee who went to high school with her. The girl who wore knee-high boots and a miniskirt to homecoming. Who flirted with the basketball team while interviewing players for the school newspaper. Who pulled all-nighters polishing articles about student government. And Caroline had been right there with her. Now, however—now she could be mistaken for one of the awkward band geeks she and Caroline had once mocked.

Deb walked down the sidewalk to her van while she reflected on her new life. She still remembered what it was like to live without so much worry. To hop in the car and drive off without looking back. To know what you wanted and go out and get it. To be confident that your body would not fail you when you needed it most. That was something Caroline would never understand.

Deb wondered about Caroline now. Could they ever be as close as they once were? Probably not—but she was willing to risk coffee. Opening the van door, Deb placed her walking stick in the passenger seat and carefully climbed in behind the wheel. While one part of her whispered, *You can never go back*, another voice admonished, *You lost her once, don't lose her again.*

Seven

After dropping off Marco, Deb had spent the next two hours of her morning on the computer at her mom's kitchen table, looking through job postings. She needed something flexible that would allow her to take care of her mom and son, but she also wanted something rewarding. Her experience in fundraising had made her an asset at her last nonprofit, and she could count on a stellar recommendation letter from her old boss. With that kind of a head start, Deb thought finding a job in DC would be easy. The reality, however, was more challenging. Although her experience was in development, demand seemed to be on the program management side. She had applied to what she could, but she kept striking out. She didn't give up hope, though. She closed her laptop, vowing to continue the search tomorrow.

All the talk of bike riding had gotten Deb thinking. Even if she wasn't going to take part in the Chesapeake Challenge, she could still get her bike ready for the upcoming season. Her troubles with fatigue and spasticity made biking difficult but not impossible. A few years ago, after her disease had progressed, she had her road bike outfitted with pedal assist. In Austin she had especially enjoyed going for a thirty-minute ride on a cool morning around Town Lake. That feeling of freedom could not be replaced.

Deb located her bike behind some boxes in the garage and wheeled it out into the open. She tested the tires. Completely flat. Hmm. Resting the bike against the van, she pulled her gloves and sport sunglasses out of her helmet, which had been hanging from the handlebars, and looked them over. The glasses were in good shape, but the gloves were stiff with sweat and starting to disintegrate. "I was probably supposed to wash these," Deb said to herself with a laugh. "Time for a new pair."

Seeing her bike was like seeing an old friend again. She recalled the many adventures they had shared. Not just the organized rides with friends, but also the training rides, the easy evening rides, the tooling around the neighborhood with Caroline or one or two others from their old high school gang, hopping curbs and riding down steps. She ached to attempt the two-day ride.

Two days on a bike? In her condition? She would have to settle for a few good half-hour tours of the local trails.

She banked the old gloves into a trash can by the door, loaded the bike into the back of her van, then went inside the house. She found her mom in her favorite seat in the living room flipping through a magazine. "Mom, I'm going to the bike shop. Do you need anything before I go?"

"No, Debbie, I'm set. I'll be here doing my yoga." Betty was barefoot and wearing black workout shorts and a fitted blue T-shirt. She looked youthful in the sporty outfit, despite the fact that her legs were more birdlike than Deb remembered.

Deb scanned the room, looking for where she could help. Betty had moved the coffee table and unrolled her yoga mat on top of the area rug. A strap and a couple of blocks were set off to the side, and a water bottle was waiting on the coffee table. Everything seemed to be in order.

"You'll be doing the online class, then?" Deb asked.

"That's right."

"Do you need me to set up the computer or turn on a fan?" Surely there was something Deb could do.

"No, I have it set. I'll be fine, I promise." Betty smiled up at her daughter.

Deb still couldn't bring herself to leave. "Marco's at school, so you'll be here by yourself."

"Yes, I know. It's Thursday. Time for yoga." Betty pursed her lips and Deb could see she was getting impatient.

"Okay, very good. Then I guess I'll go." Deb started to walk away, then stopped and turned back. "Mom, please remember, don't answer the phone while I'm out, even if you recognize the number. Let them leave a message if it's important."

"I know, I know." Betty sighed. Deb could almost hear her eyes rolling in her head.

"I don't mean to be a nag, but there are a lot of scams out there, and it's getting harder to tell the difference. It's not about you. Sometimes even I get fooled."

"Debbie, please leave so I can do my workout now." The words were a sharp rebuke but not unexpected. They had had this conversation before.

Betty stood up with some difficulty and switched on the TV, already hooked up to the computer. The screen came alive and Deb could see an empty workout studio that mirrored her mother's setup with mat, strap, and blocks. Betty took a wide stance and breathed deep yoga breaths. She seemed to be making a point of not looking at her overbearing daughter.

Deb waited until the yoga instructor came on the screen and officially started the class. Then she grabbed her cane and her purse and walked out to the garage. *Mom will be all right on her own,* she told herself, and turned her thoughts to other things. Next stop: bike shop.

The bell over the door to the bike shop jangled, announcing Deb's arrival. She struggled to hold the door open and push her bike in at the same time, until another customer came over to help. She had purposely left the cane in the car but still must have looked frail, because a bike shop attendee, dressed in cargo shorts and a shop-branded polo shirt, immediately approached as well.

"How can I help you today?" he asked.

"I'm here for a tune-up and a new pair of gloves if you've got them," Deb replied.

The shop was small, and it took some maneuvering to get past the bikes lining both sides of the aisle. Deb struggled to control the bike while keeping her purse on her shoulder.

"Here, let me get that for you," the attendee said, and using one hand he easily steered the bike down the lane to the back shop area. Then he palmed the bike as if it were weightless and clamped it onto the rack. Spinning the wheels, he shifted rapidly through each of the gears, which made a smooth, clanging sound with each jump. "Any problems?"

"No, just a couple of flat tires, as far as I know, and then the usual. Lube and such."

The mechanic inspected the chain and nodded. "Okay. I see you have a mid-drive ebike conversion kit installed."

Deb's heart sank. This was her first time in this shop. She had forgotten not every bike shop was equipped for ebikes too. "Yes, that's right. Can you work with that?"

The young man looked at her for the first time. "Sure, we handle those. We have a couple of bikes ahead of yours, but I can have this ready for you after lunch."

"Great! I'll come back for it."

The mechanic paused a moment while looking over the bike, then added, "Have you considered clipless pedals?"

Deb's bike still had the flat pedals that came with it ten years earlier and didn't require special shoes. "I've thought about it but wasn't sure they were right for me."

"Well, you can certainly get along with these here for shorter rides, but if you ever do a longer ride, you might want to think about the upgrade. The transfer of power is so much more efficient. You'll definitely notice you aren't working as hard. They also have a way of locking you in to the correct form, so you're less likely to tear out your knees."

Long rides might not be an issue, but protecting her knees did sound appealing. "Can I think about it?" she asked.

"Of course." The fellow took Deb's bike off the rack to wait its turn, and lifted another one up.

Deb watched him work for a minute or two. Not anxious to go straight back home, she looked around at the gear but didn't spot the gloves right away. "Can you point me in the direction of your gloves? I'm due for a new pair."

Another worker appeared from out of the back. The first guy said, "Joe, can you help this customer? She needs gloves."

"Oh, sure. Right this way."

Joe, who wore bike shorts under regular shorts and a company shirt, was a goofy sort but not off-putting. Leading the way, he strode smoothly on the balls of his feet to the front left corner of the store. His blond hair flopped up and down with each step.

"Right-o. Here they are," he said, stopping in front of a display of gloves, saddles, bar ends, and other accessories.

Deb took a look. She usually liked to try on a few pairs before choosing, but this shop had only one style in her size. She plucked it from the peg, then wiggled her fingers inside, saying a silent prayer that these would fit. "Perfect!" she said with glee. When she turned to grin at Joe, she discovered he'd already retired to the back of the store. She shrugged her shoulders and smiled to herself.

Deb scanned the rest of the gear, hoping something else might catch her eye. She really didn't want to have to come back to pick up the bike. Hanging next to the bar ends were the clipless pedals. "Not too expensive," she muttered. It might be nice to upgrade, but she wasn't sold just yet. She turned to the left then and discovered a corkboard with bulletins on it, and walked over to read the signs. There were so many rides coming up. If she couldn't do the Chesapeake Challenge, maybe she could do one of the shorter rides instead. She looked more closely, leaning over a display of tire treads to see better. She scanned flyer after flyer, hoping one would capture her imagination.

Twenty miles for Pride night.

Fifty miles for the firefighters.

Sixty-five for heart health.

These were all good causes, but the rides were either too far from home or not taking place until the fall. More to the point, none of them was the MS-150, the ultimate test, the one that got away. After another minute of searching, she gave up and turned abruptly around, nearly tripping in the process.

"What the . . . ?" She had bumped smack-dab into a magazine rack. Where had that come from? She stumbled backward a step before regaining her balance. That's when she noticed that someone had left a cycling magazine flipped open on the rack. The headline blazed across the two-page spread: "I Have Multiple Sclerosis—and I Won't Let It Stop Me From Crushing a 150-Mile Ride." Deb could hardly believe what she was seeing. She looked around as if she were being watched. Did someone leave it for her? Was this the sign she'd been longing for? She backed away quickly, feeling unstable, then stopped, went back, grabbed the magazine, and scrambled to the front of the store to make her purchases. Come to think of it, she would get those clipless pedals too. She just might have a long ride in her future after all.

Eight

Deb pulled open the heavy black door of Mishna's coffee shop and squirmed her way across the threshold. Her entrance was anything but graceful—the door began closing before she was fully inside. She was thankful she wasn't in a wheelchair. *Yet*, a small voice added. She shook off the thought and approached the counter.

The café was bigger than it looked from the outside, with a small front area for placing orders but with a larger adjacent room with ample seating to the right. Espresso machines whirred, competing with the noise of chatting customers. Deb ordered an apricot Danish and hot tea from the barista behind the counter. Nervous to be alone with Caroline after all this time, Deb was fighting to keep an open mind. They would catch up and maybe even enjoy each other's company. It would be fine. No commitment necessary.

The barista handed over the pastry and an empty cup, and Deb fixed herself some tea before looking for Caroline. She found her at a table by the windows in the adjoining room, a latte at hand.

"Debra! Is this table all right?" Caroline asked as she approached.

Deb gave her approval, then set down her Danish and teacup, removed her jacket, and took a seat. She looked across the table at her old friend. Caroline's smile looked like it might hurt, and Deb realized she was just as nervous as Deb.

Caroline breathed deep through her nose. "So, elephant in the

room, you have MS? I had no idea." She took a drink of her latte and
looked at Deb over her mug.

"Yeah, you know, I wasn't trying to hide it, but I haven't really announced it to everyone either. I hope I didn't make anyone
uncomfortable at the dinner party. Most people don't like to talk
about it, so I just don't mention it. Of course, some days it's pretty
obvious something's 'wrong' with me." She used finger quotes to
indicate her meaning.

"Well, you look great today."

"Thanks." Deb tore off a piece of the apricot Danish and stuffed
it in her mouth. She looked around the room, uneasy with the current topic. At a nearby table two college-age women were laughing
boisterously. Deb had missed the joke but remembered the feeling
of friendship.

"Say, how's your mom, anyway?" Caroline asked, bringing Deb's
attention back. "She was always so sweet to me back in high school."

Deb pictured her mom at home in her recliner watching TV and
reading magazines all day. "Oh, she's good. She had to retire as a
nurse last year, which was hard for her, but after two strokes, she
just didn't have the strength for it." Not to mention the beginnings
of dementia. More than just forgetfulness, Betty could become
confused and afraid after the sun set. "We have a home nurse who
checks on her a couple times a week, gives Mom her meds and what
have you. I couldn't do it without Nurse Lydia, that's for sure."

Caroline smiled wanly. "That's great you have help. You always
hear such horrible things about home nurses. With the stealing and
stuff. You haven't had any trouble, have you?"

Deb shook her head no. "I was scared at first because, yeah,
you hear stories. But not Lydia. She's late sometimes, you know,

because she's got her own family obligations, but that's the worst I can say about her." Deb was used to other people's skepticism about home health nurses. She counted her blessings that they had avoided those problems. "Now, tell me about this art show you have coming up. How did that come about?"

"Robbie's sister owns a place downtown and she offered to show my photography. I've wanted this since way back when you and I worked on the school newspaper together, remember? Finally, I'm going to have my own show!"

"Of course I remember! Good for you, Caroline. Good for you." A memory from their high school years came charging back. When Christopher Reeve—Superman himself—and Richard Avedon—the godfather of portraiture—died in the same month, she and Caroline took turns crying on each other's shoulders. Wet cheeks, wet hair. Deb smiled. "So, when is it?"

"Three weeks. I hope you'll come."

With the warmth of the old memory in her chest, Deb yearned to be there for Caroline like old times. "I'd like to, but can I bring Marco?"

"Of course! Jacob will be there, and probably PJ too."

"So, no nudie pics?" Deb said with a twinkle in her eye.

"Debra Lee!" Caroline let out a heartfelt laugh. "No, no nudie pics. No beaver shots. Not even any boudoir. It's all nature pho-tography. You remember how much I loved Ansel Adams? It's like that."

"It sounds wonderful, Caroline."

"So you'll come?"

Deb hesitated. She wanted to say yes, but she also wanted to pre-serve her own well-being. Maybe that was unfair to Caroline, but to

Deb's mind, the friend who had taught her how to live was also the one who had abandoned her when she needed her most.

Caroline was waiting for an answer.

Deb took a chance. "I would love to come."

"Oh, thank you . . . Now I'm nervous. I hope you like my art." Caroline took another sip of her drink.

"I'm sure I will. The only hitch is I can't always predict what my life is going to be like. I get tired easily. I'm not at all the party girl I once was. But you probably guessed that."

As soon as the words left her mouth, Deb realized Caroline probably had no idea what her life with MS was like. Caroline could tell from her crooked walk that things were different, but exactly how they had changed, she couldn't possibly know.

"Do what you need, Debra. Please."

Caroline swirled her latte while Deb picked at her Danish, hoping to find a new topic to talk about.

"So, what do you do when you aren't volunteering with the PTA? I noticed you weren't helping at the car loop yesterday."

Caroline perked up at the question. "Yeah, I alternate weeks with another parent. I work at a nature center not too far from here. Officially I'm a forester."

"So, all those trees and plants in your backyard—?"

"I planted them!"

Deb's mind flashed to the Certified Wildlife Habitat sign in Caroline's garden and she suddenly felt bad for judging her. She'd actually done the work herself. "That's so cool. Do you like it?"

"I do. It's very flexible with the hours and I get to give talks to school groups. And I do research when I'm not doing that. I love it!"

Caroline's passion was palpable, but Deb couldn't help wondering what she was leaving out. Low pay. Lack of respect. Parents treating you like a volunteer. She let it go.

Caroline said, "And what about you? Are you working?"

Deb's eyes flicked to her tea and back up. "Nothing yet. I left a job I loved in Austin to come back here and care for Mom. I'm still waiting for the right opportunity." She finished her Danish, then pulled out her phone and checked the time. "It's already after nine thirty. Should I let you get to work?"

"Yeah, that may be best. I have that ten o'clock call I need to prepare for. I think I'll take it from here. Too late to get to the office." Caroline pulled out her laptop from the case hanging on her chair and opened the lid. Then she blurted out, "Hey, Debra, do people with MS ride bikes?"

"What?" Deb's confusion showed on her face.

Caroline laughed. "I'm sorry, I'm being rude. I was just wondering if people with MS ride bicycles." She explained that while she was waiting for Deb, she saw a sign for the Chesapeake Challenge on the board by the front door. "I've heard of it but I've never known anyone who did it. Well, apparently Philippe, but I didn't know him then and he doesn't have MS . . ." Her voice trailed off and her face burned. "Sorry."

Deb shook her head. "Don't worry about it. Yes, people with MS ride bikes. A lot of us do. I have an ebike now because I get too tired with a regular bike, but other people ride standard bikes."

Caroline asked about balance problems. Like many people, she assumed that would make biking too hard.

"Okay, yes, for some people, balance makes biking a challenge. But for a lot of people, like me for example, my balance problems aren't about equilibrium. I stumble because I get tired and can't lift my feet properly. Biking in some ways is easier than walking." Deb was silent a minute and then made her decision. She would trust Caroline. With a slight hitch in her voice, she announced, "I'm going to do the Chesapeake Challenge in June." She held her breath while she waited for a response.

Caroline's face brightened. "You are? That's amazing!"

"Thank you. Well, I haven't done it yet, but it will be amazing if I complete it." She chuckled.

"Wow. So, are you doing it alone?" Caroline asked.

"I hadn't thought about it. Yes, I guess I am." Deb smiled. She was relieved and happy to have Caroline's encouragement.

"No. You can't do it alone."

"What do you mean? Why not?"

"You can't ride one hundred and fifty miles alone. That's crazy. I'll do it with you."

"What?" Deb didn't know how to react to this news.

"Yes, I will do it with you. This is better, trust me." Caroline looked like she had just solved a tough math problem—very self-satisfied.

"Do you even cycle?" Deb asked. She was taken aback by Caroline's offer. When she imagined doing the ride, she hadn't considered having a partner. This would be completely different.

"Sure. I ride with Jacob all the time. It'll be great. We can train together and everything. Seriously, you do not want to ride a hundred and fifty miles by yourself."

Thoughts of a spider's web came to Deb's mind as she felt trapped by Caroline's meddling. Her throat was dry and she almost shouted her response. "No! Caroline, really, this is my thing. I want to do it myself." Then, softer: "I don't want to put you out. I can do it."

"Oh, I know you *can* do it yourself, but why would you want to? Debra Lee, I won't take no for an answer. Anyway, this will be a great way for us to reconnect." Caroline grinned. She clearly was not hearing Deb.

Deb felt confused. Was this really a good idea? Caroline seemed so sure of it. Having Caroline on the route with her might be fun, and it might ease Paula's worries too. But Caroline tended to push her way into things and take over. Now Deb felt stuck.

"Y-you're so right. Let's do it."

"So I guess it wasn't a stupid question?" Caroline asked.

"Oh, Caroline. No, it wasn't a stupid question. I'm sorry you think you can't ask me about my disease. It's a big part of my life. But there's a lot more to me also."

Caroline could barely keep a straight face. "This feels like an after-school special."

"Caroline!" Deb laughed in spite of herself.

"Sorry. I've missed you, Debra Lee. I'm glad you're back."

Deb stood up, slipped her jacket on, and gathered her trash. "Bye, Caroline. See you around." She waved and turned to leave.

"Yes! I'll send you the info for the art show."

Deb walked away, still laughing at Caroline's quip. She recalled some of the funnier moments they'd shared putting together the school newspaper. Working on deadline brought out the ridiculous in some people. She felt that old camaraderie, the warmth in her chest, and grinned. Training with Caroline hadn't been her first choice, but what could go wrong? Having a riding partner was sure to be the right decision. She reached the café door to leave just as someone else was coming in. Hallelujah! She didn't have to hold the door.

At home that night, Caroline slipped off her blouse and jeans, unhooked her bra, and pulled her silk nightgown over her head. Robbie was on his side of the bed, getting his own pajamas on. Jacob had been asleep for at least two hours, but out of habit, they dressed quietly so as not to disturb him.

Caroline tossed her dirty clothes into the hamper in the walk-in closet. She would have to run the laundry tomorrow. Or maybe she would ask the cleaning service to add it to their list. She was thankful for this life she and Robbie had made for themselves and their son. Growing up, she had never expected to have a cleaning service. Now she wondered how anyone got by without one.

"Do you think I'm too pampered?" Caroline asked Robbie.

"What?" Robbie looked confused. "No, Caroline. I would never say that about you. Sure, you like nice things, but we work hard for what we have."

"Hmm. That's what I think too." She was quiet for a minute while she took off her jewelry and put it in its case. She turned back toward Robbie and said, "I had coffee with Debra Lee today. We met over at Mishna's, the little shop at the strip mall."

Robbie was checking his phone to make sure his morning alarm was set. "Oh? How did that go?"

"It went well. I was happy to see her. And it's a nice place. But I couldn't help comparing some things."

"Like what?" Robbie climbed under the covers on his side and grabbed his book from the nightstand.

"Like our shoes, for one. Debra was wearing these comfortable-looking sneakers with black yoga pants and an oversized blouse. She looked quite cozy but also, the sneakers were clearly from a discount store, and I imagine the blouse was too. Maybe I should shop at discount stores, save us some money." Caroline pulled out a sports bra, tech shirt, and athletic capris for the next morning and laid them on her dressing table.

Robbie frowned. "Honey, you hate discount stores. You've said before that it's not worth the savings if you end up with clothes that don't fit right or you have to spend twenty minutes finding what you're looking for."

Caroline considered this. "Yes, that's true. I just think maybe there are some things I could learn from Debra."

"Did she tell you her secret?"

"Not yet. I'm working on it. Anyway, I thought you didn't think she was hiding anything."

Robbie shrugged and opened his book.

Caroline had meant it when she told Debra she missed her. Deb had been an angsty fifteen-year-old when they met, not surprising after her sister died, and so suddenly. But Caroline brought her out of her slump, watching all those B movies with her until she was ready to rejoin society. They had been too young to go clubbing, but they had their share of fun together. Besides working on the school newspaper and living on the same block, they had most of the same friends and hung out almost every weekend. Caroline thought they would never lose touch. But graduation came and

Debra disappeared. Ran off to Austin with barely a goodbye. Caroline had tried to contact her at Christmas break and looked for her that first summer, but it seemed Debra had no plans to return to Silver Spring. Caroline had heard news of her here and there, mostly outlandish rumors, but nothing since the death of her husband in that awful car wreck. Until now.

"Did you know people with MS can ride a bike?" Caroline said, interrupting her husband's reading.

Robbie sighed. "Is that surprising?"

"It is to me. And MS isn't fatal. It's just a long, painful decline." She had done some research after seeing Debra at the coffee shop and was surprised by all she had learned.

"Wow, okay. Is that somehow better?" Robbie looked horrified.

"Yes. At least, *I* think it is." Caroline was miffed. How could her husband not see that one was much worse than the other? She got into bed and opened her phone. Robbie was reading again. "I invited Debra and Marco to the art show," she said.

"You did?"

"Yeah. Is that okay? You don't sound happy."

Robbie shrugged. He was looking at his book. "It's your show. Of course you can invite her. She just . . ."

"What?"

Robbie let out a breath. "She makes me uncomfortable."

Now Caroline was really mystified. "How can you say that? You've only met her once."

Robbie stared at his book. His ears turned red.

"Okay, well, I suppose you could just not talk to her." Caroline felt the pit of anger in her belly. Why couldn't Robbie be happy that she had invited her old friend? Debra was a good person. A little lonely maybe, but Caroline knew how to fix that. It was just like Robbie to write someone off before he ever got to know them. And of course he'd managed to make the art show about him somehow.

Robbie huffed. "No. It's not like that. I'll talk to her, don't worry."

"Good." Caroline paused, then added, "Because I'm also going to be training with her."

Robbie looked at Caroline as if she had just turned purple.

"Deb needed a partner for the Chesapeake Challenge. She was thinking about doing it alone, but that's ridiculous, so I said I would do it with her."

"How long of a ride is that?"

"A hundred and fifty miles over two days." Caroline braced for her husband's reaction.

"And you didn't think you should clear that with me first? How much time is that going to take? Besides the actual weekend of the event I mean. Jesus, Caroline."

"It will be fine. Jacob doesn't need constant monitoring anymore." She was aware of the irony of those words coming out of her mouth and avoided looking at Robbie.

Robbie shook his head and went back to his reading. Caroline turned back to her phone and opened her food diary. She entered the morning's mocha latte, the spinach salad for lunch, and the Lara bar she ate for afternoon snack. She reflected on the past few days. What was she going to do about Jacob? She looked over at Robbie.

"Did I tell you about Jacob yesterday morning?"

Robbie looked up from his book once again and sighed. "You mean about the homework?"

"Yeah."

"Jacob told me. He said you were pretty P.O.'d and embarrassed him in front of his friends."

"I was! I was pissed. Wouldn't you be? He's so forgetful all the time. He needs to learn some responsibility." Caroline's voice grew louder involuntarily.

"Honestly? I think you need to lay off him." Robbie closed the book and looked directly at her.

Caroline sat quietly for a moment, eyes on Robbie. Anger building. She didn't want to fight about this again. She looked at her phone and then back at Robbie, who had gotten out of bed.

"Listen," Caroline began quietly, trying again to explain herself, "Jacob is smart. He should be challenged to do his best every day. I thought you agreed with me on that. Isn't that why we go through all the effort with the language classes and the extra math lessons at Kumon?"

"I do agree with you that he's smart. And yes, he should be challenged. But he's also ten years old. Did you work as hard as Jacob does when you were ten?"

"No, but I can't say I was as gifted as Jacob is either. My parents didn't really push me and sometimes I wish they had."

"Fine, but Jacob is a good kid. He should be treated with respect. If you have a problem with something he did, you don't have to call him out in front of his friends. Jesus, Caroline. I thought you understood that by now." Robbie moved toward the door.

"Where are you going?"

"To read downstairs for a while. I need some space."

"It's after eleven o'clock. Don't you think you should get to bed?" This was a pathetic attempt to get him to stay, but Caroline was too angry to think of something better.

"Good night, Caroline. I'll talk to you in the morning."

She glared at him as he walked out. "Good night."

She put her phone on her bedside table and snuggled under the covers. She flopped onto her left side, then her right, trying to get comfortable. She knew she was right about Jacob. You can't let kids do whatever they want. They need rules and boundaries and direction. She turned onto her back and looked up at the ceiling. That's what she would say to Robbie in the morning. She was right. She lay in bed another minute, still unable to relax. Finally she got up and walked to her closet. She pulled out a body pillow, shoved it under the covers, and curled up next to it. Then she turned out the light and waited for sleep.

Nine

It was a cool Sunday morning in late March when Deb met Caroline for their first training ride. Over the past couple of weeks, Deb had made some adjustments to her routine in preparation. Besides getting her bike in working order, she'd moved her interferon injections from Saturday to Sunday nights. She would need as much energy as she could muster for training both days of the weekend. Marco would also be spending more time with friends on the weekends. Deb regretted the time away from him, but consoled herself that it was temporary.

Caroline had suggested one of the local paved trails for their first time out together. Two miles from Betty's house, Sligo Creek Trail was popular with cyclists, runners, and moms' groups. Deb had come here often before she moved away. She was curious to see how it had changed.

She arrived at 8 a.m. with her newly tuned-up road bike loaded in the back seat. Caroline was already there, riding in circles on an older-model road bike that once was considered high-end. Watching Caroline, Deb still wasn't confident this matchup was the best idea. Caroline was several inches taller than Deb, for one thing, and more fit. Deb would need to stop often to stretch her muscles to keep from getting cramps. But Deb had pedal assistance on her bike; Caroline might find it hard to keep up, especially on the uphills.

"I did some research for training plans," Caroline said, hopping off her bike to greet Deb. "I think we can definitely get in shape in time for the ride."

Deb nodded. Of course Caroline already had a training plan.

"So, should we just take it easy for our first ride?" Caroline asked.

"Actually, I think we should jump right in. I did some research of my own, and the training plan I saw suggested starting with twelve to fifteen miles. Are you up for that?" Deb could have her way too.

Caroline looked surprised but said, "Sure, I can do that. Let's start with twelve. That's all right for you?"

"That's what I was planning on. I just might need to stop to stretch. Even with the pedal assist. You'll have to bear with me. Or go on ahead without me."

Caroline looked as if she were about to argue, then paused. "Let's just see how it goes. For this ride we can plan to stay together, and in the future we can see if it makes more sense to split up. Deal?"

"Deal." Deb relaxed as she began to pedal in circles. Biking had that effect.

They started off, and a thrill of excitement went through Deb. "Here we go!" she said, grinning.

The trail was wide enough for them to ride side by side for the first mile or so, but would soon narrow. All around, the trees were just starting to sprout leaves, and the dominant color scheme was green. Bright green blades of grass, olive-green leaves on the trees, lime-green weeds poking up out of the creek that ran by the trail. Signs of new life everywhere. The perfect place to begin a new training regimen.

The cyclists exchanged stories of their most recent rides, and Deb pointed out her new clipless pedals. Caroline said, "Tell me about the pedal assistance," turning to look at the black box attached to Deb's drivetrain. "I've seen them on the trail but never up close."

Deb explained about the different kinds of ebikes. "Some increase assistance with how fast the wheel is turning. This one adds assistance the harder you work."

"That's so cool. Does it have gears, then, for getting up hills?"

"Sort of. I have six levels of assistance, so I could zoom past you if I wanted. But the higher assistance levels drain the battery faster. For a long ride, like fifty or seventy-five miles, I'll have to keep it at the lowest setting if I don't want the battery to run out."

"Oh, tricky. I never would've thought of that."

"Yeah, my plan is to keep it to the lowest setting so I'm in the best shape for the ride. Then I won't have to worry so much about battery life." This was a real concern for Deb. She didn't know if the Chesapeake Challenge would have charging stations, and an ebike without a battery was just a really heavy bike.

Several riders passed on the left, and Deb pedaled a little faster. Her competitive nature always woke up on the trail.

Caroline said, "So, who's watching Marco and your mom this morning?"

"Actually, Rosa!"

Caroline cocked her head. "My neighbor Rosa?"

"Yes, your neighbor Rosa." Deb had wondered if Rosa would have already filled Caroline in. Apparently not. "She's a big reason I decided to do the ride, and when I told her I was thinking about training for it, she offered to help out."

"I'm glad you two made the connection. Isn't she delightful?"

"That's funny. *Delightful* is exactly the word I would choose."

The wind rushed by Deb's ears as she pedaled. She felt good to be out on her bike. It was especially nice to have a friend along. Maybe this partnership would work out after all.

"So, what made you want to start training?" Caroline asked.

Deb sat back a bit on her seat and relaxed her wrists. "A few things really. Rosa reminded me that I might not be able to do this another time. When you have MS, the future is a black box. I should be doing everything I can while I can. So that made me *want* to do it. What made me think I actually *could* do it was something I read in a magazine. Another woman with MS completed the ride a few years back and—"

"Wait," Caroline cut in, "we're going to ride a hundred and fifty miles in the middle of June because of a magazine article?" She pulled her sunglasses down theatrically so Deb could see her incredulous look.

Deb laughed. "Not exactly. I've wanted to do a big ride like this for years. I've just been too scared. Scared and busy. But don't you remember, Caroline? The Chesapeake Challenge is the ride I was training for senior year of high school."

"Oh, yeah. I thought that was right, but I have no memory of you actually doing the ride." Caroline shook her head. "What happened? Did you do it? Why can't I remember?"

"I didn't do it. I had to drop out. It used to be held in October, and I was going to come back for it but didn't." She shrugged. She didn't feel like explaining why. Even now, Deb marveled at what women gave up to have babies. "I missed my chance once before," she said. "That is *not* going to happen again. For me, it's now or never."

"Wow. I like that attitude."

"We'll see how far it gets me." Deb laughed again and Caroline joined in. They pedaled a little farther, and then Deb asked, "Have you started fundraising yet?"

Caroline shook her head. "No, haven't even thought about it. I haven't officially registered yet, to be honest. You?"

"Not yet. I created my account but that's it. I'm still formulating my plan. I know my mom wants to donate. I have a mental list of some other people I think will donate, but I'm not ready to approach them yet." Deb was a professional fundraiser, but she knew this attempt was going to be different. This one was personal.

The two women focused on their breathing while they climbed a steep hill and navigated around a curve. The path was shady and the sun warm but not too hot so early in the season. About four miles into the ride Deb asked for a break. "I just need to stretch out my calves."

The cyclists pulled over and dismounted. Deb kicked out her heel and stretched over her leg. She had almost forgotten what joy it brought her to use her body this way. Meanwhile, Caroline sipped water. She'd brought a protein snack and took a nibble of that too.

"All set?" Caroline asked.

"All set," Deb replied, and they were off again.

"So, how are things with your mom?" Caroline asked.

"They're good. As good as can be expected. My big worry recently is the phone. I told Mom not to answer it while I'm gone. She thinks caller ID is going to keep her safe. She doesn't know what dangers are lurking."

"But what if you need to get in touch with her?"

Deb thought of that often. "I have to call and leave a message. It rarely comes up, but I do worry about her when I'm gone."

Deb took in more of the scenery around them as they pedaled. Tall trees shaded the path, while scrubby bushes lined the trail. Between the trunks she noticed a couple of deer having a morning snack. A new bridge spanned the creek, and two playgrounds had sprung up along the path that she didn't remember from years past.

Farther up the trail, Caroline pointed out a few of the plants growing along the creek, distinguishing the native species from the invasive ones. One of her volunteer jobs was to pull out the invasive plants. "It's a real problem," she said. "The invaders will choke out the native species if we let them have their way."

A few more pedal strokes and they dropped back into single file to allow other riders to pass.

The women passed the eight-mile mark and Deb asked for another break. She thought she saw a look of annoyance on Caroline's face. "Hope you don't mind. If I keep stretched out, I'll have a much better recovery," she explained.

"Oh, this is fine. It's not too different from riding with Jacob."

"So riding with me is like riding with a ten-year-old?" she said sarcastically.

"Oh, please, don't be like that. I didn't mean anything by it." Caroline waved her hand. "I'm used to taking breaks, that's all."

Caroline stretched her upper body and ate more of her protein snack while Deb repeated her stretching routine from the previous stop. She released her anxiety over the insult as she stretched her muscles.

"So, Debra," Caroline ventured, "when's the last time you saw Sandy Patterson?"

Deb stopped what she was doing and looked at Caroline. What had made her think of Sandy? "Not for years. After I left, I lost touch with just about everyone from around here. You?"

"It's been a few years but I was shocked the last time I saw her. She has four kids now. Four!"

"That's a lot. I don't know what I would do with four kids. But I never really understood Sandy anyway. What about Sara Burns? Do you ever see her?" Sara was one of the few people Deb would have liked to see again. A go-getter, she had never seemed bothered by the drama of high school.

"No, she did like you—left for college and never came back. Runs a TV station in Morgantown now, from what I hear."

"Good for her. I always liked Sara. The only trouble was she wouldn't go anywhere without Rachel." Deb sighed, remembering her old high school friends. She had given surprisingly little thought to them in the twenty years since graduation. "And did Rachel marry Owen the way everyone expected?"

"Yes, she did, but they got divorced, sadly. She moved away three or four years ago and I haven't heard from her since."

Deb thought about all the people who had come in and out of her life. Silver Spring, with its proximity to Washington, DC, had always been transient. Rachel and Owen had worked on the student newspaper with Caroline and Deb for just one year before changing schools. They were interested more in each other than in serious journalism. With that thought, a memory caught on the corner of Deb's brain. "Hey, what was the name of the managing editor on the school paper? The short guy who was super fit and always talking about 'the integrity of the paper,' as if we were some serious journalism school. You guys were study partners and I thought he had a crush on you. Steve something, I think."

"Oh, what was his name?" Caroline thought for a minute. "Not Steve. Seth . . . something."

"Seth Riley?"

"Yes! That's it! He's a journalist now at one of the local papers. Still short. Still super fit. I think he's happily married."

"Glad somebody is. We had a good time working on that paper, you with your photography and me with my human-interest pieces. I always thought Seth was a good guy, too, even if he did take himself a little too seriously."

"Know who I just thought of?" Caroline's eyes were wide and a big smile spread across her face.

Suddenly dread crept up from Deb's stomach and tightened her chest. She knew what was coming and put her hands up as if to stop it.

"Andy Peters," Caroline said. Deb's heart froze at the words. "He and Seth hung around together after graduation. Last I heard, he wasn't married." Caroline's voice was teasing.

"Ugh, let's not talk about Andy, okay." Deb couldn't hide her disgust.

"You had such a crush on him," Caroline continued, seemingly oblivious to Deb's discomfort.

Deb pursed her lips to master her physical reaction, keeping her voice steady. "Yes, I did, and it did not serve me well."

"What's the matter? I thought he liked you too. Even if he was a couple years older. You went off with him at that party, didn't you?"

"Yeah, well."

"It's hard to believe we did those things back then. Whose house was that anyway?" Caroline looked at the sky as she thought.

"It was Andy's," Deb replied briskly.

"I just remember we ended up out in the woods somewhere, half drunk and well outside the boundaries we usually set, if you know what I mean. We should have gone home. And then I couldn't find you when it was time to leave. I always felt bad about that, by the way, but I guess it all worked out." Caroline sighed. "I wonder where he ended up," she said wistfully.

"Who?" Deb asked.

"Andy." Caroline looked at her askance. "Maybe I should look him up."

"No. You shouldn't. Some doors are better left closed." Deb clicked the odometer on her bike computer for something to do. She wanted the conversation to end. "Hey, we better get moving. I told Rosa I'd be back before ten and we have a third of the ride left."

"You're right! Let's do this!" Caroline reracked her water bottle, mounted her bike, and pedaled onto the path. She led the way the final four miles, Deb lost in thought behind her.

Back at the trailhead, Deb loaded her bike into her van while Caroline lifted hers onto the rack attached to her SUV. Deb unbuckled her helmet and wiped the sweat off her forehead.

"That went well, I thought!" Caroline said. "How about you?"

"Yeah, good. It was the right distance for me." Deb pressed one arm across her chest, then switched sides. "It's hard to imagine when that will be our short ride, but I know it's possible." She felt strong as she stretched her muscles.

"What are you up to after this?" Caroline asked, water bottle in hand.

"After getting Marco? Job hunt. I've been putting in about two hours a day on it for the past three months. I have to admit, it's getting to me."

Caroline nodded. "What kind of job are you looking for? Maybe I can help."

"I really love working for nonprofits. My background is in development and member relations, but I'm open to other things. If you hear of anything, please pass my name along."

"Of course! Absolutely."

"How about you, Caroline? What does your day hold?" Deb kicked out her left leg and began stretching her calf.

"Studying with Jacob. We have him enrolled in extra math classes through Kumon, and he needs a companion or he won't do it."

"Oh, does he not like it?"

"He does. He likes it. He would just rather be playing video games." Caroline sighed. "Robbie thinks I'm too hard on him, but I know Jacob is an exceptional boy. He deserves to be challenged appropriately."

Deb nodded. "That's the dream. The challenge for parents is knowing what an appropriate level is." She refrained from saying more.

Caroline blew out her breath. "So, will I see you at the art show on Tuesday?"

Deb confirmed that she and Marco would be there.

"Great! And when should we ride next?" Caroline had grabbed

her foot and was stretching the front of her thigh while balancing on one leg, then switched to the other side. Deb remembered when she could balance on one foot.

"What about next Sunday for a long ride?" Deb asked. Both women would have to do short rides on their own during the week.

Caroline took out her phone to check her calendar. "Ooh, I can't next week. Robbie has a thing with the guys. How about the week after? We can try for twenty-two miles."

"Oh my!" The thought of pedaling for twenty-two miles sent shivers down Deb's spine. "But this was my idea, wasn't it?" she said with a laugh. "Count me in."

Deb said goodbye to Caroline, then climbed into her van and pulled away. She breathed deep, enjoying the feeling of having worked her body. She looked forward to getting stronger. And it was a comfort to have a friend along. She could have done without the rehash of their high school chums, but she knew it was coming eventually. *At least it's over*, she thought. No more stampeding rhinoceroses in the room. Now she and Caroline could focus on making new memories, like attending art shows and completing the Chesapeake Challenge, instead of reliving old ones.

Ten

"Debbie, the mail arrived. Can you get it for me?" Betty sat in her favorite chair in the living room waiting for her dinner to finish cooking. The TV was on but the sound was down.

"Sure, Ma. I'll be right there."

It was a little before six o'clock on the evening of the art show, and Deb was in her bedroom getting ready. She wanted to look nice for the event and was even considering applying some makeup. It would be Caroline's photography on the walls, but Deb felt as if she would be on display. Caroline had texted earlier in the day to make sure Deb was still coming. There was someone she wanted Deb to connect with. That put more pressure on Deb to look presentable. Nights were hard. The fatigue often set in around four thirty and might not lift for the rest of the night. She was doing better today. Since she wasn't working, she was able to take it easy for the afternoon. Add in the adrenaline and she could pass for a spry thirty-five-year-old. She would bring her cane and Marco for support.

Deb walked out of her room and down the hall to the front entryway, opened the outside door, grabbed the mail from the mailbox, and stepped back inside, closing the door behind her. She shuffled through the envelopes. Junk mostly, but the bank statement and mortgage were in the mix along with a couple of catalogs and a letter-size envelope.

"Marco, you have a letter." Marco, who had been reading on the couch, hopped up. "Looks like it's from Paula," Deb said, handing over the envelope. So Paula had followed through after all. Good girl.

Marco's face spread into a wide smile. "Thanks." He walked off in the direction of his bedroom, studying the writing on the front of the envelope, the grin still on his lips.

Deb shuffled through the mail again. "Mom, why don't you get your bank statements electronically? You have to be the last person alive who still gets a paper statement." She walked over to her mother and delivered the stack, keeping one envelope for herself.

"I like to be able to read it all the way through. Those electronic statements are so hard to read. Trust me, this is better," Betty explained, but Deb was only half listening. "What do you have there?"

Deb had split open the envelope and was now reading intently. "Mom, what did you do?"

"What are you talking about?"

"This is a letter from the bank. Did you close your account? I'm confused." She flipped to the back of the letter and then to the front and began to reread it.

"What is it? I don't understand, Debbie. I did not close my bank account."

"Okay, well, can you please explain what this letter means? It shows a zero balance." Deb handed her mother the letter. Betty read it over but was as bewildered as Deb. "Let me see the bank statement." Betty handed it to her and Deb read each entry. She stopped when she got to the gift card purchases. "Mom, look here.

This is showing you bought ten Visa gift cards. Is that right?"

"Yes, but before you get angry," Betty started, "you should know I only did what the internet company rep told me to do."

"I'm sorry—what? What internet company rep?" Deb was in disbelief. When would her mother have been talking to the internet company? Then it hit her. "Oh no, please don't tell me you answered the phone."

"What do you expect me to do, Debbie? They said it was an important call from my internet provider." Betty's face flushed as she spoke.

"Mom, Mom, Mom. I asked you not to answer the phone." Deb's voice was rising. This was just what she was afraid of. Her mother was lonely and easily confused; she was particularly vulnerable to these types of schemes.

"I only did what they said. I promise, it was completely legitimate." As Betty talked, however, she seemed to realize she'd made a mistake. "Are you telling me they weren't really with the phone company?"

"No, Mom, they weren't from the phone company or the internet company or any other legitimate business. Legitimate businesses do not deal in gift cards. And it looks like they stole—oh my God!—*three thousand dollars* out of your account. When did this even happen?" Deb checked the date of the transactions against the calendar in the kitchen. "I see. It was the day I went to the bike shop. Why didn't you tell me when I got back?"

"It must have slipped my mind." Betty was defiant.

"Or maybe you were afraid I would be mad at you? Why don't

you listen to me? I ask you to stop eating chocolates so you don't lose your legs, but I find wrappers all over the house. I ask you not to answer the phone so no one steals your money, but you do it anyway. Why am I here if you aren't going to change? I can't keep you safe if you won't do what I ask you."

Deb sighed and sat down on the couch. The room felt hot as she tried to master her anger. Betty continued to fume. That's when Deb noticed Marco standing in the kitchen doorway. He must have finished with the letter from Paula and come out of his room.

"Grandma, your dinner is ready," he said brightly, though Deb could see he was concerned about the argument they were having.

"Thanks, Marco," she said. "Mom, come on, I'll fix you a plate before we go. I'll have to call the bank tomorrow to see what we can do about the fraud. I cannot believe this." She stood and went to help Betty up from her chair. But as Deb took her arm, Betty pulled away and stood up on her own.

"I'm not a child, Debbie. Please don't speak to me like one."

Deb let out her breath, admonishing herself for getting upset. Her mother did not need someone to reprimand her. "I know, Mom. Just, please, don't answer the phone. They can always leave a message."

Betty looked at her for a beat, the tension slowly leaving her face. "You're right. I'm—I'm sorry."

Betty disappeared into the kitchen while Deb collected her thoughts for another moment.

"Marco, are you ready to go?" she asked. But he had gone to his room. "Marco, please use the restroom while I get Grandma her supper," she called as she followed Betty into the kitchen. "We'll be leaving in just a few minutes."

Deb served her mother supper in the kitchen and arranged the plate on the table. She filled Betty's water glass, set out silverware and salad dressing, and placed a piece of bread and butter on a small plate. Then she cleared and wiped down the counter and loaded the preparation dishes into the dishwasher while Betty tucked into her baked chicken, seasoned rice, and salad.

"I can do that, Debbie. You should get on with your night." As a retired nurse, Betty did not enjoy being the patient.

"Thanks, Mom. You can load your dishes when you're done. I'm going to round up Marco. I thought he'd be ready by now."

Deb walked down the hall to Marco's room. Laurie's room. Five years older than Deb, Laurie had had an air of mystery that Deb had always admired. When Laurie died, Deb regretted not knowing her better. Though she hadn't understood it at the time, that's what compelled Deb to watch all of Laurie's old movies in high school. It kept Laurie's spirit alive just a little longer.

Deb knocked on the door. "Marco, let's go. We need to leave now if you want to see Jacob." She waited but there was no answer.

"Marco?" She opened the door. Marco was sitting on the edge of his bed reading a book. He did not look up. "Marco, did you hear me? It's time to go."

"I don't want to go."

"What? Since when?"

"Since now." He continued staring at the book.

"Well, I told Caroline we'd be there. Don't you want to see Caroline's photographs?"

"Not really."

Deb wondered where this could be coming from. The argument with Betty? Or was there something in the letter from Paula? "What about Jacob? Did you want to see him? PJ will probably be there too." She bent to look at Marco but he continued to avoid her gaze. Instead he was silently picking at the pages of the book still in his lap. His eyebrows were knitted.

Deb sat down next to him. "Can you please tell me what's going on?" she said quietly.

"I don't want to go. I want to stay home. Someone should be home." *Flip, flip, flip* went the pages of his book.

"You mean someone should be with Grandma?"

Marco didn't respond right away but then said firmly, "Yes. She needs us. We moved here from Austin so you could take care of her, but you keep leaving. And now someone stole all her money 'cause you left her home alone." Marco kept his eyes on his book.

"Oh, sweetie. I'm sorry you see it that way." There was a time when Deb might have gotten angry with his blaming her. Not tonight. Now she just felt sad for her sensitive son.

"How am I supposed to see it?" Marco looked at Deb now, the anger apparent in his red cheeks and dark eyes.

"Listen, I'm doing my best to protect you and Grandma, but I can't be home at all times. Things are going to happen. They just are. This is really unfortunate, but we'll work it out. Staying home tonight is not going to change anything. Nurse Lydia will be here any minute. She'll help Grandma while we're out."

Marco made a low grunt by way of reply. Deb could tell he wasn't convinced.

She waited as long as she could, then said, "We need to go now. I want to stop off for flowers for Caroline. Are you ready?"

Marco scowled at Deb but put his bookmark in the book and closed it. She wished she had the magic words to make him forgive her, but they didn't come. Instead, she said goodbye to Betty, and mother and son walked out of the house with a storm cloud hanging over them. All Deb could think was, *The rest of the night has got to be easier than this!*

The art gallery was located in a storefront next to a dive bar in the suburban downtown district. The brightly lit street had just the right touch of dirt and danger to earn the gallery its reputation as bohemian chic. The building was painted lemon yellow with large red, blue, and purple petals spreading out from around the door. Marco had been gloomy for the whole ride, including the stop for flowers, but now that they were at the door, he began to loosen up. He opened the door for Deb, who entered with roses in one hand and her cane in the other.

About a dozen people were in the front room of the gallery. One wall showcased paintings and sculptures by another artist, but the two other walls and the middle divider were dedicated to Caroline's photographs. A poster on an easel greeted them at the front with a glossy headshot of Caroline and one of her nature photographs, a close-up of a bright orange rhododendron that Deb recalled from a room in Caroline's house. She didn't see Caroline but spotted Robbie standing in the corner and laughing with a tall brunette.

"Marco, let's go say hello." She walked over and greeted Robbie. "Sorry we're late. Is Caroline here?"

The woman with Robbie stuck out her hand. "Hi, I'm Jeannie, Robbie's sister." She shoved Robbie playfully, and Deb was surprised to see this carefree side to Caroline's husband.

"It's so nice to meet you. I love your gallery," Deb said.

They exchanged a few pleasantries and then Deb asked again where Caroline was.

"Right back there," Robbie said, pointing to the next gallery.

Deb said goodbye, and she and Marco went to join Caroline. They found her deep in conversation with another couple.

"Caroline, hello!" Deb said, announcing herself.

"Deb, Marco, you made it! Have you looked around yet? What do you think?" Caroline had a glass of wine in one hand and her cheeks were pink.

"We haven't. I wanted to give you these first." She handed over the flowers and looked around. "It's a nice turnout."

"Thanks, yes, I'm so pleased!" The group widened to make room for Deb and her son. "This is Meg and Jason," Caroline said, gesturing toward the couple standing with her. "Meg's the one who makes the support dog videos."

"Nice to meet you." Deb nodded at each of them. "And how are the videos going, Meg?"

"Very good. Thanks for asking. I love the dogs at Sparky's."

"And apparently everyone else does too," Jason chimed in. "How many thousands of views did the last one get?" He poked Meg in the side playfully.

"Ten thousand," Meg said, grabbing his hand and wrapping his arm around her. "I was shocked. But very happy. It's all for a good cause."

"Congratulations," Deb said. She had watched some of the videos shortly after the dinner party. She could see why they were so popular. Meg, a petite blonde whose appearance reminded Deb of the babysitter from *Scream*, had an engaging camera presence, and the dogs all showed extreme patience and ability. Sparky's was doing good work, matching support dogs with people who needed them. It was a mission Deb could get behind.

"Thanks," Meg said as she maneuvered her way over to stand next to Deb. "And I'm glad you're here. Caroline mentioned you're in the job market?" She lowered her voice, and the rest of the group took the conversation in a different direction.

A pit formed in Deb's stomach. Whether it signaled anticipation or embarrassment she didn't know. "Yes, that's right."

"Well, Sparky's has an opening that might be up your alley. We're looking for a new director of development. That's your field, isn't it?" Meg's bright blue eyes were shining.

Deb's own brown eyes grew wide. "Why, yes, it is! That was my role at my last job in Austin."

"Then you should apply. The listing just went online. It's a wonderful organization to work for."

This must be why Caroline had been so anxious for Deb to come tonight. Deb was glad she'd made the effort. Her hopes rose precipitously, then faltered. "How are they with accommodations for people with different abilities?" Although the job sounded perfect, she needed the right culture too.

"Are you kidding me? With our mission, we're all over it. Seriously, apply. Then email me and let me know you did so I can put in a good word. I know the executive director pretty well. I can at least make sure he sees your résumé."

The pit in Deb's stomach released, and she felt her hopes soar. "This is great news, Meg. Thank you so much! I'll definitely get my application in. I'm going a little crazy being home so much of the time."

Throughout this exchange, Marco's anxious energy was palpable next to Deb. Thankfully, reinforcements were coming. From behind, Deb heard someone call out, "Hello!" She turned to see Rosa wearing a black-and-white wrap dress with tiny white flowers decorating her dark hair, with Philippe and PJ close behind. Robbie was bringing up the rear.

Caroline greeted the new arrivals and her husband, then turned to PJ. "Why don't you go with Marco to the other room and get a bite to eat. See through that door?" She gestured to an archway in the wall across from where they were standing. "There's food and bottled water and even a few activities for kids. Jacob is already in there. Would you like that?"

"Yes!" PJ shouted. He looked to his parents and they nodded permission.

Marco looked at Deb and she said, "Go on ahead. I'll catch up with you soon. You can get yourself a sandwich."

"All right." Marco was reluctant to leave at first, but a smile slowly spread across his face. He and PJ ran off together to find Jacob.

The adults watched the boys go, then returned to the conversation. Deb felt more at ease with Rosa and Philippe there. She had known them only a few weeks, but she already thought of them as friends.

"How's your training going for the Chesapeake Challenge?" Deb asked Philippe.

"What's this now?" Jason asked. Deb noticed he was dressed almost identically to Robbie, with a light blue button-down shirt and khakis. The only difference was Robbie's had a faint pinstripe.

"I'm training for a hundred-and-fifty-mile bike ride. Deb and Caroline too," Philippe replied.

Jason perked up. "Really. Are you following a training program?"

Philippe shook his head. "I don't really have a schedule. I'm on my bike most days before work, so it's just my long rides that will be getting longer."

"How about you, Caroline? Are you following a program?" Jason asked. Deb got the feeling Jason didn't do anything that didn't come with an app.

"Oh, yes, Debra and I are training together." She reached out and touched Deb's arm as she spoke. "We had our first long ride on Sunday." She smiled. "Deb's done this before."

"You have?" Jason said, turning to Deb. He looked more surprised than Deb thought he should. Sure, she was a little plump, but still.

"I've trained before," she said. "I wasn't able to do the actual ride, but that's going to change. By the way, I got an email from the ride organizers about a new-rider orientation in a couple of weeks. Are either of you going?" she asked, looking from Philippe to Caroline.

Philippe shook his head. "I'm afraid I have to miss it. Will you be there?"

Deb was disappointed but tried not to show it. "I'm planning on it. How about you, Caroline? Do you want to go?"

"For sure. Wouldn't miss it!"

Deb was glad to have Caroline in her camp. She was already seeing the benefits of a training partner. They agreed to go together and work out the details later.

"Deb, how's your mom?" Rosa asked. "I wondered if she might be here this evening."

Deb shook her head. "Healthwise, she's fine. I suppose I could've invited her, but I'm not sure she would have wanted to come after what happened. I was late getting out of the house this evening because I discovered someone stole several thousand dollars from her."

"What?" Caroline exclaimed. "How did that happen?"

"Well," Deb said, "it's a lot easier when the victim hands over the money in the form of gift cards."

Deb explained what she'd learned about the scam. The others were dutifully outraged. Deb was gratified to know they also worried about their elderly parents falling into these traps. "But enough of that. Caroline, tell us about the art you have up. I'm curious to take a closer look."

Caroline's face brightened. She spread her arms out wide and said, "These are my photographs!" Then she gave the layout of the room. All of the shots on the east wall had been taken with a digital camera and processed on the computer. Most of those photos were taken in Maryland in the regional forests or at the nature center, with a few from Caroline's days in Washington state thrown in. On the perpendicular wall were Caroline's film photographs. Jeannie had wanted to show the evolution of her work over twenty years. "Which I thought was a great idea," she added. "The older pictures are from the woods behind our old neighborhood, Debra."

"You must be so excited to see your photographs hanging in a gallery after all these years," Deb said, looking around.

"I really am." Caroline was beaming.

"Well, I have to say I am so proud of you, babe," Robbie said, hugging her. "You all wouldn't believe how nervous Caroline was for tonight. But I told her she had nothing to worry about. My sister knows what she's talking about. She wouldn't have suggested a show if she didn't think the artwork was up to snuff."

"Hear, hear," said Jason.

"Well, I'm going to take a look around," Deb announced. "Anyone want to join me?"

"I think I'm going to get a sandwich," Philippe said, and the others agreed. So while the rest of the group wandered off to find food, Deb began a trip around the perimeter of the room.

The first piece she came to was a field of blue flowers surrounded by trees. A path ran along the front of the field, and strong sunshine flooded in from the upper left. Caught in the sunlight were tiny dust particles. Looking closer, Deb made out a couple of butterflies dancing above the field. The whole image gave the impression of heavenly bounty. It was stunning.

She moved on to the next piece, thankful for her cane to lean on. She was getting tired after all the standing. This photograph was of a building she didn't recognize. Once again Caroline had captured streaming sunshine, this time reflecting off the glass of a greenhouse. The way the light played, you could see the greenery from inside the building while the sunlight made the glass disappear in a blaze of white. Deb had to admit, Caroline had real talent.

The next several photographs were smaller prints of flowers floating on water, similar to the rhododendron on the poster. On the end was a composition featuring a set of stairs and trees, this time in black and white, that reminded Deb of a famous French artist Caroline used to talk about. The quality was less refined than the others, as if Caroline were still learning how to get the best exposure. *We must be moving back in time.* It was a heady trip.

As she stood in the gallery, fatigue hit Deb like a tidal wave. It had been a long day with many emotions, and it was catching up to her. She noticed a black leather bench along the perpendicular wall, the one that held the earliest photos. Deb made a beeline for the bench, willing the other patrons to stay away. This was one reason she brought her cane. People usually looked at her and saw a healthy woman in her thirties. They would never suspect what fatigue she experienced, utterly drained of all energy in a matter of minutes, and they wouldn't think to let her sit down in their place.

She reached the bench and plopped down unceremoniously. She situated her cane so that it wouldn't be in the path and took a deep breath. Where was Marco? She twisted around to look for him. Still having fun with PJ and Jacob. That was a blessing. She appreciated his help, but some days his fretting over her was a heavy weight on her chest. She recalled the weeks and months after she was diagnosed. Paula was twelve and Marco hadn't yet turned four, but he kept following her around the house, asking what she was doing and could he help. That let up over time, but after Luis died, some of those same impulses surged. Deb suspected that his uncle had fed him a line about being the man of the house now that Luis was gone, and she couldn't seem to get that thought out of Marco's head.

She closed her eyes, trying to master the fatigue. For the first time, she noticed soft music playing. One of Dido's haunting melodies. She remembered the song from high school. A sad but soulful tune. *I will go down with this ship.* She opened her eyes, feeling relaxed, and turned her attention to the photograph before her. It was a huge, beautiful print showing several knotted trees lining a trail and reaching high into the night sky. She was impressed with how clear the image was—a real feat for night photography. There was something vaguely familiar about it. This must be from the woods that ran behind their neighborhood. Deb looked closer and suddenly was washed over in a mix of emotions.

Her heart quickening, Deb's mind whisked her back twenty years. Before her stood Andy Peters, her high school crush, with that little knowing grin on his face. He wore board shorts and a T-shirt, and his blond hair was messy from the summer air. She could smell his sunscreen and sweat. What was happening? She heard Caroline and the rest of their friends from the party laughing and talking next to her, but they were not paying attention to her. Some of them were heading back to the house. *The party must be over*, she thought. But as the others drifted away, Andy took Deb's hand. "Come with me," he said, and for some reason she did as he said. Deb looked back to see the other kids disappearing and wondered where Caroline was. Caroline. Her surrogate sister. Her ride home. Andy pulled her along. "I know a place," he said.

At the gallery, shame flooded her. She squeezed her eyes shut again and then opened them. Across the room she saw a familiar face. Andy Peters! Was he really there? She blinked a couple of times, trying to focus, but the man she saw had turned away from her. She didn't know if it was him or not. Her heart beat in her ears, and she felt driven from the room. She had to find Marco.

She got up and moved quickly, her cane clicking on the wood floor, into the side room where the food and activities were laid out. Rosa was there with the boys, who were crowded around a small card table playing a marble game. Deb tried to hide the windstorm of emotions whipping through her.

"Marco, I just noticed the time. We need to get back to Grandma."

"Aw, Mom, can't we finish this game?" He didn't look up.

"I'm sorry, we need to go." Deb could hardly breathe.

"Is everything all right?" Rosa asked.

"Oh, yes, it's fine," Deb lied. "We just have a lot to do at night to get ready for bed. Marco, let's go."

"Okay," he said reluctantly. He set down the marbles and said goodbye to Jacob and PJ.

She took Marco's hand and went to find Caroline. "We have to leave now," she said when she found her standing next to Robbie in the front of the gallery. "Congratulations again."

"Is everything okay?" Caroline asked.

Deb felt her cheeks flush again and tried to keep her voice under control. "Oh, yes, we're fine. I really loved the artwork. So beautiful. You're very talented." She was vaguely aware of the look on Robbie's face and knew she was acting weird, but could think only of escape. She said goodbye one more time, then hurried out the door, Marco trailing behind her.

Eleven

The morning after the art show, Caroline sat in her office lost in thought. The opening had gone swimmingly. She sold four photographs, including one to someone who had stopped by off the street, and after years of feeling like a fraud, she finally felt like a real artist. But for as good as she felt, she couldn't stop thinking about Debra. Something had happened to drive her away, and Caroline wanted to know what it was. Not least because it had ruined Caroline's big surprise.

"Should I call her?" she wondered aloud. Debra might be busy. Or sleeping. It was ten o'clock in the morning, but Caroline had read that some people with MS take naps. Of course, she shouldn't assume. Isn't that something she was learning? But how could she know if this was a good time to call?

In the end she decided a text would be best.

She typed: *Hi!! How are you this morning? Thanks for coming to the show last night. Want to get lunch?* She hit send, then added, *We could meet at the coffee shop in the strip mall.* Caroline's work was nearly twenty minutes from Mishna's, but it might increase the odds of Debra agreeing if she didn't have to travel too far.

She had to wait several minutes for a reply. She turned back to her work. Maybe Debra really was taking a nap . . .

Hi! Sorry, can't make it to lunch today. Doctor's appointment. On hold with the bank now. Another time?

Tricky. Caroline didn't want to ask about the drama over text. She would just have to wait to find out. *Sure! Let's plan on it!*

She put her phone away and returned her focus to her computer. She was putting together a new presentation about skinks, a small lizard native to Virginia. One of their most fascinating characteristics was their ability to lose their tail and regrow it. Caroline reveled in the reactions she got from young students when she shared that fun fact. As she concentrated on the slide she was designing, a sudden sharp pain pierced her behind the left eye. She moaned at the force of it. She closed her eyes and tracked the pain as it traveled across her skull and settled behind her forehead, where it sat, throbbing with each heartbeat. She pressed her palm against her forehead to relieve the pressure. The pain was beyond any headache she had experienced before. Tears formed in her eyes and she began breathing rhythmically, as she had learned in Lamaze. Out of nowhere her stomach lurched. She jumped up from her desk as if controlled by an invisible puppeteer, ran to the bathroom, and vomited in one of the stalls.

Afterward, she got a drink of water and wiped her face. Thankfully the restroom was empty. She looked in the mirror. Her eyes were bloodshot. What in the world was that? She thought back on her meals for the past twenty-four hours but couldn't recall anything that would have resulted in food poisoning. What else would cause such a reaction?

Over the course of the day the headache slowly dissipated. By the time she was ready to leave the office, it was gone altogether. The vomiting still concerned her, but she decided not to mention it to Robbie just yet. Why spread the angst? There were lots of things it could be. He was sure to jump to conclusions or start lecturing her, and then they would end up arguing and she definitely didn't want that. Over a headache? No. It was nothing to worry about.

Getting her mother's money back was not as easy as Deb had expected. Years ago Deb had had her credit card stolen, and that took minutes to fix. All she had to do was denounce the transactions and they were reversed. Another time, someone emptied her bank account by writing fraudulent checks. That took more effort to reverse, but even that was proving easier than what she had to deal with now. Because these were gift cards and not credit cards, the money was gone from the bank as soon as Betty gave the thieves the PINs.

"Are you still on hold?" Betty asked, coming into the kitchen for some water. It was eleven o'clock in the morning and Deb had been wrangling with customer reps since nine thirty.

"More like on hold again," Deb said. "I've talked to several people already. The bank said they couldn't help me. I'm on the phone with Visa now, since it was Visa gift cards. They all know this scam is out there. I don't know why it's so hard for them to just give you back your money."

Betty sighed. She looked pained to see her daughter cleaning up after her. "I'm sorry. I messed up."

"Mom, at this point it's the bank I'm frustrated with. Don't they understand we need that money? How are we going to pay the bills?" Deb shook her head.

As a retiree, Betty lived on a fixed income. She wouldn't be able to pay for groceries if the money wasn't restored. And she wouldn't be able to donate to Deb's fundraiser either. Not that Deb was concerned about that, but Betty was.

As the minutes ticked by and she continued to hold the line, Deb considered hanging up and trying again later. She had jobs to apply for, lunch to make. This had been going on far too long. Then a voice came on the line.

"Mrs. Morales?"

"Yes, I'm here." Deb got her pen ready and sat up straight in case she needed to write something down.

"Mrs. Morales, good news. We can restore your mother's funds." Deb's heart leaped in her chest. But it was premature. "But first you're going to have to come into our offices to fill out the paperwork."

"You're kidding." Thoughts of more time spent fighting over finances filled her with dread.

"I'm afraid not. We need a copy of the power of attorney, and we need some of these forms witnessed."

All of the fight left her. She slumped in her seat. "Okay. Can I come in today? I really want to get this taken care of."

"Yes, you can come this afternoon," the service rep said. "I'll add you to the schedule."

Betty, who'd been listening from the doorway, shook her head vigorously at Deb. "Doctor's appointment," she hissed.

It took Deb a second to understand. She had forgotten all about her appointment with her neurologist. She couldn't skip that; getting the appointment had taken almost two months. Speaking into the phone, she said, "I'm sorry, I can't make it today after all. It'll have to wait until tomorrow."

"Unfortunately, ma'am, we're short-staffed at the moment and the person you need to speak to is only in on Wednesdays. If you can't come today, I can put you on the schedule for next week."

"Are you kidding me?" Choose between an unreachable doctor and getting her mom's money back? "And am I understanding correctly that the account won't be credited until after the papers are filed?"

"Yes, that's right."

Deb did some calculations in her head before resigning herself to the situation. "Fine, next week."

"Oh, actually, it looks like he'll be out of the office next week. Can you make it the following week?"

Seriously? Deb took a deep breath and let it out through her nose. She was glad her mother was there. The sight of her helped Deb control her temper. "Do I have a choice?"

"Ma'am?"

"Please put me on the schedule for two weeks from today."

At last Deb was off the phone. She marked her calendar, the pit of anger still tight in her belly. She stretched her neck. "What a mess," she sighed. She was thankful the company had finally relented. She just wished the whole affair could be over.

She looked at the clock. In a way she was glad she couldn't join Caroline for lunch today. While under normal circumstances time out with a friend held much more appeal than a doctor's visit, after last night's episode, she wasn't ready to face her. In the light of day, her extreme reaction was embarrassing. How could she explain it? Obviously Andy hadn't been at the art show. Why would he be?

She also felt guilty for not having told Caroline about Paula yet. The more time passed, the more awkward it would be. The moment just never seemed right.

What Deb really wanted was to get out on her bike and clear her head. She wondered what her doctor would say when she told him about her training. Paula's reaction had made her reluctant to tell him. At the same time, if the doctor was supportive, maybe Paula would be more comfortable with the idea too. It weighed on Deb that Paula didn't have more faith in her.

Deb spoke to Betty. "I'm going to make lunch now so I can get to my appointment. What can I get you?"

"Just a sandwich would be great. Thanks, Debbie." Betty took a seat at the table.

Deb opened the cupboard and pulled out the loaf of bread. Two skinny ends were all that were left in the bag. "Shoot. I forgot to stop by the store this morning after dropping off Marco. Now I'll have to go after my doctor's appointment. Mom, we don't have enough bread for sandwiches. Do you just want tuna and crackers instead?"

Betty was silent behind her and Deb turned to look at her mother. Betty's face was pinched in anguish, and tears had started to gather in her eyes.

"Mom?"

Betty swallowed, and a tear flowed down her cheek. "That's fine for me, but can you even go to the grocery store now? How are you going to pay for it when I lost all our money?" Deb's chest tightened as her mother struggled to speak. "I'm sorry, Debbie. I'm so embarrassed. How could I be such a fool?" Betty pounded a fist on her thigh.

Deb let out a long breath. She realized the effect her words had had on her mom and felt at once defeated and guilty. She'd been too hard on Betty. "It's okay, Mom. I'll use my own money." She sat down next to her and looked her in the eyes. "Really, it's not even about the money. We'll get it back. But you have to know there are a lot of crooks out there looking to take advantage of people. I think it's best if you just don't answer the phone anymore. Can you do that?"

Betty looked at Deb and gulped her tears. "I won't. I promise."

"Thank you." Deb squeezed her mom's warm hand, then set about making their lunch. Perhaps at last her mother understood her concern.

Twelve

Eleven days later Caroline and Debra were back at the bike trail ready for their second long ride together. It was another cool morning, perfect for getting some miles in. Caroline still hadn't told Robbie about the migraine she'd had at the office. She felt sure her recent spate of headaches was caused by stress. She had taken on new responsibilities at work, and Jacob's bad attitude lately wasn't helping. She couldn't explain the vomiting, but that had only happened once. Exercise and fresh air would be the key to fixing it. She was glad she already planned to train with Debra. She never knew how much fun it could be cycling long distances.

"Can you make it twenty-two miles?" Caroline asked now. The question she really wanted to ask was how Debra would manage the fatigue, but she was afraid to be so blunt. She had been reading up on MS ever since she and Debra reconnected. The disease, she'd learned, is highly variable, but almost everyone with MS has to deal with fatigue.

"I hope so! Getting an early start is good for me. As long as you don't mind stopping to stretch, I should be fine." Debra circled on her bike a few times. She had talked to her doctor about the ride at her last visit, and he agreed there was no reason she shouldn't try it. He reminded her that stretching and hydration were critical to her success. And of course rest when she needed it. "Actually, I've been very happy with myself," she told Caroline. "I've stuck to the training schedule and I think it's totally doable. Especially with my trusty pedal assist. But I'm not sure I'm the one we need to worry about. How's that scrape?"

Caroline touched her face. "It's fine. I just can't believe I did it." She chuckled self-consciously.

"What happened, again? You were out biking and . . ."

"And I don't know what happened! I remember it was very windy and some dust blew up at me. It was kind of miserable and I was deciding whether to call it a day when I got a migraine. I closed my eyes against the pain, and *splat!* I steered into a tree."

Debra laughed at Caroline's lighthearted reenactment. "Was that on Thursday, the super windy day? I couldn't believe the headwinds! There was once or twice I thought it was going to blow me over."

"Yes! Thursday! But I don't think the wind is why I crashed." Caroline shook her head at the memory.

"Well, I hope it doesn't hurt too bad."

"No, no, it's fine. My ego hurts the most. I just can't explain why I closed my eyes. I must've squeezed the brakes reflexively. Oy. At least my bike isn't too banged up." She brushed off the scratches on the handlebars.

When she told Robbie the story, he hadn't thought it was very funny. She tried to explain that the headache was nothing to worry about, that she used to get stress headaches every day when she was in high school, but he wasn't listening. He thought she should see a doctor. She shrugged him off. "No one goes to the doctor for one little headache," she told him. Finally he let it drop.

Caroline started pedaling and Debra fell in behind her. The path was dotted with runners and other cyclists at eight o'clock on a Sunday, and the air smelled of freshly mowed grass. They settled into a groove, and when the path opened up, they rode side by side for a bit.

"So, Caroline, you haven't lived here this whole time, have you?"

"No, I've lived all over. Ithaca for undergrad, which I think you knew, then Yale for grad school, Peace Corps in Malawi and Botswana, then a nonprofit doing conservation in Washington state."

"That's a lot of travel. So what finally brought you back?"

Caroline considered her answer. "A few things really. My parents are here, so that was a big draw, but also Robbie's job."

"And what's he do again?"

"He's a fed. Congressional Budget Office. So this is the place." Caroline shrugged.

Deb was silent for a minute as several cyclists passed. "Was it hard coming back after living abroad? I mean, I found the adjustment challenging coming from Austin, but you've really been all over."

"Yes and no." Caroline was quiet while they pedaled up a steep hill. She was breathing hard now. "I think it helps knowing I could be a forester almost anywhere. Being here is my choice. If I hadn't gotten to have those other experiences, I'd probably be saying something different."

They crested another hill and wound through a wooded area with a playground set off the path. Caroline enjoyed this part of the trail. The woods were especially beautiful in spring.

"Speaking of jobs," Deb said, interrupting Caroline's thoughts, "I applied to the position at Sparky's Support that Meg told me about." Deb's excitement rang in her voice.

"You did? That's wonderful! I hope you get it!"

"Me too. I've sent out dozens of résumés and cover letters, but this is the first time I feel like I really have a chance."

"Well, good luck, Debra Lee. You deserve it." Caroline looked at Deb. She was keeping up better than expected. That was a relief. Caroline realized then just how big of a difference the pedal assistance made. Over long distances, she might end up being the one trailing Debra. "By the way, how did things work out with your mom and the bank? That was such a crazy story."

Deb scoffed. "It was crazy, wasn't it? And it's not over." Deb explained the hoops she still had to go through to get Betty's money back.

Caroline frowned. "I'm so sorry, Debra. That's really rough." Should she offer to lend Debra the money? Too awkward.

"Yeah, I just hope my mom has learned her lesson. She was pretty embarrassed."

"I'm sure she was. Poor Betty." Caroline thought about how her own mother, a retired teacher and activist, would have reacted to falling for a scam and shook her head.

The women rode on for several miles enjoying the fresh air. It had rained the night before and was cooler than it had been in days, which seemed to keep most other riders off the path. Debra called for a stretch break at miles five and fifteen, and they were both happy to have a downhill leg for miles sixteen to eighteen. They pulled up for a final stretch and water break.

Caroline removed her sunglasses to wipe the sweat off her forehead, revealing the scratch on her cheek before replacing them.

"You get migraines?" Deb asked between gulps of water.

"Not normally. When I was younger I would get stress headaches, but I don't think I've really had one since Jacob was one or two."

"What do you think brought this one on?" Deb stretched her calves while they talked.

"Oh, I don't know. Hormones? Stress? Could be anything." Caroline took a deep drink from her water bottle.

"Are you worried about it?"

"No, not really." Caroline recalled the vomiting episode but decided not to mention it. She exhaled. If she was honest, the recent onset of headaches was a little worrisome, but she thought Robbie's reaction was unnecessary. "If it happens again I'll do something about it," she said with finality.

"What if you're pregnant?" Deb asked, grinning.

"Do not say that!" Caroline said, laughing. "Well, it wouldn't be so bad, but still. I don't think migraines are a symptom of pregnancy, are they?"

"No, I'm just kidding you. From what I've heard, migraines usually get better during pregnancy. It's postpartum when they get worse."

"So there. I'm not pregnant." Caroline looked defiant.

"Are you ready to finish this ride?"

"Yes, let's go!"

As they finished out the twenty-two miles, it crossed Caroline's mind to ask what happened at the art show. It seemed clear to her that something had gone wrong to send Debra running from the gallery. But then, Caroline decided, she was probably just worried about Betty and the bank. Caroline's parents were fairly well insulated at their retirement residence, but even they could fall victim to one of the clever schemes out these days. Sometimes it felt like having older parents wasn't much different from adding two more children to the mix.

They arrived back at their vehicles around ten thirty. "I'll see you tonight for the new-rider orientation," Caroline said as they loaded up their bikes.

"Sure thing. I'll pick you up."

Caroline skipped lightly down the stone stairs in front of her home, ready to join Deb for the new-rider meeting. Self-conscious about the scrape on her face, she had dabbed some makeup on it and applied mascara. She wasn't sure what to wear to such an event, but had settled on black yoga pants and a silk blouse. *You can't go wrong with silk.* Her quadriceps twinged as she descended each step. Twenty-two miles was nothing to scoff at.

Debra and Marco were sitting in Deb's van outside her house with the windows cracked, and as she approached, she could hear them talking. It seemed Marco was sulking.

"Listen, Marco, you just aren't old enough to stay home by yourself at night. Nine is not old enough," she heard Deb say.

"I wouldn't be by myself. Grandma is there." Marco sounded miffed.

"Yes, and Grandma is not equipped to help you to bed," Deb said forcefully.

Marco huffed. "I can help myself to bed."

"Listen, Grandma's mental state can be unpredictable after the sun sets. You know that. I'm sorry, but you're coming with me."

As Caroline listened, she discovered she was grateful to know that Debra and Marco had troubles of their own. Sometimes it seemed like she and Jacob were the only ones who struggled. He talked back; he was moody; he cried and yelled whenever she asked him to clean up his toys or work on his Kumon. She found herself making concession after concession to him and still he didn't respect her. She worried he would end up abusing drugs and alcohol or falling in with the wrong crowd and she would lose him completely.

"You know, you might even find it interesting," Deb was saying, her tone encouraging.

Tap, tap.

Deb and Marco jumped.

"Sorry," Caroline said. "I didn't want to interrupt but it's getting late." She smiled.

"Oh, no worries. I was just trying to convince Marco he'll have a good time with us tonight."

Caroline looked in at Marco in the back seat. He did not look convinced. "I have an idea," she said. "What if Marco stayed here with Jacob and Robbie? Robbie won't mind." She didn't know for sure that Robbie wouldn't mind, but she'd make him see her way. This was important. If she helped Deb out like this, maybe Deb would open up more.

Deb looked back at Marco. "What do you think? Does that sound like a good idea?"

"Yes!" Marco had unbuckled his seat belt and was out of the van before Deb could change her mind. "Thanks, Mrs. Cook. You're the best!"

Twenty minutes later, Deb pulled the van into the parking lot of Wellspring Café. Inside, it was dimly lit with a small bar of ten seats, about a dozen four-top tables, and a nook where a band might be playing on a Friday night. The walls were painted black or dark red, and the windows were tinted. A handful of people were standing at the bar getting drinks, and half of the tables were full. R.E.M's "Shiny Happy People" was playing over the sound system, and several people were bobbing their heads to the music. Off to the side, Caroline saw that one table had been taken over as a welcome desk.

The newcomers signed their names to the list and grabbed the handouts. Caroline took a Bike MS magnet from the pile of giveaways, and Deb chose a pen.

"Pennant?" Deb asked, pointing to another stack of items with the Bike MS logo.

Caroline looked at the yellow triangle and imagined attaching it to a pole at the back of her bike. She shook her head at the vision. "No, thanks." She scanned the room. Judging by the list of names she had just seen and the number of people in the bar area, not to mention the general vibe coming from the patrons, she thought everyone here must be with the event. "Want to get a drink while we wait?"

"Great idea."

At the bar, the bartender poured them each a glass of prosecco. A friendly-looking fellow in an orange polo shirt and khakis came over to chat. He had the build of a dedicated cyclist and the aura of an event host.

"Hello and welcome," he said, reaching out his hand.

Caroline took his hand and shook it. She read his name tag: "Where there's a Will there's a way." *Will* was written in bold.

"Hello. Very clever," she said, gesturing to the tag.

"You like that?" he said, grinning.

Deb also smiled. "Hello, I'm Deb."

"I'm Will, the leader of this group. I see you found the handouts. Now you need name tags. Come with me."

The trio walked back to the welcome table. Standing behind the table and off to the side was a striking woman who appeared to be in her midtwenties.

"Trish," Will said, "do you have name tags for my new friends?"

"Of course," Trish said pleasantly.

Caroline took in the sight of Trish. She hadn't noticed her on their first stop at the welcome table and thought she must've been elsewhere because she was definitely noticeable. Her hair was twisted in pink dreadlocks, and she wore a sleeveless white tank top and a black denim miniskirt. Bright eye makeup accentuated the unusual blue of her eyes. Her name tag, written in rainbow colors, read "Make-a-Wish Trish."

Trish handed Deb and Caroline each a name tag and a marker. The friends looked at each other, both clearly thinking of puns for their tags. Deb laughed as she jotted something down. Caroline thought a moment, then wrote a few words, pulled the tag from its backing, and patted it in place.

Deb read it out loud. "'Caroline Cares a Lot.' Indeed she does."

Caroline flushed and read Deb's tag. "'Debra Lee Won't Break.' Hmm. I thought you would have gone with 'Nobody Doesn't Like Debra Lee.'"

A genuine laugh burst from Deb's lips, and Caroline laughed too. "Maybe next time," Deb said.

More people had filled in around them in the few minutes since they arrived, and they went to find seats for the presentation. Caroline sipped her wine. It was crisp and light, and the bubbles tickled her nose. She discovered she had a permanent smile on her lips in this atmosphere and she liked it.

Will took to the microphone on the tiny stage, while someone turned down the music from the PA system. Several people applauded. Caroline looked from table to table. She wondered who here had MS and who was like her—here to support someone who did. In the dark of the room, they all looked the same.

"Hello and welcome," Will boomed into the microphone, and the audience quieted down. "If you are here to learn about Bike MS, you are in the right place." A few people whistled and cheered before Will went on. "We are going to start tonight with a couple of stories to remind everyone why we're here. Then we'll talk about the logistics of the ride and just exactly what it is you're getting into." The crowd erupted in laughter as Will deadpanned the last phrase.

"First up tonight is Make-a-Wish Trish. This lovely lady has been with us for more than five years and has raised an inspiring twenty-five thousand dollars."

The audience clapped as Trish climbed onto the stage and took the microphone from Will.

"Good evening," Trish began. She flipped her dreads to one side as she got comfortable speaking. "I'm here tonight to tell you that what you are about to do is going to change your life. Not only that, but the money you raise has the power to change the lives of thousands of people across the country. I know because my sister is one such person. Ashley lives in Florida with my parents. I ride for her because she can't ride for herself. Diagnosed at age twenty-six with primary progressive MS, she experienced a rapid decline that left her in a wheelchair. Although there have been many breakthroughs over the years, PPMS patients have just one drug option available to them. We must continue the search for more and better treatments. We need medicines that not only slow the progression but repair the damage. And I believe we'll get there, thanks to people like you, people who care about other people and aren't afraid to work hard for a good cause. This year I will be riding one hundred and fifty miles over two days, and I have pledged to raise ten thousand dollars. For Ashley."

Trish raised her fist in the air and the crowd cheered. Someone yelled out, "For Ashley!"

Caroline felt her face flush with excitement. She looked over at Deb. Her eyes were locked on Trish, as enthralled as Caroline.

Will took back the microphone. "Thank you, Trish. You got

this!" he said as Trish returned to her seat. "Next we're going to hear from my good friend Ben. If you join us for any of our training rides, you'll surely see Ben again. He's a committed member of our group and a real inspiration to the people around him. Let's hear it for Ben."

Caroline looked around the room to find who would be speaking next. Two tables over, a short, muscular man with graying cropped hair stood up and moved to the stage. He took each step with deliberation, and one of his hands appeared clubbed. Once onstage, he held the microphone in his good hand.

"Hello, everyone. Thank you so much for being here. My name is Ben Michaels, but most people call me Ben Bikes. I was diagnosed with relapsing-remitting multiple sclerosis in 1995. At that time, doctors still told patients that we should not exert ourselves too much. We were supposed to quit our jobs and rest our bodies and drop out of life."

Boos rose up from the audience as Ben described the old way.

"But I said no. I called bullshit on that doctor."

Caroline and Deb added their voices to the cheers.

"In 2003 I found a support group that was interested in really helping people with MS, not putting them in a corner and locking them away. That's where I met Will, and that's how I got involved with Bike MS." He scanned the audience. "My disease isn't as bad as some," he intoned, turning his gaze to Trish. "I don't need a wheelchair. Most days I don't even use a cane. But that doesn't mean it doesn't affect my life. It does. Every day. And I have my bad days, just like anyone. I've woken up only to discover I can't see out of one eye. I've woken up only to fall when I try to get out of bed. I've lost friends and lovers because they didn't understand." Ben paused and looked out at the crowd again. "But this group, being part of this group of beautiful souls—especially my teammates, Will, Lonny, and Ahmed—you make it so I can get through the rough patches. Sometimes when we are out on the road training, or sending emails trying to raise money, we might ask ourselves, Does what we do matter? Does any of it make a difference? And the answer, my friends, is yes. Yes, it does!"

The audience roared its approval.

Caroline wiped a tear from her eye while whooping with the rest of the patrons. Deb turned and smiled at her. "I'm so glad we came," she yelled over the applause.

When they turned back to the stage, Will was at the microphone again. "All right, everyone, now that you know why you're here, let's talk logistics. Get out your phones and get ready to register. You'll need to create an account and you can decide whether to ride as an individual or as a team."

Caroline and Deb both pulled out their phones and went to the Chesapeake Challenge website. "Shall we make a team?" Deb asked.

"Yes, and we should invite Philippe too."

"Good idea."

Caroline dashed off a text to Philippe to ask him to join the team.

Deb said, "It's too bad he couldn't make it tonight. He's really missing a show."

Will returned to the mike, giving more logistics about the fundraising website and how to make the most of it. Regarding how much money to pledge, he said, "My advice? Set a goal just above what you think is possible, and then get to work meeting it."

The room came alive then, with the would-be participants all chatting and clicking through their phones. Caroline considered what goal to set. Ten thousand dollars, like Trish? She knew if she didn't get enough pledges from others, she'd end up putting in the money herself, so she didn't want to aim too high. After some consideration she settled on two thousand.

"Do you know how much you're going to pledge?" she asked Deb.

"I want to be sure it's attainable," Deb said. "I'm going with a thousand. You?"

"I think the people at my work will contribute a lot, plus Robbie's friends and coworkers. I went with two thousand."

"Hmm. Do you think I should raise my goal?"

Caroline wanted to be tactful. "Well, maybe when you have a job?" Her cheeks flushed as she spoke.

Deb laughed. "Good point. I can always raise it later, or go over my goal. Did you hear back from Philippe?"

Caroline checked her phone. "Not yet. I wonder how far he's planning to ride."

"Rosa said one fifty."

"Oh, well, we don't have to do that if you think it's too much," Caroline said. She worried about Deb overdoing it.

"No, I want to do the full one fifty."

Caroline scrolled through the site. "They have routes for every level of ability here. Thirty, sixty, seventy-five, or one hundred miles for the first day, and fifty or seventy-five for the second day. Are you sure you want to do one fifty?"

"Yes, I'm sure," Debra insisted.

Caroline held her tongue. Although riding thirty miles on the

first day and fifty on the second would still be a respectable challenge, she sensed doing the full distance was a point of pride for
Deb. Better to support her than try to dissuade her. "Okay then, the
next question is whether to do one hundred and then fifty, or split
it into two rides of seventy-five."

Deb thought a minute. "I have a feeling two seventy-five-mile
rides will be more doable than trying to do fifty miles the day after
completing one hundred. We'll be completely spent after a hundred miles on the bike. I know I won't want to get back in the saddle
the next day. What about you?"

"I'm not as practiced of a rider as you are, Deb, so I don't really
know. Let's ask."

Caroline raised her hand, but before she could ask her question, Will had moved on to other important aspects of the ride.
He explained the lodging options—hotels or camping on-site—and
noted that all food would be provided. SAG support would also be
provided, including rest stops every ten miles with food, water, and
energy drinks. "We do everything we can to ensure you have a successful ride," he said.

When the presentations were over, the crowd began to mill
about, and Will and Trish roamed the room, answering questions.
Caroline and Deb looked at each other. "I can't believe we're doing
this," Caroline said, a thrill of excitement running through her.

"I can't believe it's taken me so long to get back to it," Deb said.
"Thank you for supporting me."

Caroline furrowed her brow. She wondered again why Deb
hadn't completed the ride all those years ago, but there were too
many people around for her to ask now. "Of course, Deb. I'm glad
to do it." She scanned the room. The diversity of people and back-

grounds reminded her of her time in the Peace Corps. That was another group of volunteers who had come together to change the world. It felt good to belong to something again, to know that what she was doing would make a difference in the lives of people in need.

At that moment Will walked by their table. Deb called out to him and he stopped. "How can I help you?" he asked.

Deb spoke up. "We're planning to do the full one fifty, but we don't know if it's better to do two rides of seventy-five miles, or one hundred miles followed by fifty miles. Do you have any guidance?"

Will looked at Deb. "First, what kind of bike are you on?"

"My friend has a regular road bike. I have a road bike with pedal assist."

"You have MS?" Will looked from Deb to Caroline and back.

"I do. Caroline doesn't," Deb said with a nod to Caroline standing next to her.

Will thought a minute. "I'd suggest the even split. The recovery from a century ride can be very tough."

Deb nodded. "I was thinking the same thing. Thanks for confirming."

"Also remember," Will added, "your battery might need to be recharged, or you'll need to carry a second battery. Not many can make it one hundred miles. Some get more like forty miles to a charge."

Caroline had forgotten all about Deb's battery life. She wondered what Deb would choose.

"That's right! I believe mine gets seventy-five to eighty miles at my current setting, assuming the route isn't too hilly. But I might travel with a second battery just in case."

Will nodded. "That's probably best. SAG doesn't carry chargers, although some of the rest stops will have electricity."

Deb thanked him and Will moved on to the next table, where someone else was trying to get his attention.

"That settles it, then," said Caroline with a smile.

"Yes, I'd say so. And nothing is going to stop me from completing it this time." Deb looked around. "I think we've done everything we were supposed to do. Are you ready to go? I should get back to Marco."

"Yeah, let's go." Just then Caroline's cell phone pinged. She checked the message. "Yes!" she exclaimed. "Philippe is in!"

At home later that night, Deb was floating. Marco and Betty were both in their rooms, Marco falling quickly asleep after a late night with Jacob, and Deb had the living room to herself. Sitting at the table with the half-completed jigsaw puzzle on it, she took a few minutes to process all that had happened at the new-rider meeting.

The stories Trish and Ben had shared were undeniably inspirational. She had noticed Caroline wiping a tear from her cheek. She was moved as well. She had yet to get involved in the local MS community, and even when she was in Austin, she had gone to her support group sporadically. Attending group was like eating vegetables—she knew it was good for her and she would feel better after, but she didn't always enjoy it. Although she liked being able to share her problems and hear how others had handled something similar, the meetings sometimes felt like she was staring down a bleak future she did not want to accept. Despite the walking stick, the weekly injections, the fatigue, she was still relatively healthy. She tried to be thankful for what she had.

But tonight? Tonight was different.

It was such a relief to be in a room full of energetic, positive-thinking MSers like her! It felt like coming home. There was no complaining. No pity. No puppy-dog eyes. And she knew now, without a doubt, that she would complete this ride. Even Betty had commented: she couldn't wipe the smile off her face. And why should she? She had found her place and she was happy.

Deb set up her laptop, filled her water glass, put on her glasses, and stuffed her earphones in her ears. Then she signed in to her video chat program and waited for Paula to join. They hadn't talked in over a week, and Deb was anxious to tell her daughter about her night. Just as the clock on the wall struck ten, the computer dinged and Paula's cheery face came into view.

"Hi, Mom. How are you?"

Deb smiled wide. "I'm very good, thanks for asking."

Paula grinned at her mother's bouncy demeanor. "Well, well. What's been happening that has you in such a good mood?"

Deb shifted in her chair and leaned in. "First, I submitted an application for a job with an organization that provides support dogs to people with disabilities, and just before I signed on tonight I saw an email from them that they want to interview me."

"Oh my goodness! That's great news, Mom! I'm so happy for you!" Paula's face shone brightly.

"Thanks, honey." Deb's smile grew even wider. "I'm really happy too. It's just an interview, but it's the most I've gotten since we moved out here. I really needed this. And I know a woman who works there who says it's a great place to work. I'm hoping my fifteen years of experience and the inside connection will close the deal."

"Absolutely. That's great!" Paula's smile reflected her mother's.

"There's something else too." Deb held her breath while she waited for Paula's attention.

Paula raised her eyebrows in surprise. "And what's that? Not a boyfriend."

"No, no, not a boyfriend. I've been waiting to tell you because I didn't want you to worry. But now that I'm certain I'm doing it, well . . . I've decided to train for the Chesapeake Challenge." She beamed.

Paula cocked her head to the side. "The what?"

"The Chesapeake Challenge," Deb said. "Remember? The MS-150 bike ride. I think I told you my friend Rosa's husband, Philippe, is doing it, and I've decided I'm going to try it."

"Oh." Paula's face fell.

Deb looked at her daughter, her own smile fading just as quickly. "I was hoping you'd be excited for me. I've been on three long rides and several short training rides and I'm very pleased with how it's going." She was determined to stay positive.

"Well, good, Mom. That's good. It's just . . ."

"What? You can tell me." She felt her chest tighten as she awaited the bad news.

"One hundred and fifty miles is a lot for even a healthy person. Are you sure you can handle it? Safely, I mean." Paula pursed her lips.

Ever since she was first diagnosed, Deb had had to deal with people putting restrictions on her. Doctors. Employers. Friends. Even her children. She usually tried to appease them, but this ride was too important to her. "I appreciate your concern, but I really think it's going to be fine. I talked it over with my doctor a couple of weeks ago, and he gave me some pointers on how to handle the physical and emotional stress. Plus my friend Caroline is doing it with me, so you don't have to worry about anything happening to me on the route."

"Oh, jeez. I hadn't even thought of that!" Paula exclaimed, rolling her eyes. She sighed then and regained her composure. "Listen, Mom, I'm glad you have a friend to do it with you." Despite the upbeat words, Paula's face could not hide her concern. "Please, just be careful."

"I will, honey, I promise. If something happens and it seems like it's not going to be a good idea, I will back out. Deal?"

"Deal."

"Caroline can ride with Philippe if needed."

"There you go. Good idea, Mom!"

Deb struggled to smile at the thought of dropping out of the ride. Her body had come a long way in the short time since she started training. Not to mention the commitment she had made to Philippe and Caroline. She'd been waiting for this for twenty years. She would be devastated if she had to stop now. She changed the subject.

"Tell me about school, Paula. How are your classes? You do still go to class, don't you?" She grinned.

"Very funny, Mom. Yes, I go to class. I'm actually doing great this semester. I'm taking a class on social diversity and justice and it is really blowing my mind." Paula relaxed with the change in topic.

"That's so good to hear!"

"Yeah, and this summer I'm going to apply for an internship at one of the programs here. Chicago Cares connects people to volunteer opportunities, and they need a coordinator."

"That's great!"

"If I get it, I won't be coming to see you this summer."

Paula seemed to be testing her with that statement. Deb weighed her response. She'd been conflicted about Paula's presumed summer in Silver Spring. There was a reason she'd never brought Paula back to her hometown. Perhaps this was a blessing.

"Well, I'll miss you," she said evenly.

A shadow passed over Paula's face. "I'll miss you too. I thought I'd come stay with you for at least a couple of weeks—if I'm invited, that is."

"It's not like that," Deb said, talking over her.

"I don't even have the job yet," Paula said at the same time, "so it may be a moot point."

With those words, Deb smiled and considered her daughter. "You astound me, Paula."

"Mom, you're so funny."

"What?"

Paula laughed. "Just—how do I astound you?"

"I don't know. For one thing, you correctly used *moot* in a sentence."

"Oh, Mom!" Paula laughed again but Deb just smiled.

"For another, you're doing all the things you need to do to make the life you want. That takes guts. You should be proud of yourself."

Paula's cheeks turned pink. "Thanks, Mom. I am proud of my-self. But now I need to go. My friends are waiting."

"Okay, me too. I have to get to bed soon. Have a good night."

The computer went dark. Deb took her earbuds out and scratched her face. Her cheeks were a tiny bit sore with sunburn after the morning ride. It was still early in the season, and she hadn't thought to put on sunblock. It reminded her of her child-hood, when no one wore sunscreen and her cheeks often seemed slightly singed. The discomfort had the unexpected effect of mak-ing her feel youthful. Her muscles felt good too. She rearranged her arms and her biceps twinged pleasantly, drawing a smile. She was also sleeping better now that she was exercising more regularly. She still had her fatigue to contend with, but all in all, she thought the cycling had only been a good thing.

She grabbed her phone and typed a text message, then copied it to four friends from Austin, her old boss, as well as Luis's brother, Julian. She explained that she was taking on a big challenge and could use their support, then attached a link to her fundraising page. Uncle Julian had been especially supportive of Marco since his brother's death, and Deb thought he might be willing to con-tribute. She looked forward to seeing who had replied by morning.

With that done, she reflected again on her conversation with Paula. Her daughter was worried about her overdoing it, but when wasn't that the case? She shook her head. No way was she giving up this feeling. As long as she took it slow, she would be just fine.

Thirteen

Things were moving quickly for Deb. In the past three weeks she'd had interviews with the deputy director and the executive director at Sparky's Support as well as a meeting with the HR rep. She'd been so busy, in fact, that she had to reschedule her appointment at the credit card company to get Betty's money back. She and Betty had made some changes at home to bridge the gap—buying on credit, transferring money from savings—and for as much as Deb wanted to be done with the scam, securing the income from a new job took precedence. The gamble had paid off. She passed each interview, and by the end of the second week, they were ready to make her the director of development, reporting to the executive director, an unreadable man named Calvin Abrams. Calvin wanted her to come in on Monday after his early meeting and get the lay of the land. He told her to expect a short first day.

The thought of starting a position that so closely matched her values made Deb giddy. But it wasn't all good news. She had requested to work from home two days a week so she could be with Betty, but when the offer came in, the proposed schedule was to work in the office five days a week with reduced hours on Wednesdays and Fridays. She hesitated only a moment before accepting. She'd been unemployed for too long, the salary was more than she expected, and the office was only ten minutes from her home. A commute that short was unheard of in the traffic-congested sub-urbs. Add in Meg's endorsement and Deb's own passion for the mission and she was willing to bend to meet their schedule.

Monday morning, Deb arrived at Sparky's to find Calvin waiting for her in the lobby.

"Come to my office. We'll chat," Calvin said, and he led the way to the only office with a door.

Deb appreciated the open office design and clean wood floors. The visitors' lobby gave way to the main office space, and there was plenty of room to navigate around desks. She also noticed a door marked "Infirmary," with a sign welcoming people to take a rest or enjoy some quiet time when needed. Meg was right when she had said this place took accommodating all abilities as key to its mission.

Sitting across from her new boss, Deb tried to remember every-thing she'd been told during the interview process. Sparky's, Cal-vin had explained, was made up of twelve people divided between programming and development, and she would primarily be inter-acting with six of them. Only Molly and Robin reported directly to Deb; Robin was the events manager, while Molly served as the de-velopment manager. The other four—Hannah, Lawrence, Flo, and Tom—reported to Calvin but would work with Deb's team on an ad hoc basis.

With such a small staff, Calvin explained now, each person had to do double duty, and that included Deb. Like the rest of the team, she would take an hour a day to work the front desk and catalog in-kind donations. The office didn't get a lot of visitors, but a few times a week they received donations in the form of money or sup-plies. Occasionally the dogs and their trainers would come by for a visit as well, but mostly it was a normal office that focused on the administrative work of the organization.

"Come with me, I'll show you where we keep the donations," Calvin said. "You can meet the rest of the department on our way."

Calvin escorted Deb around to each person's desk to say hello. This was made slightly awkward because they could see Deb and Calvin approach from across the room and had to pretend to be working for the few moments it took the pair to arrive. Not only that but Calvin was much taller than Deb. Together Deb thought they gave the impression of Abbott and Costello, with her cast as Costello. Or perhaps Cheri Oteri and Will Ferrell, if they had been wearing cheerleader outfits. As she thought about the comedy duos, she smiled, wondering if she and Calvin would someday have such a rapport.

Moving through the office, Deb was keen to see how each person reacted to the boss. Calvin was tall and formidable, but his employees didn't seem intimidated. Hannah, Lawrence, and Flo were all smiles, welcoming Deb to the team and offering their support. Her direct report Robin, with her bouncy blond curls, came across as professional and ready to help, just as Calvin had described the department. Deb could definitely see them working seamlessly on projects together.

Next she met Tom, an oafish blond who connected the support dogs to the people who needed them. He smelled slightly of weed, and she noticed that he and Molly kept exchanging looks. Molly, seated next to Tom, was Deb's other direct report. When Calvin and Deb arrived at her desk, Molly smiled up at Calvin as if she were starstruck. "Molly here has been an asset to Sparky's for ten years," Calvin said. "No one handles the donors better. I'm sure you'll agree."

Deb smiled, expecting a warm greeting from Molly after that glowing review. "I look forward to working with you, Molly." But Molly only grimaced, muttering "Hiya" before turning back to her work. *What was that about?*

Before Deb could give it too much thought, Calvin had walked off. She caught up to him in front of a large storeroom at the end of one hallway. "And now for the donation closet. Although what we really need are towels, dog beds, and training treats," Calvin said, "our donors insist on including at least one toy with their donations." He swung open the door.

Deb looked at the rack of shelves in front of her and burst out laughing: one entire shelf was stuffed with unopened puppy toys. "I see what you mean," she said. Calvin smiled down at her.

After the tour, Deb and Calvin walked back to the front of the office and took their seats on the facing couches in the visitors' area. The cushions were stiff, as if rarely used, and Deb sat uncomfortably on the edge. Calvin's demeanor was more open than it had been during the interview, but he still struck Deb as a businessman first and foremost. That was all right with Deb, as long as he trusted her to do her job.

"Do you have any questions?" Calvin asked, his hands clasped in front of him.

Deb spoke carefully, still feeling like she was in an interview. "On our call you mentioned one of my main tasks would be working on the annual dinner coming up in June. Can you tell me more about that?"

"Oh, yes. I have lots of paperwork for you on that." Calvin rubbed his palms together. "I'll get you the files from the previous events. We already have the venue, theme, and date set, as I mentioned, but you'll have oversight for arranging the vendors, entertainment-slash-speakers, decor, invitations, mailers, et cetera, et cetera." Deb must have looked overwhelmed because Calvin quickly added, "There's a whole checklist of items with due dates and backup materials from previous years available to you. I won't lie, it's a lot of work, but you don't need to reinvent the wheel."

"Okay, great. That's good to hear." Deb smiled to show she was on board.

"While the annual dinner is the biggest project under your purview, I want to draw your attention to the fiscal year end for meeting our donation goals, which is June 30."

"June 30," Deb repeated. She tried to calculate how far away that was, but her adrenaline was clouding her brain.

"We're nearing the end of April now, so you have about two months," Calvin said helpfully.

"Right. Great. Very good. Thanks for clarifying that." She smiled again, then said, "Who usually attends the annual event?"

"We invite a robust list of donors. About twenty percent of them will come to the event. These are businesspeople in our community, some of the local elected officials, as well as leaders of societies that serve the same constituents, such as the Cancer Institute, Wounded Warriors, and others. It's a good time. I have high expectations for this year." Calvin took a deep breath and exhaled. "Well, I think that's all for now. You'll need to take your time going through the manual and the documents I mentioned. You'll find links to those in your email tonight. I had hoped to have it all ready for you this morning, but I'm afraid my morning meeting ran long." He shook his head. "Ah, one last note. Our donors generally give because they love dogs or because they have family members who have benefited from our services. You'll need to be familiar with our mission, of course, and all of our public-facing materials. Our website is a good place to start. I suggest you go home for the day, read up on our website, and come back tomorrow ready to dive in."

"That's perfect." Deb thought for a minute, then ventured a question. Speaking softly so her coworkers wouldn't hear, she said, "I was thinking about using my lunch hour to attend a support group for people with MS. It's once a month at 11 a.m. on Tuesdays. Will that work for the office, or should I plan to make different arrangements?"

Calvin nodded and said, "I'll leave that one up to you. If you'd like to try it tomorrow, be my guest. You just might find your dance card is full when you're here." Calvin gave an enigmatic smile.

"Enough said," Deb said, nodding back at him, though she wasn't sure she understood. That was okay. She would have tomorrow to see how things went.

Tuesday morning Deb said goodbye to her mother, dropped Marco off at school, and arrived at Sparky's just before nine o'clock. Taking her cane with her, she went inside to face her first full day at her new job. She was excited and nervous. She had landed what seemed to be the perfect job, but there was still a lot she didn't know.

"Good morning," she said brightly as she walked into the office. Flo, Molly, and Hannah were settling into their workstations and said hello. Deb noticed three empty desks as she passed them.

Tom took Tuesdays off, she remembered, and Robin and Lawrence weren't in yet. Calvin's office door was closed, but Deb was sure he was in there somewhere.

She took a seat at her workstation and logged on to her messages to find links to the files that Calvin had promised. They were organized on the shared drive, with files for past galas, volunteer lists, donor lists, company documents for mission, vision, and strategic goals, the company code of conduct, and a slew of budgetary spreadsheets. Most of the budget did not fall under Deb's job description, but she did have significant funding for the annual dinner, and she had that June 30 fundraising goal to meet. She sighed at the breadth of materials in front of her.

She downloaded the files she expected to use the most and organized them into folders on her file manager. The annual dinner was set for June 27, just two weeks after the Chesapeake Challenge. She hoped to have everything well in hand by race day so she could take time off without worry. She pinned up a couple of papers with dates she didn't want to forget and printed the checklists she would need. She was known to friends and colleagues alike as an organization and neatness queen, thanks in no small part to her penchant for keeping lists.

Throughout the morning, people stopped by her desk to welcome her aboard. The programming folks she didn't meet the day before smiled or waved. One kind woman offered to show her where the refrigerator was. Deb felt pleasantly surprised by the collegial atmosphere. She had always enjoyed her work. It was good to be back among people.

Around ten fifteen, she got up to stretch her legs and make some tea. She was still working through her paperwork, and more was pouring in. Should she leave now and attend her support group, or try to get more work under her belt? On the one hand, it was her first full day and she had barely made a dent in what she was hoping to accomplish. On the other hand, she needed to take care of her mind and spirit or her body wouldn't function. But she also had her coworkers and reports to think about. Would they resent her leaving before midday, even if she did come back after lunch?

On her return trip to her desk, she remembered she needed to set up meetings with Robin and Molly. She stopped by Robin's workstation first. Robin was a heavyset white woman with rosy cheeks and a calm demeanor. She smiled easily and put Deb at ease. "Robin, I'm thinking we should talk tomorrow about where you are with your projects. Is there a time that's good for you?"

"Hi, Deb. Sure. Let me see." Robin peered at her calendar on her computer, leaning in to see better. "I don't have anything scheduled for ten o'clock. Does that work?"

"Perfect," Deb said. "I'll send you an invite." She moved on to Molly's workstation and repeated her request.

"Uh, I don't know . . . ," Molly replied with a frown. She had small features, with freckles across her nose, and glasses that gave her an owl-like appearance. Deb found her hard to read.

She waited to see if Molly would say more. When she didn't, Deb said, "Would ten thirty work?"

Molly sighed. "That's fine. I guess I won't work from home tomorrow then."

Now it was Deb's turn to frown. "Do you normally work from home on Wednesdays? I wasn't aware of that."

"No, it's fine. We can meet tomorrow." Molly's mouth formed a thin line.

"Because we could do a virtual call if you were going to work from home," Deb offered.

"I said it's fine." Molly's cheeks went red.

Let it go. "Okay, tomorrow it is. I'll send the calendar invite." She let out her breath as she walked away.

By the time Deb reached her desk, cup of tea in hand, the idea of leaving for her support group seemed an obvious mistake. She searched the online calendar of MS support groups in the area hoping to find one that met outside work hours. Not that she had loads of free time after work, what with Marco and Betty to care for, the house to run, and the ride to train for, but it might be the best option. "Aha," she said, scrolling through the list. Another group was meeting on Saturday afternoon. She had a bike ride planned for the morning, but the timing should work. She marked her calendar and made a mental note to ask her mom if she could watch Marco while Deb attended the meeting.

With that settled, she sent meeting invitations to Robin and Molly for the next day. She would need to engage them personally and find out how she could support them. Robin accepted the invitation immediately. Molly took a few minutes, causing Deb a short burst of anxiety, but when her computer pinged next, it was with a notification that Molly had accepted. Deb opened up the company handbook then and started to read. She had so much to learn about her new organization. She was excited to start meeting donors, getting to know her teammates, and raising money for the Sparky's mission.

Fourteen

That night Deb went to bed feeling good. She was happy with her choice to stay at work for the full day and looked forward to trying the Saturday support group. Lying in the dark, she realized she hadn't told her mom about the schedule change. Shoot! If Betty couldn't watch Marco, Deb would have to arrange a playdate for him. But where? She'd relied on Rosa too much lately. Maybe Caroline wouldn't mind having him over. She typed a quick note on her phone as a reminder before drifting off to sleep.

Wednesday morning, Deb woke up early, showered, dressed, and got breakfast for herself and Marco. Then she once again said goodbye to her mother, dropped Marco off at school, and arrived at work just before nine o'clock. She was already starting to feel the grind but told herself to be grateful she had a job.

By ten o'clock Deb was in the conference room for her appointment with Robin. The small room with beige walls was taken up almost entirely by the conference table and a few filing cabinets. One full wall of windows allowed some natural light into the room, though the view itself was of a brick wall. Robin came in moments later with a notepad and pen. She took the seat across from Deb.

"Robin, thank you for meeting with me."

"Of course. Happy to," she said with a smile. Her bouncy blond curls hung down to her shoulders, and she flipped the tresses behind her shoulder as she spoke.

"You've worked here for seven years, right?"

"Yes, that's right. I started out in donor relations and was promoted twice."

"And now you're the events manager. Congratulations."

"Thanks."

"Well, let me get straight to the point. My purpose in having this meeting is really just to find out what you're working on and how I can support you. As the events manager, you're crucial to the success of the annual dinner. I want to be sure you have what you need to succeed." Deb paused to let Robin respond.

"Thank you, Deb. I appreciate your offer to help. I think I have what I need. With the director position open, I was doing some of that work as well, so having you take care of that will be a load off for me."

"Well, thank you, Robin, for stepping up like that. I'm sure I'll be relying on you. I still have a lot of catching up to do." Deb looked at her notes, then said, "You're the liaison with the venue. Can you tell me about that?"

"Yes, that's right. Silver Celebrations. We've used them for the past several years. They've been a good venue. My only complaint is that they're very particular about vendors. All vendors have to be preapproved. But that's not too hard. We generally just use the providers from their lists."

"That makes sense." Deb jotted a note down. They talked for several minutes more about the annual dinner, the other initiatives Robin was working on, and what direction she wanted to take her position. Deb was very pleased with everything she heard. She saw

Robin as an asset and potential confidante in the office and was thankful to have someone on the team she could trust to follow through.

"Thanks again, Robin," she said at the meeting's end. "You can leave the door open. Molly should be in shortly."

Deb took a few minutes to clear her mind, then prepared to speak with Molly. When Molly sat down for her meeting at ten thirty, the atmosphere was decidedly stormier than when sunny Robin had been in the same seat. Molly said the right things, for the most part anyway, but her countenance was once again hard to decipher. Deb noticed her mouth always returned to a frown when she wasn't talking.

"Given your role of development manager, you must be very close with our donors," Deb said brightly. Her voice sounded strained to her ears as she tried to lighten the mood.

"I guess so." Molly's brown hair hung in lank curtains to her shoulders. With Deb's attention on her, she looked as if she would prefer to hide behind them.

"Molly, like I told Robin earlier, I most want to be sure you have everything you need to succeed. You'll be instrumental in meeting our fundraising goals. Is there anything I can help with to make your job easier?"

"No, I think I can handle it." That same grimace.

Deb paused, unsure how to respond. She was having a hard time reconciling the woman in front of her with the description Calvin had given. "Okay, well, that's great. And for the annual dinner, you're in charge of the food, correct?"

"Yes."

"Any concerns there?"

"No."

Deb searched Molly's face for signs of insubordination. Nothing. She decided to move on. "And when you think about growth in your position, what do you see as being in your ideal future?"

Molly looked at Deb as if she were speaking a foreign language. "Do you mean where do I see myself in five years?"

Deb nodded. "Sure, you can think of it that way. I was thinking of a more immediate future. Say, next year, where do you see yourself?"

"Here." Molly's face was inscrutable as she looked blankly at Deb.

"Okay, great!" This meeting seemed to be taking a left turn, but Deb sensed she wasn't going to get a more specific answer today, so she dropped it. "Thank you for your time, Molly. Please know I'm here to help." Deb smiled.

"Can I go?" Molly asked with a frown.

Deb stuttered her reply. "Uh, yes, we're finished. Thanks." She smiled again and held her breath while Molly walked out. When she was out of sight, Deb exhaled and placed her forehead on the table. *Like pulling teeth.* She sat up just as Calvin was passing by the conference room. He looked in at her, but she couldn't tell if he was amused or dismayed by her theatrics.

The rest of the day passed quickly. She had lunch at noon, then worked at her desk until three, when she left for the day. Her first early release day! She planned to take advantage of it with a bike ride. She checked in on Betty at home, rode her bike for forty-five minutes, then took time to stretch when she returned home. She silently applauded her discipline in stretching. She had been on the go all day; slowing down to stretch required a Jedi mindset.

Finally, around four thirty, she picked Marco up from Rosa's house. Marco and PJ were supposed to be working on their Spanish together, but when Deb arrived, that did not seem to be the case. Instead Jacob had joined them, and the three boys were in the back-yard playing soccer. She walked to the back gate and called over the fence. "Marco, let's go. It's time."

"Aw, Mom, can't I stay a little longer?" Marco was chasing PJ, who had the ball. Deb's son was three years older than PJ and caught him easily with his longer, stronger legs.

"Not tonight, sweetie. We need to go."

"Okay," Marco said in a pathetic voice. But instead of dragging out his goodbyes as he sometimes would, he quickly ran to Deb's side and followed her out. Deb smiled as he hugged her, and they walked toward the van.

"I'm going to say goodbye to Rosa real quick. You can climb in."

Just as Deb was turning back to the house, Rosa opened the front door. "Deb, good to see you!"

"Rosa! Thanks for hosting Marco this afternoon. I really appreciate it."

"No worries. It was a pleasure listening to Marco and PJ read together."

"So they actually did it?" Deb was floored.

"Yes, they did! Jacob arrived about half an hour ago and they all went outside then." Rosa laughed at the shocked look on Deb's face. "I know, I know. I was as surprised as you are."

Deb waved goodbye and joined Marco in the van. When they arrived home five minutes later, the exhaustion from a long day hit Deb hard. Dinner was going to have to be something simple. She went straight for the couch while Marco ran to his room to do his homework.

"Mom, how are you feeling today?" Deb asked, sitting back on the couch.

Betty was seated in her favorite chair working on a word search. "I'm good. Why? Is something wrong?"

"No, nothing's wrong. I just wanted to see how you are. Things have been busy. How are you holding up?"

"Fine. Just fine. Is there anything I can do?" Betty looked at Deb with concern in her eyes.

Deb thought for a minute, then said, "How would you feel about making dinner?"

Betty was stunned. "You mean it? I would love to make you dinner. What did you have in mind?"

Deb immediately felt ten pounds lighter. She'd been solo parenting for the past three years, putting the loss of her husband aside as much as she could to make sure the house ran smoothly. She'd forgotten the pleasures of having someone else to lean on. "Something simple. Spaghetti and salad? I can make the salad. I can sit at the kitchen table and chop while you brown the meat and boil the noodles."

"Wonderful!" Betty beamed at Deb. After a pause she said, "Thanks, Debbie."

Deb looked at her mom with new eyes. Maybe she should ask for help more often. "Don't mention it."

The two women cooked together in a contented silence in the small kitchen. Chopping lettuce for the salad, Deb remembered her schedule change. "Mom, I had to reschedule my support group. I'm not going to be able to make the Tuesday group anymore."

"Oh, I'm sorry to hear that. You liked them, I thought." Betty was at the stove with her back to Deb, minding the ground beef.

"Yes, I did. The one time I went, anyway. But it's not going to work with my new schedule. So I found another one. It's once a month on Saturday afternoons."

"And where is it?"

"In Rockville, so a little ways away but not too bad. There's a meeting this Saturday. Are you able to be with Marco while I go?"

Betty didn't answer right away and Deb said, "I can also try to get him a playdate with Jacob or PJ. Would that be better?"

"No, no, I can watch him." Betty turned to look at Deb, careful not to drip grease from her spatula onto the floor. "If you're sure you can trust me."

Deb blinked. Had Marco said something about Betty not being well enough to watch him at night? Or could this be about the gift card scam?

"What do you mean?"

Betty turned back to the beef in the pan without responding.

Deb sighed. "Daytimes I would be happy to have your help, Mom. Nights are harder. I think we both know that." She hated to hurt Betty, but she had to do what was best for Marco. She just hoped Betty could understand.

They worked in silence for a while, Deb lost in thought.

"I love you, Ma."

"I love you too, Debbie."

By the time Friday morning arrived, Deb felt like a wet leaf that had dropped from a tree. She had worked until 5 p.m. the day before, and the hectic pace of the morning scramble, working all day, making dinner, and caring for Betty and Marco at night had left her spent. She was looking forward to an early end to her day and the week. She would also be taking her first turn at the front desk today. There didn't seem to be much to it, but after three days of reading background material for her job, an hour of answering the phone and cataloging donations would be a welcome respite.

Just before eleven o'clock Deb grabbed her purse and her cane and walked over to reception to relieve Molly. She made a separate trip for her mug—she could carry only one thing at a time with her cane in her good hand—causing Molly to raise her eyebrows. Molly was a few years younger than Deb but had been with Sparky's the longest of anyone else on the team. It occurred to Deb then that Molly might have tried to get the director position. It would have been an obvious next step in her career. If she did, she was passed over, and after working with her for the past three and a half days, Deb had a good guess as to why. Her negative demeanor and shy attitude left most people feeling cold. It was hard to imagine her rallying a team around a common goal. That was Deb's task now, and that included personalities as different from hers as Molly's.

"Hi, Molly. I'm your relief," Deb said cheerfully, setting down her mug.

"Oh, great. Thanks," Molly said flatly. She got up from her chair and started to walk off.

"Uh, Molly?" Deb called.

"Yes?" Molly turned back. She sounded perturbed.

"Do you have any notes for me?"

Molly sighed then said, "We had three phone calls. One was a wrong number. The other two were people looking to adopt a dog. I forwarded them to Tom to handle."

Deb nodded and asked if there was anything else she should know.

"If any trainers take supplies, you have to record that on the inventory sheet."

"And that's this sheet here?" Deb touched one of the papers on the desk and Molly confirmed that was it. "Do you want your mug?" Deb asked, picking up a Mickey Mouse coffee cup with ears for handles.

Molly took the mug and attempted a smile, then walked back to her desk.

Deb sat down and got ready to answer the phone. What was she going to do about Molly? It was up to Deb to break through the gruff exterior. A lunch date? Too soon. Most likely Molly just needed time.

Deb didn't have much time to consider it, however. She fielded five calls in the first twenty minutes. Three people had questions about what Sparky's did and who might benefit from a support dog. This was good practice for Deb, who had newly learned all the different types of support dogs available and how patients could qual-

ify for government assistance. Two calls were about in-kind donations, and Deb directed the callers to stop by the office during the
specified times. This was all very exciting for Deb, who was both
pleased to have the interaction and happy to help, and she congratulated herself for each successful call resolution. But the real
excitement was yet to come.

At eleven thirty Meg walked in with Taylor, one of the support
dogs Deb recognized from the website.

"Meg! How good to see you!" Deb said from her seat behind the
welcome desk.

"I wondered if I would see you today. I saw the announcement
that they hired you. Congratulations!" Meg smiled broadly, her big
eyes shining.

Deb thanked her for turning her on to the opening. As they talked, Taylor waited patiently at Meg's side. He was a full-breed yellow
Lab and looked every bit the part of a support dog. "Is that Taylor
you have with you today?"

Meg confirmed it was. "Today is Taylor's turn to star in one of
my videos. I came by to use one of the rooms and to get a box of
treats. Do you want to watch us film?"

"I'd love to, but I have to work the front desk until noon. How
about I come find you after that and see if you're still filming." Deb
had wondered where Meg filmed. The videos she had seen online
were in a nondescript room, apparently right down the hall from
where she now sat.

"Works for me!" Meg clicked her tongue and Taylor stood up.
"Enjoy the rest of your morning," she said to Deb, and she and Taylor walked down the hall to the storeroom.

Deb remembered she needed to record the box of treats Meg was taking. She flipped over the paper that Molly had said was the inventory sheet and paused. Rather than an inventory sheet, it appeared to be a running tally of donations for the week, complete with donor names and dates. She scanned it quickly to see if there was a place for recording what was taken as well. She flipped the sheet over again and stopped dead. Halfway down the list was a name that struck her like a bolt of lightning: Andy Peters. According to the sheet, he had stopped by Monday to donate towels.

She instantly flashed back to that cunning smile. *"Come with me. I know a place."* A knot formed in her stomach. She shut her eyes tight but could not chase the memory away. Her heart pounding, she opened her eyes and checked the time: 11:50. Close enough. She grabbed her cane and her purse and rushed outside. When she returned from her lunch break almost an hour later, she had forgotten all about Meg, the video, and the inventory sheet.

Fifteen

Deb lay in bed Friday night bone weary. What a week. Even Marco had been acting out of character when she picked him up from school.

"What's for dinner?" he had asked when he got in the van. His voice was sullen and he leaned his head against the glass.

"As I can hardly stand the thought of working a stove, how about takeout?"

"All right," Marco grumbled.

"Well, don't sound too excited." Deb didn't like the idea that takeout was so commonplace it wouldn't warrant even a little enthusiasm. She looked at him in her rearview mirror trying to discern if something else was bothering him.

"What?" Marco huffed, looking back at her.

It wasn't like him to be gruff with her without a good reason. That was more Jacob's speed. Deb wondered in passing if the boys had been spending too much time together.

"Let's just enjoy a little music," she'd suggested, and they were quiet for the rest of the ride home. Little did she know what troubles this blip in her sweet boy's mood portended.

Now Marco was safely in bed, Mom was asleep too, and Deb

had only her thoughts to listen to. Strains of Andy Peters returned to her now. She shut her eyes but allowed the memory to stay with her. How could something twenty years old still feel so raw and new?

There he was, standing in front of her, pulling her along. She had the vague notion her friends were leaving her. Where was Caroline? She followed Andy deeper into the woods. How far had they walked? They kissed then, deeply, and he guided her to sit on a short hill. It was rocky there and uncomfortable, but he didn't seem to care about her or her feelings. Her head was spinning from all the beer she'd drunk, and in her memory she was unable to speak. Andy laid her back against the hill, then slipped her skirt up to her waist. Finally she found her voice. "I'm not going to have sex with you," she whispered. He kissed her again, then pulled down her panties. "I know you like me," he said. Debra was confused. Did he hear her? He didn't seem to be stopping. She tried again to speak but couldn't form the words. He got on top of her and her mind drifted. All she could see were knotted tree trunks reaching high into the midnight sky. They seemed taller and more threatening than any trees she'd ever seen. Tears leaked from her eyes as fear bubbled up inside her and she whispered, "Stop." Then, louder, "Stop!" She felt Andy shudder then roll away from her. "Thanks," he said.

Young Deb's mind struggled to catch up. She sat forward with her arms around her knees. What just happened? Why'd he do that? Hadn't she said she wasn't going to have sex with him? Andy lay on his back nearby for a moment longer, then sat up. He was acting like everything was normal, which was even more confusing.

They each tucked in their shirts and straightened their hair, and he put out his hand to help her up. She walked back to his house holding his hand. Shame colored her face. When they reached the house, nearly everyone had left. Caroline, her ride home, was gone.

Tears came to Deb's eyes in the darkness of her room. Why hadn't she pushed him off her? Fought back or done something, anything, to stop him. Guilt flushed her cheeks. And Caroline. Deb's best friend. Why did she leave her? Weren't there rules about these things?

Her friends at the party guessed they'd made out; some knew Andy enough to assume they went all the way. School let out the next weekend and she never had to worry about setting the record straight. Not even Caroline knew the full story. Why bother when Deb was on her way out of town. *Austin, Texas, here I come!*

When she turned up pregnant two months later, Betty wanted her to end it. She had already lost Laurie. She didn't want Deb's life ruined too. But just the thought of an abortion sparked nightmares in Deb, and she couldn't bring herself to do it. Instead, she moved in with her aunt, deferred college for a year, and had the baby in Texas. By never returning to Silver Spring, she kept the assault and baby Paula her secret.

Lying in bed Deb tried to think of other things. She had expended enough energy on goddamned Andy Peters. She'd moved on, hadn't she? Sure, she was back in town, but she was thirty-eight years old, a professional woman and a mother. A good mother. She should be able to survive seeing his name on a piece of paper. Yet she worried what she would do if he ever came into the office while she was there. Would he recognize her? What would they say? She couldn't imagine having a conversation with him all these years later. What if he found out about Paula? What if he tried to butt into her life?

Stop! She had been through this so many times. She knew she couldn't let thoughts like these keep her awake. She had a busy Saturday to look forward to: a bike ride in the morning, her new support group in the afternoon. She should be thinking about that, not ancient history.

Deb took a deep breath and, using an old relaxation trick, took an assessment of her full body. She scanned from toes to soles to ankles, then calves, knees, thighs, hips, up to her chest, arms, fingertips, and the top of her head. As she moved up the length of her body, her focus left her inner turmoil and shifted to her physical body. She had done this many times to get her mind under control, only this time she paused when she got to her big toe. If she wasn't mistaken, it had gone numb.

"Debbie! Debbie!"

Betty's scream cut through the silence of the house and Deb sat up. She looked at her clock. 3:10 a.m. She threw her legs over the side of the bed, stood up, and immediately fell to the floor.

"Mom! I'm coming!" she called. She tried again to stand but her legs were spastic. Walking on them would be very difficult and painful. She pulled herself up into a seated position on the floor and began to scoot along the carpet.

"Debbie! Please help me!" Betty called again.

"Mom! I'm coming as fast as I can. Where are you?" Deb called back. The room was dark and she could barely see. The bed blocked her view of the door.

"I'm in the bathroom. I fell." Deb could hear the anguish in Betty's voice.

"Okay, just wait there." Deb realized then that she would probably need her cell phone, which was now several feet behind her on her bedside table. She backtracked across the ground, retrieved the phone, and tried again to stand. No go. She scooted along the carpet until she reached the chair by the door, where her cane was resting. With much effort, she levered herself to standing on one leg and used the cane for support. Now the phone was a problem. If only her pajamas had a pocket. She tucked the phone in her waistband, using one hand on the cane and the other to lean against the wall.

It was slow going, but eventually Deb reached the bathroom. The light was on, the door was open, and Betty lay on her side on the floor.

"Mom, are you hurt?"

"Yes. What took so long?" There was only concern in Betty's voice.

"I fell," Deb said, and the two women started laughing.

"You fell?" Tears came to Betty's eyes.

"Yes. My leg was stiff when I woke up and I fell. Also, I think my big toe is numb again."

"Oh, Debbie, I'm sorry." Her mom looked up balefully.

"What did you hurt, Mom?" Deb leaned against the doorframe, trying to see.

"I hit my head. I think I'm bleeding." Betty reached up to touch her forehead and looked at her fingertips. "Yep, there's blood."

"Okay, I'm going to call an ambulance."

"I think that's best."

Deb chuckled. "Thanks for the vote of confidence." She dialed 911 and explained to the operator what had happened. When she hung up she told Betty, "I need to go to the front door to let in the paramedics. Stay here. I'm not able to tell if you broke something."

"I don't want to just lie here on the bathroom floor by myself." Betty sounded pitiful and Deb was sorry to leave her.

"I know, but I think it's for the best. I don't trust my legs if I were to help you up, plus you hit your head. You should stay there. Would you like me to wake up Marco? He could sit with you."

"No, no, don't wake him. If he's lucky enough to sleep through this, we should let him."

Deb nodded her agreement. "Okay, then I'm gonna leave you here. They said it would be five minutes, so you shouldn't have long to wait."

"They'll see me in my nightgown."

Even though Betty had been a nurse, Deb knew modesty was important to her mother. She offered to get her mother a robe, but then there was the problem of how she would get it on, so they opted to forget it.

Betty took a deep breath and exhaled. "I'm sorry, Debbie."

"It's going to be all right. Just sit tight."

Deb picked her way down the hall to the front door where she sat on a straight-back chair to wait. Out the window she saw the lights of the ambulance. Her mind conjured images of Luis's accident and her sister's untimely passing. The sirens. A sharp knock on the door brought her back to the present.

Deb let the paramedics in, a man and a woman in full gear. "It's my mom. She's in the bathroom. Straight down that hallway."

Deb peered down the corridor after them and saw Marco standing in his doorway. Laurie's doorway. "Marco, come here."

"What's happening?" He was bleary-eyed from sleep.

"Come here and I'll tell you."

Marco slipped past the medics and wrapped his arms around his mom, burying his head in her chest.

"Sit with me," she said, still holding him tight, and while the medics tended to Betty, Deb explained all that had happened.

Sixteen

Caroline's Friday night took a far different turn than Deb's. Though the day had started off well, with a pleasant walk to school with Jacob, something they hadn't done in weeks, by 10 p.m. she was contemplating taking a sleep aid just to be sure she slept through the night.

Fridays at the nature center often entailed a visit from school groups, and it was Caroline's job to give age-appropriate presentations on wildlife. These events were always unpredictable and had become one of Caroline's favorite parts of her job. Just this morning she had spent several hours preparing for a group of sixth graders who would be learning about the new skinks and other lizards at the nature center. She relished preparing new talks, and had included all the gross-out facts she could find, plus plenty of hands-on interactions with the animals. The kids were sure to reward her with groans and laughs and shouts of "Yuck!"

As it turned out, however, she would not be leading the skink program that day. Ten minutes before showtime her phone rang. She checked the number. Jacob's school.

The call was from Mr. Weebly, the social worker at Woodlawn Elementary. "There has been an incident at the school. We need you to come down and pick up Jacob."

Fear shot through Caroline. Was he hurt? Sick? "What happened? Is Jacob all right?"

Mr. Weebly's voice was calm. Jacob was fine. He was waiting in the principal's office. If Caroline could please come down, Ms. Juno would like to speak with her.

"Of course. I—I can come now."

She hung up the phone and thought for a moment. What could possibly have happened? The principal's office? Maybe she had been right to worry about her son falling in with the wrong crowd. This was the first sign. She opened her phone again and started to text Robbie but deleted the message and pressed the call icon instead. Robbie answered on the first ring.

Caroline filled him in on the call from Mr. Weebly. "I'm supposed to be giving the skink program in five minutes. What am I going to do?"

"Do you need me to go to the school instead?"

Caroline really wanted to give the presentation, after all the work she'd put into it. But Robbie didn't ask as many questions as she did. If Robbie went, they would get home tonight and she still wouldn't know why Jacob was in trouble. Besides, these talks were scheduled multiple times a year. Most likely, she would be able to lead the presentation the next time it came up.

"No, no. I want to go. I'll see if Susan can cover for me," she said finally.

"All right. Well, if she can't, text me and I can go to the school."

"I will." Caroline hung up.

After quickly explaining the situation to her boss and her co-worker Susan, Caroline handed over the slides and other materials for the program and left the nature center at high speed. She arrived at the school twenty minutes later to find Jacob in Ms. Juno's office and Mr. Weebly and the principal waiting for her.

The room smelled of coffee and dust. Large windows on two walls were darkened by blinds, and fluorescent lights hummed from above. Caroline's forehead pulsed in response. Jacob, frowning into his chest, arms crossed, was seated in a plastic chair opposite Ms. Juno. Mr. Weebly was leaning against a bookcase off to one side. Caroline dreaded hearing what they had to say.

Ms. Juno invited her to have a seat. Caroline chose a black plastic chair next to Jacob and looked between Ms. Juno and Mr. Weebly. "Can someone please tell me what's going on?" She took Jacob's hand in hers while she awaited the news.

"Mrs. Cook, I'm afraid your son is in serious trouble this afternoon," Ms. Juno said gravely.

Caroline looked at Jacob for answers but found none coming. "Okay," she said slowly, looking back at Ms. Juno. Her chest tightened. "Can you tell me why?"

The principal nodded at Jacob. "Jacob, please tell us what happened."

Caroline turned to face her son, who wriggled uncomfortably in his seat. His brow was furrowed and when he finally spoke, Caroline could barely make out what he said.

"What was that, honey? Someone had a knife?"

Jacob repeated his words, but Caroline still couldn't understand.

"I'm sorry, sweetheart. Who had the knife?"

"I did!" Jacob's face was suddenly red and he looked as surprised by the volume of his voice as the others in the room.

"You had a knife? Here?" Confusion washed over Caroline.

"Yes, here."

"At school." She needed to be perfectly clear about what she had just heard.

"Yes. That's what I said."

Jacob had raised his voice again, and Caroline worried he might lose control. She felt her breath quicken and her voice rise to match his. "Where did you get the knife? What kind of knife?"

"I don't know."

"You don't know where you got the knife?" Caroline was aghast. Her heart was beating rapidly. Of all the trouble she expected, never in all her life did she think her son would be the one to bring a weapon to school.

Jacob fell silent.

Caroline was emphatic. "Jacob, now is not the time to hold your tongue. Please tell me where you got the knife." She looked at Ms. Juno impatiently. "Can I see it?"

"Of course." Ms. Juno took a pocketknife out of her desk drawer and handed it to Caroline. "I'm afraid we will have to call the resource officer about this as well."

Caroline couldn't believe what she was hearing. The police? "No, no, no. Hold on. Can't we work this out as a family first?"

"I'm afraid the county has a no-tolerance policy about weapons at school. We have to report every incident, no matter how minor." The principal's tone conveyed she would not be moved on the subject.

As Ms. Juno spoke, Caroline couldn't help but think how incredibly useless Mr. Weebly seemed to be. Weebly. Like a Weeble toy, wobbling to and fro. What was the point of having a social worker there if they were going to bring in the police anyway? Surely there was no need to escalate this when it was a first offense.

Calling on all her diplomacy, Caroline said, "I'm sure there is some misunderstanding. Jacob, please explain." That's when she finally looked at what Ms. Juno had handed her. The knife had a red-and-white handle and a silver blade. A small Mexican flag decorated the handle. "I've never seen this before. Jacob, where did you get this?"

Jacob didn't answer. His eyes were trained on the floor.

She looked back at Ms. Juno. A ray of hope entered her mind. "How do you know this is Jacob's? Did someone see him with it?"

Ms. Juno leaned forward, taking the knife back from Caroline as she spoke. "He took it out of his backpack in math class this afternoon. After lunch. Another student saw it and told the teacher. The teacher, following school protocol, alerted me, and I alerted Mr. Weebly."

"Who was this other student? What's his name?" *Tattletale.*

"I can't tell you that," Ms. Juno replied.

"What?" Now Caroline was angry. "You can't tell me the name of my son's accuser? How do you know this other kid wasn't lying?"

"We found the knife in Jacob's bag."

"Fine. But how do you know someone else didn't plant it there? For all you know, the other kid put it there."

"And why would he do that?" Ms. Juno asked.

"How should I know? Jealousy? Looking for attention? You won't tell me who the kid is, so how can I guess what his motives might be?"

"Mrs. Cook, please lower your voice."

"Lower my voice?" Caroline was nearly screaming now. "I just can't understand why you're going to take some kid's word for it when Jacob has never been in this kind of trouble before."

Ms. Juno said quietly, "For the record, this is not Jacob's first time in my office."

Caroline narrowed her eyes and bit her lip. The fight. Shoving match, really. She knew that would come back up eventually. It had been the start of the school year and tensions were high, with Robbie working overtime, Caroline busy with the PTA, and Jacob struggling to adjust to harder classes. He pushed a kid in the hallway. According to Jacob, the other kid had started it, but the school didn't care. Both boys got detention.

"Mrs. Cook," Mr. Weebly said now, speaking for the first time, "please listen. We found the knife in Jacob's bag. All he will say is he doesn't know how it got there. This is why we are handing it over to the resource officer. They will investigate. If your son is innocent, they will come to that conclusion."

Caroline did her best to calm down. She needed to get them on her side. "I'm very sorry this happened. I don't know what we're supposed to do now. Can you explain the next steps? I mean, can we go home? Or maybe I should be asking, is Jacob welcome back on Monday?"

Ms. Juno spoke then. "The good news is, Jacob is not being expelled. We are asking that he take the weekend to write a formal apology to demonstrate remorse for his actions. The police will be by your house to discuss next steps."

Caroline thought of Robbie. What would he say to all of this? "We are ready to talk to the police anytime. But this is a pocketknife. If it was folded up—"

"That's a big 'if,' Mrs. Cook. The student said Jacob opened the blade and was pointing it at people. That's an act of violence." Ms. Juno's look was smug.

"And you believed him?"

"At this point we have no reason not to."

The injustice of the situation struck Caroline like a slap. *Let me out of here.* "Are we free to go now?" she asked, standing. The question seemed straight out of a trashy crime drama and Caroline laughed at her own bad dialogue.

"This isn't funny, Mrs. Cook," Ms. Juno scolded.

"No, it isn't," she agreed, and the smile vanished.

"We expect a full explanation and apology on Monday morning. Please come to my office first thing to make sure this is taken care of."

"Yes, ma'am." She looked down at Jacob, still sitting in the chair. "Jacob, let's go."

He stood up and walked out behind her, shuffling his feet.

Jacob sulked on the ride home, and Caroline was too upset to say anything. She knew if she opened her mouth, the wrong words would pour out. What was she going to say to Robbie? He would be livid. Or would he? Caroline felt bringing a pocketknife to school was wrong, but she also thought the school was blowing things out of proportion. It wasn't a gun or drugs or any of the things she had begun to worry he might get into. And it wasn't like he planned to hurt someone with it. Shouldn't Ms. Juno know her son well enough to see that? With Jacob not willing to speak to defend himself, however, there wasn't much she could do. And now she had the police to contend with.

By the time Caroline reached the house, Robbie was home from work. He greeted them at the front door hesitantly. "Hi. I came home early. How did it go at school?"

Caroline watched the look on her husband's face morph from optimistic to concerned as he took in her own sour countenance and Jacob's shuffling feet. "Not good," she said. "Jacob, do you want to tell Dad what happened?"

Jacob stood next to his mom in the front hall but didn't say anything.

Caroline looked down at him and then back at Robbie. She shook her head. "He hasn't spoken since the principal's office. Apparently he brought a pocketknife to school." The thought of it made her angry all over again.

"What?" Robbie's voice was loud. "Jacob, is that true?"

Jacob looked at his father then spun around. He shook his arms and legs and let out a guttural scream in frustration.

Caroline watched her son vent, then turned back to Robbie. "I'm not happy either. They said he took it out of his book bag and another kid saw it and tattled. At least, that's the story Ms. Juno told me." Caroline stalked into the kitchen and got a bottle of water. Her throat was suddenly dry. She opened the bottle and took a drink. A dull headache had taken root and she hoped the water would help.

Robbie followed her into the kitchen but Jacob didn't.

"Jacob, please come in here," she called. She looked at her husband and rolled her eyes.

"So, what now?" Robbie asked. "Is he expelled?"

"No, not expelled. He has to write an apology letter over the weekend, and we should expect a visit from the police." She drank more water. "Jacob! Get in here!" She sounded angrier than she intended.

"Maybe he should spend some time in his room," Robbie suggested. "Let us talk a bit."

Caroline heard the unspoken message: she needed to calm down. She was irritated by Robbie's apparent composure, but admitted they needed some time to get on the same page. When Jacob finally appeared in the doorway to the kitchen she said in a measured tone, "Jacob, go on to your room. Dad and I will be with you soon to talk."

Jacob walked away and Robbie asked, "What's for dinner?"

"I don't know. Are you really asking me that right now? I would like to focus on the crisis at hand."

Robbie put his hands up in self-defense. "Fine. I was just thinking if we needed to get something cooking we should do that now."

"We'll order a pizza, how's that?" Caroline felt her own emotions rising the calmer Robbie acted. He was always so put-together in a crisis. She really couldn't stand it. She paced the room drinking water, trying to regain her composure.

"Sure. Fine. Pizza it is."

"Now can we talk about this knife situation?" She came to a stop behind a kitchen chair.

Robbie sat down at the table across from Caroline, who remained standing. He took a deep breath and said, "Yeah, let's talk. We have the police coming over, you said?"

"Yes, but I don't know when. Mr. Weebly said this weekend." Caroline started pacing again.

Robbie watched her walk back and forth. "So—what? Are we supposed to hang around all weekend waiting for them to show up?"

Caroline didn't know.

At that moment, the doorbell rang and Caroline's phone buzzed. The doorbell app on her phone showed two uniformed police officers standing on her porch. She imagined Rosa and Philippe across the street seeing the cruiser in front of their house. What would they be thinking? She strode on long legs to the front of the house.

"Somehow I thought they would call first," Robbie said, walking up behind her.

Caroline opened the door and welcomed the officers inside. They walked into the living room as if this were a social call, but no one sat. Caroline said, "Just a minute, I'll get Jacob."

She returned with her son, and the two officers, both short men, one Latino, one white, with dark hair and thick waists, began their questioning. Caroline tried to focus on what they were saying, but her head was starting to throb. *Not now.*

"Jacob, how old are you?" Officer Chavez asked. He spoke with authority but managed to seem concerned with Jacob's well-being just the same.

Caroline held her breath. If Jacob didn't answer the officers, would they hold her in contempt? Was that even a thing?

"Ten," Jacob said. He sat on the edge of the couch, his eyes flicking from the floor to the officers, while his parents stood nearby. The light from the table lamp shone on his red hair, emphasizing his resemblance to his mother.

"Ten. And you're in what grade?"

"Fourth."

"And you brought a pocketknife to school."

Jacob muttered affirmatively.

"And where did you get the pocketknife?"

"I don't know."

"You don't know where you got it?"

"No." Jacob's voice trembled. Caroline wondered if the officers had noticed. Would they think he was lying?

"Did someone give it to you?"

"No."

"Did you buy it?"

"No." He spoke firmly now, and for the first time, Caroline thought he might be telling the truth. A whisper of empathy flitted by.

Officer Chavez looked at Caroline, but she couldn't read his expression. Was he asking her to step in? She looked at Robbie for help but got none. She put her hand on her son's shoulder. "Jacob, sweetie, please tell the officers where the knife came from."

"I don't know where it came from," he said harshly, shrugging her hand off.

"But you took it out of your book bag, right?" she prompted.

"Yes, but I don't know how it got there." Though it sounded far-fetched, Caroline knew how sloppy her son was with his belongings. What if he really didn't know where it came from?

"You didn't put it there?" Officer Chavez asked.

"No."

"Do you know who did?"

"No."

"Jacob," Caroline cut in. Even if she believed him, she didn't expect the police to buy this story. "You have to tell the officers what you know. The truth is the best policy."

"I'm telling the truth!" Jacob cried. He crossed his arms in front of his chest and fumed.

"Ma'am, do you have any idea where the knife came from?" Officer Price asked.

"No, actually, I don't. I never saw it before today in Ms. Juno's office." She turned to Robbie. "Do you know where he might've gotten it?"

Robbie raised his eyebrows, appearing surprised to be included. "Not off the top of my head. What did it look like?"

Caroline flushed at Robbie's ignorance. Couldn't he have asked that before the police arrived? She described the knife for him.

Robbie thought a minute. "It doesn't ring a bell. Could it have come from PJ?"

"Oh, good question!" For the first time since walking into the principal's office, Caroline felt hope rising. She turned to Officer Chavez and quickly explained. "Our neighbors across the street. They have a boy named PJ. His mom is from Mexico. He and Jacob play together all the time. He probably put it in Jacob's bag by accident." Caroline smiled and let out her breath.

Officer Chavez looked at Jacob. "Is that what happened, son?"

"I don't know."

Caroline was exasperated that Jacob couldn't confirm what she knew must have happened. She would have to trust the police to follow up.

Officer Chavez nodded. Speaking firmly to Jacob he said, "Regardless, you should not have had the knife at school, and you most definitely should not have taken it out in class. And you absolutely should not have opened the blade in the classroom."

"Yes, sir," Jacob mumbled.

"Officer Price and I will have to write this up. We'll be in touch in the coming days with any further actions."

Caroline stepped forward. "But, Officer, what do you mean? If it was an accident . . ." Her face fell as she realized that her tidy explanation was not going to be the end of it.

"Ma'am, sir, I know it might seem like a minor thing to you, but bringing a pocketknife to school is often a first test before something more serious happens. We don't charge crimes for anyone under age thirteen in this state. However, there is something called a delinquent act. For children ten and older who commit an act of violence, there are consequences. We'll do our best to keep this simple, but we cannot just sweep it under the rug. Now, we have everything we need, so we'll be going."

"Excuse me," Officer Price said, then spoke quietly to Officer Chavez. Caroline kept her eyes on the two policemen. Maybe this Officer Price would come to the rescue. She held her breath.

Officer Chavez quickly dashed those hopes. "Right. Ma'am, if you can please give me the contact information for this neighbor."

Caroline pulled out her phone and, with shaking fingers, found Rosa's contact information. She recited their phone numbers. "The husband is Philippe Thompson. I believe 'PJ' stands for Philippe Jr." She was speaking quickly now, very aware of whatever impression she must be making. The indulgent mother. Suburban housewife. Overeducated elitist liberal. When the two men walked to the front of the house, she nearly bumped into them trying to open the door for them. They left, saying they would be in touch soon.

"Time to order a pizza?" Robbie asked when the lock clicked shut behind them.

Caroline slumped against the door. "Ugh. I'm too exhausted for that. Let's just make sandwiches." And she strode into the kitchen, unaware of the bewildered look on her husband's face.

Seventeen

Saturday morning came early for Deb. The paramedics took Betty to the hospital for tests and observation. A third stroke was suspected as the cause for her fall in the night. She wasn't convinced, but all agreed it was best to be sure.

Deb's legs were still spastic at breakfast. She poured cereal and milk for herself while sitting at the table and asked Marco to help himself.

"What are we going to do today?" he asked as he slurped a bite of cereal.

"I don't know. I need to try to get an appointment with the acupuncturist. I was also supposed to go to a support group meeting this afternoon. Not sure that's going to be possible now." Deb pursed her lips. The first time Betty was going to watch Marco, and she had ended up in the hospital.

"I thought those were on Tuesdays."

"They were but I had to reschedule." With Betty out of commission, would she have to skip the support group? It was too late to ask Rosa. She hated to give up on it, though. Maybe Caroline was available. Deb would text her after breakfast.

Mother and son ate their cereal, then shared an apple. "Drink your water, Marco. It's good for you."

Marco did as he was told. Deb considered him as he cleared the dishes and loaded them into the dishwasher. He was a good kid. She was sorry he had to see her like this. It only fed into his tendency to think he needed to take care of her.

"Want to go for a bike ride with me this morning?" she asked.

"Yeah!" Marco whooped. "Oh, wait, should you do that with your legs?"

Deb shrugged. "I was thinking just fifteen or twenty minutes. I don't want to miss too much riding time." She was just finding her groove with her training. No need to get derailed now.

"Then, yes, let's go for a bike ride!" Marco bounced with excitement.

"Great! I'm going to text Jacob's mom and see about a playdate for you this afternoon. You can do that while I go to the support group and pick up Grandma from the hospital."

Marco's face fell. "Can't I go to PJ's instead?"

This was a surprise. "I thought you liked Jacob. Is that not true?"

"I don't know. I just would rather go to PJ's."

"Oh, I see. Well, I've relied on PJ's mom an awful lot lately. I'd rather spread the favors around."

Marco pinched his face and sighed.

"Why don't you go get dressed for our ride. I'll do the same."

Marco agreed and ran to his room.

Deb grabbed her cane and slowly made her way to her bedroom. She was very tired and did wonder if she was pushing it too far trying to go for a bike ride. Her legs ached from the hours of spasms. But what else was she going to do this morning? *Clean the house*, a small voice replied. Of course they would clean. But that wasn't a full day's work. No, the bike ride was a good idea. And the sooner the better. She just needed to make some arrangements first.

She started with the acupuncturist. The office didn't open until ten, but she left a message requesting a same-day appointment. Maybe they could squeeze her in. Next she texted Caroline.

Hi! Any chance the boys could have a playdate at your house this afternoon? I have a support group meeting to attend and Mom can't do it. (Long story.)

She didn't like to text so early in the morning, but she was hoping to reach Caroline before her day filled up. Deb imagined Caroline to have an endless calendar of social engagements. If she didn't reach her before nine, she was sure to miss the opportunity.

With some difficulty, she got into her bike clothes while she awaited a reply. She took her time, checking her phone periodically while trying not to obsess. She still hadn't heard back by the time she was lacing up her bike shoes, so she brushed her teeth and started on her sunscreen. Finally, her phone chirped.

Can't today. Sorry!!! Jacob is grounded. He was caught with a knife at school!!! So mortified! Tell you all about it when we ride tomorrow.

Deb read and reread the message. Jacob brought a knife to school? Also, now what was she going to do with Marco all afternoon?

One thing at a time.

By Saturday morning Caroline was certain of only one thing: Jacob was grounded until this pocketknife business could be sorted out.

She didn't know if she was allowed to talk to Rosa before the cops did. Or maybe they already had. In either case, her first stop was Rosa's. She still didn't understand why Jacob hadn't just told her the knife wasn't his.

"Jacob," Caroline said carefully while she sat at the breakfast table with her husband and son, "you need to write the apology to Ms. Juno and the school today."

"All right," Jacob mumbled.

"Before you do anything else."

"He said all right," Robbie said.

Caroline looked at Robbie and blinked. Trying to sound more pleasant she added, "Okay, good. Just get it done." After a pause she announced, "I'm going over to Rosa's now. I need to ask her about the knife. I'm just sure it came from PJ. She'll want to know what happened."

She got up and cleared her dishes. She was already dressed for the day. Despite the exhausting night before, she had risen at six thirty for her usual workout. Actually, six thirty was sleeping in. During the week she was up at five thirty, but she couldn't bear to do that on a Saturday. Robbie and Jacob were still at the breakfast table when she walked out the front door, down the fifteen stone steps, and across the street.

Rosa was in her pajamas when she answered Caroline's knock. "Caroline. How are you this morning?" She looked tired and a little surprised. The family dog, Sarge, was by her side, ready to investigate the new arrival.

"Got a minute? I need to talk to you about something." Caroline regretted not having a gift to offer. Morning coffee at least.

"Sure. Want to come in?" Rosa opened the door wide.

"That would be great, thanks."

Rosa's house, though across the street from Caroline's, was much less grand than her neighbor's. Like Caroline's it had a formal living room and a family room, plus dining room and kitchen, but the floors were a scuffed hardwood and the kitchen was dated. Clean but cluttered. When Caroline sat down on the living room sofa, the springs squeaked.

"So, what's up?" Rosa asked, smiling.

Caroline's mind began to swirl. How would her friend take the news? "Uh, well, there was an incident at school yesterday. Did you hear about it?"

"Yeah, someone had a weapon?" Caroline winced. Rosa continued, "I got the email from Ms. Juno but didn't know what it was about. Was Jacob involved?"

Caroline explained what she knew but added that she was still trying to get the full story.

"Oh my goodness. Is Jacob in trouble?" Rosa's eyes were wide.

"Yes, he is. You may have noticed the police cruiser in front of our house last night."

"Actually, no, I didn't. We went out for dinner and must have missed it." Rosa's full attention was on Caroline.

"Well, you might be getting a visit from the police." Caroline flushed. Had she thrown Rosa under the bus by suggesting it was PJ's knife?

Rosa turned around at a noise behind her. PJ and Philippe were coming in from the kitchen. Both were in their pajamas, and PJ had a milk mustache, as if he had just finished his morning cereal.

"Hi, PJ!" Caroline said brightly. "Hi, Philippe."

"Good morning," Philippe said. His tall frame towered over the women sitting next to each other on the couch. "What's going on? Everything all right?"

"Caroline was just telling me about some trouble they're having. Jacob brought a knife to school."

"What?" Philippe motioned for PJ to leave the room.

"By accident," Caroline clarified. She put her hands up as if to calm Philippe. "At least, I think it was an accident. That's why I'm here."

Rosa said, "Yes, what was it again? Why do you think the police will be coming here?"

"Because I told them I thought the knife might belong to PJ," Caroline blurted.

"You did what?" Rosa and Philippe spoke in unison, incredulity and anger evident in their voices. Their faces were ashen.

"I'm sorry, I wasn't trying to get PJ in trouble," Caroline said quickly. "I think this whole thing is just a misunderstanding. The knife had a red handle with a Mexican flag on it, and I thought maybe it belonged to PJ. A gift from a relative? I thought it might have ended up in Jacob's book bag one day when they were playing together." Seeing the horrified looks on her friends' faces, Caroline backpedaled. "I don't think he did it on purpose. He's little. I thought he might've hidden it there to be funny or something. I don't know." She paused. "I'm sorry for bringing trouble. But could it have been your knife?" Caroline crossed her fingers.

Rosa shook her head. "PJ doesn't have any pocketknives that I know of. Do you, Philippe?"

"I have a pocketknife, but it doesn't look like what you described. It has a black handle, and it's safely on my dresser." His voice was tight, not the usual melody that put listeners at ease.

Caroline visibly deflated. "Oh." She sighed and tears pricked her eyes. "I was really hoping it had come from you." She blinked and smiled up at her friends.

Philippe glared back. "I can't believe you told the police to come here. How thoughtless can you be?"

Caroline flinched.

"Philippe, please." Rosa looked at him pointedly. "It was a mistake, right, Caroline?" She leaned over and patted her friend on the shoulder. Rosa was only half succeeding at hiding her own anger.

"I'm sorry. I was desperate. I don't know what's going to happen to Jacob. Please forgive me."

Philippe blinked at her and walked out of the room, his face full of fury. Heat seemed to radiate from his body as he left.

Caroline looked at Rosa for help. Rosa just shook her head.

"I'm so sorry." There was nothing left to say, so she got up. "I better get back to my family."

"That's probably best," Rosa said.

As Caroline walked back across the street, her shoulders slumped with the weight of her situation. What had she done? Not only was the knife not PJ's, but now her best friends were mad at her. And she couldn't blame them.

"Marco, I've made a mistake." They were less than two blocks from their house but Marco was well ahead of his mother. Deb pedaled harder to catch up, increasing the amount of assistance. "Marco,"

she called. He looked over his shoulder then circled back. When he was in hearing range, Deb began again. "I've made a mistake. My legs feel awful. I have to go back. I'm sorry." She stopped pedaling and exhaled.

"Oh, okay."

"Are you disappointed?" Deb asked gently. She searched his face for signs.

"No . . . yes . . . I don't know. Maybe a little, but it's okay." Marco rode in a circle around his mom while he talked.

"Let's go back."

With significant effort, Deb made a wide circle and pointed her bike toward home. Marco followed.

Deb's legs had gotten even more stiff in the short time they were gone. They stowed the bikes in the garage, and she struggled to walk into the house. She placed a hand on Marco's shoulder and leaned on him as if he were her cane. "Sorry about this. I hope the acupuncturist called back. Then I can get my legs back."

"When are we going to see Grandma?" Marco asked as he led her into the living room.

"This afternoon. I told her I would be there around two." She sat down on Betty's favorite chair and began massaging her legs. The support group was scheduled for three o'clock. If the stars aligned, she would be able to see the acupuncturist, get Betty from the hospital, and still make it to the meeting. She had a lot riding on this acupuncturist calling back. She pulled her cell phone out of the pocket of her bike jersey and checked for messages. "Nothing yet," she reported. "I'll try again."

She called the number but had to leave another message. Her legs seemed to be getting tighter by the minute and without being able to reach the therapist she started to panic. It was bad enough she might have to miss her support group. How was she going to manage getting her mom from the hospital when she could barely walk? She wasn't even sure she could stand upright long enough to make a morning snack for her son.

"Maybe Mrs. Cook can help," Marco said, responding to the worry on his mother's face.

"Maybe," Deb said thoughtfully, though she didn't really see how. "Maybe PJ's mom can help. She works in a doctor's office." She dialed Rosa's number but when it went to voicemail, she decided not to leave a message. Finally she called Caroline. After Caroline recovered from her shock at hearing Betty was in the hospital, Deb explained that what she really needed was an acupuncturist.

"Do you want to try mine?" Caroline offered. "I see an acupuncturist for my tennis elbow. Dr. Walden. She's wonderful!"

Deb lit up at the suggestion. "I'll try anything at this point!" She laughed. "I actually tried to go for a bike ride earlier, but it was a mistake. I'll have to cancel our ride tomorrow, I'm afraid."

"Oh, no problem. I forgot all about it, honestly. Here, I'll text you the contact info for Dr. Walden. Let me know if it comes through." Caroline sounded happier now that she had found a way to help.

Almost immediately Deb's phone pinged. "Got it! Thank you. I'll give her a call now."

Deb ended the call and dialed Dr. Walden. She could hear Marco in his room drumming on the wall. She crossed her fingers while she waited for someone to answer.

"Walden Spa and Acupuncture, how can I help you?"

Relief washed over Deb at the sound of the receptionist's voice. She asked to make an appointment, noting that Caroline had referred her, in case that held any sway.

"Okay, and when would you like to come in, Mrs. Morales?"

"Do you have any openings today? My legs are spastic and I need help. I have multiple sclerosis." She waited to see what effect those words would have. The receptionist took a moment, then offered an appointment at 12:45. The lunch hour, but it would have to do. She was grateful just to have gotten hold of someone.

When she hung up with the doctor's office, Deb sent a quick text thanking Caroline. Then she scheduled an Uber to take her to the appointment.

"Good news, Marco," she called from the living room. She waited until he appeared around the corner before continuing. "I have an appointment with an acupuncturist. You'll have to come with me and we'll have to go to the hospital straight afterward to get Grandma."

"Okay. Is it snack time yet?"

Deb took a deep breath and let it out. The laser focus both of her children had on food always astounded her. "Yes, it is. You'll have to get it yourself, though. We have apple slices or yogurt."

"Yogurt!" he yelled and ran into the kitchen.

"Will you get me one too, please?" she called after him. It pained her to ask Marco to care for her. When she was diagnosed with MS, she had vowed not to let it get in the way of her relationship with her children. Now, she was thankful he was a capable child who didn't mind helping her. She and Luis had done that much right.

By the time Deb walked out of Dr. Walden's office at two o'clock that afternoon, she felt like a new woman. She could only hope the feeling would last. She and Marco grabbed another Uber and went straight to the hospital to pick up Betty. They located her in a double room sitting in bed watching TV with the sound down. Betty wore a gauzy bandage on her forehead and a hospital gown. The smell of disinfectant filled Deb's nostrils, and the ventilation system clanged in the background.

"Mom, we're here to take you home!" Deb walked to the second bed and hugged her mother. She opened the curtains and began straightening up the bedside table.

Betty said hello with a smile for Deb, but when Marco came around the curtain wearing a baseball cap, Betty looked up at Deb with a question on her face.

"Hi, Grandma." Marco plopped in the chair next to the bed and opened his book.

"Who is that? Why's he calling me grandma?" Betty's voice was rigid. Red blotches broke out on her cheeks and she curled up against the pillows in fear.

"Mom, Mom, it's all right. It's Marco. My son." Deb touched her mother's arm to calm her, but Betty yanked it away, almost hitting Deb in the face. Her eyes were clouded with fear.

"Get that demon out of here," she hissed.

Marco's face turned pale. He'd seen his grandmother discombobulated in the evenings, but he had never been the focus of her delusion.

"Debbie, help me. Get him out of here." Betty began to tremble.

Deb heard the urgency in her mother's voice. She wrapped her arms around her mother and began to rock. "Marco," Deb said gently but firmly, "go out. Just for a minute. Please."

Marco stood up, eyes wide and starting to brim with tears, then walked out of the room.

With Marco out of sight, Betty relaxed into Deb's arms. Deb held her tight, shushing her like a small child. After a minute, Deb felt the episode subside. She decided to try again.

"Mom, Marco is here with me. My son. He's going to come in now."

Betty looked at her and nodded.

Deb went around the curtain and did her best to explain the situation to Marco, then instructed him to remove his hat. When he came in again, Betty seemed watchful, but she didn't tremble. Deb let out her breath.

According to a nurse at the nurses' station, they were waiting on paperwork from the doctor. Deb settled in, making herself comfortable. She'd hoped to sweep in and carry Betty away so she could get to the support group. She held out hope that the doctor would be in shortly to see them.

The two women sat in silence for a bit, watching the moving pictures on the television. After a while an ad came on with a cat and a fish playing tag. Betty laughed. "Know what that reminds me of?"

"Uh, the time the neighbor's cat ate Laurie's fish?" Deb asked.

"Yes!" Betty started laughing harder. "I felt so bad for her. She really loved that fish."

"So did I. We buried it in the backyard."

"Did you?" Betty looked at her, surprised. "I didn't think the cat left anything to bury."

Deb crooked her head to the side, remembering. "You're right, we couldn't have. The cat ate it." She laughed. "But we buried something! I think it was a shoebox of fish supplies."

"Oh my. I do miss that girl." Betty fell silent and Deb looked out the window. She wondered at the workings of her mother's mind. Betty recalled the events of thirty years ago with clarity, yet mistook her grandson for a demon roaming the hospital halls.

After a few minutes, Betty spoke again. "Have you talked to Paula lately?"

"We're supposed to talk tomorrow. Why?"

"She isn't much younger than my Laurie was when she passed. You might want to talk to her."

Deb didn't like the implication. "She's safe and healthy, Mom. I know she isn't getting into the stuff Laurie got into."

"That's what I thought about Laurie. You can never be too sure."

Deb couldn't remember her mother ever speaking so openly about her sister's death. Laurie had been like a cherub her whole life. When she died suddenly, and of a drug overdose, everyone was taken by surprise. That unexpected loss, at a critical time in Deb's life at age fourteen, had made her value every minute. But Betty didn't want to talk about how it had happened. She only wanted to remember the good side of Laurie, the bright eyes and cheery smile, the volunteering and straight A's in school. She had died of an overdose at a party off campus. Betty told everyone it was Laurie's first time stepping out of line, but Deb knew different.

"Where you going?"

It was after midnight and Laurie was at the back door, dressed in a miniskirt and ripped tights, with a bag over her shoulder. A silver necklace with a bicycle pendant, a birthday present from Deb, glinted around her neck.

"Go back to bed, Debbie."

Deb went back to her room, but she didn't fall asleep. She traced the

cracks in the ceiling with her eyes, listening for Laurie to come home.
It was four o'clock in the morning when the lock clicked and Deb was
able to sleep.

"You don't have to worry, Ma. You don't know Paula like I do."

"And whose fault is that?" Betty asked, eyebrows raised.

Deb shot a protective look at Marco, who was now absorbed in
his book. In a low voice, Deb retorted, "This is not the time to talk
about this, Ma. Paula's fine. Mind your own business."

Knock, knock. The door to the room swung open. "Good afternoon, Mrs. Lee!" a loud voice announced.

Mother and daughter, faces flushed, turned to see Dr. Strauss
appearing from around the curtain.

Deb recovered her breathing, thankful the doctor had arrived.
Dr. Strauss was a tall white man with a potbelly and salt-and-pep-
per hair. Friendly beyond measure, he always treated Betty with
respect. If Deb had one complaint it was that he wasn't more particular about Betty's diet.

"Good news! You are free to go. The nurse will be in with some
paperwork for you. Mostly it says how to handle that wound. Just
soap and water should do it. Nothing to worry about. I did see you
have slightly elevated blood pressure. We'll keep an eye on that.
But as I said this morning, no sign of a stroke and no broken bones.
Since the fall took place in the bathroom, the nurse will have a
handout for you with information for adapting your bathroom to
be more accessible. This means a raised toilet seat, a shower chair,
railings in the shower, that sort of thing. I'll leave it to you to deter-
mine which adaptations are needed. But as we age, we need more
help. Do you have any questions?" He looked Betty in the eye and
waited patiently.

"No, no questions," Betty replied with a serene smile. Deb thought she was flirting.

"How's her blood sugar?" Deb cut in.

Betty shot her an accusing look, as if Deb were ratting her out to the principal.

Dr. Strauss looked at his papers. "Hmm. A bit high." He looked back at Deb and then at Betty and smiled. "Stay away from the sweets, Mrs. Lee, and you'll be all right."

That's it? If anyone had the power to keep Betty from her nightly chocolates, it was him.

"If there are no more questions, I'll send the nurse in with the paperwork. Should be just a minute. Have a good afternoon!"

For the next twenty minutes Deb twisted in her seat waiting for the nurse. What was taking so long? She and Betty had said all they were going to say. Betty turned the volume up on the TV and they watched in silence. After a while, Deb got up and peeked out the door at all the white coats and scrubs bustling by. No one seemed to be coming their way. She let out her breath and sat back down. Her chances of attending the support group were slipping away.

Finally, a nurse arrived with the promised paperwork, and Deb, Betty, and Marco were on their way home. In the cab, the three of them jammed in the back seat, Betty asked, "Did you go to your support group, Debbie?"

Deb took out her phone and looked at the time. "No. It's happening right now. I'll have to try again next month." Her mom murmured consolation at missing the meeting, but Deb wasn't really listening. She clicked an icon for a notification on her phone and her lips spread wide in a smile. "I got a new donation!" She tapped the buttons for more information.

"Who from? Is it for the ride?" Betty asked, leaning over to see.

"Yeah. Julian. Looks like he got my text the other day after all. I was starting to wonder." Wow. Two hundred dollars. She felt a warm glow at the message he had included with the donation. *You're a force to be reckoned with, mujer. Buena suerte!* She closed her phone and put it away, still grinning.

Marco, who had been looking out the window, was suddenly animated. "What's for dinner?"

Deb groaned at the thought of it. "Sandwiches," she and Betty said in unison.

Eighteen

Caroline was on a mission. Her son could be facing serious consequences over bringing a weapon to school, and she didn't even know where it came from. Not only that, but now her best friends were angry with her for implicating their son. She'd been a fool. She had been certain the knife was PJ's. If not his, then whose?

When she returned to the house Saturday morning, Jacob was alone at the kitchen table writing his apology. She'd walked into the room ready to report what she learned at Rosa's, but quickly backed out when she saw what he was doing. Better to give him space. Later, when Jacob had finished the letter and gone to his room to pick up his toys before the cleaning service arrived, she asked if she could read it.

He looked at her sideways. "If you want to."

Standing in the doorway of his bedroom, she watched him work. He was a good kid. She hoped the letter would give her some clue as to what had happened. She needed to know for certain that he wasn't lying. That some other kid hadn't led him astray. "Where is it?"

He gestured to the top of his dresser, which held four Lego sculptures, several old birthday cards, two stacks of Uno cards (as if he were in the middle of a game), a dozen plastic fidgets, and three broken watches—all presents from his grandparents. The sight of the clutter raised Caroline's blood pressure. Where her in-laws saw harmless fun, she saw environmental destruction. She plucked the single flat sheet of paper from on top of the watches and stepped into the hall to read it.

Dear Ms. Juno,

I'm sorry for taking a pocketknife out of my bag in class. I didn't mean to cause any trouble. I didn't know the knife was there. I've never seen it before. When I found it in my bag, I pulled it out to see what it was. I never intended to hurt anyone with it and I don't know how it got there. I wish I knew whose knife it was because everyone is mad at me. I'm sorry.

Sincerely,

Jacob Cook

She read it over several times, leaning against the wall. The simplicity of the explanation touched her, and she knew he was telling the truth. Someone had put that knife in his bag. But who? She walked back into her son's room. He was sitting on his bed playing with two action figures he was supposed to be putting away.

"Jacob," she said quietly. She was standing just inside the doorway.

"Yes?" He looked at her only briefly before going back to his toys. He looked like he expected to get in trouble for taking a break from cleaning.

"I want to tell you something. Can you put the toys down, please?" She walked over and stooped in front of him.

He looked at her and frowned but said nothing.

"I read your letter and I want you to know, I believe you. I believe you didn't put the knife in your bag. I talked to PJ's mom and it's not his either. I don't know whose it is, but I'll find out, okay? I'll make sure your name is cleared."

Jacob looked pensive. "Really?"

"Yes, really. Can I give you a hug?"

Tears had gathered in Jacob's eyes. "No, thank you," he whispered.

Caroline's breath went out of her and she swallowed. "Oh. Okay." Her heart ached at the rejection. She still had a lot to make up for.

The next morning she said goodbye to Robbie and Jacob at eight o'clock and headed out on a bike ride. She hoped some time on the bike would clear her head. She was disappointed Debra couldn't join her. Caroline hadn't had a chance to tell her the full story. Maybe Deb would have an idea about where the knife had come from.

It was the first of May, and the weather that morning was beautiful. The sun was shining, the air around her was cool, and the native ferns growing by the creek were the bright green of spring. Caroline checked her odometer. Twenty miles to go. Funny how quickly fifteen miles passed now that she had been training. Her legs were stronger than they'd been in years, and the time alone on her bike had given her space to think. She had even begun to miss her family at times.

Around mile twenty-five she came to a wide intersection and stopped. A fellow cyclist pulled up next to her. Together they waited for the light to turn green.

"Good morning," he said collegially.

"Good morning," Caroline returned.

"Out for a leisurely ride?" he asked. He pulled his water bottle out for a drink.

"Thirty-five miles." Her pride was evident in her smile.

"Oh, no, not leisurely. You must be in training."

Before answering, Caroline looked more closely at the man. Around sixty, very fit, in full bike gear with puffy white hair sticking out from under his helmet. Riding atop a silver road bike with an orange pennant flying off the seat. "I am," she said. "Are you?"

"Oh, not exactly. I ride every day. Done that for the past five, ten years. Rain or shine. Keeps me healthy." The man racked his water bottle, and Caroline noticed a slight tremor.

"Good for you."

The light changed and the two riders kicked off.

"Enjoy the rest of your ride," the man said.

"Same to you."

As the fellow took the lead, Caroline noticed a logo on the back of his jersey—"I Ride With MS."

Small world.

By the time she finished her thirty-five miles, she'd been gone the whole morning and was anxious to get back to Jacob. The plants she'd seen that morning had given her an idea for a collaborative art piece, and she hoped he would do it with her. But first she would swing by Deb's house. She wanted to tell her about the man she met and see how she was recovering. Maybe trade ideas about the knife situation too.

She arrived at Debra's house sweaty but happy. She leaned her bike against the outside wall and knocked on the front door. The house was just as she remembered it, a redbrick bungalow with a yellow front door and cement porch. How often she'd stopped here to pick up Debra for some teenage outing. The house was the same, but was Caroline? She couldn't say.

The door opened, interrupting her reverie. "Mrs. Lee!" Caroline said when Betty came into view.

"Yes, that's me." Betty looked curiously at the woman on her porch. Her voice was raspy and a little faint.

"It's Caroline. Debra's friend from high school," she said, raising her voice and enunciating.

"Oh, yes. Hello." Betty nodded with recognition.

"Is she home?" Suddenly Caroline thought how foolish she was for just stopping by. Debra was probably out. She should have at least texted first. She started to turn away but Betty said, "Yes, she's here." Then she turned and called over her shoulder, "Debbie, you have a visitor." To Caroline she said, "Please, come in." She opened the door wide.

"Thank you. It's so good to see you, Mrs. Lee."

"And it's so good to see you, Caroline. It must be twenty years. You are as sprightly as ever."

Caroline laughed. "Thank you for saying so. I'm afraid thirty-eight isn't all it's cracked up to be."

"I'm afraid sixty-eight isn't all it's cracked up to be either," Betty said kindly, touching the bandage on her forehead.

Caroline laughed. She'd forgotten how much she used to love Debra's mother.

"Come in. Everyone is in the living room."

When Caroline entered the room, Debra and Marco looked up.

They were seated at a coffee table eating a snack and playing video games. The light from the TV shone on their faces, and several beeps and boops resounded. Caroline didn't recognize the game.

"Caroline!" Deb gave a welcoming smile. "Marco, pause the game." Looking at Caroline she said, "Are you just back from your bike ride?"

Caroline noticed how at ease Debra was in her own home. She held up her helmet. "Yep, I'm all sweaty too. Hope you don't mind my stopping by. I just wanted to see how you were doing after yesterday."

"I'm good. Not quite as fabulous as I felt after seeing Dr. Walden yesterday, but I'm good." She explained that she had another appointment scheduled for Wednesday afternoon. "I'm looking forward to that."

To Caroline's eyes Debra looked exhausted, her face puffy and her hair wild, but she seemed happy too. Whatever physical pain she was dealing with, being with family seemed to have washed it away.

Debra thanked her again for the referral. "I don't know what I would have done without it. I never did hear back from my usual practice, the bums."

Betty offered Caroline some ice water but she declined. "I can't stay long. I just wanted to see how you all were doing. And Mrs. Lee, how are you? I heard you bumped your head." Caroline touched her own head where Betty's bandage was.

"Oh, yes, yes. I'm fine now. A little bump is all it was. Thank you for asking." Betty took her seat in the recliner.

"So, how was the ride?" Deb asked.

"It was gorgeous!" Caroline gushed. "I'm sorry you had to miss it. I made great time, and the weather is just perfect for biking." She stopped herself. Was she rubbing it in Debra's face that she wasn't able to ride? Maybe she shouldn't have come by.

"I'll be back on my bike soon," Debra said as though reading her thoughts.

"That's so good to hear," Caroline replied. "There was one funny thing that happened." She told them about the man she met at the stoplight. "The funniest thing was when he rode away. He had a jersey that said 'I Ride With MS.'"

"Aha! What a coincidence!"

"Do you think he has MS?" she asked.

"Well, yeah, they don't give those jerseys to just anyone. You have to earn that."

Caroline thought about the other reason she'd stopped by. She hadn't envisioned the whole Lee-Morales family being in on the conversation about the pocketknife. She'd have to talk to Debra another time.

"How's Jacob? You said he's grounded?" Debra asked, seeming to read her mind once again.

"Yes, he's grounded. At least for now. I'll have to tell you about that later." She looked pointedly at Marco.

"Gotcha."

"Mom," Marco interrupted, "can we play?" He motioned toward their game.

"I'm visiting right now, Marco. We can take a break."

Caroline stood up. "No, no. You play your game. I should be going. I'm sure Robbie is waiting on me."

"Well, thanks for stopping by. I hope to be up for a long ride next Sunday. Can we plan on that?"

"For sure," Caroline said. "Sounds perfect."

She said goodbye and headed out the door. As she mounted her bike and pedaled home, Caroline felt an unexpected stir of envy. Debra and Marco had the easy relationship she'd always envisioned for herself and Jacob. It had been ages since they did one of their collaborative art projects, and they had never played video games together. She wasn't sure she was even invited.

That night, Deb signed into the video chat ten minutes early. After the weekend she'd had, she was anxious to talk to Paula. Hard as she tried, she couldn't shake Betty's warning about Paula getting into the drug scene. Losing Paula would be unthinkable. Deb was sure her daughter was on the straight and narrow, but it wouldn't hurt to check in.

The computer chimed and Paula's face appeared in the little box. "Good Sunday night," she said. Deb scanned Paula's face for any signs of drug use. Her hair was unkempt, as if she'd been sleeping in her ponytail. Her normally cheerful eyes were rimmed with red, and her face looked puffy. Deb pictured a freight train coming. *Is this it?*

Trying to keep the worry out of her voice, Deb asked, "How was your week?"

Paula puffed out her cheeks, then wiped her nose with the back of her hand.

Oh my God. Cocaine?

"Not so good actually. I had a fight with one of the girls in my study group this afternoon, and now I have to find a different group. I've been crying for the past hour."

Crying! Of course. Deb relaxed and smiled.

"What?" Paula asked, looking confused.

Deb realized her reaction didn't fit the news. "Oh, nothing. Just something Grandma said. I'm so sorry that happened to you. What was the fight about?"

"It was stupid. She thought I was flirting with her boyfriend, who's also in the group. She's never liked me because he laughs at my jokes. She called me a slut and I let her have it."

"Oh, no!"

"I really liked that study group too." Fresh tears came to Paula's eyes.

"Do you think it will blow over? Or do you need to apologize?"

"Why should I apologize? She's the bitch."

Deb knew that when Paula dug in, she could be as stubborn as a Saint Bernard and just as difficult to move. She considered her words before responding. "I used to be like you, Paula. Immovable when I knew I was right. Sometimes I still am." She thought of the arguments with Betty about the phone and chocolates. "But I've learned it's usually best to say sorry even when you know the other person started the fight. Luis taught me that."

Paula looked skeptical but said she'd think about it.

"It all depends on how much you want back into that study group," Deb added.

Paula thanked her for the advice. "And how about you, Mom? How was your week?"

Deb thought back over the past seven days. "This week was a doozy."

Paula leaned in, a smile on her face for the first time that evening. "Do tell."

Deb described her first days at the Sparky's office, including Calvin, whom she was finding hard to read, and the rough start with Molly.

Paula nodded. "I'm sure you'll win her over. You always do."

"I hope so. She's just very temperamental. For example, one of my tasks is cataloging donations—" And that's when Deb remembered seeing Andy Peters's name on the donor list. Her face flushed. Not a discussion to have with Paula.

"What?" Paula had noticed the hitch in her mother's speech.

"Nothing," Deb said, recovering. "That's going well. Oh, and Grandma is on the mend after her fall."

"Thank goodness. And what happened exactly?"

Deb filled Paula in on what the paramedics had done and the information Dr. Strauss had given them. "So, we might be updating the bathroom to make it more accessible."

"That's probably a good idea anyway, don't you think?" Paula said, eyebrows raised with meaning.

"I do. I've been having a rough time myself." She recounted the acupuncturist's visit and Betty's fall. "There were a lot of Lees on the floor Friday night." Deb laughed darkly.

"Ooh, I'm sorry to hear that. Is it serious?" Paula's voice was tense and her face pinched.

"I don't think so. I took the weekend off from training just to be safe." Deb thought of her numb toe but didn't mention it. She didn't want to worry her daughter any more than she had to.

"Good." Paula nodded her approval.

"I plan to get out on my bike again later this week."

Paula's reaction was immediate. "No way, Mom. Don't you think you should rest? What if you're having a flare-up?"

Deb was taken aback. "Uh, no, I don't think I should rest. I don't want to lose my momentum with the training."

"What do you mean?" Paula's voice was rising. "If you injure yourself, then you'll really lose momentum." Her eyes were wide with exasperation

"You're right, Paula. That's why I'm being careful about what rides I do." Deb's voice was beginning to rise as well, as she started to lose her patience.

"Honestly, I don't know why you're training for this ride in the first place. It's really crazy to think you can do it." Paula looked straight at her mother through the screen. Deb stared back, dumbfounded. She took a breath and then spoke as calmly as she could. "I am working towards an important goal. I need your support, not your advice. Please don't forget that I *am* your mother." There was much more Deb wanted to say, but she forced herself to hold her tongue.

"You said—no, you *promised*—that you would drop out if it looked like you were overdoing it. Now you're telling me you fell in the night and you couldn't walk without seeing an acupuncturist. Doesn't that say to you that you're overdoing it? Have you even talked to your doctor? You're being irresponsible." Paula's face was red with emotion.

"I'm sorry, Paula, but I am not going to give up this ride. You don't understand. I have people counting on me now. People have donated on my behalf. Friends and family. People I haven't heard from in years donated. They expect me to follow through. I *want* to follow through. I had to drop out once before; I am not doing that again. And it's not your place to tell me how to handle my disease."

Paula was quiet for a moment and nodded grimly. "You're right. It's not my place." She breathed deeply and looked down at her hands. "I've got to go."

Deb paused. Should she try to keep her on the line until they could smooth things over? Fighting with Paula was painful in a way she couldn't describe. She longed for her support; she wanted her blessing as well as her admiration. But from the look on her daughter's face, it was going to take more time than she had to make things right. "Good night, Paula. I love you."

Paula's screen went black.

Nineteen

Monday morning found Deb back at Sparky's headquarters. She was happy to be at the office after the treacherous weekend at home. By comparison, work would be a vacation.

At least, that's what she was thinking when she left her house. When she pulled into her parking space, she remembered Andy Peters had dropped off donations one week earlier. The pit in her stomach pulsed, like a traffic sign warning her of danger. Did she really have to worry about her whatever-he-was turning up at her office with puppy dog beds and chew toys? What would she do if he did?

But Andy wasn't the only thing on her mind. She had started her day with another full-body assessment, and it wasn't good. The effects of the acupuncture were wearing off, and the numbness in her toe had not gone away. Rather, it had spread to the ball of her foot. She made a mental note to tell Dr. Walden about it at her appointment on Wednesday. She had neglected to mention it at their first meeting; the pain of her legs had overshadowed her toe problem. She wasn't sure Eastern medicine could reverse the lack of feeling any more than Western medicine ever had, but it was worth a try.

She was also experiencing some brain fog this morning. This most frustrating of MS symptoms came and went, but she usually was able to manage it by slowing down and focusing on one task at a time. She also kept meticulous notes. The stress of the weekend seemed to have exacerbated things, however, because that approach was only sort of working. She decided to get herself a cup of tea—decaf, of course—and meditate at her desk for five minutes before starting work.

The agenda for the day included her first full event-planning team meeting. They would be discussing arrangements for the annual dinner, and after reading through as much of the backup paperwork as possible, Deb was ready to make a few suggestions. She had no intention of reinventing the wheel, as Calvin had called it, but she did see room for improvement.

At ten to ten, she grabbed her cane and her papers and went to the conference room to await the rest of her team. To Deb's surprise, Molly was already in the meeting room. Deb took the seat at the head of the table.

"Good morning, Molly," she said cheerfully. She would seize this prime opportunity to build a bridge.

Seated in the middle of the long side of the table, Molly had her laptop open in front of her, and she was reading something on her phone. "Morning," she said, not looking up.

Deb looked at Molly's bent head. Her brown hair was hanging down, half hiding her face, and Deb wondered if she did this intentionally. No matter. She would win her over anyway. "How was your weekend, Molly?"

Molly turned and looked at her. Then, perhaps realizing her new boss was trying to have a conversation with her, she sat up straight and pushed her hair behind her ear. "Good. My weekend was good. How about you?"

Deb considered her answer and realized none of her weekend

was appropriate for the office. "Let's just say I'm happy to be back at work."

Molly looked at her quizzically, then went back to her reading. By then the other team members had started to arrive. Robin, Hannah, and Lawrence took seats across from Molly, and Tom and Flo filled in the spaces between Deb and Molly. They were seven in all, leaving half of the conference table empty.

"Good morning, team," Deb said, launching the meeting. "I hope you've had time to settle in on this Monday morning." The faces around the table nodded. Robin smiled. "As I said in the email invitation for this meeting, today's agenda is really about getting on the same page with various aspects of the dinner. We still have a couple of months to prepare, but as you know, some decisions need to be made sooner rather than later. After we discuss the planning, if there's time I would like to get an update from each of you on the funding goal for the fiscal year ending June 30."

Deb turned to Robin sitting beside her. As events manager, Robin was the point person for the event vendors. "Robin, can you fill us in on where things stand with the venue?"

"Of course." Robin flipped her curly hair behind her shoulder as she looked through her notes. "So, Gene, our contact at Silver Celebrations, has reserved the large pavilion for us for June 27. We can begin setup as early as noon. Gates open at six thirty and programming starts at seven. We're expected to be off the premises by midnight. I've submitted our deposit to hold the date, and the final payment is due June 20."

"Perfect. Thanks, Robin." Deb referred back to her notes. "Now, it looks like, Hannah and Tom, you've been working on programming?"

Tom and Hannah looked at each other and nodded. Tom said,

"Yes, Hannah is inviting speakers, and I've been coordinating the volunteer spotlight. We have a couple of suggestions for that. Kevin Berger has been a dedicated volunteer for years. He's donated a lot of money and time as well. We thought he would be a good candidate."

Deb looked at Hannah. She had the sense Tom was overstating the consensus. "And Hannah? What do you think?"

Hannah looked at Deb. "I like Kevin. I also like Meg Shaeffer. She's been doing videos with the dogs, and those have been a real attention-grabber."

"Oh, yes!" Deb said. "I know Meg. She would be great to have. I suggest we start with her—if no one has any objections. Tom?"

Tom leaned forward, folding his hands in front of him. "Kevin has been with us longer than Meg. I would like to recognize his efforts."

Deb nodded. She was really hoping for consensus. She thanked Tom for his thoughts. "Anyone else?" She surveyed the team. Tom and Molly seemed to be close. "Molly, what do you think?"

Molly sighed. "About what?"

"About having Meg Shaeffer as our volunteer spotlight at the annual dinner," Deb said carefully.

"I'm not a fan. I think it's gimmicky what she does with the dogs. I vote for Kevin." Molly's tone was flat and her expression was blank.

"Oh, I see." Deb was quiet for a moment. She was excited to have Meg but was anxious not to look like she was playing favorites.

"I like Meg," Robin said. "She's done a lot of good for Sparky's."

"I like her too," said Lawrence. "I'll be running the social media for the event, and Meg would give us a lot of fodder for that."

Deb nodded. "Okay, I think that's a majority. Let's ask Meg.

We'll start with her and if she is unable to make it we'll ask Kevin Berger. All right, Tom?"

Tom nodded. Deb thought he was disappointed but willing to go along with the decision. She was afraid to ask Molly if she agreed with the compromise. The sour look on her face would indicate no, but you couldn't be sure with her. Deb made some notes, then moved on to the next order of business.

"Flo, I see you're in charge of decorations. Is there anything you need from me at this point?"

"No," Flo said. "I have my shopping list from last year. To go with the backyard barbecue theme, I chose red-and-white gingham tablecloths and streamers. I plan to place orders next month to be sure it arrives in time. For now, I'm just here."

Deb wrote that down, then said, "Okay, the last thing I wanted to cover today is food. Molly, that's your realm, correct?"

"Yes, that's right. I have my notes from last year and I plan to repeat that."

Here Deb knew she needed to tread lightly. Although Robin was events manager, she had delegated finding a caterer to Molly a couple years back to help even out the workload, and Molly had taken ownership ever since. Deb did not want Molly to react poorly to feedback and put the task back on Robin, who had her hands full. She said evenly, "I noticed that food was our biggest expense."

"Yes," Molly said slowly, her eyes narrowing.

"I also read through the comments we received from attendees. People want more variety, especially with gluten-free and nondairy options. One of our biggest donors apparently is nondairy, so that raises the level of importance for us."

Molly's lips disappeared into a straight line.

Deb plowed on, determined to remain professional. "Do you

know if your current choice for food vendor has more gluten-free and nondairy options we can choose from?" she asked as delicately as possible.

Molly looked right at Deb and frowned. "No."

Deb paused then said, "No, you don't know if they have more options; or no, they don't have more options?"

"I don't know what their nondairy options are," Molly said stiffly. She crossed her arms in front of her chest.

"All right. That's understandable. This hasn't come up before. Please look into that and report back to me next week. We need to evolve with the times, and if our guests want more variety we should be providing that."

"Yes, ma'am," Molly said.

Deb looked at Molly for an extra beat. She didn't know if Molly was being insubordinate or not, so she chose to give her the benefit of the doubt. "Our last order of business, team, is meeting the funding goal for the fiscal year. Obviously this dinner is a big part of that. We need to get our invitations out. Lawrence, that's you." Lawrence saluted with two fingers. "And we need to get our mailers out. Flo, that's you."

Flo smiled sweetly. "I'm happy to do it. I'm waiting on the text from Molly before having the invitations printed."

"Molly?" Deb said, looking at her. Molly's head was down again.

"I'm waiting on Robin to proofread my draft."

"No," Robin said. "I haven't received anything as of this morning."

"I sent it before the meeting. You should have it now," Molly said.

Deb recalled the open laptop at the start of the meeting. Was Molly sending the draft as everyone came into the room?

Robin's brow furrowed. "Well, in that case, I'll have it to you by end of day tomorrow."

The tension between Robin and Molly was palpable, and Deb sensed the meeting slipping away from her. Putting on her best cheerleader's voice, she said, "Thank you, everyone, for your contributions. We are making a real difference here and we couldn't do it without working together. We'll meet again in two weeks."

Seven chairs pushed out from the table at the same time. Molly was the first out the door. Deb caught Robin just before she walked out. "Thanks, Robin, for your diplomatic response with Molly."

Robin sighed and shook her head. "You're welcome. That's typical Molly."

"Really? Why does she get away with that?" Deb's voice was just above a whisper.

Robin looked behind her. The rest of the team was already gone. "She seems to have a problem with women. Haven't you noticed? She doesn't pull that stuff with Calvin. Or Tom. And she didn't with your predecessor, Sanjay, either."

Deb tried to recall her other experiences with Molly. Maybe Robin was right.

"She's also very good with the dogs," Robin added. "She seems to like animals more than people."

"Well, that's good to know. Thanks for telling me."

As they walked out of the conference room and into the main office area, Robin asked, "How was your weekend?"

"It was . . . interesting." Robin gave her a questioning look and Deb decided on the one detail she felt comfortable sharing. "I wasn't able to go for my bike ride as planned."

"Oh, are you a cyclist?"

"Yes, I am. I'm training for the Chesapeake Challenge." Deb beamed as she spoke.

Robin gaped. "I had no idea. That's great. That raises money for MS research, right?"

"So you've heard of it! Yes, each rider is supposed to set a goal and get donations. I'm about halfway to my fundraising goal. Which reminds me, I need to raise some money!" Deb and Robin shared a laugh as they made their way back to their desks in the open office.

For the rest of the day Deb felt good about herself. She updated Calvin following the team meeting, and she made sure Robin was able to approve the draft invitation from Molly. She also enjoyed her one hour at the front desk, fielding questions and cataloging donations. She convinced herself it was unlikely Andy would be back so soon, and she put that possibility out of her mind. She was very happy with where things stood with the annual dinner, and she really did enjoy her coworkers. They were thoughtful, and they were good at their jobs. It would have been a stellar day. But then, right at the end, it took a sour turn.

Shortly after five o'clock, Molly and Tom were walking out of the building ahead of her. They must not have known she was behind them, or maybe they did, but she heard Molly spit out, "I was not at all surprised she supported Meg. Didn't Meg practically get her this job?" Tom made a reply that Deb couldn't make out but sounded like agreement. Then Molly spoke again. "Did you hear her say she's raising money for MS? I really hope she doesn't come asking me for money. Some people just can't get enough attention. Wah, wah, wah."

And they both laughed.

Deb's shoulders slumped. The words hurt. She had never been one to seek attention, and Molly's flip tone made her angry. But there was something more concerning. Molly's malignant negativity was spreading.

Twenty

Deb felt the tears dripping from her eyes and soaking into her pillow. She was in so much pain. Grueling waves of spasms started at her feet and rippled up her legs. At the same time, her big toe and the ball of her left foot were numb, making it very difficult to stand, much less walk. She already had an acupuncture appointment scheduled for three thirty, after work. Would she even last that long?

"Marco," she called from her bedroom. It was just now seven o'clock on Wednesday morning. "Marco, sweetie, can you come here, please?" A wave of electricity traveled up her legs and fresh tears coursed down her cheeks from her eyes into her ears. She arched her back in response to the pain.

Soon Marco appeared in the doorway. "Hi, Mommy," he said.

"Hi, sweetie," Deb said, breathless. "Thank you for coming. Can you please bring me my cane? It's there on the chair at the end of the bed."

"Sure." Marco picked up the cane and handed it to his mother. "Is that all?" His eyes were dark with worry.

Deb sat up in bed and winced as her legs shot through with fire. "That's all for now. I'm going to need your help this morning. Do you think you can get your own breakfast?"

"Of course." He was nearly vibrating with energy, and Deb knew her state was causing him stress.

"Okay, then please do that. And, Marco," she said, as her son started to turn away, "can you please tell Grandma that I'm not feeling well."

"Yes, Mommy." Marco ran off in the direction of the kitchen.

Deb picked up her cell but realized it was too early to phone her boss. She had an hour and a half to get herself in shape. Maybe she could go to work after all.

"Debbie, is everything all right?" Betty, still in her dressing gown, poked her head through the doorway.

"Hi, Mom. I'm fine. I just can't really walk very well."

"Oh, is that all?" Betty said facetiously. "Here, honey, let me help you." She walked over to Deb, picked up the cane, and stood in front of her daughter. As a nurse, Deb's mother had years of practice helping patients get out of bed. "Place your hands on my shoulders, here," she said, guiding Deb's arms. "Now . . . lift up." Mother and daughter stood a moment looking like awkward teenagers at a dance. They took a few steps away from the bed and into the center of the room. "Can you use your cane now?" Betty asked.

"Let me try." Deb eased one arm off her mother's shoulder and onto the cane. She settled her weight on her two legs and the cane. "Yes, I think I can make it now. But don't go too far."

"I'm right here, Debbie. I won't leave you." Betty placed one hand on Deb's back.

Deb shuffled a few steps until she felt sure she wouldn't fall, then took a few steps with more confidence. "I have an appointment with the acupuncturist this afternoon, but I might try to move it up. I'm debating going into the office."

Betty raised her eyebrows doubtfully. "Could you work from here?"

"That's what I'm going to suggest. I have to call Calvin. But it's early yet. First I need some breakfast."

"Good idea," Betty said. "Come on into the kitchen and I'll fix you something."

After a light breakfast of toast and fruit, Deb called Calvin. She explained about the unrelenting pain in her legs, and he listened attentively.

"This has happened before. I just need to get to the acupuncturist and then I'll be fine," she said, aware her new boss had no reason to believe her. "I felt off yesterday evening, so I brought a few files home with me, just in case. I'd like to work from home this morning and come in after I see the therapist, if that's all right with you." That assumed she could move the appointment up, of course, but she didn't want to bother Calvin with the details.

Calvin spoke in his deliberate manner. "Deb, I'm happy to flex when I can, and this seems like a no-brainer to me. Come in when you are able. Tomorrow if need be."

"Oh, thank you! Thank you for understanding. That makes this much easier. I plan to be in this afternoon." She was anxious not to press her luck.

"Very good. See you then."

"Thank you!" she repeated. She hung up and laughed out loud. "Thank you, thank you, thank you!" she said to the empty room.

Betty, who'd been getting dressed during the call, returned to the kitchen. "How did it go?"

Deb beamed. "He completely understands. Oh my! I hadn't realized how stressed I was about that. I mean, he could've told me I had to come in or I'd be out of a job." The smile on her face spread even wider.

"Did you really think he'd react that way?"

"Well, no, I suppose not," Deb said, considering the possibilities. "But this is only my second week on the job. He doesn't have much reason to give me a break." Deb stood up then sat back down again. "I need to call Dr. Walden's office now. Cross your fingers they can see me early."

Betty patted Deb's shoulder. "Fingers crossed," she said.

Before she dialed, Deb remembered something else and hung up. "Shoot!"

"What now?" Betty asked.

"I was supposed to go sign those papers at the credit card company today! I forgot all about it. I've been putting it off for weeks. Now how am I going to get there?" Could she somehow get to the acupuncturist, go sign the papers, and still make it to Sparky's? She felt the weight of it all pressing down on her, and her legs seemed to spasm in response. "Mom, help. I don't know if I should go sign those papers or try to go to work."

"Both are important," Betty said diplomatically.

Deb's immediate reaction was anger. She was in too much pain to make a decision. She wanted someone to tell her what to do. Why was her mother always so neutral about everything? "Do you really have no opinion, Ma? Please, I need your help. What should I do?"

"I don't know, Debbie. I think you should stay home and not go to either office."

"Okay, but that's not an option." Deb looked at her mother, exasperated.

Betty looked back at her daughter. "Then I don't know what you should do."

Deb sighed. She'd already told Calvin she would be in. That's what she would have to do. The money would have to wait. Again.

Deb was sitting on the couch while Marco stood before her, dressed and ready for school. "Marco, you know the way to school. You're a big kid and I'm trusting you to walk straight there with no detours. Do you hear me?"

"Of course, Mom. Where else am I going to go?" He looked at her like she had a third arm.

The innocent question conjured memories of all the places Deb used to go when she and Caroline skipped school. "Let's not think about that," she said. "It's time for you to leave. Do you have everything you need? I see your book bag. Do you have your folder and workbook? Lunch box and water bottle?"

Marco took his backpack off his shoulder and peered inside. "Yes, yes, yes, and yes."

"And it's not P.E. day or anything like that."

"Nope." Marco began to shift his weight from foot to foot.

Deb smiled. "Okay, then get going. Be safe. I love you and will see you this afternoon."

"I love you too," Marco said. He hugged his mom tightly. "Bye, Grandma," he said to Betty, who was sitting in her favorite chair, then he went out through the front door.

"What time is your appointment?" Betty asked Deb.

"They said noon but I'm planning to go at eleven and see if they can squeeze me in sooner. Sometimes it's like flying standby—if you're there, they'll get you in."

"So you've got some time. Do you need to lay down for a while?"

"Are you trying to get rid of me?" Deb joked. Then more seriously she said, "I don't want to get back in bed. That will only make things worse. I'm going to set up in the kitchen and try to get some work done."

Betty picked up the remote. "Do you mind if I watch my program while you work?"

"That's perfectly fine, Mom. Pretend I'm not here."

Deb stood up and steadied herself on her cane. Then she gathered the items she would need to do her work: her files, a notepad and pen, her laptop, and her cell phone. With her cane in her strong hand, she ferried each item to the kitchen one by one and arranged her workspace. Ten minutes later, she settled down at the table.

From the kitchen she could hear the news program her mother was watching. The sound was innocuous at first, but then a commercial came on. She tried to block it out, but marketers, she realized, are very good at getting a person's attention. She read and reread the same paragraph several times. By the fourth commercial she determined she needed headphones. She looked in her purse but didn't see them. She got up and, using her cane, went into her bedroom to look for them. She rooted around in the drawer of her bedside table but couldn't find them. She checked the top drawer of her dresser, the tiny drawer under the stereo in the living room, and all three drawers in the kitchen. Finally she decided to ask Betty.

"Check the front pocket of your computer bag," her mother answered, not looking up from the TV.

At last Deb found the earphones. They were, as Betty had suggested, in the computer bag, which had been sitting next to her impromptu workstation the whole time. She let out a deep sigh, then plugged them into her computer, stuffed the other end into her ears, turned on some soft music, and returned to the document she was reading. The music blocked the commercials, but with no outside noise to distract her, the pain in her legs became unbearable and her mind felt cloudy. She was too distraught for even a simple task like filing emails. At last she gave up. She closed her laptop without completing anything, then scheduled an Uber and got her belongings together. Her legs were still on fire; the spasms undulated through her body. To get through it she focused on how good she would feel after the session with Dr. Walden.

"I'm heading out now, Mom. Remember, don't answer the phone while I'm away."

"Yes, Debbie. I won't."

Deb paused to think. "I was considering going straight to work from the therapist's office, assuming I'm feeling well enough. That would leave you to get your lunch and everything yourself. Are you up for that?"

Betty rolled her eyes. "That's what I do most days. It's been fine."

"All right, all right." Deb started to leave again then added, "Just one more thing." Betty pressed her lips together waiting for her daughter to speak. She looked like she might scream if Deb said the wrong thing, so she spoke quickly. "Would you be willing to watch Marco for the weekend that I'm doing the ride? I know it's a lot to ask, but he's pretty self-sufficient most of the time. You wouldn't have to do much."

The frown on Betty's face turned into a grin. "Sure, I'd like that."

Deb explained the plan for the weekend. She and Philippe and Caroline would drive to Easton, Maryland, the Friday night before the ride and stay in a hotel. They would drive back Sunday afternoon after completing day two. Betty would need to get Marco his lunch and dinner—prepared by Deb ahead of time—and make sure he went to bed on time.

"This is all assuming I'm able to lick these spasms," Deb added. She was not entirely sure it was a good idea to leave Marco with Betty for such an extended period, but her options for childcare were limited. Short of flying Paula or Julian out to stay with him, she didn't know what else to do. Thankfully Betty was willing to try it.

"Thanks, Mom. I really appreciate it." Deb's phone buzzed. "Uber's here. See you this evening."

Given how much faith Deb had put in Dr. Walden, it was perhaps no surprise that she should be let down. Her attempt to get in sooner with the acupuncturist had failed, and she'd spent the time alternately sitting in the waiting room and scouring the vending machines for something that could pass for lunch. When she finally got in for treatment, the results were less than miraculous. Although she could walk with greater ease, her legs felt like stilts, stiff and painful, and her big toe and the ball of her foot remained numb. Deb knew what she needed: steroids.

The troubles with steroids were manifold. Yes, they worked well—most of the time—but they had wearisome side effects. It would also mean taking at least one more day off work if not a whole week. Calvin had been patient so far, but Deb knew from experience, bosses have their limits. She liked her job too much to want to risk it. That said, if her legs were going to be coursing with fire like this, she didn't have much choice. She couldn't work, not even from home.

She arrived at Sparky's at one o'clock, and her first order of business was to call the neurologist. She spoke with the schedule coordinator.

"I believe I'm having a relapse. I need to schedule steroids."

"You'll need to see the doctor first. When can you come in?"

"Can I do a telehealth visit?" Anything not to have to miss more work.

"I'm afraid not. The doctor will want to assess your symptoms, make sure more isn't going on, and confirm it's not a pseudo-relapse."

Drat. "Okay, then, do you have anything Friday afternoon? I get out of work at three o'clock."

"He's booked that day. I could squeeze you in between patients, but you might have to wait."

Deb calculated the effects. Marco would need somewhere to go after school, with either Betty or Rosa, but at least it was after the workday. She accepted the appointment and crossed her fingers she wouldn't be in the waiting room too long.

"I have you down for Friday at three thirty," the coordinator said. "Dr. Gill will schedule the steroids with the hospital. If you need an MRI, we can schedule that as well."

Deb hung up and sighed. She knew she should be thankful the doctor was squeezing her in, but the wait until Friday seemed interminable. And that didn't even include the time it would take for the steroids to take effect. Plus an MRI? All the while she had work to do, a son to raise, Betty to care for, and the ride to train for. She could scarcely afford to be off her bike for so long. How would she make up the training time? Her shoulders slumped under the pressure, tears stinging her eyes, as much from fatigue as from the pain. Maybe Paula was right. Maybe the whole idea had been a mistake.

Twenty-One

That evening Caroline was in her kitchen preparing dinner. She'd stopped by the store on the way home and bought chicken breasts, fresh garlic, green onion, spaghetti, cream, shredded Parmesan, and sliced almonds. She put a pot of water on to boil, then set the chicken breasts poaching. She made a roux with butter and flour, added the green onions and garlic, and stirred. The room filled with the welcoming aroma. When the roux was smooth, she added the cream and Parmesan to make a sauce. By the time Robbie arrived home with Jacob, she had combined the sauce, noodles, and chicken into a casserole, sprinkled toasted almonds over the top, and placed the whole glorious concoction into the oven.

"Something smells awesome!" Jacob said as he came into the kitchen.

"Thank you," Caroline said with a smile. She had begun chopping vegetables for a salad to go with their chicken tetrazzini.

Robbie came in behind Jacob. "Hey, babe, what are you up to?"

"Just making dinner. I got out of work early and decided we could all use a delicious meal. There's pinot in the fridge if you'd like."

"Great." Robbie kissed Caroline, then got out two wine glasses and poured them each a drink.

"Jacob, how was school?" Caroline asked.

Jacob groaned. "I don't want to talk about it."

"Okay, we don't have to," she said. She was feeling more optimistic than she had in weeks, and Jacob's angst wasn't going to change that. Nothing objectively had changed; she still didn't know whose knife Jacob had pulled from his bag. But experience had shown her that good things happen when you believe. "All I'll say is, you did your part with the apology, turning it in Monday, and we'll find out whose knife it was soon enough. It will all work out, I'm sure." She put the chopped vegetables into a large bowl, tossed it, and set it on the table. "Five minutes till dinner. Please go wash your hands," she sang out.

Robbie and Jacob both left to wash in the bathroom, while Caroline washed her hands at the sink. She enjoyed the feeling of cool water as it ran over her hands. Now that she knew Jacob was innocent, she felt lighter. Happier. More appreciative of her surroundings. She felt like laughing for the first time in days.

The timer for the casserole dinged, and taking an oven mitt from the wall, she removed the hot dish from the oven and placed it on the dining room table. Jacob and Robbie took their seats. Caroline topped off the wineglasses, then pulled out her chair. Before she could sit down, however, the doorbell rang. She sighed and smiled. Darn. "I guess I have to get that. I'll be right back. You can serve yourselves."

She went to the door and looked out. "You've got to be kidding," she muttered. Instantly, Rosa's and Philippe's angry faces flashed through her mind and all of her lightness went out.

"What is it?" Robbie called from the dining room.

Caroline didn't answer. She opened the door and said, "Good evening, Officer Chavez. Officer Price. What brings you by?"

"Mrs. Cook, may we come in?" Officer Chavez asked. The yellow porch light illuminated his face. He wasn't smiling.

"I have dinner on the table. Can you come back another time?" Worth a try.

"This will only take a minute," Chavez said.

"All right," Caroline relented, and she opened the door for the two men to enter.

Robbie came over to see what was going on. "Officers, what can we do for you this evening? Jacob turned in his apology letter yesterday. He's well on his way to being done with this mess."

Officer Chavez nodded. "Yes, well, there's still the matter of the provenance of the weapon. We spoke to Mrs. Gamez as you suggested, Mrs. Cook, and she doesn't know anything about a pocketknife with a Mexican flag on the handle."

"Yes, I know," Caroline said.

"You know?" Officer Chavez's face was pinched and Caroline realized her mistake.

"What I mean is, I found that out after you were here Friday night. I spoke with Rosa myself and she said PJ doesn't own a pocketknife."

"I see. In that case, do you have any other ideas about where this knife may have come from? Because it didn't just fall into your son's backpack out of thin air."

Robbie said gruffly, "My wife is aware of the laws of physics."

The tension in the room was thick.

"It's okay, Robbie," Caroline said, taking his hand. "I'm the one who suggested it was PJ's. It's only natural they would think I might have other ideas when my first idea didn't pan out." She smiled at Officer Chavez. Again she became aware of what judgments they must have of her. This time she tried to shake it off. "Officers, I'm afraid I'm all out of ideas. I don't know where the knife came from. Jacob doesn't know where it came from either. He had no intention of hurting anyone with it. I think you know that."

"No, we don't know that," Officer Price said, red blotches appearing on his cheeks. "What we know is that your son took out a pocketknife in the middle of class, opened the blade, and was pointing it at people. Those facts have not changed."

Caroline blinked a few times. *According to one little pipsqueak who isn't even willing to be identified.* She squeezed Robbie's hand and bit back her retort. With her emotions under control and in the most neutral voice she could find, she said, "What happens now?"

"Now the matter will be referred to juvenile court."

"Is this where we say we want a lawyer?" Robbie asked.

"That's within your rights," Officer Chavez said.

"But Jacob is not under arrest," Caroline said.

"That's correct." Officer Chavez handed Caroline a piece of paper. "This is the contact information for the state's attorney's office. They can answer your questions from here on out."

Caroline took the paper and looked at it, but her mind was moving too fast to make sense of it.

"Good night, Mrs. Cook, Mr. Cook," Officer Chavez said with a grim smile. "Dinner smells delicious."

The officers walked out, leaving Caroline and Robbie reeling.

Twenty-Two

The forty-eight hours between getting her acupuncture and seeing Dr. Gill were hellish. Deb fumbled through the days barely able to think straight due to the waves of pain still roiling her body. She was careful not to schedule any meetings while she was feeling and thinking like a rag doll, but that didn't keep Calvin from stopping by her desk to check on her.

"Good to see you in the office, Deb," he said Friday morning.

"Thank you, Calvin. It's good to be here," she lied. She looked up at him from her desk. She hoped he wouldn't stay long.

"How are you feeling?"

"I'm good." She tried to sound cheerful but when she looked into his face, she could tell she wasn't fooling him. She decided to come clean. "I've been better. I'm afraid I'm having a relapse."

"I'm sorry to hear that." He frowned but still did not leave Deb's desk.

"Yeah, me too. It's terrible timing. But I have an appointment this afternoon that should help."

"Okay, well, whatever you need. I would rather you take time off so you can do your best work than have you try to muddle through." He gave her a fatherly look.

"I understand. I'm managing the workload. Thanks for your concern." Deb smiled to show she was being sincere.

Calvin walked back to his office and Deb let out her breath. In hindsight she should've asked for the afternoon off. The toughest thing she had in front of her for the day was tracking down Molly and the caterer's information. She still hadn't gotten back to Deb after the last event-planning meeting. On second thought, she just might leave that unpalatable task for a day when she had her full strength.

It was after five o'clock when Deb arrived at Rosa's house to pick up Marco following her appointment with Dr. Gill. As was often the case, Jacob was in the backyard with PJ and Marco, and the three boys were avidly undertaking soccer drills while Sarge looked on. Deb passed through the gate.

"Mom!" Marco called as he ran up and down the lawn.

"Hi, sweetie, having fun?" she asked, moving cautiously over the uneven ground. She leaned into her cane.

"Do you want to play with us?"

Deb's soul hurt at the question. "I can't, honey. My legs aren't up for it. But maybe next time. You can play a while longer. I'm going to talk to Miss Rosa for a bit. Hi, PJ. Hi, Jacob."

The neighbor boys both called hello as they tried to steal the ball from Marco.

Deb entered through the back door, which led into the kitchen. She found Rosa getting ingredients out for dinner.

"Good afternoon, Rosa. Thanks for having Marco over," Deb said. "Mind if I have a seat?" She pointed to the stool at the counter.

"Deb, hello! Please sit. Here, have some water," Rosa said, filling a glass and placing it in front of her guest. "You would've been proud of Marco today. He and PJ were reading PJ's bilingual books together before heading out into the yard. I think it's really helping. PJ got a note from his teacher saying his English has improved."

Deb congratulated Rosa, feeling good that she'd contributed to PJ's success. Rosa asked how things went at the doctor's office, and Deb took a long drink before answering.

"I had to wait for almost an hour to be seen. Good news is the doctor agreed to do a round of steroids so I can get my legs back." She rubbed her thighs subconsciously. If the MRI showed new lesions on her nerves, she would also need to start a new medicine. Switching meds meant even more unknowns. "The biggest bummer is how much time I have to be off my bike. There's no telling how long it will take for the steroids to kick in. A long ride like I was planning for Saturday and Sunday is out of the question."

Rosa frowned sympathetically.

Deb twisted her water glass thoughtfully, watching the water swirl. "I really want to do this ride. I know it could be my last chance. I just don't know how I'm going to make up the time."

"No, no, no. You still have lots of time. The ride is a month away. You'll be able to catch up," Rosa said firmly, coming over to stand next to her.

"You really think so?" Deb asked, feeling hopeful.

"I do. And you know, if you end up doing only one of the days, that's okay too. But don't give up. I know you'll regret it if you do." Rosa patted her on the shoulder.

Rosa's attitude was just the counterbalance Deb needed in the face of her recent challenges. "You're right, I would regret it. I have to at least try."

"That's the spirit!" Rosa said with a big smile. She went back to the counter and began chopping peppers and onions.

Deb sipped her water. "How is Philippe's training going?"

"Oh, very well. He trains year-round, so this is more like fine-tuning. But he's not thrilled about the fundraising aspect. That has been . . . challenging."

"Really? But Philippe is so outgoing and likable. I assumed he could talk anyone into supporting his ride."

"He is a great talker, yes, but he does not like to ask people for money. He grew up poor. He knows people work hard for their money and he doesn't always feel right taking from others. He feels like a thief."

"Oh, yes, I see. That makes sense." Deb thought a minute about Philippe's predicament. After all he and Rosa had done for her, she was anxious to help. "I'll tell you what has worked for me. Tell him to remember the money isn't going to him. It's going to the research. He's not a thief. He's Robin Hood."

Rosa nodded, considering her words. "I'll tell him that. Yes. Robin Hood. Thanks, Deb. I think that will help."

"So, I was surprised to see Jacob here. Do you know if everything got settled at the school?"

Rosa stopped slicing the onions to answer. "I only know a little about it. Caroline says the knife wasn't his. Or that's what he says. I really don't know." She resumed her chopping, and Deb could see Rosa was holding something back.

"Is there more?" she asked.

Rosa didn't respond right away. She threw the peppers and onions into a pan, then added several spices and stirred, her lips pressed tight as she worked. Finally, she said bitterly, "Caroline thought the knife came from PJ. She directed the cops here. It all worked out, but I wasn't too happy being visited upon by the police." Rosa looked at Deb with raised eyebrows.

"Oh, gosh. I'm sorry you had to go through that." Deb realized how inadequate her consolation sounded.

"Yeah, me too. Philippe was even more upset than I was. You know, where we come from, you don't send the police to a friend's house." Rosa shook her head.

Deb winced. "Oh, Rosa, I'm sure Caroline wasn't even thinking about it like that."

"I know, I know. You're right. I'm over it now. I do feel for Caroline. She still doesn't know where the knife came from."

There was a heaviness in the air then. Rosa returned to her cooking, and Deb took a final drink of water. She felt bad for Rosa. Deb knew firsthand how oblivious Caroline could be. She trusted the two women to work it out.

"Okay, well, thanks for the water and the chat. I need to get home to Mom and get our dinner made. What are you making, by the way? It smells delicious."

"Chicken tinga. A family favorite. I'll send you the recipe if you like."

"I would love that. Luis loved *tinga de pollo* tacos. He didn't have a recipe, though, so I've never been able to duplicate it. It would be great to surprise Marco with that one night."

Rosa set her spatula down and gave Deb a hug. "Then I'll send you the recipe."

As Deb walked out and she and Marco went home to Betty, she thought again about the ride. After talking to Rosa, she felt more upbeat about recovering the lost training time. Completing this ride was about more than getting in shape physically. It was about achieving what she set out to do. Following through on a plan and seeing what her body could do. And it raised money for a good cause. She had reached seventy percent of her fundraising goal just from friends and family. She hoped her body would not betray her again now that she was so close. Getting Paula's support too? She wanted that nearly as much as finishing the ride.

Twenty-Three

Deb opened her eyes and checked the time. Six forty-five on Wednesday morning, day five of the steroids. Her doctor had agreed to oral steroids, which meant she didn't have to go to the hospital after all—no missed workdays and no extra care for Marco. It was a new type of steroid from what she took in Austin, where she was living the last time she had a relapse, and so far she was pleased with the results. By Monday she was walking better, and although she had been wired during the days, she was able to sleep by Tuesday night. Scheduling the MRI had been trickier—there was a four-week lag time. She would have to wait until after the bike ride to find out if she needed a new medication.

Now, on Wednesday morning, she assessed her body. She felt . . . good. The numbness in her big toe that had spread to the ball of her foot had finally retreated to her big toe once again. That was positive, though Deb did wonder if she would ever get feeling back in that toe. The more pressing problem of stiffness and painful spasms in her legs had abated. The doctor had increased her dose of baclofen, and that seemed to be working. In the early years of her disease, baclofen had caused headaches, but she was hopeful that would not occur now.

She got out of bed, took her medicine, and went into the kitchen, leaning on her cane for support. Marco was still sleeping, but

Betty was up and sitting at the kitchen table. After thirty years as a nurse, she was an early riser by habit. Deb sat down across from Betty and tucked into a bowl of cereal.

"Would you like me to pour you some coffee?" Betty asked, rising. "It's decaf." Deb accepted the offer and Betty poured her a mug.

Betty leaned back against the kitchen sink. "So, tell me about your work. You've been there a few weeks now. Do you like it?"

Deb thought while she chewed her cereal. "You know, I really do. I love the mission, I like the people, and it's something I'm good at. I find my boss . . . what's the word? Enigmatic. But also very accommodating. One woman's been a challenge, and I'm worried her negativity is spreading to others on the team. She was supposed to get some information to me last week about the food for the annual dinner and I never heard from her. So I need to deal with that. And we have a fundraising goal we need to meet by June 30 that I'm nervous about, but I'm trying to stay positive."

"You seem happy, being part of a team."

"I am, Ma." Deb smiled.

Betty grinned back. "I'm happy you're happy. I know you weren't too keen to move back here after all that happened—"

"No, Mom," Deb interrupted, but Betty powered on.

"I know this wasn't your first choice. You were happy to do it because I needed you, but you had a life in Austin and you gave it up to come here. And I thank you for it. I know I don't always show it, but it warms my heart to have you and Marco nearby, and the fact you have a rewarding job and a new hobby with the cycling, well, that makes it all okay. I never wanted to be a burden, and this feels good. Like family."

"What are you talking about, Grandma?" Marco asked, taking Betty's seat at the kitchen table.

"Oh, just how much I enjoy having you and your mom here with me."

"Well, Mom," Deb said, getting up from the table, "I'm thankful I was able to come here and be with you. I know some people see times like these as challenges or burdens, but I think we are all so fortunate to have each other to lean on. And you're right, I wasn't sure about coming back here after all this time. But it's worked out." She thought fleetingly of the face in the crowd at Caroline's art show. There had been no more mention of Andy Peters and she was relieved.

Betty nodded rhythmically. After a pause, she said, "Paula called me."

Deb looked at her mother, confused. "She did? When?"

"Yesterday. You were at work." Betty seemed to know that what she was saying might be disturbing to Deb, but Deb couldn't figure out why. Was it because she had broken her promise?

"You—you answered the phone?"

"I did, yes. It was Paula. She wanted to talk to me."

Deb tried to keep her response even. Her frustration at her mom not keeping her word was displaced by the uneasy feeling that Betty had a bigger bomb to drop. Was this about Betty not getting to know her granddaughter, like she said at the hospital? *Tread carefully.* "Okay. What did she say?"

"She doesn't want you to do the ride. She thinks it's too strenuous." Betty looked up from her coffee mug and met Deb's gaze.

"That's what she said?" Confusion was giving way to anger.

"Yes. She's worried about you. I told her it was going to be all right, that you were doing what you needed to do. I'm not sure I changed her mind. Anyway, I thought you should know." Betty's voice was calm and even. She sipped her coffee.

Deb didn't know what to think about this news. On the one hand she wanted to scream at her mother for answering the phone when they had agreed she wouldn't. On the other hand, Betty had defended her, and that had to count for something, didn't it? Her feelings about Paula were equally muddied. What was she thinking calling her grandmother like that? Was she trying to turn Deb's own mother against her? This was a headache she did not need.

"Are you still able to watch Marco while I'm in Easton?" Her mind was puzzling through all the ramifications of this news.

"Yes. I haven't changed my mind about that."

Marco had been silent for the whole conversation. Deb tried to keep these kinds of confrontations out of his view, but some things couldn't be helped. She tidied the dishes on the counter, preparing them for the dishwasher. The kitchen was otherwise spotless, as was the living room, Marco's room, Deb's room, and the hall closet—a side effect of the steroids.

She was still processing what her mother had revealed. She needed time to think. "I'm getting in the shower now. I'm going by the Visa office after work to finally sign those papers and get your money back. Marco, please load the dishwasher when you're finished with your breakfast."

"I will."

"Just three weeks left of school. Can you believe it?" Deb ruffled his hair as she walked out of the kitchen.

Deb was in the conference room with the event-planning team later that day. She had gathered the group to discuss preparations and any progress toward the fundraising goal. Each person had retaken their seat from two weeks ago, with Deb at the head of the table and the six teammates seated around the horseshoe. With all of the drama in her personal life, not to mention the residual brain fog from the relapse, she had lost track of some of the pieces for the annual dinner. She had a good team, though, and knew she could rely on them. Molly stood as the lone source of consternation.

Deb called the meeting to order and everyone quieted down. She had sent out an agenda ahead of time, alerting Molly that she would be speaking first. Deb still hadn't heard the final word about the caterer, but Molly had assured her, in her usual clipped manner, that it was under control. Robin had also hinted she had some big news to share.

"Molly. Let's start with you. How are we doing with the gluten-free and nondairy options?"

Deb knew from her previous job that the food was what everyone remembered most from events like these. Perfectly cooked pasta prelude. Jumbo shrimp in a spicy cocktail sauce. Plentiful desserts. These made a positive impression. Not enough food, overcooked meats, and meal choices that didn't respect a restricted diet left attendees questioning why they'd come. And when one of those attendees with a restricted diet was one of your biggest donors, getting the menu right became a top priority.

Molly had her laptop open and made several swipes on the track pad before responding. Deb held her breath.

"I asked what gluten-free and nondairy dishes they had, and they seemed reluctant to make any changes to our menu. But I told them that if we couldn't add more options, we would have to change food vendors. Gene, our contact, said he'd be in touch. I got a message at the end of last week with an update. We now have three new dishes to choose from." Reading from her screen Molly listed them: "Tofu and green bean stir-fry, served with rice; quinoa salad with artichokes, red onion, black beans, and a balsamic vinaigrette; and pepper steak with nondairy creamed corn. They also have appetizers: plant-based Swedish meatballs, and beets with vegan goat cheese."

Deb was stunned. "That's fantastic!" she said. "Well done, Molly. I'm really impressed."

Molly blushed. "It was nothing."

"You told me earlier you had a sample menu planned. Can you tell us about that?"

Molly pulled out a few sheets of paper and passed them around. "You'll recognize most of the menu from last year's event. I've added the quinoa salad and the steak with creamed corn, and I swapped the mini quiches for the vegan Swedish meatballs."

Deb nodded as she read over the menu. "Works for me." She had picked up her pen to note the decision when Molly spoke again.

"It's going to increase the cost."

Deb detected a challenge in her tone. "I understand," she said. "Send me the numbers and I'll make it work. We might have to drop one of our desserts, but it's worth it. Any other thoughts on this before we move on?"

Everyone was quiet. Then Tom said, "Nice work, Molly. Sounds delicious."

"Yeah," Robin added. "I'm looking forward to it. I love steak with creamed corn."

Heads nodded around the conference table. Molly allowed herself a smile, and Deb let out her breath. Maybe she really could win Molly over.

"Now, Tom and Hannah, any movement with inviting Meg Shaeffer?"

Tom reported that they sent the invitation and Meg accepted right away.

Hannah picked up the thread. "Meg suggested playing some of her YouTube videos during the gala. I thought that was a great idea. We would need a screen and projector, but I think it makes for excellent background entertainment."

Molly sighed heavily and Deb asked if she had something to add. Molly was already on record as saying the dog videos were too gimmicky. She reiterated her stance now.

"I hear what you're saying, Molly. I know Meg wasn't your first choice. But the donors love her videos and it's a donor event. I'm going to approve the projector and screen." As an olive branch, she added, "We can schedule Kevin Berger for next year's event. I'll put it in the files."

Lawrence made a motion and Deb nodded for him to speak. "I'd like to invite Meg in to film a few clips for social media before the event. We can show that as well."

"Great idea!" Deb was so impressed with her team. "Wow, we are really moving along. Flo or Robin, any updates from you?"

"Nothing at this time," Robin said.

"Ditto," said Flo.

Deb laughed quietly and muttered, "I love you too." When she realized her team was looking at her, she said, "Don't you also think of Patrick Swayze and *Ghost* when someone says 'ditto'?"

"What?" Tom asked, baffled. "What's *Ghost*?" Then everyone

laughed. Deb hadn't felt so good about being on a team in a long time. She could be herself with these people.

"Okay," she said, calming everyone just a bit, "last point of business. Does anyone have an update on our fiscal year fundraising? Any new donations or promises?"

Robin raised her hand. "I almost forgot. I received a commitment for a donation of twenty-five thousand dollars!" Her eyes were wide. "It happened when you were out Friday afternoon, Deb, or I would've told you."

"That's great!" Deb said, astounded. "Who's it from?"

Almost before the words were out of Robin's mouth, Deb knew the answer. "Andy Peters," she said. "He usually makes several small donations throughout the year, but this year his company chose us for their charity, so he can make a bigger commitment."

"Wow," Deb said. Her mind spun. She tried to listen while Robin and the others celebrated but didn't quite follow everything.

When she tuned back in Robin was talking. "He'll present the check at the annual dinner. He's looking forward to meeting you."

Deb mastered her breathing and said, "That's really something. Great news, Robin. Just terrific!"

No one else had news to report after that, so Deb adjourned the meeting. She spent the rest of the day crunching numbers, trying to make the new menu items and the projector and screen rental work with their budget. All the while, she had a pit in her stomach and one thought in her mind: Sparky's had accomplished so much, and this donation could make a big difference for a lot of people. Did it really matter whose name was attached to it?

Deb got out of work at three o'clock and headed for the credit card office. Finally she was getting her mother's money back. It sure demanded a lot of effort for what now seemed like not a lot of dough. Compared to the cost of remodeling the bathroom, it was a pittance. But it was done. Cross one thing off the list.

When she arrived home that evening, Nurse Lydia was just leaving. Deb parked on the street so she could have a word with the home health aide. A tall and slender Black woman who often smelled like strawberry perfume, Nurse Lydia greeted Deb warmly outside the house. The sky was heavy with clouds as if rain were on the way, and the nurse was moving quickly toward her car.

"Heading home?" Deb asked, walking toward her with her cane at her side. She stopped about ten feet from Lydia and leaned on the stick.

"Trying to. It's college night at the high school and I need to get Kelly there."

Deb remembered searching for colleges with her own daughter. "Bittersweet, isn't it?"

"Indeed it is." Lydia made a move to unlock her car.

"Real quick, how's my mom today?" Deb asked.

"She's in good spirits."

"How are her blood sugar numbers?" Deb asked, cutting to the chase.

Lydia looked her in the eye. "Not bad. They could be better, of course. I suspect she's been sneaking chocolates again."

Deb nodded. "Yes, I suspect that too. Anything else?" In caring for her mother, Deb had discovered there was always something.

"Nothing comes to mind. She takes her medicine regularly; the yoga is paying off with regards to mobility on her left side. I believe we talked about a speech therapist a while back. Your mother is borderline there. You may see some improvement if she went regularly, but that's your decision, and hers."

Deb took all of that in. "What about dementia? Did she tell you about getting ripped off last month?"

"No, she didn't. I'm sorry to hear that. She does have some early signs of dementia. She doesn't always recognize me when I first come through the door. I announce myself when I enter, but I can tell she's frightened."

Deb thought of the episode at the hospital with Marco. "Do you have any suggestions for how to handle that?"

"I'm afraid I don't. If you're concerned, you could talk to the neurologist about it."

Dr. Strauss. "We just saw him."

"Oh, yes, the fall. Well, her head is fully healed. That's one positive. Truly, with her medical history, I think you're both doing very well."

Deb had to agree. She said goodbye then, and Nurse Lydia went on her way.

Twenty-Four

Caroline arrived at the trailhead Sunday morning at eight o'clock. It was a beautiful day, fifty-six degrees and sunny with just a few clouds and a light breeze. She wore her long-sleeved jersey zipped up to her chin, with bike pants, gloves, and sunglasses protecting the rest of her. She was anxious to get started. She was going to attempt forty-five miles for the first time, and she expected it to take her nearly four hours to complete it.

It had been eleven days since the police last stopped by her house to announce Jacob was still under suspicion. She had no answers for where the knife had come from, no new leads. She thought back on the fights they'd had earlier in the year about Jacob being forgetful, leaving his folder at home. How many water bottles did that child lose in the first month alone? Now she was wondering what would happen if he were referred to juvenile court. She had expected it all to move much faster, but she seemed to be the only one who felt any urgency over the situation.

A blue van pulled over and parked on the gravel patch near the trailhead and Debra Lee climbed out. "Caroline! I was hoping to beat you here. I'll be ready in just a minute."

The rear side door of the van slid open. Debra pulled out her bike, strapped her helmet in place, and wheeled the bike over to where Caroline stood waiting.

"I am *so* excited to be here today," Deb said. Her eyes were bright with enthusiasm. "I was off my bike for more than two weeks, but I finally was able to get a short ride in on Friday after work. Oh, it is so difficult not being able to ride." While she talked, Deb quickly arranged various items in her back pocket: food, keys, phone. Like Caroline she was wearing long sleeves and pants, as well as gloves. "Let me just do a couple short stretches and then we can get going."

"For sure," Caroline said. She pulled out her phone to look at the map while she waited. "The training plan calls for forty-five miles this week. Is that what you were planning?" She was doubtful, after how long Debra was off her bike and why, but was learning not to put restrictions on her friend.

Debra stretched her arms over her head and bent first to the right and then to the left. "No, I'm going to have to modify. It's been too long and I don't want to risk an injury. Especially after the agony I just went through. I'm aiming for twenty-five to thirty miles. But you go on ahead. We're meeting for lunch at your place?"

Caroline confirmed that was right. She'd arranged a late lunch with Debra, Rosa, and Philippe so they could talk through race-day logistics. Robbie was smoking a brisket, and Caroline had bought a triple berry pie to go with it. She also had a surprise for Debra.

"Now I can't wait," Debra said.

The women pedaled off down the trail. Because the route was so long, they would be doing some trail and some road riding. Caroline's route would take them across two different creeks and through a regional park. Deb would have to miss some of the more scenic areas when she turned back early, while Caroline would ride along the Potomac River into Washington, DC. But they both would experience a mix of hills and flats, high- and low-traffic areas, and lots of natural beauty. The varied landscape was one of the features of Silver Spring that Caroline appreciated most. You could pass through urban and natural terrain in a matter of minutes.

After they'd gone eight miles, Debra called for a stretch break. They pulled over near a public restroom in the park, and both ladies guzzled water. The day was heating up.

"I should've worn my cooling vest," Deb said, fanning herself. She sprinkled some water on her chest.

Caroline shook her head. "What's that? A cooling vest?"

"Yeah, it's a neat little vest that holds ice packs to help you stay cool in hot weather. For people with MS, which gets worse in the heat, it can make a real difference." Deb stretched her legs in a methodical routine while Caroline stretched her shoulders and upper back. "I'm going to pop into the restroom to see if there are any paper towels. Be right back."

Caroline waited patiently for Deb. She had never considered something as simple as a cooling vest before. She realized there was a whole world of problems, and another whole world of products meant to solve them, that she never knew existed.

When Deb returned she had two or three wet paper towels wrapped around her neck. "This should help at least a little."

"Very clever."

They rode more or less together for another several miles, with Caroline leading the way. Deb was right about the effect taking two weeks off her bike would have; Caroline could tell she was struggling. Caroline suggested she turn up her pedal assist, but Deb was dead set against it. "I want to train under the same conditions as the ride." A worthy goal, but it meant Caroline crested the hills before her companion almost every time.

A few miles on, where the road was closed to traffic, the women pedaled side by side.

"Can I ask you something?" Caroline said.

"Shoot."

"Are you scared? About your MS?" It was a question Caroline had wanted to ask ever since she first learned of Deb's diagnosis.

Deb let out a breath. "Yes, I'm scared. I mean, of course I'm scared. I've known people who lost almost all of their mobility seemingly overnight. That could be me. That's why I want to do this ride and do it now."

Caroline swallowed. "Wow."

"But you know me. I've felt that way ever since Laurie passed. We have limited time on this earth. We have to make the most of it." Deb smiled a crooked smile. "But I'm also very fortunate. I don't really have the vision changes that others have. And my MS has responded to medication. That isn't true for everybody." She shrugged. "We really never know what the future holds, do we."

Caroline was silent, marveling at how different their circumstances were. She'd been healthy her whole life, her parents vibrant, her husband and son the picture of good health. Other than a few headaches, she really had no complaints. It was humbling.

"I see your face finally healed. How are the headaches?" Deb asked, and Caroline wondered if they'd been thinking the same thing.

When was her last headache? Not since around the time Jacob was caught with the knife. "They seem to have abated. I'm happier generally, things have settled down at work, and miraculously, Jacob is listening more and doing what he's supposed to do. So there you go. I think it was just the stress." She shrugged.

"Oh, that's good. I was worried about you. Headaches can be caused by so many things."

"True." Caroline had done some research and confirmed what she already knew. Stress was the most common cause. Everything else was too horrible to think about.

At mile eighteen, Caroline indicated she would be branching off. She showed Deb the map on her phone. "I'm going to make this loop here, to the right—or north and east. You have a couple of options for how to end. If you cross this bridge here"—she pointed to a spot on the map—"you can make it to thirty miles before getting back to the cars. If you turn before the bridge, that should get you twenty-five."

Deb took the phone so she could memorize the route, then handed it back to Caroline. "Thanks, C. I think I'll go for thirty. I'm feeling good."

Caroline paused before remounting her bike. "Wish me luck, Debra. I've never done forty-five miles before." She gritted her teeth in mock angst.

"You can do it!" Deb clapped her gloved hands together, making a muffled thud.

The two women parted ways, Caroline to the northeast and Deb heading southwest. As she pedaled off, it occurred to Caroline that those were the directions they had traveled when they left town for college twenty years earlier.

Back then, Caroline had been confused and hurt that Deb didn't try to reconnect after she left town. Caroline still didn't know what had kept Debra away for so long. If she asked now, she was afraid Deb would disappear again. For a while Caroline had thought it must've been something she did, but as time passed, she decided that was just the self-centered teenager talking. Whatever it was had nothing to do with Caroline. Odd, though. Betty was here. Why wouldn't Debra come home? Caroline had heard the rumors, of course. That night with Andy Peters. Debra supposedly fleeing town to have their love child. But Caroline didn't believe it. Deb would have told her something like that. Now that Debra was back, Caroline was more convinced than ever that the rumors were false.

Andy was a different story. As it turned out, he played golf at the same country club as Robbie. Caroline had looked him up after that first ride with Debra. Deb had said not to, but what could it hurt? Sure enough, still single. Meanwhile, Debra had no love in her life. Caroline knew just what she needed to do.

Twenty-Five

Deb arrived at Caroline's house for lunch shortly after two o'clock. The afternoon was sunny and warm with blue skies, and the alluring scent of homemade brisket was in the air. As Deb climbed the stone steps, her legs ached from the long ride with Caroline that morning, but she also felt solid. She could see a way forward with her training. Making up the lost time no longer seemed impossible.

She went through the side gate to the patio, where Rosa, Philippe, Caroline, and Robbie were already assembled. The scene reminded Deb of Caroline's dinner party months earlier. She wouldn't have even considered trying the Chesapeake Challenge if not for that night. She smiled, thankful she had taken a chance on Caroline.

Caroline had arranged for Jacob to go to his grandparents' that afternoon, and PJ was with a sitter. Marco was home alone with Grandma for the first time, a small point of concern for Deb. But he'd shown himself to be capable during her relapse, and Betty always did better during the daytime. She reassured herself it would be okay. So this gathering was just the adults. What a relief it would be to have a conversation uninterrupted by the needs of little people.

Deb took her seat at the table next to Caroline and immediately noticed the nervous energy coming off her friend. Caroline stood up, went inside, came back, sat down, stood again. Walking back and forth to the house, she brought bowls of chips and salsa. Old Bay popcorn. Candied nuts. Meanwhile, Robbie had busied himself with the brisket and salad. Deb squinted at Philippe and Rosa. Their faces showed a tension Deb had rarely seen. "So, how are you two?"

"I need the restroom." Rosa stood up briskly and went inside, leaving Deb alone with Philippe.

The knife. Caroline had sent the cops to Rosa's house, and they had yet to sort everything out.

Deb clapped her hands together lightly, trying to soothe the ripples of anxiety in the air. She cast her gaze around the garden, hoping for something to talk about. She laughed when she saw the Certified Wildlife Habitat sign. It really was impressive that Caroline had done all this herself. Finally she looked at Philippe across from her. "Tell me about yourself, Philippe."

Philippe smiled his welcoming smile and leaned back in his chair. "What do you want to know?" The chance to talk seemed to put him at ease.

"Hmm." Deb realized she knew very little about her new friend. Although always cordial, he wasn't forthcoming with his history. She decided to try something safe. "How did you and Rosa meet?"

"At a bar!" Philippe's face lit up with the memory.

"Really? At a bar? I thought for sure you were going to say you volunteered to build the same Habitat house."

"Oh, no. We both enjoy volunteering, but that's not how we met. I was new to the area, just moved to DC, and I'd gone to see a band. I read about this tiny club that was going to have a band from Haiti playing, and I thought, no way, I've got to see this. So I went, and there was Rosa, standing at the bar, listening to the music. And she had this vibe about her. She was just so welcoming and open, I knew I had to meet her." Philippe had a boyish look as he recalled meeting his future wife.

Deb smiled wide. "That's so great! Was the band any good?"

"You know, I don't remember them at all. I wasn't paying attention. Maybe Rosa remembers. That was nearly fifteen years ago now."

"Wow, fifteen years. Is that when you came to the US?"

"Oh, no, I came to the US twenty-five years ago. First I came to Florida, like so many of us. I came on a boat in the middle of the night. Can you believe it? I came on a boat like a thief in the night. I was twelve years old. My mother put me on a boat with my uncle and said, 'Go.' And who was I to question? So I went. I left my family and arrived in Florida with nowhere to stay. I think they thought the US would welcome us with open arms. You know, we hear that a lot in Haiti: The US wants us to come, we're welcome here. We'll find work and things will be better. But when you get here, the reality is much different." Philippe shook his head.

"Wow," Deb said. "I had no idea, Philippe. That's an amazing story." She wished she had something more insightful to say. Her own family had immigrated three generations earlier, so she didn't have much to contribute. She absorbed what she had heard.

"Yeah, it is. Even I am amazed sometimes. How did I get from there to here? I do not know. As a Black man in America, I struggled. I really did. But I have my papers now. I have a degree. I have a job. And I have Rosa and PJ. I am blessed."

Deb allowed the melodic sounds of Philippe's voice to echo in her ears. After a moment she said, "You're not a thief."

"What's that?"

"You said you came here like a thief in the night. You're not a thief. You're one of the most generous people I know. I'm glad you came here."

Philippe considered her for a moment and nodded. "Me too."

Rosa came back then, and Caroline and Robbie joined them with the lunch dishes.

"Should we talk about race day?" Deb asked after everyone had served themselves. Her mouth watered as she looked at the pile of shredded beef on her plate. Her appetite after the long ride was the size of Utah.

Everyone seemed to relax a bit with the food out, and they had a good time discussing how to get to the race (Deb would drive her van), where to stay (the race hotel), and how they would all get back. Deb was relieved to see Caroline and Philippe laughing together. They seemed to remember why they were friends.

"We'd be happy to have everyone back here for a celebratory barbecue on Sunday evening," Caroline said. She looked at Robbie. "Right?"

"Yes, definitely," Robbie agreed.

The group talked some more about what they would need to pack and who would be taking care of each of their children. Caroline got up to bring the pie out, and Deb thought she heard the doorbell ring while she was gone. When Caroline came back, she was carrying the pie. And she wasn't alone.

"Surprise!" she announced. Her face was split into a huge grin.

Deb looked at the pie in Caroline's hands, then looked at the guest beside her. It took a few seconds for the years to wash away and the picture to resolve but when she could focus again, she was certain she had once known the man standing next to Caroline. Deb's heart was in her stomach.

Caroline said, "You remember Andy Peters, don't you, Debra?" She was beaming as if she'd just brought home the prize turkey.

Deb could hardly bring herself to respond. Her throat was tight and she was desperate not to let her fear overwhelm her. She nodded. "Yes, I remember."

Caroline set the pie down and invited Andy to have a seat. He said something to Deb but she didn't really hear it. Her mind was plotting an escape. She felt repulsed and was sure her face would give her away. Here he was. And here she was. At the same table. What had Caroline done?

He was shorter than she remembered, hair a little darker. His skin was clear, eyes brown and shining. A red ball cap with the white Nationals *W* on the front cast a shadow over his face. He was talking to Philippe and Rosa now, explaining how he'd reconnected with Caroline. Something about golf at the country club. What struck Deb most was how normal he seemed. He wasn't a monster. He could have been anyone.

Thoughts of Andy finding out about Paula rose up in her mind. What would she do then? Her life would be ruined. Paula's life. Marco's. Thank God she hadn't told Caroline everything.

She sat glued to her seat for as long as she could stand it. She wanted to be strong enough to stay, to be over it. But she just wasn't. She had to leave. For her own survival.

"Well, I have to go now. Good to see everyone."

Her voice sounded strained. She was desperate not to make a

scene even as she felt herself moving too quickly. The others said goodbye, and at last she was free. She fled through the gate and around to the front of the house, still trying to master her feelings. Then footsteps. Caroline was following her.

"Deb, don't go. Are you mad?"

Caroline tapped her shoulder and Deb turned around. By then the anger had boiled up and was coloring her face.

"Am I mad? Caroline, what do you think? Yes, I'm mad. I'm livid. I'm absolutely livid." She was trembling with the effort to control her voice.

"But—" Caroline stammered. And then, as if to explain why she had chosen today to reveal this surprise, she added, "I invited him to the art show, but you left before I could introduce you. Don't you want to catch up?"

Deb blinked, trying to comprehend where Caroline could possibly have gotten that idea. "No, Caroline. Just no. I told you, some doors are better left closed."

"If you're worried about what he'll think of your MS, don't. I already told him and he's fine with it."

"You did what?!" Deb could hardly believe her ears. Caroline had always been pushy and occasionally oblivious, but it had come from a place of love. Now? Now she had crossed a line. "Humility, Caroline. Try a little humility."

"What do you mean?"

"Your family. Your friends. You treat them like playthings, never apologizing for the harm you've caused, and then wonder why they don't want to be around you. You think you know what's best for everyone, but you don't even see what's in front of your face."

Caroline's eyes narrowed. "I see very clearly what's going on. Everyone deserves a little love in their lives, Debra. Even you."

Now Deb thought her head might literally detonate. She imagined her exploded brain leaving bone chips and blood spatter all over Caroline's pristine front porch. Maybe then Caroline would understand the magnitude of her mistake.

"I never want to talk to you again."

Deb grabbed the railing and hustled down the steps. This time Caroline did not follow.

Twenty-Six

That night Deb logged in to chat with Paula. She had calmed down from her fight with Caroline, but still she felt off-kilter. Her body ached in response to the adrenaline, and she hadn't stopped worrying about Andy finding out about Paula. Betty and Marco had noticed how shaky she was. For once she was grateful to have MS to blame her problems on.

She was nervous to talk to Paula after their last argument and still miffed that her daughter had tried to circumvent her. Paula had her own relationship with her grandmother, Deb acknowledged, but that did not include trying to undermine Deb. She was ready to let that go, however, in the interest of keeping the peace. She took a few deep breaths and released them, settling her body and mind. This call would solve everything. Once Paula saw for herself how far Deb had come with her training, she would be on board.

Deb checked the time on the clock over the stove. A few minutes past ten. Paula was late. She pulled her phone out of her purse and woke up the home screen. Two new notifications. The first text was from Paula.

Can't talk tonight. Killer exam tomorrow, have to study. Sorry!

The time stamp read 9:55. Deb's shoulders slumped. Was her daughter avoiding her? Now Paula wouldn't get to see for herself that the ride was a good idea. Feeling deflated, Deb took the earphones out of her ears, closed her laptop, and stored them both in her bag. She preferred to assume the best of her daughter. She picked up her phone and typed:

Good luck, sweetie. I love you!

She hit send, then navigated to the next message, this one from Julian. She kept in touch with him, her closest connection to her beloved husband, but they didn't text often. She wondered what he could be writing about. She quickly found out.

Everything all right over there, mujer? Paula called me yesterday. Said you had a flare-up after all the riding and she doesn't know what to do. Asked me to step in if I could. She doesn't want you to do the ride. I told her I had no sway over you, you're too pigheaded to listen to a nice guy like me, lol. But I couldn't let down my niece, so here I am. Should I be worried?

Deb's pulse soared as she read the message, and her disappointment quickly spiraled into indignation. Now Paula wasn't just trying to turn Betty against her, she had called her uncle too? Deb tried to talk herself down, but she felt her anger writhing out of control. Before she could think better of it, she found Paula's number in her phone and called it. She would tell her what she thought of these underhanded tactics.

"Mom?" Paula picked up on the second ring.

Deb let out a harsh breath before speaking. "I heard from Uncle Julian and Grandma that you've been lobbying them, trying to turn them against me. I think that's really low." She was shaking with emotion. Her heart was racing, and adrenaline was making her throat feel tight.

Paula didn't miss a beat. "I didn't want to go behind your back, Mom, but you won't listen to me. You said so yourself. It's not my place. So I went to people I thought you would listen to. I would've called the doctor if I had his number. I don't want you to do the ride. I think you're being irresponsible and selfish."

Deb closed her eyes. She hated fighting with her daughter. She tried speaking calmly to keep from saying anything she would regret. "Paula, you have to trust me to make good decisions."

"Then make good decisions! Drop out of the ride!"

That was the one thing Deb couldn't stand to hear. She let loose her tongue. "Listen, miss, I dropped out once before because of you and I'm not going to do it again!"

Paula hesitated before responding. "What are you talking about?"

The words tumbled quickly out of Deb's mouth. "Last time I trained for this ride. When I was eighteen. I dropped out to protect my unborn baby—you. Not this time. I am not being selfish just because I'm doing something for myself. If you hadn't canceled our call you would see that I am totally healthy. I just need you to support me."

"Totally healthy? Mom, I don't buy it. You may have recovered this time, but who's to say it won't happen again, and worse? What if you crash your bike or get stranded because your legs give out?"

"They have SAG support. And I told you, I have my friend Caroline." Deb paused. She didn't have Caroline anymore. She would be facing the ride alone.

"SAG support isn't going to help when you get hit by a drunk driver like Dad!"

Paula's words echoed down the phone line. Deb was quiet. She knew she should be more sympathetic to her daughter's fears. They had both lost enough people. But in Deb's heart, this was different.

She wasn't being irresponsible. She was finally doing something for herself, and she wasn't going to give that up.

"Never mind, Paula. I'm not going to change your mind. I see that now. I'm sorry you can't trust me, but I'm doing the ride whether you like it or not."

Silence rang in Deb's ears.

"I'm sorry to hear that." When she finally spoke, Paula's voice was quiet and Deb wondered if she was crying.

Oh, Luis, I could really use your help right now.

"I'm hanging up now," Deb said gently. And then the line went dead. Paula had hung up first.

Deb sat down and cried.

Twenty-Seven

Deb had reached the point in her training where her long ride had become her short ride. When she began, she could barely do fifteen miles without feeling it for a couple of days afterward. Today, she was heading out for a light ride of . . . fifteen miles. She grinned as she buckled her helmet and slipped on her gloves. The Chesapeake Challenge was two weeks away, and for the first time since her relapse, she felt confident she would be ready in time.

"Mom, I'm going out for a quick ride before I get Marco from school," Deb said. It was Friday afternoon and Betty was doing a large-print word search in her favorite chair in the living room, waiting for *Jeopardy!* to begin. "I'll be back in an hour. Please don't answer the phone while I'm out." *Even for Paula*, she thought bitterly.

"Yes, Debbie, I know. Enjoy your ride."

Deb, dressed in bike shorts and a sleeveless jersey, took in the view of her mom in the living room. The shades were pulled down against the sun and the lamp was on for light. "Are you sure you don't want to spend some time outside? It's seventy degrees out. I could set up a chair on the back porch," she offered. "Near the rose bushes." Betty loved her rose bushes.

"No, I'm happy where I am. But thank you. Nurse Lydia should be here shortly anyway."

Deb hesitated. How could her mother stand to be inside all day when the sky was an impossible blue, the clouds light and fluffy? "Are you sure?"

Betty looked at her overbearing daughter, sighed, and forced a smile, tucking her pen inside her puzzle book and closing it. "Okay, Debbie, why don't you set up a chair for me. I might go out in a bit."

Deb skipped out the back door, brushed off a chair, set it next to the rose bushes, which were just starting to bloom, and reappeared in the living room.

"Okay then. I'm off now."

Betty waved goodbye. Deb walked out through the garage, hopped on her bike, and set off.

What a beautiful day! Deb breathed in the fresh air and relaxed her legs while she pedaled. Riding brought her such joy. She was thankful for the pedal assist that made her rides possible. What once seemed like cheating she now recognized as simply leveling the playing field.

Around mile five she stopped to stretch her calves and shoulders. Her muscles were tired from all of the training, and she felt a little sluggish, despite the charged air. But she had learned that an early stretch break could make a big difference in her stamina as well as her recovery.

Back on her bike, a stray cloud passed overhead, casting a shadow over her. She had not talked to Caroline since their argument several days ago. Caroline had texted her a few times with GIFs and non-apologies, but she clearly had no idea why Deb was upset, and Deb was in no mood to set her straight. She was still so angry at the way Caroline had meddled in her life, she couldn't see ever forgiving her. Granted, Caroline didn't have the full story. But Deb had been clear that she didn't want to reunite with Andy. Caroline just couldn't help herself.

What really pissed Deb off was that Caroline had managed to taint the one really good thing she had going right now: the Challenge. But Deb was defiant. She would do the ride alone—she had already reserved a second room at the race hotel. Whether Caroline was on the route or not was up to Caroline. Deb would control what she could, and she refused to breathe the same air or wake up in the same room as Caroline.

Deb still hadn't heard from Paula either. She felt bereft when she thought about it, like a balloon without its air. Paula had always been the cautious type, but going behind Deb's back felt vindictive. She was worried, yes, but did that justify her attempts to turn Betty and Julian against her own mother? Yet Deb knew she needed to fix this one. She'd seen rifts in other families that lasted years, sometimes ending only with death. She would not let that happen to her and Paula.

That Betty had stuck by her was heartening. She and Deb had a complicated relationship, starting with Laurie's death and including the unplanned pregnancy. *"You're too young to have a baby. There are other options."* At eighteen Deb had fully supported a woman's right to choose, and she chose to have her baby. She hadn't told Betty much, not even the name of the boy responsible. She had wanted to leave it in the past. That Deb refused to return to Silver Spring, always finding an excuse to stay away, had further strained their relationship. But eventually Betty accepted it was Deb's decision to make.

Now that they were living together again, Deb saw how similar her own life was to her mother's. No wonder Betty worried. A mother's love for her children was unsurpassed. They still fought— about the phone, the chocolates, Paula—but Deb felt closer to Betty than ever. She couldn't imagine life without her.

Before she knew it, Deb had returned to the edge of her neighborhood. She recalled her cycling days as a teenager, hopping curbs and stones, riding down steps not far from here. She wasn't crazy enough to ride her bike down cement steps anymore, but she bet she could still hop a curb. As she rolled across the side street, she gave it a try. *Ca-chunk.* "Ooph." The bike was heavier than she'd expected. She was a little late pulling up on the handlebars, and she heard a worrisome *pfft* when her back wheel hit the curb. She pedaled on and felt the telltale drag. She looked back, hoping somehow she was wrong. Would it be better if her legs were just really, really tired? But there was no denying it: the back wheel was flat.

"Damn!" She slowed her bike, wobbled in her new clipless pedals, and toppled to one side still trying to free her feet. "God damn it." Somehow her feet came loose from the pedals during the crash, and she stood up. Brushed herself off. Picked up the bike. Tested the flat back tire uselessly. "Damn," she said again. She had a spare tire in her seat bag, but she didn't know how to change it with the pedal assist. She was so close to home—less than two miles—she could walk it. But she needed to get Marco soon. She pulled out her phone and called home. Maybe Betty could come get her.

The phone rang once. Twice. Three times. "Of course." Deb shook her head. After five rings, voicemail picked up. "Hey, Ma. It's Deb. I have a flat tire. Can you help? Call me back."

Sighing, Deb stowed her phone in her jersey and started walking her bike through the neighborhood. It was heavy with the battery, and her legs were tired. She felt as graceful as a penguin out of water walking along the pavement in cleats. She kicked gravel, wishing Betty had answered, but knowing it was her own damn fault she hadn't.

Walking was a heck of a lot slower than biking. She was going to be late picking up Marco. Trudging up one short but steep hill, she had to walk in the street as there were no sidewalks. From behind, she heard the honk of a pickup truck. She tried to hurry out of the way but was too slow. The air brushed her arms and legs as the truck zoomed past her. She stopped to get reoriented. Sweat dripped down her back. She hadn't worn her cooling vest, since this was supposed to be a quick jaunt. She was going to pay for this in more than "spoons" when she got home. Two more blocks to go.

Deb arrived at the house shortly after 5 p.m. and stowed the bike and her helmet in the garage. She was wrecked! Inside, Betty wasn't in the chair where Deb had left her. "Hi, Mom! I'm home," she called down the hall. "Did you get my message?" She walked into the kitchen, washed her hands with cool water. The house seemed quiet. She dried her hands and listened. Where was Betty? An unknown feeling of dread crept into Deb's chest, and she moved quickly down the hall looking for her mother.

"Mom?" She passed the bathroom and peered in. The door was open and the light was out. No one was there. Marco's bedroom was also dark and empty. Hustling farther down the corridor, she reached Betty's room and looked in. Empty. She turned back down the hall, wondering where else to look, then stopped and backtracked. Pushing the back door open, she peered out into the rose garden and her world shattered. Betty was lying on the porch motionless. "NO!" Deb screamed. She ran to her and knelt beside her. She checked her mother's pulse. Nothing. "MOM!" How long had she been here? Deb cursed herself for not knowing CPR. *"No, no, no, no, no!"* She pulled her cell phone out of her jersey pocket and dialed 911.

"I need help," she told the operator. "My mother is passed out in the garden and I can't find a pulse." She looked at Betty, eyes closed, lips slightly parted and pale. She'd never been so frightened for her mother.

"Have you tried CPR?" the operator asked.

"No. I don't know how." Deb flushed with anger and resentment. "Can you please send the paramedics?"

"Yes, ma'am. What's your name?"

"Debra Morales. My mother is Betty Lee."

"Location?"

"20003 Daffodil Drive, Silver Spring, Maryland 20901. It's the corner house."

"I'll send someone right away."

"Okay, thank you." Tears stung her eyes.

"Do you want me to stay on the line with you?" the operator asked. "The ambulance is two minutes away."

"Um." Deb didn't know the right answer. "Uh," she stammered. "Yes. Yes, please." She looked at her mother. Was there a feeling worse than helplessness when someone you loved was in danger? She thought of Marco and Paula and Laurie. She thought of Luis. She thought of Nurse Lydia and her mother's old friends and of Rosa and Caroline too. Already she was translating the events into a story. She had found her mother comatose in the rose garden and was worthless to help her.

She heard the siren of the ambulance approaching and moved quickly through the house to the front porch. She watched as it pulled up. "The ambulance is here," she told the 911 operator. "I'm going to hang up now."

She ended the call as two paramedics exited the ambulance. "This way," she called, and stepped out of the way to allow them to pass. The paramedics trotted through the house and into the backyard. Deb looked on as they approached her mother. She was too frightened to cry. Too frightened even to think.

"Is this your mother?" one asked.

"Yes, it is."

"What's her name?"

"Betty. Betty Lee."

"Betty! Can you hear me?" Getting no response, the paramedics worked together to perform CPR. Minutes passed and Deb began to absorb what was happening. Her mother, her beautiful, caring, devoted mother, was not responding. As time clicked past ten minutes, tears rolled down Deb's cheeks. She wanted to call off the CPR. Absurdly, anger at Betty welled up. How many times had Deb asked about end-of-life decisions and do-not-resuscitate orders, and every time Betty demurred. Now Deb held her breath, hoping with each compression her mother might come back to her.

And then, exchanging words Deb didn't comprehend, the paramedics stopped. One, a small woman with a blond ponytail, stood and approached Deb. "I'm afraid your mother has expired. Would you like us to take her to the hospital?"

Deb gulped air. "Uh, is that normal?"

The woman's blue eyes connected with Deb's. "Some families

want their loved one to go to the hospital even after they are declared dead. Others choose to have them taken to the funeral home."

"Oh." Deb was dumbfounded. "Let's go to the hospital. I don't know what funeral home . . . Or, can it wait a minute? Can I think about it? I . . ." Deb covered her face and turned in a circle, then broke into sobs. Every emotion seemed to hit her at once. She could hardly breathe as her chest heaved. What was she going to do?

"Mrs. Lee?" the paramedic said calmly and touched Deb's arm.

The feel of the woman's rough hand on her bare arm brought Deb back to herself. She blinked and looked at the woman. "It's Morales. Debra Morales."

"Mrs. Morales, take your time," the medic said firmly.

And with that comment Deb realized there was no rush anymore. Her mother was dead. That was not going to change, whether she went to the hospital straight away or if they never went. She spoke with new clarity. "I don't want to go to the hospital. I want to call my mom's doctor and ask where he thinks she should go. Is that all right?"

"Yes, ma'am, that's fine with us."

Deb breathed through her nose, and a fresh set of tears came to her eyes. She found the box of tissues in the bathroom, located her phone, cleaned her face, and dialed Dr. Strauss. One thing at a time. She had lost people before. One thing at a time. That's what she had to do. That was the only way she would make it through.

Deb was in the living room on the phone speaking to Dr. Strauss when the front door of her house opened. It was still unlocked from when she let the paramedics in. Nurse Lydia appeared, looking flustered and worried. Deb realized she must have seen the ambulance out front. It was well past five o'clock. The nurse was late.

"Deb, what's happening?" Lydia said carefully. She scanned the living room for clues.

"Just a minute, Dr. Strauss," Deb said into the phone. "The home health nurse is here." Deb took the phone away from her ear and said, "My mom died this afternoon."

Lydia gasped and blinked rapidly. "Oh my goodness! I'm so sorry. When?"

"I'm not sure. I went out for a bike ride after work and when I got home, I found her. The paramedics tried CPR but it was too late. They're with her now."

"Oh my goodness," Lydia repeated. "I should have been here. I'm so, so sorry for your loss."

Deb wasn't prepared for the nurse's heartfelt response. Fresh tears came to her eyes and she wiped them away with her tissue.

"It's okay," she said to Lydia. "The paramedics are taking her to the funeral home as soon as I get off the phone with Dr. Strauss."

Nurse Lydia nodded and breathed out through her lips. "Is there anything I can do?"

"I don't think so." Deb ached for the woman who had taken such good care of her mother.

"I was supposed to be here," Lydia said in a quiet voice. "I got caught in traffic. There was an accident on the Beltway. That's why I'm late." She looked shaken.

"It's not your fault," Deb said kindly. "It was her time to go, that's all."

Lydia gave a grim smile. "Yes, I'm sure you're right."

The paramedics came out from the back of the house at that moment and spoke to Lydia. Deb went back to her conversation with Dr. Strauss.

"I'm here," she said. "Sorry about that."

"No worries, Mrs. Morales. Do you have any more questions?"

"Not that I can think of. I have a thousand phone calls to make, and I need to pick up my son, but I can handle that. Thank you for all you did for my mom." Her voice grew thick as she spoke.

"You're very welcome. She was a special lady. The apple doesn't fall far from the tree."

Deb laughed through her tears as she hung up.

"Mrs. Morales? We're ready to take your mother to the funeral home now."

Deb's mind split again. This was it. "Okay. Can I see her?"

"Of course."

The medic stepped to the side, and that's when Deb noticed the gurney now standing in her living room. She started to walk up to it but stopped before reaching it. There was a sheet over the body. Was she going to turn down the sheet? No, she wouldn't do that.

"You can take her," she said.

"Are you sure?" Nurse Lydia asked. "Deb, come with me." And she took Deb's hand and walked her up to the gurney. "This is your last chance to see her before it all becomes a big show," Lydia whispered. "Say goodbye."

Deb's heart beat faster and her voice caught in her throat. "Goodbye, Mom," she whispered. "I love you."

Lydia put her arm around her. "Good girl," she said. Deb turned to her and welcomed the embrace that followed. Nurse Lydia signaled the paramedics, and they took Betty out of the house while

Deb cried on Lydia's shoulder. She stayed that way for a long time. Finally, she straightened up and wiped her face.

"I have to get my son now," she said.

"I'll help you to your car."

"Thank you, Lydia."

"You're welcome. Where's your cane?"

"By the garage door. We can get it as we walk out."

"You're going to be all right."

Arm in arm, the two women left the empty house.

Twenty-Eight

Betty Lee's funeral was on a Wednesday morning at ten o'clock. A modest crowd of about fifty gathered at the Unitarian church on University Boulevard to bid farewell. Deb remembered the capacity turnout that Luis received in his hometown of Austin three years earlier. Her heart had soared to see so many friends and family touched by her husband's life. That may have been the case for Betty, too, had she not suffered two strokes already. She could no longer get out the way she used to, and her friendships dwindled. Still, many of Betty's old friends and work acquaintances showed up to see her off.

Deb tried to be a good host to those people, especially at the wake the night before, but many of them were shadows on the periphery. She was focused on Marco, a boy who had already lost more people than was right, and on Paula, who had flown in from Chicago to be with her family. The significance of Paula's first trip to Silver Spring was not lost on Deb.

Telling Marco his grandmother had died required the fortitude of a Buddhist monk. Deb had expected him to be sad. She had not anticipated the anger. When he learned Deb had been on a bike ride when Betty died, he exploded.

"We moved here so you could take care of her. You didn't do what you said you would do and now she's dead!" The words still echoed in Deb's ears. She had picked him up from after-care after the ambulance pulled away carrying her mother to the funeral home. Sitting in the van with the engine off in front of the school, she explained why she was late.

"I did my best, Marco. I couldn't be with her all the time. She would have hated it if I had even tried. You have to know this was no one's fault. It was just her time."

Marco's dark eyes burned. "How do you know that? How do you know you couldn't have saved her if you were there?"

Deb let out a long breath. She had no good answer to Marco's interrogation. And she already expected to be asking herself the same questions for years to come. Had she been selfish in her decisions? Had she been too hard on Betty? Whatever her misgivings, Marco deserved some peace of mind, and Deb did her best to provide it.

"Listen, Grandma was unwell. We did what we could to get her healthy, but sometimes our bodies just don't live as long as we want them to. You can be mad at me if you want. I'm mad too. But eventually I hope you will understand that we can't control everything, and you will be happier if you don't try."

"I already know that. If I controlled everything, Dad would be with us and we would still live in Austin with all my friends and Uncle Julian and my old school, and Grandma would be alive and none of this would have ever happened."

The hurt and anger in his voice cut through Deb like a knife. She was silent after that. They drove home without speaking, ate a quiet dinner, and then Marco went to bed while Deb made phone calls. She accepted it would be some time before he forgave her.

Her first call that night was to Paula. But Paula didn't pick up.

Deb didn't want to leave the news on a recording, so she simply said it was important, please call.

Deb thought of Caroline next, but she couldn't bring herself to dial her number. Instead she called Calvin's cell phone. It was after hours, but he picked up anyway. Deb explained what happened, and Calvin was understanding. When she said she was concerned about taking more leave, he encouraged her to take the time she needed. "Deb, take the week off. You will be occupied every minute of it, I'm certain. As I've said before, I would rather you take leave and do your best work than try to power through." Deb thanked him before hanging up. She silently vowed to get back to work as soon as possible. She didn't want Calvin to think she was taking advantage of his kindness.

She texted Julian and a couple of friends from Austin—the same people who had so generously donated to her Bike MS fundraising—then fielded reply texts decorated with hearts, hugs, and crying emojis. By ten o'clock she could barely keep her eyes open. She walked into Betty's bedroom to put some papers away and recalled finding her mother in the rose garden. The panic. The fear. The overwhelming sadness enveloped her. She blinked the teardrops away and walked to Betty's dresser. On top were various pill bottles, some old prayer cards, a rosary, and a wooden jewelry box. Curious, she opened the wooden box—and found what she was looking for. Mixed in with her mother's pendants was Laurie's bicycle necklace. Betty had kept it all these years. Using two fingers Deb picked up the delicate silver strand with a bicycle charm and slipped it over her head. Then she climbed into her mother's bed. She slept for nine uninterrupted hours.

The next morning, Paula still hadn't returned Deb's call, so she tried again. No answer. Finally, she sent a text. *Paula, please call me. It's about Grandma.* Paula had never been angry with Deb for so long. Her heart ached from the separation.

Deb began the work of arranging the funeral. Half an hour later, the phone rang. Paula. Deb explained everything. Paula seemed trapped in an internal struggle. "Are you sure you want me there?"

Deb's heart broke again. "What? Yes, I'm sure. Why do you say that?"

"You've—you've never invited me to Silver Spring before. I thought maybe you didn't want me there."

"Oh." Deb was speechless. She had hurt her daughter with her shame, and she had no excuse. Was she any better than Caroline, oblivious to what was right in front of her? She grasped for the words that could make it better. "Paula, please come. I want to see you. I need you with me." Tears streamed down her face.

Paula was on a flight the next day.

Most of the rest of the days were a blur. But one event stood out. Caroline turned up at the wake.

She found Deb sitting by herself, a rare moment alone. "Rosa gave me the news. I only came to pay my respects."

Deb fought the anger in her belly and determined to keep their interactions short. She was surprised to see Caroline, but part of her was glad she hadn't allowed their fight to keep her away. Caroline knew Betty when she was still vibrant, and it meant something that she'd come out for the wake. But Deb also wasn't ready to talk.

Paula returned from the bathroom then, and it felt to Deb like two worlds colliding. She hadn't had time to explain anything to Caroline; not the fact that she had a nineteen-year-old daughter, and not who the father was. Still, she saw the recognition on Caroline's face when Paula entered the room. Paula wore a black backless jumpsuit that set off her figure perfectly. Her warm blond hair was long and streaky, and she had applied a neutral palette of eyeshadow, blush, and lipstick. She was stunning. She also was the spitting image of her father.

To Deb's eyes, the secret she had harbored for nineteen years was on full display. Of course, Caroline was the only person there who would even know who Andy Peters was, much less guess the relation. Deb said a silent prayer that Caroline wouldn't say anything to Paula. But she needn't have worried. Caroline was the picture of good manners.

"It's so wonderful to meet you, Paula. I'm an old friend of your mom's. I'm sorry for your loss." She squeezed Paula's hand in both of hers.

"Thank you," Paula said with a smile. Caroline had started to ask a question when Paula turned to Deb with a jolt. "I almost forgot—Marco needs you. He asked me to send you to the boys' room."

"Do you know what the trouble is?" Deb was reluctant to leave Caroline and Paula alone together.

"I think he spilled something on his pants."

Deb pictured her son with mustard stains on his dress pants and rolled her eyes. "I'll be back in a minute. Maybe you two can talk photography while I'm gone. That's something you have in common." She patted Paula's shoulder and walked away.

Caroline could hardly believe her eyes. When Deb introduced Paula as her daughter, it took all the diplomacy she could muster not to exclaim out loud. If Andy Peters had a daughter, this is what she would look like. That meant the rumors were true—Deb had Andy's baby. Suddenly Caroline's own actions twenty years ago took on new significance. She'd been oblivious to what was right in front of her face.

"Are you a photographer?" Paula asked, bringing Caroline's thoughts back to the room.

"I dabble. You?"

"Not really," Paula said. "I took a class last year, but I think my mom was the only one who really liked how my photos turned out."

Caroline detected a hurt in Paula that she recognized. She was drawn to her the same way she'd been drawn to Deb when they were teenagers. "It's good she supports your interests."

Paula shrugged. "I'm lucky, I guess. She encourages me to try new things."

"It runs in the family." Then, in a conspiratorial tone, she said, "Can you believe your mom's going to do this crazy bike ride?" She made a dramatic face. "She was going to do it alone, but I told her that was ridiculous, so now I'm doing it too."

Paula was quiet, and Caroline continued. "And it's for such a good cause that I know is close to your heart. Together we've raised almost three thousand dollars. And I've learned so much too." She recalled the night of the new-rider meeting and felt a pang in her chest. She'd messed up inviting Andy over. How could she make it up to Debra? "It's opened my eyes to what MS is all about. Really, I feel very fortunate to be a part of it."

"I'm very happy for you," Paula said politely. "I worry about the strain, though. It's one thing for a healthy person to take on that kind of challenge." She allowed Caroline to complete the logic.

Caroline put her hand on Paula's shoulder. When Caroline was in Botswana more than a decade before, her mother had broken her ankle on the ice and was laid up at home for a couple of weeks. It wasn't MS, but Caroline did know what it felt like to be too far away to help.

"I get it," she said. "She's your mom. You need her to be safe and to make good decisions."

Paula nodded.

Caroline continued, speaking slowly. "She also needs to test her boundaries once in a while, try new things. Just like you." After a moment she added, "I think she could really use your support."

Paula's jaw muscle flexed. "She has my support."

"Does she?" Caroline looked Paula in the eye. Her resemblance to her father was uncanny. But her personality was clearly shaped by Deb. "Listen, fear is a powerful thing. It will keep you from living your dreams if you let it. I can't promise nothing bad will happen to your mom, but I'll do whatever I can to keep her safe."

"Do you mean it?" Paula's tone was cautious.

"Yes, I do," Caroline said sincerely. "Your mother is very dear to me. I definitely don't want her to come to any harm."

"Well, thank you," Paula said, visibly relaxing. "That does make me feel better. I'm far away from her now and it's hard. If something happened to her, I don't know what I'd do. She's all I have left. Her and Marco."

"I can only imagine what it must be like for you," Caroline said.

"You are a strong woman. And so is your mom. It'll be okay."

Paula smiled, revealing a charming dimple in one cheek. "I think I'll go find my mom now."

"I'm going to go up to the casket now. Will you come with me?" Paula was at Deb's elbow. Marco was sitting in a chair a few feet away with a wad of paper towels on his thigh, poorly hiding a wet spot, and Deb was speaking with Lydia near the guest book.

"Hi, sweetie, yes, I'll go with you. But first I want you to meet Nurse Lydia." Deb put her arm around her daughter. "Lydia, this is Paula. She lives in Chicago. She's studying social work at UIC."

Lydia greeted Paula warmly. The three of them spoke for a few minutes about social work and nursing and the crossover that a home health aide represented. Deb was proud to introduce her daughter. Her chest swelled as they talked.

"Mom, will you come with me now?" Paula asked.

"Yes, I can go with you now." Deb took her arm from around Paula and grasped her hand. "Take care, Lydia. Thank you for all you did for my mother. I know I said it before, but truly, I couldn't have made it without you."

"You're welcome, Deb. Take good care."

Deb and Paula turned and headed to the far side of the room, where the casket was. They walked slowly, hand in hand, through the small crowd that had gathered. Deb had already greeted everyone there. She had been surprised by some of the faces. Neighbors and acquaintances from the school. Nursing colleagues of Betty's and their children. Even one friend of her father's. She didn't know how they had heard about it. Social media, perhaps, or the required announcement in the newspaper. Uncle Julian couldn't make the trip on such short notice, and her Austin friends sent flowers. But Rosa and Philippe had come earlier with PJ, and Meg also stopped by briefly and dropped off a plant. Calvin and the Sparky's gang sent a huge bouquet with a card. The outpouring for Betty meant more to Deb than her logical mind said it should; it was nice to feel cared for.

The most important guest was the one holding her hand. She was so pleased to have Paula close by. She still wanted her daughter to support her, but it would no longer come between them. They reached the casket and Deb released Paula's hand. A look of fear came over Paula's face. She had lost her stepfather just three years earlier and her grandfather years before that. She was not new to the ways of wakes and funerals. Yet, it also was not something a young woman took in stride. Trembling ever so slightly, she knelt by the casket, bowed her head, and was silent. Deb wondered if she was saying a prayer, the way some people do, or recalling favorite memories of her grandmother.

After a minute, Paula rose and it was Deb's turn to kneel. She looked in at her mother. This was it. One step closer to the final goodbye. They would have the funeral and burial to get through, but this was their last semiprivate moment together. Tears filled Deb's eyes. She felt the blame Marco had laid heavy on her shoulders. She felt the guilt of not being there when her mother needed her most. She remembered the hurt and anger they had inflicted on each other through the years. The arguments about answering the phone, taking care of their health, whether Deb would be coming home for a visit, whether she was calling often enough. And she recalled the love, the unquestioning support for Deb and her baby after Paula was born, and again when Marco was born. Of her new husband and her life in Austin. Deb dabbed her eyes. Betty had not been effusive in her love, but she had been steady. And now she was gone. The hurt in Deb's heart manifested as a physical pain in her chest, and she allowed the tears to stream. Then she felt Paula next to her on the kneeler, Paula's arms around her shoulders, and from behind, Marco's arms wrapped around her middle. She turned around and gathered her children to her, feeling loved and cared for and forgiven. She felt whole.

Twenty-Nine

Deb started her day with hot tea and buttered toast. It was Saturday morning, one week before the Challenge. Marco was sleeping in, but Paula had stepped out before Deb was out of bed. At least, that's what Deb assumed when she saw the couch empty and the sheets folded. When she heard rustling in the garage, she took the last of her toast and tea with her to investigate. She found Paula in the garage hunched over Deb's bike, the bike upside down and the rear wheel removed.

"Hi, Mom," she said without pausing her work.

Deb surveyed the scene. "Hi there. What's that you're doing?"

"Just fixing your flat tire. You don't mind, do you?" Paula paused and looked up.

"No, no, I don't mind. Do you know what you're doing? I mean, is it going all right? I've been meaning to do it, but I wasn't sure how, with the pedal assist on there."

"That's what YouTube's for. I watched three different videos to make sure I could do it without screwing things up. It's not as hard as I expected. It's just getting the last bit of the tire in place that's tripping me up." Paula was finagling the tire levers while she spoke.

Deb emptied her tea cup and put the last of the toast in her mouth. "Let me help you with that."

Deb, still in her pajamas, shuffled over, set her cup on the garage floor, and with a grunt, helped Paula lever the tire into place. Straightening back up, Deb said, "I have to admit, I'm surprised to find you out here. I didn't think you were particularly interested in helping me with anything to do with the ride."

Paula was quiet for a couple of beats. "I . . . I changed my mind. I talked to Caroline at the wake, and she pretty much called me out on letting my fears dictate my life. After I thought about it, I decided she was right. This is something you really want. And look at you. You're glowing. I know Grandma just died, but still, you seem happier than I remember ever seeing you. Certainly not since Dad died. I . . . I want to support you."

Deb was taken aback. "You mean it?" Her emotions were still so raw, tears pricked her eyes in response to Paula's kindness.

"Yes, I do." She had the wheel back on the bike and flipped it right side up. "You've always supported me when I want to do something crazy. My trip to Prague. This internship I'm hoping to get. It should go both ways."

"Well, thank you, sweetie. That means a lot." Deb wiped tears away before they traced down her cheeks. "Have you had breakfast?"

"Not yet. I wanted to surprise you with the bike." She smiled and extended one arm. "Surprise."

Deb smiled at her daughter. "Well, come on, then. I'll fix you something." She put her arm around Paula's shoulders and they walked back into the house.

Out on the road by herself, Caroline thought about the wake she'd attended earlier in the week. She'd gone hoping there might be a crack in Deb's armor, but she didn't see one. Instead, they barely spoke, and she spent most of her time with Paula. Paula's very existence seemed to substantiate those old rumors of Debra leaving to have Andy's baby. It was so out of character, though. Caroline needed to get the full story from Deb. But how, when her oldest friend wouldn't talk to her?

And that's when she made up her mind: it was time to make amends. She knew she had work to do with Jacob as well as Rosa and Philippe. But today she was starting with Deb. Meeting Paula had been a turning point for Caroline. For the first time she saw with her own eyes the consequences of her actions on someone else's life. When she returned from her ride, she would invite Deb over for a private conversation.

Deb spent a lazy Saturday morning at home with Paula and Marco. Thanks to Paula's handiwork, she would be able to get a few miles on the bike before lunch, but for now they were all reading their own books in the living room. Deb wasn't really focusing on hers, however. She had other things on her mind.

For one, Paula had credited Caroline with changing her mind about the ride. What was she supposed to do with that? She was thankful Caroline had shown up at the wake. It had touched her heart having her oldest friend there, even if they were on the outs at the moment. And she was relieved to have Paula's support at last. Still, she was having a hard time forgiving Caroline. Who in their right mind would have done what Caroline did?

But as Deb thought about it, she considered whether she was being entirely fair. It was wrong of Caroline to not listen when Deb told her to leave well enough alone, but Caroline didn't have the complete picture. And that was Deb's doing. Deb was wondering if it was time to change that when she got the text from Caroline. After some hesitation, she accepted the invitation. At two o'clock that afternoon, she left Marco and Paula at home and drove over to Caroline's.

Caroline's den was comfortably furnished with two overstuffed facing couches and a plush rug. A large TV and game system took up one wall (Robbie's), while a built-in bookcase covered the opposite wall (Caroline's). Four of Caroline's most impressive flower close-ups hung in simple white frames over the two sofas. This was her favorite room in the house for entertaining or relaxing, and it was the perfect place to welcome Debra.

It was awkward at first. The two women each sat on a couch, Deb's face not giving away anything. Caroline thanked her friend for coming and offered her some snacks or something to drink, but Deb declined each time. She could've asked about Paula and Marco, but finally decided to just get to it.

"I'm sorry I invited Andy over when you told me not to. I should have listened to you. There's clearly more to the story that I don't know. I should have respected your wishes."

Caroline looked Debra in the face and was relieved to see acceptance there.

"I appreciate your apology. I really do." Deb squeezed her fingers. She looked like she might speak, but Caroline wasn't finished yet.

"There's more," she blurted. Was she ready for this? "I'm sorry for leaving you with Andy that night in high school. I should never have done that. I was your ride home and I should've waited for you."

Caroline's heart beat fiercely in her chest. She hadn't expected that to be so hard. Now she waited for Deb's response, and it seemed to be taking a long time.

Finally, Deb swallowed. Her cheeks were flushed when she spoke. "Thank you, Caroline. I came here today because I realized maybe if you knew everything that happened that night, you would understand why I was so mad."

Caroline nodded. *Mad* was an understatement. She had never seen such intense hatred in Deb's face as she did the day they argued.

Deb's voice trembled. "I don't think you even know what that night, what that whole experience, has meant for my life. It changed . . . everything." She whispered the last word. "Where did you go? Why did you leave me?"

Caroline was taken aback. She answered simply, "I went back to Andy's house. We were all going inside. Don't you remember? There was lightning and we went inside before it started to rain. I thought you were coming but when I looked back, you and Andy were headed the other direction. I was scared for you. Andy didn't have a great reputation. But you liked him. I said a little prayer to the gods and went back to the house. It was late by then, close to midnight, and I needed to get home. I waited as long as I could. But then someone said the cops were going to raid the party. I don't know if that was true or not, but it scared me. I couldn't lose my place at Cornell. I remember asking Rachel what I should do and she said Andy would probably take you home. So I left."

Caroline's brow furrowed. "I always thought something happened that night. People talked. But you had a crush on him, so I figured it was mutual. Was it not what I thought?" Fear now gripped her.

Deb swallowed again. "No, I'm afraid it wasn't what everyone thought." A tear slipped down her cheek. "I don't want you to tell anyone anything I'm about to say. And I don't want you to think I blame you for what happened. It wasn't you. It was just unfortunate that you left when you did. I . . . I could've used a friend. But you couldn't have known what was going to happen."

For the first time in twenty years, Deb shared the full story of the night at Andy's house.

"Oh my God, Deb. That's rape." Caroline was silent. Then she breathed, "Paula."

Deb inhaled deeply. "Yes, Paula. She doesn't know about that night and I don't plan to tell her. All she knows is that her dad left before she was born. I do *not* want her to know how she came to be. She's one of the best things to happen to me."

Caroline kicked herself for not having asked about that night sooner. Never did she imagine Debra would have carried a secret like that for so long.

Deb continued. "I was crushed when I had to drop out of the

ride that fall. I would get so scared out on my bike. I had terrible pregnancy paranoia, and I couldn't do it."

"I'm so sorry," Caroline said. "I'm so, so sorry." Threads of sadness and guilt made a knot in her belly.

"Caroline, it was a long time ago. I'm all right. At least, I was. Until I came back here."

That's when Debra told her about seeing Andy Peters's name on the donor sheet at Sparky's. "Not only that, but he's supposed to attend the annual dinner I've been planning. I'm terrified. When I saw him in your backyard, I flipped. I don't know if I could keep it together in front of my coworkers."

Caroline took a breath, then asked gently, "Are you sure it's the same Andy Peters? That's a pretty common name."

"You think it might be someone else?" Deb asked, the thought just dawning on her.

"It could be," Caroline said encouragingly. "Why don't you investigate. See if it's the same guy. You might be worried over nothing."

"I'm scared. Will you help me?"

"Of course I will. I'm here for you."

They were quiet for several minutes, both letting out big sighs and weighing what they had just revealed. Deb asked for a glass of water then, and Caroline brought back two tumblers with ice and set them on the coffee table between them.

Deb said, "Did the drama with Jacob ever get settled?"

Caroline was grateful for the change in topic. "No, it didn't. School's almost over and I still don't know what's going to happen. I'm really worried. They said since he's ten, it could be referred to juvenile court."

"What do you mean, 'since he's ten'?"

Caroline explained what the officers had told her about Maryland's laws for delinquent acts.

"So if he was nine, this wouldn't even be an issue?" Deb asked, incredulous.

"That's what it sounds like to me. But he's ten, so he's in trouble. I don't even know where the damn pocketknife came from! It's so frustrating, Debra. I really don't know what to do. The only thing I'm sure of is, it wasn't Jacob's."

"I didn't realize it was a pocketknife. I thought he had some kind of steak knife or something. Seems like they're making a big deal out of nothing."

"Yeah, well, it might not have been so bad, but he opened it up in class. The foolish boy. He says he never saw it before and was curious, so he opened the blade to get a better look. Some kid thought he was pointing it at him and told on him." Caroline shook her head.

"Rosa mentioned you thought it came from PJ." Deb took a long drink from her water glass, watching Caroline.

"She did? Oh, I'm so embarrassed. I did *not* think that through." How she wished she could take back that mistake.

Deb tilted her head to the side and looked at Caroline curiously. "What made you think it was PJ's?"

"It almost sounds racist now." Caroline covered her face with her hands, then looked at Deb. "It was this tiny red-and-white knife with a Mexican flag on the handle. I'd never seen it before. And Rosa is Mexican. I thought maybe she bought it for PJ and PJ put it in Jacob's bag for some reason. It sounds ridiculous now." Caroline exhaled and clasped her hands together. She had rarely regretted anything as much as she regretted that.

"It might not be completely ridiculous. You just picked the wrong Mexican kid," Deb said with a laugh.

"What do you mean?" Caroline asked.

"I mean, Marco's uncle sent him a pocketknife like that shortly after we moved here. I don't know where it is now. Somewhere in Marco's room, I assume. Or maybe not. Maybe he gave it to Jacob."

"Do you mean it?" Caroline said breathlessly. Hope swelled in her chest. "Do you really think that's possible? Well, no, he couldn't have given it to Jacob because Jake had never seen it." Caroline's mind was racing with the possibilities.

"Maybe it got mixed up in their bags one of the days they played together. I don't know what happened, but I can talk to Marco. I'm sure there's an innocent explanation."

Caroline felt tears of happiness prick her eyes. "Oh, Debra, this is the best news I've heard in so long. I hope you're right." As she thought over the implications, a twinge of angst shot through her. "You're not worried about the cops?"

"Well, not yet. If it was an accident, there shouldn't be anything to worry about. But first I have to go home and talk to Marco. See what he knows."

She took one last drink of her water and set her glass down. Then they both stood up.

Caroline's heart fluttered. "Call me right away and tell me what he says. Marco might not realize it, but Jacob's future is hanging in the balance."

"I'll tell you, I'm a little bothered Marco hasn't spoken up before now. Surely he's heard the hullabaloo at school about Jacob. That's why I think if it is the same knife, it must've been an accident."

Caroline nodded as they walked from the den to the front of the house. "I agree. I think the whole thing has been a misunderstanding. Please tell Marco, whatever happened, we won't be mad, okay?"

They reached the front door and Caroline opened it for Deb. Deb turned to look at Caroline, and her friend wrapped her in a close hug. "I'm so sorry, Debra."

"Me too," Deb said. They broke apart and smiled at each other. "I'll call you as soon as I talk to Marco."

"And then we'll investigate Andy Peters."

"Deal."

Thirty

Deb returned home to find Paula and Marco playing video games in the living room, Betty's favorite chair sitting empty. Deb took a seat on the couch. She watched for a few minutes before interrupting.

"Marco, pause the game, please."

"Hi, Mom. What did you say?" His eyes were glued to the television set.

"I said pause the game, please," she said more forcefully.

Paula must have noticed the tone because she asked, "Everything all right, Mom?"

"Yes, I hope so, I just need to ask Marco a couple of questions."

"Would you like some privacy?"

"That might be good," Deb said. "Thanks, Paula."

Paula got up and went into the kitchen, grabbed a soda, then went out onto the front porch. In the small house, there weren't a lot of ways to give someone else privacy.

Marco paused the game and looked at his mom. Deb waited until the front door had closed, then spoke. "I was at Mrs. Cook's house just now," she began.

"Yeah," Marco said, "I know." He sounded suspicious.

"Do you remember the incident at school a few weeks ago with Jacob?" Deb looked Marco in the face, keeping his full attention.

"You mean about the knife."

"Yes, that's the one. Mrs. Cook was telling me it was a pock-etknife, but Jacob didn't know how it had gotten in his bag." She searched his face for recognition. Marco was silent, so she contin-ued. "She said she'd never seen it before. When she described it to me, it sounded a lot like the knife Uncle Julian sent you from Austin."

Marco began to fidget and looked down at his hands.

"Please look at me, Marco. Does any of this sound familiar?" There was an edge to her voice. She wanted him to know this was serious stuff.

"Yes," he said gruffly. His face turned dark and Deb decided to take a different tack.

"Sweetie, is it possible the knife Jacob brought to school is actu-ally your knife?"

"Yes."

"Was it your knife?"

He shrugged.

"Marco, this is very important. Jacob is in serious trouble. Mrs. Cook said the police have already been to their house twice. If you know anything, please tell me now."

The boy was silent, but Deb could see he was working out the words to explain. Finally, he spoke, but Deb couldn't understand. "Can you say that again, please?" She was struggling to stay calm. "Take a deep breath and try again."

Marco exhaled then said, "I put it in his bag. I was mad at him and I thought . . ."

"You thought what?" Deb prompted.

"I don't know what I thought." He hung his head.

"Well, can you tell me what had you so mad at him? Did he beat you at soccer or something?" She didn't think her son was that petty but she didn't know what might have driven him to do something to harm his friend.

"No, it was nothing like that."

Deb nodded. "Okay. Did he make fun of you? Try to exclude you?"

"No, not exactly." Marco kept his eyes on his hands while he talked.

"Marco, look at me. Mrs. Cook said to tell you they won't be mad at you no matter what. So tell me, why did you put the knife in Jacob's bag?"

Marco pursed his lips, then mumbled, "He was making fun of you."

"Of me?" Deb raised her eyebrows. That was not at all on her radar.

"Yeah. We were at PJ's and he picked up a stick and was using it like a cane and saying, 'Look, I'm Marco's mom,' and he was walking crooked. I told him to stop but he kept doing it."

Now Deb's anger was changing course. "What did PJ do?"

"He was laughing, of course. But I don't blame PJ. He's just a little kid. He thinks everything we do is funny."

"But you do blame Jacob." Finally, Deb understood.

"Well, yeah, I did. He was being mean. So I thought I would, I don't know, get back at him, I guess. I'd brought my pocketknife over to show him, but I hid it in his bag instead. I felt bad about it later and tried to get it back, but it was too late. I was surprised when they said he opened it up in class. I never expected that." Marco looked at Deb. His brown eyes were burning. "I don't care if I'm in trouble. He shouldn't have been making fun of you. Serves him right."

Deb took a deep breath and exhaled. Then she gathered Marco

to her. "It was not right of Jacob to make fun of me, you are right about that." Marco relaxed into her embrace. "And you also made a mistake. We don't 'get back at' our friends when they do something that hurts our feelings. We can forgive them, or we can decide we aren't going to be friends anymore. But we don't get revenge." She hugged her son tighter. "Thank you for telling me," she said, and squeezed him, then covered his face with kisses.

Marco started laughing and pushed away from her. "You're welcome," he said.

"And now the hard part."

"What's that?" Marco asked. He was looking at Deb suspiciously again.

"You have to tell Jacob it was your knife."

"What?"

Deb had thought this through. Marco needed some kind of punishment, though not what the legal system might have in store. "We can tell the police it was an accident, that it was yours and not Jacob's and it was all a misunderstanding, but Jacob deserves to know the truth."

Marco's eyes grew wide and his voice shook. "I don't think I can do that."

"You at least have to tell him where the knife came from. We can't go on with things as they are now, with Jacob's future being decided by the police."

Marco slumped back on the couch. "Okay," he said in a singsong.

"Great. I'll call Mrs. Cook right now."

"What? Right now? Can't it wait until after dinner at least?" Marco was on the edge of his seat again.

"Nope. This is like removing a bandage. Better to get it over with." Deb retrieved her phone from her purse and came back to the center of the living room.

Marco pouted half-heartedly. "Fine."

Deb dialed the number. It rang three times, then Caroline answered.

"Hi, C, it's Deb. I talked to Marco." Deb watched her son as she spoke. He was slouching on the couch and kicking his feet up and down.

"And? Was it his knife?" Caroline asked.

"Yes, it was."

"Oh, wow, that is such good news!" Caroline let out a sigh and laughed. "Oh, thank you, thank you, thank you."

"Is Jacob around? I told Marco he needed to explain himself to Jacob."

"Uh, yeah, he's here. I think he's in the den. Let me find him."

Deb could hear rustling while Caroline moved through the house. Then she heard Caroline speak again: "Jacob, Marco is on the phone for you." Deb handed the phone to Marco. At first, he stared at it.

"Speak," she urged.

"Jacob?" There was a pause and then he said, "I'm sorry I put the pocketknife in your bag. You can tell the police it was me." A longer pause followed, and Deb didn't know if Jacob was speaking or not. Then Marco said, "Yeah, I don't know. Maybe." He handed the phone back to Deb.

"Everything all right?" Deb whispered.

Marco nodded. "Yeah, it's fine."

"Deb, is that you?" Caroline was back on the line.

"Yes, I'm here." She put her fingers up to signal to Marco to wait.

"Are we good now? I mean, can we tell the police it was Marco's knife and this was all a mix-up?"

"That's what I had in mind. Do you think Marco will talk to the police?" Caroline asked.

"We'll do whatever we can to clear this up." A white lie to the police for the greater good suited Deb just fine.

"Did he say how it got into Jacob's bag?" Caroline asked, then quickly added, "You don't have to tell me if you don't want to."

Deb looked at Marco while she thought for a moment. She said, "I'll tell you another time."

"Oh, okay." Caroline exhaled. "Well, that's one mystery solved. Do you want to come over this week and try to solve the other?"

With Betty gone and Paula leaving the next day, no one would be home with Marco. "I need to stay close to home," Deb said. "Could you come here?"

"Sure. How about Tuesday?"

"Perfect."

The two women said goodbye and Deb put her phone away. Teaming up with Caroline again felt like walking a tightrope without a safety net. She was still processing all that had happened, and as far as she was concerned, Caroline was high risk. But she had other concerns at the moment.

"Good job, Marco." Deb sat down next to her son and wrapped her arm around him.

"For what?"

"For apologizing. You aren't out of the woods yet, however. You might have to talk to the police. Mrs. Cook is going to tell them what happened, but you might have to confirm her story. Do you think you can do that?"

"I can if I have to."

"Well, you have to. Now go let your sister back in the house."

Deb checked the time. It was already five o'clock. "What's for dinner?" she asked. Before Marco could reply, she went into the kitchen to investigate. As she opened the refrigerator, her mind returned to her conversation with Caroline from earlier in the day. The business with the pocketknife was unexpected. She was glad she could help there. Now what would they find out when they searched for Andy?

Thirty-One

Caroline was overjoyed. As soon as she hung up the phone with Debra, she went to tell Robbie what she'd learned. She found him sitting in the TV room watching classic football. The volume was up so loud he didn't hear her come in.

"Robbie." She walked over and stood by his chair, watching the game.

He was eating red-hot potato chips out of a bag even though he knew it would give him indigestion, and Caroline stuffed down her commentary. She had something more important to say.

"Robbie," she said again, a little louder. This time he looked up at her. "Did Jacob tell you the news?"

"Uh," Robbie stumbled, "I don't think so. What news?" He sounded frightened. He muted the TV.

"I just got off the phone with Debra," she said brightly. "The pocketknife belongs to Marco." She explained that when they talked that afternoon, Deb thought it sounded like one he'd gotten from his uncle. "She just called to confirm. Marco apologized for putting it in Jacob's bag."

"Why would he do something like that?" Robbie asked, his face reddening.

"I don't know and I don't really care. All I care about is that

Jacob is going to have his name cleared. He didn't do it!" Caroline's chest swelled.

"Well, I want to know why Marco would do such a thing. He turned our lives upside down and you aren't even a little curious?"

"Of course I'm curious. Deb said she'd tell me another time. I think Marco was there and she didn't want to embarrass him. But you know how kids are. Marco probably thought it would be funny and didn't think through the consequences." Caroline hoped Robbie would take off his poop-colored glasses and see what good news this was.

Something caught their attention on the TV and Caroline said, "You can go back to your game now. I'm going to call Officer Chavez and tell him what happened." She leaned down and gave him a peck on the lips, then walked out.

Caroline dialed Officer Chavez's number from the sofa in the formal living room. She recalled the night the two detectives came to the house and questioned Jacob about the knife. It felt like years ago now. She was mortified when she thought about sending the police to Rosa's home. She'd been desperate then. Now she finally knew the true origin of the knife.

While the phone rang she realized she had no idea if the detective would answer or if she would be leaving a message. All she could think about was clearing her son's name.

The phone rang four times before someone answered. It was not Officer Chavez, to Caroline's disappointment, but the person took down her name and number. "And is there a message?" the person asked.

Caroline said, "Please tell him I know where the pocketknife

came from." It sounded cryptic as it came out of her mouth, but she
didn't know what else to say.

"I will give the detective your message. Would you like him to
call you back?"

"Yes, please."

Caroline hung up and waited. When Jacob was a tiny baby, she
would often call the after-hours line at the doctor's office. The answering service always said to call back if she didn't hear from the
on-call doctor within thirty minutes. She wondered if the same applied here. The difference now was that Jacob wasn't crying incon-
solably or delirious with fever. Like those old times, Jacob seemed
oblivious to the danger he was in. Now, thanks to Debra, she had
the cure.

Ten minutes later, Officer Chavez called back. Caroline gave
him the information she had and he said he would follow up with
Debra. When she hung up, she tossed the phone on the couch and
danced a jig.

Jacob was sound asleep. Caroline had checked on him before retir-
ing to her own room that night, kissing the top of his warm head
just like when he was small. She was still feeling elated now that
her son was going to have his name cleared. What a nightmare it all
had been! She reminded herself that it wasn't over yet. The police
needed to speak to Marco. But she couldn't worry about that. It was
going to work itself out, she could feel it.

She started to undress. Should she put on a nightie and surprise Robbie? It had been over a week since they made love, even longer since she wore something sexy to bed. She opened her top drawer and reviewed her options. Black lace? Red satin? She settled on a royal blue and white teddy.

When she finished dressing, she opened the calendar app on her phone and made a notation. While she was there she noticed she hadn't had a headache in more than seven days. She'd started tracking her headaches after she crashed her bike, hoping to piece together a pattern. When that failed, she did some more research. She bypassed the more unpleasant causes of headaches, and learned some women get migraines just before starting their periods. That didn't seem to be the case for her. But her hormones were raging. How many times had she cried lately? Plus, her breasts were just the tiniest bit tender, and here she was, putting on lingerie!

The hall floor creaked, signaling Robbie had finished washing up. Caroline struck a sexy pose on top of the covers and waited for him to open the door.

Robbie walked in and halted, hand still on the doorknob. "Well, hello there!" He grinned and raised his eyebrows at his wife playfully.

"Hello." Caroline attempted a seductive smile.

Robbie shut the door behind him and walked over to Caroline's side of the bed. "You look ravishing. Mind if I join you?"

"I don't know," Caroline teased. "Are you sure you're up for it?"

"You look amazing." He caressed her firm thigh and calf. Caroline was pleased with the changes in her body since she started training.

"Well, come on then," Caroline said, and Robbie removed his shirt, then climbed in over her, pausing to kiss her. She exhaled as the weight of him settled on top of her before he rolled on to his side of the bed.

"Don't go too far," she said, and rolled over to kiss him some more.

She ran her hand over his chest, up his back, and through his hair. He moved closer to press his body against hers. His hand caressed her back and buttocks, then roamed over her full breasts and flat belly. She responded to his touch with a gasp, and he kissed her more passionately. She sensed he was taking his time, and she felt cared for in a way she hadn't in a long while.

"I've missed you," she breathed.

"I've missed you too," Robbie replied. He tugged at her panties and they both giggled as she contorted to help.

After their passionate diversion, Robbie left to clean up. When he came back, Caroline hadn't moved.

"So, that was pretty good?" he asked with a knowing grin.

"It was terrific." Caroline yawned. "You know, I've been so stressed out. After this whole ordeal, I can't imagine getting worked up about forgetting a folder at home."

Robbie lay next to her, wrapping his arm around her waist. "I'm glad to hear that, honey." He snuggled a little closer and was soon breathing as if asleep.

As Caroline tucked her head against his chest, she thought again about the headaches and Robbie's opinion that she needed medical help. Maybe it wasn't just Jacob she'd been too impatient with. She owed it to her husband to take care of herself. If it happened again, she would see a doctor. Of course, now that her stress was so much lower, that was a big "if."

Thirty-Two

Tuesday found Deb back at the Sparky's office for the first time since her world had fractured. With the funeral services over and Paula back in Chicago as of Sunday night, Deb was grateful to have a moment's peace in the office. She would be playing catchup for some time on all aspects of her life: work, health, family.

Her extended weekend had been taken up with going through her mother's file cabinets so she could better understand Betty's assets. Betty had left her the house, but Deb had not yet decided if she wanted to stay in Silver Spring or return to her old life in Austin. With Paula gone and Marco in school, the bungalow was oppressively quiet and her mother's absence hurt that much more. She didn't know if she could face every day surrounded by memories.

The one point of light was that her MS was stable. Other than a little numbness in her left big toe, this morning's full-body assessment had come up clean.

Around midmorning, Deb was working the front desk waiting for something to do. She had scheduled an afternoon meeting with Calvin to discuss the annual dinner. Only good news there: the team was executing, and thanks to Andy Peters, the bastard, they'd already met the fundraising goal. Deb shuddered at the thought of seeing him again. She hoped with all her might it wasn't the same guy. She and Caroline would be investigating this afternoon. And after that, she planned to relax with Marco, finally make that chicken tinga recipe Rosa had given her. She would be relieved when she could put the whole Andy thing behind her.

Another mystery had been laid to rest the day before, when the police stopped by Deb's house to talk to Marco.

"Marco, this is Officer Chavez and Officer Price. They're here about the knife that Jacob accidentally brought to school." The foursome were standing in the living room. Deb emphasized *accidentally*, in case the officers needed convincing.

"Hello, Marco," the officers said.

Marco looked up at them. "Hello."

"Tell them what happened," Deb prompted.

"We just need to know how your knife came to be in Jacob Cook's backpack. You do admit it was your knife, right, son?" Officer Chavez said.

Marco looked frightened. He swallowed, and Deb rubbed his back to reassure him. "Yes, it was my knife. It got mixed up with his stuff one day when we were playing." His brown eyes were wide.

"It got mixed up. Okay. Is that because you put it in his bag or because he took it?"

Marco looked at the floor. "I put it in his bag."

"And can you tell us why you did that?"

Marco shuffled his feet. "I don't know."

"Officers," Deb said, breaking in, "is this part important to the investigation? Marco had no intention of using the knife at school, and he didn't intend for Jacob to use it at school either. He's nine years old. He isn't exactly careful with his things. We were both surprised and dismayed to find out what had happened. Isn't that right, Marco?"

Marco looked at his mom with appreciation. "Yes."

They both turned to face the officers. Deb said, "It was just a crazy mix-up. We're very sorry."

Officer Chavez nodded. Deb couldn't tell how this ploy was going over. Was Marco really going to have to own up to framing Jacob? Would it make any difference that he did it as a way of sticking up for her? But then Officer Price said something to Officer Chavez, and Deb remembered what Caroline had said about children under ten not being held responsible. For a split second she worried *she* would be in trouble now. Thoughts of parents on trial for the children's actions raced through her mind. But no. Officer Chavez said, "Yes, I think that's all it was. Thank you for coming forward, Marco. It's important to be honest in matters like these." And the two officers walked out of the house.

When Marco and Deb were alone again, Deb started laughing with relief.

"What's so funny?" Marco asked.

Deb hugged him. "You know, I don't know. I'm just glad that's over." She squeezed him tighter before letting go. He still looked confused. "Marco, there's one more thing I want to say to you. I appreciate your wanting to stick up for me. That's admirable. But I'm not gonna break just because someone makes fun of the wonky way I walk. Promise me you won't do anything like this again." She gave him her best "stern mother" look.

"I promise." Marco looked up at his mom, and Deb wrapped her arms around him once more.

"Deb, can I see you in my office?"

Deb jumped. Calvin had come up behind her while she was lost in thought.

"Yes, of course. Can it wait until my turn at the desk is over? I just have ten more minutes." She tried to read his face. He was always a businessman first and foremost, but this morning he was even more brusque than usual. What had him in a twist?

"Fine. Ten minutes."

Deb's thoughts ricocheted around her head as she watched her boss stalk back to his office. At noon, she gathered her purse and cane and went to Calvin's office. She paused at the doorway. She'd spent the previous ten minutes writing notes about what had happened before she left for the funeral. Everything seemed to be in order. The annual dinner was less than three weeks away and the preparations were well in hand. She was at a complete loss as to what this meeting could be about.

The door was open but Calvin was engrossed in his work. "Calvin?" she said.

He looked up from his computer and spoke. "Come in, Deb. Have a seat." His voice was gruff. Deb had never seen Calvin out of sorts, and she didn't know what to make of this new situation.

"Is something wrong?" she ventured, taking the seat across the desk from him. Calvin looked as though someone had just stolen his life savings.

"I'll say. While you were out last week, I received a call from the event venue. They tell me you're using a new food vendor, one that isn't approved."

Deb was dumbfounded by this assertion. "No, that's wrong. Molly coordinated with the caterer to get more nondairy and gluten-free options. That's the only major change I've made." She racked her brain for more information but was foggy on the details. She'd been gone too long.

"Well, that's not what I'm hearing from our contact at Silver Celebrations. They said Molly canceled the old contract and chose a different food vendor, one not on their list. Molly is your direct report. Isn't that right?"

Deb shook her head, feeling blindsided. Heat rose in her cheeks as she tried to figure out what had gone wrong. "Yes, of course. I'm sorry. I'm really not sure what happened. Molly said she was able to get the old vendor to add some new options. They're going to cost a little more, but I think we can offset the price."

"No, no, no. You aren't listening, Deb. It's not the cost. She canceled the vendor. We need this fixed now. I know you have been unwell and you just lost your mother, so I'm sorry to lay this at your feet. But there is one thing I have said over and over and that is, take the time you need to do your best work." Anger, disappointment, and frustration were vying for domination on Calvin's face.

"Yes, you did say that." Deb looked at her hands. Her mind swirled as she tried to make sense of what her boss was telling her. She was certain Molly had said nothing about changing vendors. But then she remembered she had been having some brain fog the day of their meeting. Had she agreed to something she didn't understand? She wanted to defend herself but thought it best to focus on solutions. Looking up she said, "I'm very sorry. I will follow up with Molly and the vendors and get it taken care of."

"Thank you, Deb. I knew I could count on you."

Deb took her cue to leave. She stood and started for the door, then stopped. "Do you still want to meet about the June 30 fundraising deadline? I had you on my calendar for two o'clock."

"That won't be necessary. We're on target, correct?"

"Yes, we are. Thanks to Andy Peters. He came through with a big donation." Deb flushed as she spoke. She felt self-conscious just saying his name aloud.

"Very good. Cancel the meeting. We have to get this vendor situation straightened out. The venue said we need it settled by Friday. I'm sorry to say it, but you might have to stay late this week to get it done."

"Yes, I understand." Deb's vision of a relaxing night with Marco floated through her head and out the window. "I'm sorry again."

Calvin nodded his acknowledgment and Deb walked out. She would have to cancel with Caroline too. So much for an easy day back at work.

Thirty-Three

Caroline powered her bike up a short hill not far from her house. After months of training, she registered the changes in her body and felt satisfied. In April this hill had taken her breath away. Today she glided up it, barely breaking a sweat. She wasn't looking for a tough workout, however. Day one of the Chesapeake Challenge was tomorrow, and all she wanted was one last easy ride to get the kinks out.

She took a left out of her neighborhood and pedaled until she reached the bike path. The tall trees offered shade and a cool breeze, and the creek that ran along the path tinkled melodically. She had taken the afternoon off to prepare for the ride and she was so glad she did. Not many people were out, and for once she was able to forget herself. No need to dodge strollers, runners, and other cyclists today. It was glorious.

As Caroline breathed the fresh air, she recalled the day Deb told her about this ride. She had invited herself along on impulse, even though she was unsure how her renewed friendship with Deb would develop. Debra had been so guarded when she came back to town. Standoffish even. Now Caroline understood why. And to think, it wasn't far from here that Debra was assaulted.

Deb had canceled their plans to research Andy earlier in the week. Something about having to work late. Instead they would take their opportunity while alone in the hotel before the ride. What would they find? She hoped for Debra's sake it was all just a coincidence. When she apologized to Deb, she didn't know what a storm she would unleash.

The perfect storm. That's what Jacob's knife incident had been. She was still mortified about what she'd done to Philippe and Rosa. The day after the call from Deb, she'd gone over to Rosa's to apologize. It was easier when she could explain the knife's origins. She sensed some hard feelings, but she could at least face Philippe. He was on their cycling team, after all.

The knife incident had been a turning point for Jacob. Caroline had to admit, their relationship was better because of it. The silver lining, if there was one. Why Marco would do such a thing she still didn't know. Kids. They just didn't always see the ramifications of their actions. But in a way she was grateful. Jacob was listening to her more now, and he was doing his homework without being nagged. She had mentioned it to Robbie the other night before bed.

"Did you notice Jacob did his Kumon work without complaint?" She slipped off her shoes and sat down on the mattress.

"I did notice that." Robbie was already changed and starting to read.

"I'm really proud of him these days," Caroline said. "He deserves a lot of credit."

Robbie looked at her. "Yes, I agree."

"I think it has to do with the pocketknife. Maybe he realized what he could lose."

"Maybe. Or maybe he appreciated that you took his side for once."

Caroline stared at Robbie for a beat. "Do you really think that's it?"

"Yes, I do." Robbie looked evenly at her.

Caroline finished getting her pajamas on and climbed under the covers. She pulled out her phone, opened up the diary, and recorded the day's food intake. Then she opened the calendar view and made some notes. She smiled with anticipation as she counted the weeks, remembering when she gave Robbie the news. All the while she was processing this new idea.

"Did Jacob say something about it?" she asked.

"What's that?" Robbie asked. He'd gone back to his book and lost the thread.

"Did Jacob say something about me taking his side for once?"

Robbie cocked his head, like Caroline was a curiosity. "No. He didn't have to. I've watched him and I know what it's like. My parents were always taking my sister's side in things. If I'd gotten caught with a pocketknife at school and tried to say it wasn't mine, there's no way they would've believed me. I think Jacob sees things the same way. Only, you did believe him. And so did I. And that's what made the difference."

Caroline sat quietly for a moment. She nodded her head as she thought it through. "I think you're right. But of course I took his side. It makes me sad that he thought I wouldn't."

Robbie nodded. "I know." He went back to his reading, then paused, put the bookmark in, and placed the book on his bedside table.

Caroline had returned to her calendar when Robbie spoke again. "At least we did this one thing right."

She looked at him and their eyes met. They leaned in to each other and kissed and Robbie rested his hand on her belly. "Good night, little one," then, "Good night, babe," and he turned out his light.

On the bike trail, Caroline still was stung by the idea that Jacob had not expected her to take his part. She was thankful things had turned out the way they had.

She turned back toward home and was now riding down the short hill she had climbed at the start of the ride. Out of nowhere, a migraine took hold of her. The pain was so sudden and violent, she instinctively squeezed the hand brakes. The bike stopped but she didn't. She landed with a thud on the concrete. Flat on her back, she opened her eyes and looked up at the sky above her. A lone cloud dotted the deep blue sky. Her head ached behind her eyes and she closed them tight. When she was pregnant with Jacob, she never had migraines. What could possibly explain this?

Deb sat at her computer at one o'clock on the afternoon before the ride, waiting for the email that would set her free. She was supposed to be out on her bike for a final spin to stretch her legs. The blue sky out her office window was calm and clear, and it pained her to be stuffed in a chair at Sparky's. She stood up and raised her arms overhead to lengthen her upper body, bending first to the right and then to the left. Tom, Flo, and Robin were all seated at their desks working. Not far away was Molly, her lank hair hiding her face. She started to look up, but Deb turned her back in time to avoid her gaze.

After Deb left Calvin's office on Tuesday, she went back to her desk in a daze. How could this problem with the vendor have snuck up on her? She knew she would have to confront Molly about it, but first she wanted to get a handle on everything that had transpired. She needed to be crystal clear about what had happened before she had any more conversations with lying Molly.

Thankfully, Deb was a highly organized person. She had separate email folders for each aspect of the annual dinner. Although Robin was the events manager, Deb was Robin's manager, and she liked to be able to put her hands on whatever item she was looking for. She clicked on the folder labeled "Food" and scrolled to the bottom. Molly had copied Deb and Robin on a handful of emails to the caterer, and she had forwarded a few more messages. Deb didn't have the full picture, but she had enough.

As she pieced together the story Tuesday afternoon, she'd felt anger rising. She went back to her notebook from the team meetings for the final nail in the coffin and was stunned. Her usually meticulous notes were incomplete. The last note she had made was "New Donation" followed by a colon. She hadn't even written in the name of the donor. She'd been so distracted by her fear and shame she had missed crucial information. And now that Deb looked more closely at the email string, she saw that the sender's name and address had changed. Whereas the original vendor was Montgomery Eats, the latest emails were from MoCo Eatery. Dammit! How had she missed that? With the names being so similar, the deception almost seemed intentional. Is that what Molly had been counting on?

She thought about taking the evidence to Calvin, incomplete as it was, but she remembered what Robin had said. Molly had a way of hiding her ugly behavior when she wanted. Deb had seen it for herself. Molly doted on Calvin. He'd never believe her without an ironclad case.

Deb sighed. She would have to talk to Molly herself. More than that, she needed a solution to the problem. She'd already signed a contract with the new food vendor, but they were not approved by the venue. Should she cancel the contract and lose whatever deposit they had put down, or should she somehow try to get the venue to accept the new caterer before Friday? How much paperwork would that be? She closed her eyes tight to keep herself from screaming.

After a late lunch, Deb had approached Molly while she sat at her desk.

"Can I talk to you for a minute, Molly?" she asked politely.

Molly looked up. "Hi, Deb."

"Hi, Molly." Deb waited to see if Molly would answer the initial question. When she didn't, Deb said, "I need to speak with you. Can you please meet me in the small conference room?"

By now the other workers had noticed the exchange. Deb wondered if they could hear the strain in her voice as she tried so very hard not to tip her hand.

"I'm in the middle of something. Is it urgent?" Molly simpered.

"I'm afraid it is."

Deb looked hard at Molly, and at last Molly got up from her desk and followed Deb into the conference room. Deb closed the door. "Have a seat," she said, and took a seat herself.

Molly rested back in the chair opposite her. She looked at Deb expectantly but offered nothing.

"Molly," Deb began. She paused, unsure where to start. She should have practiced. She always did better when she was prepared. Nevertheless, she plowed on. "Molly, I had a conversation with Calvin this morning and it wasn't very pleasant."

"Oh?" Molly had an innocent look that Deb didn't quite buy.

"Yes. Do you know what we talked about?"

"How bad you are at your job?" Molly muttered, looking away.

Deb blinked. "Excuse me?"

"I just . . . What did Calvin have to say?" Molly asked, shifting in her seat.

Deb's heart was racing now and her hands were beginning to shake. "He said the food vendor you arranged wasn't approved by the hall where we're having the dinner. He said we have to change vendors or get this one approved. But what I'm wondering is how this happened. You did not tell me you were changing vendors. You said you worked with our usual vendor to add new offerings."

Molly looked at Deb like a defiant teenager. "No, I didn't."

"Yes, you did, Molly. Yes, you did."

"No, you're mistaken. I said I tried but they wouldn't budge. So I found a vendor with new options for us to choose from."

"That is not what you told me at our meeting." Deb tapped her notebook where the evidence should have been recorded. Molly didn't need to know Deb hadn't written it down.

Molly was undeterred. "Yes, it is." She looked pointedly at Deb.

Deb's head was spinning with the lies. What had she expected? She took a deep breath before she spoke again. "Molly, I need you to own up to this mistake. I don't know how we're going to fix it, but it is fixable. But for you to keep your job here, you need to be a team player. That means owning up when you mess up. You don't hide your mistakes or cover them up!"

"I'm not hiding anything. You have the email from the vendor. You're the one who wanted to add the specialty items. And you signed the contract. I did what you asked. How can you be mad at me? Just because you didn't read the email."

Deb was stung. Molly was right. She hadn't read the email closely enough. Or the contract for that matter. She had been so distracted by her fears of Andy Peters that now she was paying for it.

"Okay, Molly. Okay. You're right. I should have read more carefully. You also should have told me you were changing caterers so I could give my informed consent to the change. I'm going to be working all week trying to fix this."

Molly scoffed.

"Do you have something to say?" Deb asked curtly.

"No." Molly pursed her lips and looked at Deb.

"All right then. You're excused."

Molly stood up. "I hope you don't have to miss your bike ride." She left the room with a smirk on her face.

Deb sat in the quiet conference room staring after her. Did Molly just admit to sabotaging her? She had no proof, but it was written on Molly's face. And while Deb cleared her head, Molly was spreading her lies to Tom and the rest of the team. Deb let out a long breath and dragged herself next door to the kitchen for a cup of tea. Robin was in the room refilling her water. They acknowledged each other, then Robin went to the vending machine to view the offerings. Deb decided to take a chance.

"Robin, do you recall if Molly said she'd found a new caterer for the annual dinner?"

Robin put her card in the machine and punched a few numbers. "No, I don't remember that. I thought we didn't need to because the old crew was adding new menu items."

"That's what I understood too." A wave of vindication washed over Deb. "I apparently was mistaken."

"Silver Celebrations is pretty strict about which food vendors they allow. Did she choose an approved vendor?"

Robin's firm grasp of the situation was a relief to Deb. "No, and that's the problem. I signed a contract with an unapproved vendor. I'm not sure what to do now."

"Well, what are your options?" Robin asked. She opened the granola bar she had chosen from the vending machine. "Cancel the contract and lose the deposit?"

Deb said, "That's one option."

"Or get the new caterer approved."

"That's the other option."

"I like option number two," Robin said, taking a bite.

Deb nodded. "Me too. I haven't done that before, though. Do you know what's involved?" Robin, she realized, might be the answer to all her problems.

Robin pointed out that getting the vendor approved was part of Molly's tasks, but Deb didn't trust Molly to do it. Delegating to responsible people was one thing. Delegating to someone you believed was actively trying to undermine you was quite another. She would do it herself.

Robin chewed and swallowed. "It's not too tough. A little paperwork. A little time. It usually takes a couple weeks. You might have to offer to help the caterer get approved."

"Could you help me with that? We have three days."

"Oh, I wish I could but I'm swamped and I'm heading out of town tomorrow. I can't."

"Rats." Deb pressed her lips together, thinking. "In that case, can you show me where the forms are?"

The process wasn't quite as simple as Robin had implied, but Deb figured it out. She worked late that night sorting through the various papers to track down the needed information. She worked late the next night too, missing Marco's end-of-year celebration at school, so she could communicate everything to the caterer. Marco's reaction was a mix of anger and disappointment, despite her attempts to explain.

Now, three days later, Deb was waiting for the final approval from Silver Celebrations saying that the venue would work with the new vendor. She wouldn't be able to leave for the weekend, or the bike ride, until it came in. Calvin had been explicit about that. She was fidgeting in her seat she was so ready to leave.

Bing!

A new email. Sender: Silver Celebrations. Subject line: "Application approved."

"Woo-hoo!" Deb blurted out. Moving as quickly as she could, she rose from her desk and found Calvin in his office. "We're approved!" she exclaimed.

"I saw," he said, nodding. "Are you leaving?"

"Yes, I'm starting my weekend early. The bike ride starts tomorrow." Deb couldn't hide her joy.

"Well, good luck," Calvin said.

"Thank you. See you next week."

And she walked out, carrying her cane and purse on one arm, strutting with confidence.

Thirty-Four

Deb flew home. She pulled the van into the garage, climbed out, and scrambled into the house to change for her ride. It was quiet as she entered. No television tuned to the local news channel, no Betty sitting in her favorite seat. A surge of sadness came over her, followed by a ripple of relief and then guilt. Sometimes, she appreciated having the house to herself. She exhaled and moved on. It was Marco's last day of school. He would be home in just a couple of hours to make the place noisy.

In her room, she slipped off her skirt, pulled on her padded shorts, exchanged her blouse for a jersey, and tied her hair back. Then she donned her cooling vest to help with the June heat. She moved quickly and fluidly, having done the same thing many times over the past three months. Managing her MS, with frequent stretching, plenty of water, and riding during cooler times of day, was all part of the routine.

On her bike, Deb felt easy. Today's ride was just about keeping her legs warmed up and relaxed before the big event tomorrow. She would avoid any significant hills and simply absorb the beauty of the day. What joy!

She breathed deep. As she pedaled she made a mental packing list for the next day. She would take a clean jersey for Sunday's ride, her medications, an extra battery for her bike, just in case.

The ride organizers would provide food, water, energy drinks, and some other supplies and gear. She was still planning to drive down with Caroline and Philippe, though she would be sleeping alone. Somehow sharing a room with Caroline was still a bridge too far. At the last minute Rosa had agreed to take Marco for the weekend, bless her. Since the boys had started reading Spanish books together, Deb's house had a little more bilingual talk. She was happy to have the Spanish return to her life.

Deb planned to drop Marco off after dinner, then the three cyclists would drive to the hotel near the starting line in Easton. There had been talk of Rosa bringing PJ and Marco to the finish line on Sunday, over an hour's drive, but Deb told Rosa it was okay if they didn't make it. Robbie and Jacob would be waiting back in Silver Spring with a celebratory barbecue for the riders Sunday night.

Deb completed her circuit and arrived back at the house still feeling fresh. She stowed her bike and helmet, then went inside to pack. Marco would be home soon. They had talked it over and Deb agreed he was old enough to walk himself home. It hurt to give up the commute time together. While it was nice to reclaim some time to herself, she could see how much he was growing and she hated to miss even a minute of it. She looked forward to a pleasant afternoon and evening with her son.

"Mom," Marco said when he came in from school, "there's a package on the front porch."

Deb had been listening to an audiobook and paused the sound when the door opened. "Oh, I wasn't expecting anything. Did you see who it's from?"

"Uncle Julian!" Marco exclaimed. He set down his backpack in the hall and found his mom for a hug.

"Okay, first things first," she said, holding Marco close, "please unload your book bag and put it in your room. You're sleeping at PJ's this weekend. You'll need to pack an overnight bag."

While Marco attended to that, Deb brought the package in from the porch. It was about the size of a large shoebox but heavier. Deb hoped there wasn't another pocketknife inside, cringing at the thought. She grabbed the mail out of the mailbox while she was at it. Sorting the bills from the junk, she found a card-size envelope addressed to her. It was from Paula.

Marco came out of his room. "Can I open the package now?"

"Yes, you may. You'll need scissors."

Marco ran to the kitchen to find the scissors, then ran back to unseal the box. It took a few tries but he managed to rip it open. Inside were another soccer jersey, red, with the number 20 on the back; a couple of books; a scratched-silver pocketknife (Deb rolled her eyes); and a letter. Marco pulled everything out to look at it more closely but set the letter aside.

"Honey, what does the note say?" Deb asked, slightly exasperated.

"I don't know. Will you read it?" Marco was busy flipping through the books. He handed Deb the letter and she began to read it aloud.

Dear Marco,

What's happening, my man? I miss you so much. I heard there was a mix-up with the pocketknife I sent you, so I'm sending you a replacement. DO NOT TAKE IT TO SCHOOL! Ha ha! I know you won't make that mistake twice!

I'm also sending a couple of books I know you will love. Your mom mentioned you didn't know who Manno

Sanon was, so I got you a biography of him. He's just the most famous footballer in Haiti. You're going to love it.

I was sorry to hear about your grandmother. I wanted so much to come to Maryland for the funeral so I could be with you and your mom. But I think I know how I can make it up to you. I would like you to come to Austin for the summer. You can stay with me and visit your old friends. We'll have a great time. I promise.

Enjoy the jersey and the books. Tell your mom I'll be calling her soon to discuss your trip here. I can't wait to see you. I love you, little man.

Tío Julian

Marco looked expectantly at his mom. "Can I really go to Austin this summer?"

"I don't know, sweetie. We can talk about it. Uncle Julian shouldn't have said anything until we made plans."

Marco huffed. "I really, really want to go, Mom. Can I please go?"

"We'll talk about it, I said." Deb loved Julian, but she didn't always appreciate his seat-of-the-pants ways.

"Fine," Marco sighed. He bounced back quickly from the disappointment, however, running to his bedroom with his new jersey. "I'm going to put this on," he called as he charged out of the room.

Deb chuckled in disbelief. Alone for a moment, she opened the card from Paula. She wondered what her sweet girl had to say. The front of the card had a picture of an old-time bicycle with flowers in the basket. The words *Thinking of You* were printed across the top. She opened it and read,

Mom!

I hope this card gets to you in time. Good luck at the bike ride. I'm sorry I can't be there to cheer you on. I know you'll do great. You have worked so hard, you deserve it. I love you and miss you. See you in August!

Love,

Paula

P.S. Marco, be good for Mom! Love you, buddy!

Deb's heart swelled and she let out her breath. She had yearned for her daughter's approval and now she had it. She felt momentarily weak, but that was quickly replaced with a sense of buoyancy.

Half an hour later, Marco entered the kitchen wearing the red jersey while Deb was setting the table. She pulled out three dinner plates, then paused, shook her head, and put one back. Old habits. She arranged silverware at the two places and filled their water glasses.

"Dinner's ready," she said. "Please have a seat." She served them each two chicken tinga tacos, black beans, and salad.

"Thanks, Mom."

Deb looked at her son approvingly.

"Are you excited for your ride?" he asked.

"Yes, I am," she said. "Thanks for asking."

"We should play the game."

"What's that?" Deb asked. Sometimes Marco skipped from topic to topic so fast, she couldn't keep up.

"Grandma's game. We haven't played it in a long time." Marco cocked his head to the side, expecting Deb to remember.

"Oh, yes, of course. Do you want to go first?"

"Okay." Marco thought a minute. "First, the rose. Getting Uncle Julian's package. That was definitely the highlight of my day." He beamed as he appraised his new jersey. "The thorn would be not getting to see my friends at school tomorrow."

"You mean because you're on summer vacation?" Deb was incredulous.

"Yeah."

She laughed lightly. Never mind that he was spending the weekend at a friend's house. She was happy he had finally connected with the other kids in his class. "Okay. And the bud?"

"That's easy. I'm looking forward to hearing how your ride went." Marco smiled. "Your turn."

"Oh, Marco, aren't you sweet. I thought for sure you would say spending the night at PJ's."

"Oh yeah! That too!" He laughed at himself, his cheeks turning red.

Deb laughed too. "For me, the rose was getting a card from Paula and having dinner with you. Paula says hello, by the way. The thorn was . . ." She paused, trying to recall something negative from the day. "I don't have a thorn today, except maybe not having Grandma and Daddy here on the eve of the big event. I know they would've wanted to be here. And the bud is the bike ride this weekend. Hard to believe it's already here." Deb raised her eyebrows in mock surprise at Marco.

Marco laughed, then he turned somber. "I miss Grandma and Daddy," he said, swinging his legs.

"I know you do, sweetie. I do, too."

"We should get a dog."

"What?" Deb was taken aback.

"This house is too quiet now. We should get a dog. PJ has a dog and it makes so much noise, you never feel alone over there."

"Interesting," Deb said, not wanting to commit, but she did like the idea.

"Can we?" Marco asked. He had clearly noticed she did not immediately say no.

Deb smiled and patted his hand. "Let me think about it."

"There are lots of reasons to get a dog." Marco was excited now. "We could even get one of those helper dogs that you're always talking about."

"You mean a support dog? Like at Sparky's?"

"Yes! Then you wouldn't need to worry so much."

"And you wouldn't need to worry so much either."

"Can we, Mom?" Marco was bouncing in his seat.

"I still have to think about it, Marco. Maybe. It's not the kind of thing you should rush into." Deb took a bite of her dinner. A dog? She had always wanted one, but she wasn't sure now was the right time. She didn't even know if they would still be living in this house in six months.

They finished their meals quickly after that. After dinner, Marco packed his overnight bag, Deb finished packing hers, and they loaded up the van together, each thinking about what they had to look forward to.

Deb said goodbye to Marco at Rosa's and picked up Caroline and Philippe for the drive to the race area. Traffic was heavy on the Friday evening as hundreds of tourists made their way east for the first weekend after the end of school. Easton was east of Silver Spring, past the capital city of Annapolis, on the Eastern Shore, and the drive was taking longer than expected. Deb worried they wouldn't arrive in time to retrieve their race packets. Despite being bumper-to-bumper, crossing the four-mile span of the Bay Bridge was breathtaking. The sun was on the horizon behind them at 7 p.m., and the golden rays reflected off the rippling water below. The race route was described as flat, and as they neared Easton, Deb noticed the change in terrain. While Silver Spring was all rolling hills and tinkling waterways, Easton had been leveled by the same force that shaped the Eastern Shore.

They pulled up at the central building for packet pickup with five minutes to spare. A thrill went through Deb as she parked the van and the threesome climbed out. Everywhere she looked were other people just like her: women and men, many of them living with MS, who had spent months training for this event. The trio found the welcome tables and got in line. Deb kept an eye out for familiar faces from the new-rider meeting, but there were vastly more riders here than had attended the meeting. Her skin tingled with the electricity of so many excited cyclists all in one place. When she received her packet, complete with bib, bike light, and other freebies, she smiled with pride. She was really doing this! Twenty years later and she was finally here.

After everyone had their packets, they set a meeting place for the next morning and dropped Philippe off at the campsite. While Caroline and Deb would be staying at the ride hotel that night as planned, Philippe had decided to save some money and camp on-site. The campgrounds were noisy, with cars and cyclists clogging every artery and several campers playing music. Philippe got out at a corner and unloaded his things before turning to find his lot. Deb and Caroline honked goodbye as they drove off, both grateful not to be sleeping on the ground before the big ride.

Deb stood in her hotel room, looking out the large window at the pool deck below, where a small crowd had gathered. Although it was after eight o'clock at night it was still light in mid-June. During check-in, Deb had regretted the awkwardness between her and Caroline. They should've been sharing a room. Instead, Caroline was three doors down the hall and Deb was alone. Rebuilding after what Caroline had done was going to take time.

Someone knocked at the door and Deb answered it.

"They're having a mixer down by the pool for the cyclists," Caroline said, standing in the doorway. "Care to join me?"

"I was hoping to get some things settled first, if that's okay." Deb looked behind her at her computer bag sitting on the bed.

"Oh, right. Andy. Do you want to do that now?" Caroline was nervously squeezing a plastic fidget, the kind Marco brought home from school as a prize for bringing in his folder.

"Would you mind? I feel a little silly asking you to be with me just for this."

Caroline shook her head. "Don't feel silly. We all need support." She came into the room and sat on the bed. "Now, what do you know about Andy Peters? I mean Andy II, from Sparky's."

"Nothing off the top of my head. But I snagged his donor file from Sparky's this afternoon." Deb showed Caroline the flash drive that held the file.

"Good for you," Caroline said approvingly.

Deb opened her laptop and sat next to Caroline. "I searched 'Andy Peters' without the address and got hundreds of hits. I don't think I could find anything definitive without the address." Deb fumbled as she tried to put the drive into the slot. Her hands were shaking, and she laughed nervously. "Sorry. Let me try again." At last, she inserted the drive, opened the file, copied the name and address, and pasted it into the search engine. She hit enter and held her breath. Ten entries came up.

"I was expecting more," Caroline said, leaning in to scan the page.

"That's what the address does for you, I guess," Deb replied.

Caroline pointed at an entry. "Click that one. Instagram. He'll have pictures."

Deb's heart beat faster as the cursor hovered over the link. She clicked it and a new page opened. It was hard to see the profile picture. She put her glasses on and leaned closer to the screen to get a better look. Then she clicked one of the images and waited for it to load.

Time stood still. This was the moment she had been waiting for since way back in May when she first saw Andy's name on the donor sheet. She had been terrified of running into him at the office. She had nightmares about him somehow finding out about Paula and butting into their lives. Living in Austin she thought she was over the assault, but coming back to Maryland had dredged it up again. And, of course, Caroline had made it all so much worse. Now Deb hoped with all her might that Caroline was right and it was just a coincidence.

At last, the picture loaded.

"It's not him!" she shouted. She leaned back and laughed. "Oh my God, it's not him." Tears rolled down her cheeks as the relief washed over her.

Caroline smiled wide and put her arm around Deb's shoulders. They both stared at the picture. The image showed a British-looking man with a sharp nose, mousy brown hair, and blue eyes. He appeared to be in his fifties. "There you go!" she said. "Nothing to worry about."

Caroline sat back while Deb scrolled through the rest of the images. This Andy had posted several pictures of himself with his two dogs. He also had pictures of vacations in the mountains out west and a blond woman, maybe a girlfriend or wife. He often posted about taking care of the earth, and he included selfies of himself biking to work. He was the CEO of a small biotech company. That explained where the money came from.

Deb wiped the tears from her cheeks. "He could be Watson from Sherlock Holmes. Completely harmless. I can't believe I was so worked up over nothing."

Deb took another good look at the photos on Andy's Instagram before shutting down the computer. She realized Caroline was staring at her, lips tight. Deb waited for her to speak.

"So, you were going to tell me why Marco put the knife in Jacob's bag." Caroline's cheeks flushed.

"Oh, right, yes, of course." Deb had hoped not to have to explain, but she saw she couldn't put it off any longer. "You might not like the answer."

"Try me." Caroline smiled weakly.

"Okay." Deb took a deep breath and let it out. "It seems Marco was defending me." Caroline cocked her head and Deb continued. "Jacob made fun of me one day when the boys were playing at PJ's, and Marco put the knife in his bag as a way of getting back at him."

"Jacob was making fun of you? How do you mean?"

"The way I walk. He picked up a stick and pretended it was a cane. Apparently, he and PJ were laughing pretty hard about it, and Marco got mad. We talked about it. I told him it's not right to try to get back at your friends. You tell people when you're angry; you don't get revenge."

Deb was aware of how appropriate that advice was for her own situation with Caroline. It might even explain the mess with Molly, though Molly's actions seemed to be driven by jealousy rather than any vindictive or harmful actions on Deb's part.

"Oh, gosh. I'm sorry Jacob did that. But Marco must've been really angry to plan something so cruel."

Caroline's gaze turned inward, and Deb tried to soothe her.

"I don't think he planned it. He said he brought the knife to show PJ and Jacob, but when things went south, he hid it in Jacob's bag instead. He tried to get it back, but it was too late."

Caroline huffed. She had said she wouldn't be mad, but Deb knew promises like that were hard to keep.

"Our lives were turned upside down over that?" Caroline started to pace, pulling again on the plastic fidget.

"We're both very sorry about all the trouble he caused."

Deb watched Caroline and wondered what the fallout would be.

Was their friendship going to crumble after all? It was hard to see a way forward if Caroline was going to stay mad about what Marco had done. Deb was truly sorry for the trouble her son had caused, but she and Caroline did seem to be about even at this point.

Caroline abruptly stopped pacing and looked at Deb. She shook her head as if coming to the same conclusion and said, "Forget about it. We all do things we regret. Shall we go to the mixer now?"

Whew. "You go on ahead. I'll join you in a bit."

Caroline walked out while Deb looked around the room, soaking up the peace and quiet. Already so much had happened on this trip. What did the rest of the weekend hold? She let out a sigh. What was Marco up to? He didn't spend the night out often, and two nights in a row seemed like a lot. She missed him. She sent a quick text to Rosa's phone.

Good night, Marco! I love you and miss you!

She added three heart emojis, one for each member of her family, and hit send. Then she typed a message to Rosa.

Thanks for watching my son. I couldn't do this without you!

A few minutes later, Rosa wrote back. *Happy to do it! Good luck tomorrow! Marco says good night and good luck!!*

Deb smiled. She loved her kids more than anything. It warmed her heart that they thought of her. She realized then that she hadn't thanked Paula for the card that arrived earlier in the day. She dashed off another text.

Thanks for the card. It made my day! I'm in the hotel getting ready for the ride. I'm SO nervous!

Paula's reply was almost immediate.

Hooray! It arrived! You got this, Mom! Can't wait to hear all about it.

Deb read the message several times. She again had that feeling of weakness and strength that came from seeking support and finding it. She sent back three heart emojis, then put her phone away. She sat up a little straighter, feeling lighter now. She exhaled deeply, rubbing the bicycle charm resting on her breastbone. Then she pulled the race packet out of her bag and opened it. Inside was her very own "I Ride With MS" jersey. She fingered the fabric, then shook it out and held it up to herself. Should she wear it tomorrow? No. She would save it for Sunday's ride, when people living with MS were invited to lead the other cyclists out onto the route. She still hadn't decided if she would take part in that ritual, but she wanted to be prepared. Deb flipped through the other tchotchkes that came in the packet, then stood up, laid out tomorrow's outfit on the extra bed, and slipped out the door.

Thirty-Five

Saturday morning, Caroline woke from a nightmare moments before the alarm was set to go off. She caught her breath. The room was artificially dark thanks to the heavy drapes over the window, but a tiny slice of bright sunlight was visible between the panels. She eased out of bed and went to the bathroom, taking her phone with her.

Sitting to use the facilities, she woke up her phone and checked messages. Eyes still bleary from sleep, she wiped them with the back of her fist, then blinked rapidly. She could see just well enough to tell there was nothing she needed to deal with in her email. She finished on the toilet and washed her hands. Put some water on her face and blinked again. She still looked blurry in the mirror but it was improving.

She dressed in silence, applying sunscreen liberally to her freckled skin, and gathered her bike and gear. Then she went into the hall to wait for Deb. The start time for the seventy-five-mile route was 7:15 a.m., and it would take ten minutes to get there from the hotel. They had plenty of time to arrive, park, unload, and reconnect with Philippe.

Deb came out of her room a couple of minutes later, wheeling her bike next to her. She looked as tired as Caroline felt.

"I wonder how Philippe slept," Caroline said. "I do not envy him sleeping in a tent."

She remembered what they'd heard at the mixer the night before. Will from the new-rider meeting was staying at the hotel. So was Trish. Caroline asked about Ben Bikes and heard he was greeting people down at the campsite. From the sound of it, the campers tended to stay up a bit later and drink a bit more alcohol—under the radar, of course.

"I wonder if he met Ben Bikes," Deb countered. "I hope he knew to lay off the beer." Both Deb and Caroline had abstained the night before. Neither wanted to deal with the effects on their muscles. "Is your clock working?" Deb asked. "Mine was flashing when I woke up."

"You mean the room clock? Now that I think about it, maybe. The electricity must've flickered in the night."

As they passed the hotel breakfast room, Caroline said, "Hold this," and gave Deb her handlebars. She trotted off and came back a few minutes later with two bananas and two plain bagels clutched to her chest.

"Perfect," Deb said. They wheeled both bikes out through the automatic doors. Once inside the car, they ran through the checklist one more time. In addition to keys, IDs, and two water bottles each, Deb had her cooling vest and her extra battery. Anything else they wouldn't need or could get at a rest stop.

They arrived at the parking area for the ride at six forty-five. They finished their power breakfast seated in the car. "Are you ready?" Caroline asked Deb. They were scheduled to meet Philippe in just a couple of minutes.

Deb breathed in through her nose. "Yes, I am," she said. They mounted their bikes and she let out a whoop of excitement as they pedaled off.

They spotted Philippe waiting at the port-a-johns near the packet pickup table ten minutes before go time. The tall, well-muscled man was imposing in his bike shorts and jersey, but his broad smile conveyed his friendly nature. "Caroline, Deb, hello!" he called as they rolled up on their bikes.

"Philippe!" they chorused.

Caroline looked up at her friend, thankful they had reconciled before ride day. "How was camping? Did you get any sleep?"

"Sure, I slept. Just maybe not as much as I was planning," he said with a grin. He grabbed his left wrist with his right hand in front of him and rolled his back in a dramatic stretch. "How about you?"

"I slept like a baby," Deb said, smiling.

"Afraid I can't say the same for myself," Caroline admitted. She thought of the nightmare that woke her. Something about a violent intruder armed with a pocketknife. She'd woken with the sensation of being stabbed in the eye.

Philippe nodded. "Sorry to hear that, Caroline. Are you going to be all right?"

Caroline smiled. "Absolutely! Lead the way to the starting line."

The paths were overflowing with people, and the trio had to roll slowly in and out of the crowd, weaving around bikes, trash cans, and tents, to find the starting line. They pedaled up to a thick cluster of bikes waiting to start with just a few minutes left before launch.

An emcee was welcoming the riders and making last-minute announcements about the route. Deb could hardly believe they were here. It had taken twenty years for her to get this far. She was trembling with electric energy.

"I should have used the port-a-john while I had the chance," she whispered to Caroline, who laughed.

"Don't worry, once we've started you'll forget all about it." She was grinning from ear to ear.

Deb sat up straight on her bike to look around one last time. An ocean of cyclists surrounded her, with smaller puddles of riders off to the sides. The seventy-five-mile route appeared to be the most popular, as a good two hundred riders were getting set to take off. She saw bikes of all shapes and sizes, including adult trikes, ebikes, several recumbents, and one high wheel—a bicycle with a very large front wheel and tiny back wheel, a throwback from the 1870s. She noticed dozens of pennants flying with the Bike MS logo, along with jerseys, bumper stickers, hats, and other paraphernalia. She knew some of the garb had been earned by the highest fundraisers. Others were riders taking part in their fifth, tenth, or even twentieth event. Their dedication was inspiring, and she felt invigorated.

At last the announcer released the riders for the seventy-five-mile route, and Deb was off like a shot.

Caroline and Philippe caught up with Deb once the crowd thinned. The race organizers had shut down roads for the ride, so there was enough room for everyone to spread out. When they had a couple of miles under their belts, Deb asked Philippe about his camping experience.

"Did you meet Ben Bikes? We heard he was the emcee at the campsite."

"Ah, Ben Bikes! Yes! He doesn't just bike, you know. He also plays soccer." Philippe's eyes flashed as he gave a genuine smile of pleasure. "We had a little pickup game after supper. It was a grand time."

"Sounds like it!" Deb said. She looked at Caroline. "C, are you all right?"

Caroline darted a look at Deb. "Yes, I'm fine. Why?"

"Oh, nothing. You just seem to be rubbing your eyes a lot."

Caroline took her hand away from her face. "I'm having something weird with my eye. I woke up with it. I keep blinking to get it to clear but it's not clearing. I don't know what it is."

Philippe frowned. "Is it your contacts?"

"No, I don't wear contacts."

"Could it be allergies?" Deb suggested.

"I think that must be it," Caroline conceded. She didn't often have allergies in June, but what else could it be? She blinked a couple more times. She was getting used to looking out of one eye. "How's Rosa?" she asked Philippe.

"Oh, very good. We talked last night. She and the boys ate popcorn and watched a movie before bed. Today they're hitting the park. Rosa bought a couple of kites to surprise them."

"How wonderful!" Deb said. "She told me about the park, but I didn't know about the kites."

"What are Robbie and Jacob up to today?" Philippe asked Caroline.

"It's Saturday so they will probably do some chores around the house before the cleaning service arrives, and then watch a baseball game. Of course, if I'm not there they might skip the chores and just watch baseball all day." Caroline laughed. "Not that I'm complaining," she added. "I *am* taking a whole weekend to ride a bicycle, so . . ."

Philippe and Deb both nodded. "We're lucky our spouses let us do this," Philippe said.

"I'm lucky your spouse is watching my son," Deb said to Philippe. "I don't know what I would've done without Rosa's help. Not this."

They reached the first rest stop at mile ten and pulled over. Several riders flitted about. Volunteers in yellow jerseys were behind the tables, refilling boxes of bananas, bagels, and energy bars. Five-gallon jugs of Gatorade and water were set up, with riders at each jug refilling their bottles. The air was crisp, it was just past eight o'clock in the morning, and everyone was in good spirits.

Deb immediately ran to the port-a-john while Philippe and Caroline topped off their water bottles. Philippe was on his bike when Deb came back. He said, "Well, ladies, I think I'm going to go on now. I'm trying to finish in under four hours. See you at the finish line?"

"Sounds good," Caroline said. "Be safe out there."

"Good luck," Deb called to Philippe as he pedaled off. "I know you can do it!"

Philippe nodded his goodbye.

"He is *strong*," Deb said, eyes on Philippe, his calf muscles bulging. "Under four hours? Is that even possible?"

Caroline shrugged, also entranced by Philippe. "Maybe. It's worth trying, I guess."

Deb completed her stretch routine, and she and Caroline started out again.

"We have a long way to go," Deb said.

"Yes, we do."

The weather was beautiful, and Caroline felt strong as she rode. It was exhilarating to be surrounded by so many other cyclists, and the route was a pleasant one. The pack stuck mostly to rural roads, often skirting along a lake or creek running through pastureland. She and Deb marveled at the cows chewing grass in one pasture. They quacked at the ducks in a pond on another farm. And so they covered miles and miles of ground.

Caroline's eyesight had never fully cleared, which worried her, but with her sunglasses on, she was able to accommodate the awkwardness of seeing better out of one eye than the other. That is, until she felt the stirrings of a headache.

"Oh no," she muttered.

"What?" Deb asked. They were riding side by side along a wide grassy field.

Caroline sighed. "I think I'm getting a migraine."

"I thought you were over those."

"Me too." Caroline shook her head. She stretched her neck side to side as she pedaled, hoping to ward off the headache. But it was no good. The force of the pain caused her to close her eyes.

This time she remembered not to squeeze her handlebars, but she couldn't help from yelling out.

"Caroline, what is it?" Deb asked. She stopped her bike just ahead and Caroline pulled up next to her.

"I feel awful." Caroline dismounted. She pressed her hands to her eyes to try to alleviate the pressure. A sudden wave of nausea rose up from her belly. "Oh God," she cried, before heaving. She threw up the Gatorade and water, the banana and bagel from breakfast. She heaved again and moaned. Deb came to her side and rubbed circles on her back.

"Caroline, I'm so sorry. Are you okay?"

Caroline sat on the ground where the grass was shorter, away from where she had lost her stomach. "No, I don't think I am." Tears welled up in her eyes.

"What's happening?" Deb asked.

Caroline sat without speaking and attempted to master her breathing. She pressed her hands into her eyes again. When she had recovered enough she said, "I'm pregnant."

Deb blinked in disbelief. "What? You're pregnant?"

"Yes, I'm pregnant. Two months. A little over."

"So this is morning sickness?"

"I guess so." Caroline wiped tears from her face and smiled wanly. "But I was never sick like this with Jacob. I'm worried."

"Oh, Caroline. I'm sorry. Well, wait. I mean, congratulations! You're pregnant! That's awesome!" Deb rubbed Caroline's shoulders. "I'm sorry you're having such a rough time. Do you think you can go on?"

Caroline let out a breath. "I don't know." Fresh tears came to her eyes. "I don't think I can." After all the work she had put into training and fundraising, she felt crushed by the thought of dropping out. But her body was telling her to stop. She had to listen.

"That's okay. It'll be okay. Let's just get to the next rest stop and we'll get you some help. Can you make it that far? I think we're about two miles from the fifty-mile stop."

"Two miles?" Caroline steeled herself. "Yes, I can do that." She wiped her nose with the back of her gloved hand. She stood up and walked back to her bike.

A couple of riders saw them coming out of the grassy field. "Everything all right?" they asked as they passed.

"Yes, we're fine," Deb called and waved her thanks. "Ready?" she said to Caroline.

Caroline put her sunglasses back on and mounted her bike. "Yes, I'm ready."

They pedaled a few feet in silence. Caroline felt embarrassed by her emotional reaction. "I'm sorry I didn't tell you before," she said to Deb.

"Oh, Caroline, I know how it is. You don't have to apologize."

"It's just, you had so much going on already, with your mom and everything."

"It's okay, Caroline. Really, it is." She gave a faint smile. "I just want you to get better."

When they reached the next rest stop, Deb found a volunteer and explained what had happened. The volunteer came over to talk to Caroline.

"We can take you back to the starting line," she said. "I'll call SAG and have a van pick you up. You're having a migraine?"

"Yes, that's right." She opted not to mention the pregnancy. She vaguely remembered pregnant riders being prohibited.

"Okay, why don't you have a seat in the shade and drink some water. Someone will be here soon."

The volunteer walked off to make the call to SAG. Deb sat next to Caroline on her bike.

"What are you going to do tonight?" Deb asked.

"I think I have to go back." Caroline looked at Deb. She hated to abandon her friend. Not again. Not after all that had happened.

"Go back to the hotel or back to Silver Spring?"

"Silver Spring. I don't think I can ride tomorrow. I want to be with Robbie." Caroline's eyes glistened with tears. This yearning for her husband made her realize how much she had taken him for granted.

"Okay." Deb was silent.

"I'm sorry to leave you."

"That's okay. You aren't well. You should go. I'll be fine."

"Are you sure?" Caroline frowned. "I feel like I'm abandoning you. Again."

"It's really okay. Please, I know it's not ideal, but I won't fall apart. I promise."

"I know you won't. It's just that I promised Paula I would look out for you. Ha! I guess I was the one who needed looking out for." Caroline tipped her face up and noticed the sun high in the sky, then looked at Deb. "Thanks for waiting with me. Did you want to go on? You're losing a lot of time."

"No, I can wait. Look, there's the van now."

A white van pulled into the rest area and onto the grass before parking near where Deb and Caroline were waiting. A man stepped out of the driver's side.

"Ben Bikes, at your service." The man trotted over.

"Ben!" Deb and Caroline laughed to see the iconic cyclist. "I thought you were riding," Caroline said.

"No, not this year. I had a flare-up that kept me off my bike for a month. I knew I couldn't bike it, but I didn't want to miss the event, so I volunteered to do SAG. So, what's up? Are you both going back?" He looked from Caroline to Deb.

"No, just me," Caroline said, raising a hand. "Deb here is going to complete the ride." She patted Deb on the arm and smiled at Ben.

"Good for you, Deb," Ben said, bowing his head slightly.

Deb smiled. "Thanks. Speaking of which, I should get moving. Caroline, call me and tell me what happens."

"I will."

"Come with me," Ben said, helping Caroline into the van. Deb watched as Caroline got seated. Her face was drawn and her eyes puffy. Ben put the bike in after her. His clubbed hand didn't slow him down.

"Bye!" Deb called.

"Bye!" Caroline waved from inside the van. The door closed, and the van pulled out of the rest area, leaving Deb behind.

Thirty-Six

Deb had already pedaled fifty miles before Caroline was escorted away. That left twenty-five miles for day one, seventy-five more the following day. A lot of road to go. But she was determined. She had trained for months, weathered several setbacks—recovered from a relapse, fought and made up with Paula, lost her dear mother—and still she was here, out on the route. She was not going to stop now.

The thing that struck Deb first was how quiet it was riding alone. Her wheels whirred over the pavement. Every plunk of a rock hitting her tire echoed in her ears, every sensation in her legs was something to ponder. But after a few miles, she forgot to listen to the road noise. Instead, she was listening to her thoughts. And goodness, did she have a lot of thoughts.

What was going on with Caroline, for one? A baby! How crazy. Jacob was already ten. Were she and Robbie really trying for another child? Or was this new baby a surprise? It didn't seem like Caroline to let anything happen by accident, but then, Mother Nature had a way of making things happen. Deb chuckled to herself. Even Caroline couldn't control everything.

There seemed to be more than just a pregnancy, though, didn't there? Deb knew from her experience with her fellow MSers that migraines could cause vomiting, sensitivity to light, and other problems. Pregnancy hormones usually calmed migraines rather than inflaming them. But what was it she and Luis used to joke about? When she was pregnant with Marco, she had so many symptoms she didn't have with Paula. But the doctors always wrote it off. No matter what she said, the response was, "Don't worry, that happens in half of all pregnancies." So maybe for some women, migraines got worse, not better.

Deb climbed one of the last hills on the route, careful to keep her assistance setting minimal, especially now. Although she was tempted to pour on the juice, the last thing she needed was to run out of battery. All the hard work was making her hungry. She began daydreaming about hamburgers. Even with the food she'd had en route, she would be ready to eat when she got back to the finish line.

And then a strange feeling enveloped her. The trail weaved through a grove of trees that reminded her of the woods in her neighborhood. She thought of Andy Peters, that bastard, and of Caroline leaving her with him, and she got scared. A ripple of emotion passed through her and she pedaled faster. She looked back and didn't see any other riders. How long had it been since she'd passed another cyclist? It seemed like ages. Had she gotten off the route? Caroline had downloaded the route GPS onto her device before the ride, so she told Deb every time a turn was coming. Without Caroline, there was no one to tell Deb which way to go. She looked for markings on the road now but didn't see anything. Her heart beat faster as she felt more and more uncertain. Surely another rider should have come past by now. She fumbled for her phone in her jersey pocket so she could check the route on the race app. How could she have been so stupid? She was so caught up in her fears that she wasn't being careful, and now she was lost. Dammit! She started to sweat but not from the exertion. Phone in hand, she pulled over and opened the race app. What would she do if she was off course? Head back, obviously, but how far off could she be? How many more miles would she have to pedal? "Debra Lee, you idiot," she breathed. She tapped through her phone until she finally had the route map she was looking for. That's when she noticed another rider coming by.

"Everything all right?" the young woman asked, slowing as she approached.

Deb's chest swelled with relief. "Uh, yeah. Is this the right road for the seventy-five-miler?"

The young woman grinned. "I really hope so or I'm in deep trouble."

"Oh, good," Deb said, and laughed at herself. "Have a good ride!"

"Thanks, you too," the rider called as she pedaled away.

Deb stored her phone back in her jersey pocket, had a few gulps of water, and got back on her bike. Her heart rate soon returned to normal. She realized then that she might never fully get over what happened to her all those years ago. She couldn't muscle it into place and make her feelings obey. But she could accept it and forgive. Not Andy. Forgive herself.

Fifty feet later, she saw the markings on the road for the next turn. Five miles to the finish line. More riders were up ahead, and she decided to catch up. No way was she getting lost again.

Deb rolled across the finish line on day one of the Chesapeake Challenge with her legs burning and her body like a rag doll. How in the world was she going to do it all again tomorrow?

She stored her bike on an open rack in the parking lot and found a spot of grass for stretching. Dozens of cyclists sat and stood in groups, recovering from their individual rides. Deb wondered how many had done each length. Some resembled fresh spring daisies. Others looked the way she felt—trampled. And still others, she realized, were out on the route. Anyone doing the century ride had nearly two hours of pedaling left to go.

The finish line was at the parking lot for a community building, a squat brick one-story structure that was functional if not pretty. Lunch was inside. She took out her phone and texted Philippe.

I made it! More than five hours of pedaling! Are you still at the finish line?

She continued to stretch and hydrate while she awaited Philippe's reply. She didn't have to wait long.

Hoorah! I'm inside. Come in!

Deb entered the building and was greeted by the sound of over a hundred riders eating and talking amid the smells of hot dogs, hamburgers, beer, and sweat. Her mouth watered at the thought of food. It was dim inside compared to the bright sun she had just left. She scanned the room.

"Philippe!" she called when she spotted her teammate.

"Deb! Welcome!" Philippe was sitting at a table with three other cyclists. "Have a seat. I heard about Caroline. So sad." He shook his head.

"Isn't it awful? I feel so bad for her."

Deb looked at the others at the table and Philippe said, "I met these guys last night while camping. We finished around the same time, so we had lunch together."

"That's awesome!" Deb smiled at the other riders. She was suddenly aware of the smell coming off her. Not much she could do about that now. "I am *beat*! And hungry! Where do I get the food?"

The other riders laughed as she hammed up her hunger.

Philippe pointed to the end of the large room. "Start there. The burger was delicious, if you eat meat."

"The veggie burger was surprisingly tasty too," a tanned and muscular man of about thirty said. "I recommend it."

"Oh, thank you, I might do that," Deb replied.

She quickly filled her plate with a hot dog, a veggie burger, chips, carrot salad, coleslaw, and a cookie. When she returned to the table, Philippe was still there but the others had left. Deb discovered she was slightly disappointed.

"What happened to your friends?" she asked.

"Ah, they needed to head on. They finished a while ago and were ready for showers. But I'm happy to stay and keep you company."

"Thanks, Philippe. I'd appreciate that." Deb settled her things at the table and got ready to eat. "So, did you do it? Did you meet your goal?"

Philippe smiled. "Not quite. Four hours, six minutes. But I'm happy."

"That's excellent. You must be very proud." Deb took a bite of her food and said, "You talked to Caroline?"

Philippe nodded slowly. "Yes, I did. She said she got ill and had to be carted back by SAG."

"Yeah, I'm worried about her. She was not doing well at all. I don't know how she was getting home." Deb was careful not to give too many details.

"Robbie and Jacob came and got her shortly after I crossed. I think she was really bummed. I know she wanted to do this with you. She asked me to look out for you while she's gone."

"Oh goodness. Well, you don't have to do that, Philippe. I'll be okay."

"I know. She's just trying to be a good friend. She worries about you, same as you worry about her."

Deb thought about that while she chewed. Did Caroline still feel responsible for her? Did Deb still think she should? She didn't exactly blame Caroline for what had happened, but sometimes little feelings snuck up on her. How different would Deb's life be if Caroline hadn't left her at that party? She would never know.

Philippe tilted his head. "Everything okay, Deb?"

"Oh, I'm fine. Just lost in thought. Your friend was right, this veggie burger is delicious." She smiled to show she was okay. "So, Philippe, I wanted to thank you personally for doing this ride. Rosa told me months ago that you were inspired to do it partly because of me."

"Yes, that's true," he said, sitting up. "I know from Rosa's cousin how much trouble MS can be. Seeing you living with it, raising your son—who, by the way, is a wonderful young man—and caring for your mom too, I thought, *That's someone who deserves more.* And I don't know. Doing this ride seemed like a good way to honor that."

"Well, thank you. Because you also inspired me. Knowing you were going to be out here made me want to do it too. MS is unpredictable, as you know. I wanted to do it while I still could."

"I think that's truly amazing," Philippe said. He tapped on the table. "So, what are you going to do tomorrow? Are you going to ride or call it quits?"

"Are you serious right now?" Deb tried to read the look on Philippe's face but was unsure what she was seeing.

"Of course I'm serious. You always have a choice, Deb."

"I'm going to ride!" she exclaimed and slapped the table.

Philippe laughed. "Well, all right!"

Deb finished her meal, and then she and Philippe walked out. He would be camping another night, and Deb had her room at the hotel, so they said their goodbyes and agreed to meet back at the same port-a-johns the next morning. Deb planned to stretch, ice her knees, bathe, and rest as much as she could over the next sixteen hours. She would prepare herself for any circumstance. Because who knew what the next day might hold?

Thirty-Seven

Deb woke early the next morning with the barest strip of light peeking between the drapes. The room clock was flashing again. She was alone in the hotel room, and as she lay there, she felt as if she had never been so alone. This was not a sad feeling but rather a curiosity. When was the last time she had been completely alone for this many hours? With her mother's passing and her friend dropping out of the ride, she felt as solitary as could be. Of course, she had Marco waiting for her in Silver Spring, and Paula in Chicago, and she had Caroline, Rosa, Philippe, plus growing friendships at work and in the network of riders she had met. But at this moment, she knew she had herself to rely on and herself alone to finish the ride.

She assessed her body, starting at her toes. Her left big toe was numb. That hadn't changed in weeks. She could deal with that. She flexed her feet. Her calves were tight and tired from yesterday. Her knees were there, which was more than she could usually feel. They would need stretching before she got back on her bike. Her thighs felt good, hips tight, waist strong, back a little tired. More stretching there. Her upper body was tired but not overly so. Neck? She swiveled it from side to side. Pretty good. Face, eyes, nose, and forehead: all working and without pain. She was in good shape. She sat up.

After washing up in the bathroom, she laid out her towel and went through her stretches. She thought of Betty and her Thursday yoga class. Betty had attended every week since before Deb and Marco moved in. She was no master yogi, but Nurse Lydia had been pleased with the improvements she saw, and Betty had sworn by it. Maybe Deb would pick up a yoga class of her own. It certainly couldn't hurt.

She stood and pulled back the curtain of the picture window to get a look at the day. The sun was up but the sky was white with thick clouds. This was good news for Deb. The longer she could put off the heat of the day, the better her ride would go. She just hoped it wouldn't rain. She closed the curtains again and dressed. Pulling the new yellow-and-blue race jersey over her head, she felt muscles in her back she didn't know she had. A second full day of riding would be a challenge. She stretched her neck from side to side and let out her breath. She was up for it.

She had charged her ebike battery overnight and had stored the freezer packs for her cooling vest in the tiny hotel freezer. She gathered them up now and put them in their proper places. She paused in front of the room's mirror to admire the new jersey. A perfect fit. She smiled a crooked smile at her reflection. Then she wheeled her bike out of the room, through the lobby, to her van. The bike loaded up, she zipped back into the hotel to grab some breakfast: an orange today, and two mini bran muffins. The lobby was buzzing with other riders, but no one Deb knew. She went through her checklist again before getting back in the van. She had prepared the bottles of water and Gatorade the night before. She was set.

She arrived at her meeting place with Philippe at 6:55 a.m. and waited. There were fewer riders about on the second day. Many people had gone home, choosing to ride just one day. Still, she saw fifty or sixty cyclists and knew more were lurking in the building or yet to arrive for the fifty-mile ride. She looked to her left and saw Philippe pedaling up.

"Good morning," he called, sounding a bit sleepy. "Sorry I'm late. How are you this morning?" Before Deb could answer he added, "Nice jersey."

Deb grinned. "Thanks. Ready to roll. How're you?"

"Ah, wishing I'd sprung for a hotel room," Philippe said, twisting his waist.

"A bit stiff, are you?" Deb asked playfully. She could not imagine sleeping on the ground after the punishment she put her body through yesterday. Definitely not when she planned to do it all again today.

Philippe was upbeat about it. "Yeah, but it's all right. Let's get over to the starting line."

"Okay, but first, let's get a picture." Deb pulled out her phone and Philippe came close, tilting his head toward hers. *Snap!* The photo showed two happy if tired-looking cyclists out for an early-morning ride. The starting line was visible in the distance. Deb sent the image to Caroline with the message *Wish you were here!* Then she sent it to Marco, Rosa, and Paula with the message *Ready or not, here we come!*

As they wheeled over to the start, she heard her phone ping several times in her jersey pocket, signaling various messages coming in and bringing a smile to her face. She looked forward to reading them later.

The atmosphere at the park was much more casual on day two. It seemed the riders were more relaxed, and so were the race organizers. The announcer was playing some funk over the sound system, and several cyclists were dancing to the groovy beat. At 7:15 a.m. the DJ came over the PA.

"All of you folks who ride with MS, please come to the front of the pack. Step right up. You are going to lead us out onto the route."

Deb hesitated. Did she really want that much attention? She looked at Philippe.

"What are you waiting for? Go up there," he said encouragingly.

"Will you come with me?" She felt the adrenaline rushing through her.

Philippe looked her in the face. "Have you seen *Joe vs. the Volcano*?"

"About a million times." Deb looked at him questioningly. Then she remembered. "'Certain doors we need to go through alone.'"

"Exactly."

Deb wound through the crowd, gathering at the starting line with about a dozen other cyclists also wearing their "I Ride With MS" jerseys. Someone snapped a few photos of the group. Then came the announcement: "Okay, riders. Lead us out." Deb and the other MSers took off, followed by a hundred more riders.

Philippe caught up with her after about a quarter mile. It would be the same route as the day before. That meant no surprises, little chance of getting lost, but it carried the risk of boredom. By mile fifty-five, some riders might be wondering what they were doing it for. Deb was determined not to let that be her fate.

"Thanks for riding with me this morning, Philippe. You know, I don't expect you to stay with me the whole time." Deb knew she would run out of steam if she tried to keep up with someone with Philippe's physique.

"That's very considerate of you, Deb. Are you sure you'll be okay?"

"Yes, I'm sure. I'm actually looking forward to it. I want to see if I can make better time than yesterday."

"Ah, ambitious! I like it," Philippe said. "In that case, I think I'll see you to the first rest stop and go on from there. What do you think?"

"Perfect."

Deb looked around. The clouds were starting to thin out some, but the temperature was still fairly cool. "We couldn't have asked for a better day," she said.

They pedaled up the first hill and followed the bend around a churchyard. Although the course was largely flat, they couldn't avoid every incline. Deb was grateful for her training to get her up the hills. Several riders were ahead and they all rode in a group for a while.

"Do you have brothers and sisters, Philippe?"

"I do. A brother. Antoine. He lives in North Carolina."

"Do you get to see him much?"

"On occasion. We take PJ down every other summer. Antoine has two kids, so it's nice to get the cousins together. You?"

"I did. A sister. She died when I was in high school."

"I'm sorry to hear that."

Deb nodded her acknowledgment.

"And who was the young woman at the wake who looked so much like you?" Philippe asked. "I thought maybe your sister?"

"That's Paula. My daughter." It felt good to say her name aloud. "She goes to college in Chicago, but we talk once a week."

"I didn't know you had a daughter."

"Yep. I do. From a previous relationship." Carrying so many secrets had been like carrying a sack of rocks over her shoulder. The more she shared, the lighter the sack became. "She'll be back in August. I'll bring her by so you can meet her."

"I'd be honored."

They rode on until they could see the first rest stop up ahead. "Are you going to stop for a refill?" Deb asked.

Philippe peeked down at his water bottles and touched his jersey pocket. "No, I think I'll skip this one and stop at the next one. I have enough on me."

"Okay, well, I'm going to stop. Thanks for riding with me. Will I see you at the finish line?"

"Yes, I'll be there. And then we can drive back to Silver Spring together."

The thought of a car ride after this day made her cringe, but Deb kept that to herself. "Okay, then. See you at the finish line! Be safe!"

"You too," Philippe said, and he pedaled off while Deb pulled into the rest area.

After a quick tour of the rest stop and routine stretching, Deb was on her way, this time alone. She wondered what Ben Bikes was up to, and Will and Trish. If Ben Bikes could be knocked out of the ride, and Caroline too, it could happen to anyone. The thought made her more determined than ever to reach her goal.

She discovered, the second time through the course, she could avoid some of the delays from the day before, knowing to skip the fruit chews and stick with nuts, energy bars, and water and Gatorade. She recognized several riders, and enjoyed a little chitchat with the volunteers and loyal cyclists. At some point between rest stops, she joined up with a small cohort of riders.

"I like your jersey," a young guy said to her as he pedaled at her side. Deb guessed he was half her age.

"Thank you."

"Is this your first time or are you one of the regulars?"

Deb knew what he meant. Some people had been doing this ride every year for the past five or ten years. She overheard one gray-haired fellow saying it was year twenty-six for him. "First time. How about you?"

"Semiregular. This is my fifth, but I don't do it every year. The last one was four years ago."

Deb explained that it had been even longer for her, but she enjoyed getting back in shape.

The man nodded. "Indeed. That's the great thing about the bike. It always welcomes you back."

"Are you doing the full one fifty?" Deb assumed that's what most people would do, so she was surprised when the fellow said no.

"I did a hundred yesterday. I've got nothing to prove."

Deb thought about that a minute. Maybe her own approach had been skewed. Maybe it was better to ride with nothing to prove. They rode together a little longer, but separated at the next rest stop.

It was harder to ride alone after being with the crowd. Deb was still hoping to beat her time from the day before, but her body was feeling the wear. Every time a faster rider passed her, a surge of competitiveness went through her. She would pedal faster for a few yards and then drop back, unable to keep up. What if she increased her assistance just a little? She had trained all spring on the lowest setting. A little boost would be just what she needed to get her to the finish line. And if she used up all the battery, she had the spare. *Might as well take advantage of it if I'm going to lug it for the whole ride.* She bumped up her assistance one notch, then two, and enjoyed the instant increase in her speed. In a short while, she was zipping past people who had passed her two or three miles back. She grinned.

For the rest of the ride Deb watched her mileage tick up on her odometer and recalled the events of the previous day. This was where they saw the ducks. This was where they watched the cows. Here was the hill where they saw kites flying. This was the field where Caroline threw up. And here was the length of road, twisting through the tree grove, where Deb panicked and thought she was lost when really she was in the right place the whole time. She shook her head when she made it through the woods. *The tricks our minds play on us.*

She missed Caroline, even as she enjoyed the time to herself. She couldn't ignore the irony of her friend dropping out for the same reason Deb herself had quit almost twenty years earlier. The things women give up to have babies, men couldn't fathom. As she rode, she remembered something else that had been bothering her. Caroline's eye problem. Could that be related to the migraines? Certainly that wasn't a result of pregnancy, not even in half of all women. What did it mean? Tumor? MS? She certainly hoped not. As she neared the end of the ride, Deb became anxious to talk to Caroline. Something was wrong. Something needed to be done about it.

Coming into the final rest stop, she could feel the bike starting to drag, much like a car low on gas. She checked her battery gauge and noticed the low-battery symbol was flashing. Weaving between riders, she pulled over to a bike rack and leaned her bike against it. Good thing she'd remembered the spare. She unlatched the used battery from its mounting and put it on the ground. Then she removed the spare from its harness on the back of her bike and put it in place. Two clicks and it was done. She lashed down the used battery and dusted off her hands. She smiled. That was easy. Increasing her assistance was absolutely worth it. Still stretching her upper body, she headed to the snack stand looking for a sleeve of peanuts.

She downed the snack and, after a quick trip to the port-a-potty, returned to her bike and mounted it. She checked the route, just to be sure, then pedaled off. She did love the feel of the warm wind on her face. It was hard to believe she was so close to completing her goal. Less than ten miles and she would have achieved something she first set out to do twenty years ago.

But at mile seventy-two, the low-battery warning was flashing again. How could that be? Deb slowed her bike to a stop at the side of the road and dismounted. Her cleats scraped the pavement and sweat dripped from her temples as she wheeled the bike into the short grass. Several riders she'd seen at the last rest stop passed her now, reminding her how much time she was losing. She let out a low whistle.

"Everything all right?" one older fellow asked. He looked like he might stop but Deb waved him and his friends on.

"All good. Just have to get my battery connected."

"Okey-doke!" And they pedaled past.

Deb squatted to get a closer look at the battery. She pressed it. Seemed firmly in place. She pulled it out and put it back, making sure everything was lined up correctly. The low-battery symbol continued to flash. "Are you kidding me?" She recalled the flashing alarm clock in the hotel and bit her lip. It seemed the electricity hadn't just flickered last night. It had kept her battery from charging. Great! Now she was wishing someone really would stop to help, but no riders were in sight. Should she call SAG? Should she try to ride the bike with the low battery? She was so close! Why did this have to happen now? She sat down on the grass while she weighed her options.

She felt the heat of tears in her eyes, but what good would crying do? She needed a solution. She took a deep breath and looked around. The sky was a clear blue with high clouds. The tall trees across the street from her were in full leaf, and the grass was the dark green of summer. She closed her eyes and turned her face up to the sun. The warm rays caressed her face. She heard a vehicle pass and her hair whipped in the breeze from its wake. Opening her eyes, she saw birds flying above the trees. How she wished to be free like the birds. Nothing would hold her back. Not a flat tire. Not a low battery. Not even MS. She sighed. What was she going to do?

That's when she remembered what Will had said: SAG doesn't have chargers. If she called the support team it would mean not completing the ride. Riding without the pedal assist would be hard, like carrying a twenty-pound sack while pedaling a standard bike. She hadn't trained for it, and that scared her. But she couldn't fail now. Not when she was this close. She would walk if she had to.

Slowly, she stood up and began to walk her bike along the road. After a few feet, she mounted it and began to pedal. *Ooof!* The bike was heavy. She recalled something Marco had said Friday night at dinner. They were talking about one of his favorite movies, *Finding*

Dory, and he said, "If you get too tired, just do what Dory would do." Deb looked at him curiously and he sang, "Keep on pedaling, keep on pedaling." Deb laughed now at her son's wise words. She began to chant quietly to herself, "Keep on pedaling, keep on pedaling." And wouldn't you know it, it helped. Having a rhythm made the task bearable. It was slow going. And it was hard work. An old man on a bike passed her. A jogger passed her on one incline. In fact, it felt like every rider on the route had passed her by the time she had gone one mile. But she was doing it, and that was all that mattered.

And then, sooner than she thought possible, the finish line appeared before her. She watched as her odometer ticked over from seventy-four to seventy-five miles. She clicked a button and saw the total mileage notching one hundred and fifty miles just before she crossed into the parking lot. "Woo-hoo!" she yelled, pumping her fist. Other riders heard her and started clapping. The announcer's voice intoned, "Welcome back, Number One-Thirty-Nine. Welcome back, Debra." The smile on her face reached from ear to ear. She had done it! She had completed the ride!

"Wahoo!" she yelled again, tracing a large circle in the parking lot. She coasted to the grass and dismounted. First she poured the remains of her water bottle on her face and wiped it off with her sleeve. Then she took out her phone and texted Philippe. *I'm here!!!!!* Thoughts of Luis and Betty skirted through her mind—how she would have loved to have them here to witness this. She jumped up and down, feeling her rubbery legs wobble beneath her, aware that she was alone. She had done it!

"Mom!"

Deb turned, unsteady on her feet, and located the familiar voice.

Marco was running out of the community center and right toward her.

"Marco! You're here!" Rosa hadn't let on that she would be bringing the kids. She must be here somewhere.

"Mom, you did it!" Marco bowled into Deb, nearly knocking her over.

She wished then she had her cane to steady her. "Careful, sweetie," she said with a chuckle. She stepped back to regain her balance and then wrapped her arms around her son. She looked around for the others. Coming out of the building were Rosa, PJ, and Philippe. Rosa was carrying something.

"Debra! Congratulations!" Rosa exclaimed.

"Oh, thank you, Rosa. Thank you so much! Thanks for bringing Marco." Deb grinned, taking everything in.

"You're welcome. I know you said we didn't have to come, but this was too big a deal. Isn't that right, Marco?"

Marco jumped up and down. "That's right."

Deb laughed to see her son's unbridled enthusiasm. "Well, I'm exhausted and hungry. Do you mind if we go back inside and eat?"

"Not at all," Rosa said. "We brought this for you." She handed Deb a walking stick.

Deb took it and leaned on it, feeling relieved. She looked more closely and realized it was hers from home. She shook her head in a question.

"Marco thought you might need it, so we stopped by your house," Rosa explained.

Deb turned to Marco. "Thank you, sweetie."

"You're welcome." He beamed back at her. "You're really sweaty."

"I'm not surprised. You wouldn't believe what I just went through."

"Congratulations, Deb," Philippe said.

"Congratulations to you too, Philippe," she replied.

As they walked back inside, the significance of the day's events hit Deb. She realized then that the ride wasn't about showing MS who's boss. Much like the memories of the assault, she couldn't muscle her MS into line and make it do what she wanted. No. This ride was about accepting it as part of her life and doing the things she loved anyway. She grabbed Marco and squeezed. "What a day. What a day!"

Thirty-Eight

Exactly two weeks had passed since Deb completed the ride. In that time, she had settled back in at work with a new attitude of accomplishment. The ride had only lasted a weekend, but the experience had changed her. She was more confident and buoyed by the knowledge that she could achieve her goals, even when they seemed impossible. She could trust herself to come through.

She had also started her new medicine. The MRI confirmed she had new lesions, meaning the old medicine had stopped working. She was disappointed but not surprised. She'd made this transition before; she would get through it again. She counted herself lucky that there were new medicines to try.

Now the night of the annual dinner had arrived. Thanks in large part to Andy II, Deb and her team had surpassed their fundraising goal, and all the moving pieces were in place. One week earlier, she had told Calvin the full story about Molly. She wanted the truth to be known. It did not go well.

"I hate to say it, but this sounds like sour grapes, Deb." They were in Calvin's office with the door closed. Deb had stayed late on a Monday to ensure their privacy.

"Calvin, she misled me and the rest of the team. And her attitude towards me has not been professional. Others on the team have noticed. I think it's time we let her go."

"It just doesn't sound like the Molly I know. I've been working with her for ten years. The donors love her. You said yourself you were having some brain fog. Couldn't that be the source of the confusion?"

Deb didn't have a rebuttal to that. So, like it or not, Molly was still on the team. She would have to figure out how to work with her or move on to a different job. For now she chose to accept it.

Deb's phone buzzed. *Call me when you get a chance.*

She frowned. Caroline didn't usually send cryptic messages like that. The last time they spoke, after the ride, Caroline was still having headaches and vision changes. She'd seen several doctors but didn't have a good explanation for them. Deb was worried. She checked the time. Just shy of six o'clock. She was resting against her walking stick amid a sea of tables under a wide pavilion decorated and set for the night's festivities. Flo and Robin had done a beautiful job, with help from Tom, Molly, and several volunteers. Lawrence had set up the video display for Meg's dog-training videos, and Hannah was chaperoning the guest speakers. Calvin was around here somewhere; he would offer an address at the top of the programming. The caterers were bustling about, getting the food tables set and ready for serving. The donors and guests would be arriving shortly. Could she squeeze in a call before the night got going?

"Hello," a voice said, interrupting Deb's thoughts.

She looked up from her phone. "Oh, hello." Standing before her was a distinctly British-looking man in his fifties, with a sharp nose, mousy brown hair, and blue eyes. She recognized him from his Instagram account and flushed. "You must be Mr. Peters."

"Andy. That's me. Thanks for meeting with me. I know the event doesn't officially start for a few more minutes." He smiled and his eyes twinkled.

Deb looked into his eyes. She could hardly believe how different he was from the Andy of her youth. She couldn't imagine ever being afraid of this gentle man. Her anxiety dissipated as she began to talk.

"Of course. Thank you for coming. Thank you for your generous donation."

"You're welcome." Andy held her gaze with a steady, kind expression. "Everything looks very nice here."

Deb surveyed the pavilion one more time. "Thank you. I have a great team." She smiled, wondering what more to say. Andy had asked to meet before the event got underway, but he hadn't said why. The video display caught her attention and she said, "We'll be showing some of Meg Shaeffer's popular videos tonight. Would you like a sneak peek?"

"Absolutely."

Deb and Andy walked over to the projector, the thud of Deb's stick punctuating each step. One video was just ending and a new one started when they arrived. They each took a seat to watch. On the large screen, Meg and a chocolate Lab named Tyson came into focus. While the video played, Deb's mind went to Caroline's backyard and the other Andy, and she felt sweat gather in her armpits. But even though she never wanted to see the other Andy again, Deb realized she could handle it if she had to. She'd tackled a one-hundred-and-fifty-mile bike ride on her own. She could face Andy. She sat up a little straighter. That one thought helped her make up her mind: she would stay in Silver Spring and make her life here.

She had her mother's house, and she had Caroline, as imperfect as their friendship was. She was ready to put down roots.

The video ended, and Andy and Deb clapped.

"Deb! You're here! The place looks great."

Deb turned to see Meg and Jason walking over. "Oh, Meg, perfect timing. We were just watching one of your videos." Meg looked curiously at the man sitting with Deb, and Deb said, "Have you met Andy Peters? He's one of our donors. He makes what we do possible."

Andy stepped forward and shook Meg's hand. "Well done," he said, hooking a thumb toward the video. "You really know your stuff."

Meg accepted the compliment. Jason put his hand on her back. "That's my girl."

"Well, Deb," Andy said, turning to her, "should we take care of business before the rest of the guests arrive?"

"Yes, good idea." They said goodbye to Meg and Jason and walked back to the welcome table.

"My wife should be along shortly. She works at the hospital around the way. We both really appreciate what you do. She has epilepsy, and our dogs have made such a difference to our lives. I wanted to meet with you so I could tell you personally what your work means to both of us." Andy handed over a check for twenty-five thousand dollars.

Deb's heart fluttered at the thought of the value of the check she was holding. She had often received large donations over her career, but they still made her nervous. "Thank you, Andy. This donation will make a huge difference to so many people." She put it in her pocket and hoped it didn't evaporate. When she looked up, a dozen or so people were walking across the lawn toward the pavilion. "Oh! Looks like the guests are arriving."

"And here comes my wife," Andy said. A slender, blond woman stepped under the pavilion and greeted Andy. Deb welcomed her to the dinner and thanked her for coming. Deb thought she was even more beautiful in person. At last Andy and his wife left to find their table, and Deb let out her breath. Everyone seemed to have arrived at once. The tables were full now, and the programming was about to get underway. She would be exhausted by the night's end. Deb remembered the text from Caroline and decided to call her before it got too late.

When Caroline answered, Deb said, "You won't believe who I was just talking to."

"You're right," Caroline said. "Who was it?"

"Andy Peters."

"What?" Caroline gasped.

Deb laughed. "Not that Andy Peters. Andy II. I'm at the annual dinner. He's here."

"Oh my God, you had me going for a second." Caroline laughed. "Did it go all right? Was it weird?"

"Only because I thought he might realize I was stalking him on Instagram. Of course he didn't. He's a nice man actually. Soft-spoken and very kind. And thanks to him, my team surpassed our fundraising goal for the fiscal year."

"Wow! Congratulations!" Caroline whooped.

"But you had something on your mind," Deb said. "Is everything all right?"

Caroline paused. "You know what, I think I'd rather tell you in person. I forgot you had your event tonight. Can you come over tomorrow? Bring Marco. You can stay for dinner."

"It's a date."

Deb hung up, then found her place next to Robin and Lawrence and took a seat. The rest of the night went according to plan. Even Molly didn't cause any disturbances, and Calvin was as charming as could be, crediting Deb and her team for the flawless event. As Deb was driving home that night, her thoughts returned to Caroline. She hoped it was nothing serious, but something told her she would not be getting her wish this time.

Thirty-Nine

Caroline trembled when the doorbell rang. She'd been practicing what she would say to Deb all morning. It seemed surreal, a conversation she never dreamed she would need to have. How would Deb take it? Could she even get the words out? She took a deep breath and exhaled, then walked from the den to the front of the house.

She opened the door, and Deb and Marco came in. While Caroline and Deb said their hellos, Marco hopped around next to his mother like a puppy ready to play. "Go on and find Jacob," his mom said, setting him free. He rushed up the stairs.

"Robbie is making dinner in the kitchen. We're free to visit in the den," Caroline said, leading the way. She had an eye patch over her left eye and was a little unsteady walking down the corridor. "I took the liberty of pouring you a glass of wine. I hope that's all right," she said when they arrived in the cozy room.

"Sure." Deb took a sip from the glass that was offered. "Mmm. Very crisp." She smiled at Caroline pleasantly.

Caroline returned the smile. She took a deep breath then, steeling herself for the difficult conversation. "So," she began.

Deb looked at her expectantly, eyebrows slightly raised.

"So, congratulations on finishing the ride!" Caroline stalled. "I'm so impressed you did it. I mean, I knew you could do it, but it's really astounding that you did it. You should be very proud of yourself." She beamed at Debra. "And the annual dinner last night? How did that go?" She sipped her wine and waited for Deb's response.

Deb looked pointedly back at her friend. "Caroline, out with it."

Caroline let out a long breath. She knew she couldn't delay any longer. What had she practiced? "Okay, here's the thing. You know I've been vomiting and having migraines."

"Yes," Deb said, nodding encouragingly. "And you thought that was because you're pregnant?"

"Well, yes, I did." Caroline stumbled. "I did think that, but I was wrong."

"You're not pregnant?" Deb asked, looking confused.

"No," Caroline said, laughing, "I'm pregnant. It's just, that's not all." Another sip of wine. Her nerves were jangling.

"Oh." Deb went silent.

How was she going to do this? All her practice wafted away. She cleared her throat and started again. "I've had some tests done over the past couple of weeks and it turns out that . . ."

Deb waited patiently.

"I have a brain tumor." Caroline winced, closing her eyes after she made the announcement. She slowly opened them to see Deb's reaction.

Deb was dumbfounded. Her mouth was slightly open in a comical expression of disbelief.

Caroline laughed. "Wow. I guess that's not what you were expecting."

"I'm so sorry, Caroline. I don't know what to say," Deb said. She looked at Caroline and blinked several times, her eyes moist.

"It's okay. You don't have to say anything. I just wanted you to know. So far only Robbie, Jacob, and my parents know." Caroline took another sip of her wine, more relaxed now. "I'm not really supposed to be drinking, but what the heck. You can't take everything away from me, right?"

"What's the prognosis? Do they know?" Deb's eyebrows were knitted.

"Right now they're saying if it's what they think it is, twelve to eighteen months."

Deb nearly coughed on her wine. "Eighteen months!" Her face flushed and tears sprang to her eyes. She set the glass down and gaped at her friend. "No, no, no. That can't be right." She covered her cheeks with her hands.

Caroline moved over to sit next to Deb. She laid her hand on her back and rubbed it gently. "I'm sorry," she said quietly.

Deb turned to Caroline. "You don't need to apologize. No, no. *I'm* sorry. I'm so, so sorry." And she embraced Caroline in a long hug.

Caroline trembled. "You know," she said, "I've cried so much over the past two weeks, I didn't think I had any tears left." She laughed a sad little chuckle. The women separated, and Caroline reached for a box of tissues. She handed one to Deb before using one herself.

Deb looked at Caroline, searching her face. "So you told Jacob?"

Caroline nodded. "Yes. I think that was the hardest conversation I've ever had." She'd never been so thankful to have Robbie by her side as the day she had to tell their son she was both expecting a baby and fighting brain cancer. Jacob didn't know what to say. He was more concerned about the baby on the way than the disease. He didn't know everything that would come with a brain tumor, and Caroline had provided limited details. He was ten; what's "age-appropriate" when your mother has a terminal illness?

Deb shuddered. "I can't even imagine." Fresh tears began to stream down her face.

The women sat in silence for a few minutes, taking it all in.

"You know I'm not going anywhere," Deb said firmly. "Right?" She looked pointedly at Caroline. "I will be with you through it all. You are not alone."

Caroline smiled, her one good eye rimmed with red. "Thank you, Debra."

There was movement at the doorway and the two women looked over. Robbie was standing there with a dishrag in his hand. "Dinner's ready."

"Oh, Robbie, I'm so sorry," Deb said. She stood to face him but did not hug him.

"Thank you, Deb. I know your friendship means a lot to Caroline. We're glad you're here."

Deb looked from Robbie to Caroline, worry lines creasing her forehead. "What should I tell Marco?"

Caroline said, "Nothing for now, if you don't mind. I mean, maybe later you can tell him I'm sick? For now let's just have a nice meal."

"Agreed," said Robbie.

Deb nodded. "Okay, agreed." She was quiet a minute and then said, "I just can't believe it. I feel like I just rediscovered you, and now I'm going to lose you? It can't be." She shook her head slowly, wiping fresh tears from her eyes.

"Debra, do you remember what you said when you decided to do the Chesapeake Challenge? Why you were doing it?"

Deb thought a minute. "I believe I said something about doing it now before I couldn't. MS is progressive. You never know what the next day will be like, much less the next year."

Caroline nodded. "Exactly. That's exactly right. You never know. The doctor says eighteen months. Well, I don't know if he's right or not. What I do know is, I have to make the most of every minute."

Deb smiled at her friend.

Robbie cleared his throat. "Let's eat before our dinner gets cold. Follow me. The boys are already there."

Caroline linked arms with Robbie, and Deb followed them all the way to the dining room.

Techno-sounding beeps and boops emanated from the attic playroom that night after dinner. Caroline walked in to find Jacob sitting on the floor ten feet from the TV, playing *Minecraft*. She sat down on the couch behind him to watch. She was not a fan of video games and wondered how her son, who came from her own body, could stand to spend so much time in a dark room playing them. The outdoors was where kids belonged, and it was where Caroline spent much of her time. She encouraged Jacob often to go outside, to run, to play soccer with PJ, to simply sit in the sunshine and absorb the fresh air. As she took a seat, she reminded herself that he was his own person, with likes and dislikes that were different from hers, and that a little time playing video games could be healthy escapism.

Jacob had taken notice of her entrance, but he hadn't said more than hello. He looked surprised to see her. He continued the game but said, "I just started this. Can I keep playing?" He turned to look behind him.

"Yes, you can play. I just wanted to see what you were up to. Can I sit next to you?"

Jacob turned back toward the TV. "Sure." He sounded skeptical.

Caroline moved over to sit on the floor next to her son. She was quiet for a minute, watching him whacking away at digital trees and building new structures. She took a deep breath, then said, "I wanted to tell you, Jake, I'm very proud of you."

"You are?" Jacob frowned but did not look at his mother.

"Yes, I am. I was thinking again about your ordeal with the pocketknife. You handled it with more maturity than most ten-year-olds would have." She leaned her head toward his, and finally he looked over.

"Thanks." His frown turned to a smile as he continued building different structures in his game.

"Things are going to be changing around here. My belly's going to get big, and I might even lose all my hair."

"Really?" He was frowning again while concentrating on the screen.

"Yes, really. But it will be okay. I will be okay."

Caroline watched a few minutes longer. She wanted her son to know how much she loved him. She wanted to tell him she respected him and had high hopes for his future and didn't want to miss any part of his life. That he was an exceptional boy, and she loved him even when he misbehaved. She said, "Can I play?"

Jacob hesitated and Caroline thought he might say no. He said, "Do you really want to?"

"Sure I do. It looks fun. You'll have to teach me, though. I was never very good at video games."

"You used to play video games?" Jacob asked, eyes wide.

"Of course! Every kid plays video games. I played *Super Mario Bros.* and *Tetris* and *Sonic the Hedgehog*. I even played *Grand Theft Auto* once, but I didn't like it." She scrunched up her nose, remembering a gamer boyfriend from college.

Jacob handed her the controller. "Wow, Mom. I'm surprised. This one's different. First you have to gather materials, and then you can build cool stuff."

"Like *SimCity*?" Caroline had played lots of *SimCity* at college, killing time between classes or when she should've been studying.

"What's that?"

"Oh, never mind. Just tell me what to do." She focused on the TV screen.

Jacob explained the game and Caroline did her best to follow his instructions. She was surprised by how much fun it was. After she'd built a few structures of her own, she said, "I see why you like to spend so much time on this."

"I don't spend that much time on it," he said defensively.

She sighed. "I didn't mean it like that. I meant, this is fun!"

He looked sideways at her. "Oh."

"Thanks for teaching me." She handed back the controller.

"You're welcome. Maybe we can play two-player mode sometime."

This was a first. Caroline's stomach fluttered. "I would like that."

Forty

Three Weeks Later

"I still don't understand what's happening with Mrs. Cook," Marco said.

"It's like I told you," Deb replied. "She's ill. She's taking a leave of absence at her work for a few months while she tries to get better."

"Okay," Marco said, sounding unconvinced.

"Listen, all you need to know is that Jacob is going to need a friend while his mom goes through treatments. If you can find ways to be nice to him and help him take his mind off things at home, that would be a help. Can you do that?"

"Yes, of course."

Deb and Marco had just arrived home from the animal shelter, and they had a new dog with them. The as-yet-unnamed two-year-old yellow Lab bounded into the house. Marco ran after her.

The dog settled down on the rug in the living room to chew on a stuffed lobster, and Marco planted himself next to her. Deb perched on a chair nearby. She knew getting a dog was going to complicate their lives, but she couldn't deny the elation she felt watching this silly pup with her floppy ears and pink tongue. After the struggles of the past several months, Deb welcomed the positive energy of a pet.

"Does this mean we're staying at Grandma's house?" Marco asked, eyes fixed on the dog.

"Yes, it does. I thought about it and I realized, Grandma's house is just right for us. She left it to me in her will, and I want us to stay here. It's perfect, really. We even have a room for Paula when she comes home." Although Deb struggled with the glut of memories that sometimes made the house feel cramped, she was learning how to make new memories and still live with the old ones. Having space for Paula too made Deb feel grounded in a way she hadn't realized she missed.

"You're right," Marco said. "When is she coming home?"

"Not till August."

Marco turned back to look at the puppy next to him. "This doggy is so cute. What should we name her?"

Deb considered the question. "I don't know. Do you have any suggestions?"

Marco thought a minute. "How about Rosie? You know, like Grandma's game."

Deb liked that but thought better of it. "Too close to *Rosa*."

"I know! Black-eyed Susan! Like Grandma's flowers."

The name was perfect for the yellow dog with a black nose.

"I love it. And Grandma would love it too." Deb smiled and gathered Marco to her. "You are really something special, Marco. I'm so lucky to have you."

"Mom!" Marco exclaimed, pushing Deb away. "You're so weird."

Deb grabbed him back again. "I know. But that's why you love me."

Marco giggled and allowed his mom to hug him a while longer.

"You'll have to let me go eventually," he teased.

"I know, sweetie. But not yet."

Call to Action

At the time this book is going to print, the US government has taken aim at our most vulnerable citizens. People with disabilities, people living in poverty, immigrants, and the elderly—people like Deb and Betty, Rosa and Philippe—and most especially trans people and members of the LGBTQIA community are being targeted. Government funds are being withdrawn and civil liberties are under attack.

While this fight continues, our friends and neighbors will be relying on nonprofit organizations more than ever. And those nonprofits rely on volunteers and donors like you.

If you would like to make a difference in the lives of other people, or if you are looking for support in these challenging times, please check out the following organizations. If you can, sign up to make a small monthly donation.

Multiple Sclerosis

Multiple Sclerosis Association of America, https://mymsaa.org/
Multiple Sclerosis Foundation, https://msfocus.org/Home.aspx
National Multiple Sclerosis Society, https://www.nationalmssociety.org/

Support Dogs

Assistance Dogs International, https://assistancedogsinternational.org/
Fidos for Freedom, https://fidosforfreedom.org/
Pet Partners, https://petpartners.org/

Immigration and Civil Rights

American Civil Liberties Union, https://www.aclu.org/
Asylum Access, https://asylumaccess.org/
National Immigration Law Center, https://www.nilc.org/
Southern Poverty Law Center, https://www.splcenter.org/

Women's Rights

Center for Reproductive Rights, https://reproductiverights.org/
Ms Foundation for Women, https://forwomen.org/

Sexual Assault

National Sexual Violence Resource Center, https://www.nsvrc.org/survivors
RAINN: National Sexual Assault Hotline, https://rainn.org/about-national-sexual-assault-online-hotline

Acknowledgments

I owe a debt of gratitude to the many people who read this book in draft form and gave feedback. Stephen Murphy and Meri Robie-Craven were my first and last readers, respectively, and both provided invaluable criticism and advice. The book is so much better because of their generosity. Amy Moore provided helpful insights into nonprofit work and office life. Barbara Morrison encouraged me to be more daring with the story.

Several people from the "Stay-at-Home" Virtual MS Support Group were kind enough to read an early draft, for which I am extremely grateful. My deepest thanks to Evelyn Caldwell Zeidman, Joe Rea, and Jenny Barbieri, as well as other group members who shared insights and experiences at the meetings. Besides being kind and thoughtful people, they also helped me to accurately depict life with multiple sclerosis. A special thank-you to Evie, the group's fearless leader, who allowed me to join the meetings after I reached out to her and explained my mission with this book; and to Joe, whose faith in me buoyed me during the rough times.

Caroline McCallam, Mark Brighton, and Matt, who responded to requests for help on Mastodon, answered my questions about ebikes, multiple sclerosis, and more. Hannah Steenbock critiqued a chapter when I ran out of critique partners. Todd Ceveris spoke with me at length about long-distance cycling with MS, balance problems, staying cool, and much more. My sincere thanks to each of you.

My thanks to the fine people at the Maryland Writers Association, the Writers Center in Bethesda, the Independent Book Publishers Association, and the very active participants of the Authors Guild Discussion Forum, all of whom have shared wisdom, experience, and learning opportunities that have made me the writer I am. A shout-out to the ZigBabes, who entered my life late in this process but quickly became an important part of my writing circle.

A warm thank-you to my publishing team: copyeditor Sarah Rutledge; cover designer Paul Nylander; proofreader Em Syth; and publicist Cherrie Woods. Your time and expertise are greatly appreciated.

And last but not least, I am grateful every day for my husband, Chris, and our two dynamic daughters, Nancy and Hazel. Thank you for giving me your love, support, and encouragement to follow my passion, in this and all things. I love you.

Book Club

Discussion Questions

In chapter one, Deb receives a call that changes the trajectory of her life. Have you ever had your plans derailed by a single phone call?

In chapter two, Deb is reluctant to reunite with her old friend Caroline. Why, then, do you think Deb accepts Caroline's invitation to dinner?

Betty loses a significant amount of money when, like many vulnerable people, she falls for a gift card scam. Yet she continues to answer the phone, despite Deb's pleas. Have you or someone you know ever fallen for a scam? What would you have done to help protect Betty?

Early in the book, Caroline and Robbie discuss which is worse, a long, slow decline (chronic illness) or something that kills you (terminal illness). How does this theme play out in the rest of the novel?

Have you ever had a friend like Caroline? Are you still friends?

Calvin repeatedly tells Deb to take the time she needs to do her best work. In what way does this become a trap for Deb? Do you blame Deb for the way she handles her work challenges?

When Paula first tells Deb she's worried the ride is too strenuous for her, mother and daughter make a deal: Deb will drop out if her health takes a downturn. What does Deb do when Paula reminds her of this deal? Do you agree or disagree with Deb's decision?

Molly and Deb have a contentious relationship working together at Sparky's Support Dogs. How would you have handled Molly's bad behavior?

It quickly becomes clear that Deb had a bad experience with a young man as a teenager. How common do you think Deb's scenario is?

Near the end of the book, Caroline gives a name to what happened to Deb. Do you agree or disagree with the label Caroline uses? Why or why not?

About the Author

Katherine Pickett is the owner of POP Editorial Services, LLC, and the author of the award-winning book *Perfect Bound: How to Navigate the Book Publishing Process Like a Pro*, now in its second edition. She earned her bachelor's degree in English from Loyola University Chicago and has been involved in publishing for 25 years.

Katherine's creative work can be found in *Lowestoft Chronicle*, *Voice of Eve*, *Grande Dame Literary*, and *Defunct Magazine*. Her industry articles have appeared on Publishing Perspectives, Jane-Friedman.com, Writer Beware, *IBPA Independent*, and elsewhere. Katherine is a frequent speaker at writing and editing conferences nationwide and an instructor at the Writer's Center in Bethesda.

Like Debra Lee, she is also an avid cyclist and took part in the real-life Chesapeake Challenge in 2023. She lives in Silver Spring, Maryland, with her handsome and strong husband, Chris, and their two awe-inspiring daughters.

Katherine Pickett at the 2023 Bike MS Chesapeake Challenge